The Big Book of Bootleg Horror: Volume 3

By Invitation Only

A Charity Horror Anthology
by
HellBound Books Publishing LLC

A HellBound Books LLC Publication

www.hellboundbookspublishing.com

Printed in the United States of America

This Book is dedicated to all the amazing authors found in these pages for without them our dreams and nightmares would never come true. Thank you for all the amazing adventures we would never have gotten to experience without you.

Forever and Always!

Edited by Xtina Marie

FOREWORD

It's always nice to give something back, they say. And indeed it is; to be in the fortunate situation to be able to do something to help a worthy cause such as the incredible *Hilarity for Charity* has to be amongst the best feelings this all too brief life has to offer.

And to be able to do so along with some of the horror industry's finest names just keeps on putting cherries on that cake.

There are names skulking within these pages that are personal heroes – old and new – and it is a delight to be included amongst them, although I do feel a tad like the little kid who snuck in the rear exit of the movie theater to catch *The Exorcist* – exhilarated at being there but not entirely convinced of his worthiness.

One thing that hit me, upon reading the superlative contributions to this most charitable of tomes, is the leaning towards cats as horror tropes (almost 10% of this anthology concerns the feline – as a dog person, this merely reinforces my decision towards the canine, as well as my deep suspicion towards statistics

In a buck to the trend, we have a short movie screenplay, preserved as written by the incomparable Chizmars – be sure to check out the movie when Richard and Billy finally release it – there's a cameo from one Stephen King that you certainly won't want to miss!

And so, it is on to the reason you purchased this assemblage of words – the stories themselves. We do hope that you enjoy them as much as we did upon compiling them, and please accept our sincerest thanks for supporting a more than worthy charity that helps fight a despicable disease that has touched the loved ones of more than author within these pages.

For you, Dear Reader…

James H Longmore

HellBound Books Publishing LLC
2017

https://hilarityforcharity.org/

Contents

The Big Book of Bootleg Horror: Volume 3

By Invitation Only

Alien Face
Jeff Strand

I fired four more shots into his chest, emptying my pistol. Matthew V. Cloak, the Lakeland Mangler, dropped his knife, looked at the growing bloodstains on his shirt as if confused by how they got there, and then fell to the ground.

I walked over and crouched down next to him. I reached into my inside jacket pocket and—*dammit!*—realized that I'd left the picture of my niece in my other jacket.

"That was for Abigail," I told him. Not as effective without the visual aid, but hopefully he'd figure out who I was talking about.

It didn't take long for Cloak to bleed out. After I was sure he was dead, I called it in.

We were deep in the thick woods. It would take at least an hour for backup to get here. I didn't think anybody was alive inside his cabin, but I had to go in and make sure. My experience as a cop leaned much more toward breaking up drunken fights in bars than taking down serial killers, so I was certain that this was going to be the most horrific thing I'd ever seen.

I opened the front door and stepped inside. The cabin had an odd smell but not the rotting smell I'd expected. The smell of preservatives, maybe?

The sight, however, was every bit as bad as I'd expected.

We'd believed that the Lakeland Mangler had killed seven people, but just a quick glance around his cabin proved that the number had been at least twice that. His souvenirs were proudly displayed. Hands. Feet. And faces. Lots of faces.

"Mangler" had never been an accurate description. Cloak, an ex-surgeon, did careful work. Many of the faces, all young women, on the mannequin heads were still recognizable, including Abigail's. When I saw her, I simultaneously wanted to fall to my knees and sob, and to go back outside and kick Cloak's corpse until there was nothing but red.

I did neither. I kept searching the cabin.

"Hello?" I called out. "Is anybody in here?"

Nobody answered.

"I'm a cop," I said. "He's dead. You don't have to—"

I froze.

What the hell was *that*?

There were four artificial heads, the kind you keep wigs on, lined up on a shelf. Three of them were being used to display the cut-off faces of young women. But the second one from the left had a long, gray, oval-shaped face with enormous eyeholes.

It looked like an alien. *Exactly* like an alien, the kind you see in the sketches when attention-seeking whackos swear that they were abducted and probed.

I touched its cheek. It didn't feel like rubber, or plastic, or anything synthetic. It's not like I could say, "Yep, that's a real alien face, all right," but despite having no basis for comparison, it sure *felt* real.

Had one of the Lakeland Mangler's victims been an alien?

No. That was insane. I was quite understandably in a state of shock right now, and I could be forgiven for a brief moment of crazy whacked-out madness where I thought it had any possibility of being an actual alien face.

So what was it? A collectible? A practical joke for the inevitable police discovery of this cabin? Something to amuse him as he gazed into the lifeless faces of his real victims?

I touched it again. If he'd preserved it as he had the human faces, it wouldn't feel real anyway, so the fact that it *did* feel real meant that it *wasn't* real.

I was confusing myself.

The most crucial things to remember were that, a) my brain wasn't functioning normally right now, and that b) aliens did not exist. That second point was the most important one. Aliens did not exist. This was the equivalent of digging through a child's toy chest and believing that an action figure was incontrovertible proof of the existence of Bigfoot.

I was in a cabin surrounded by the body parts of a serial killer's victims, and somehow I thought I'd discovered life on Mars. This was not okay. I needed to pull myself together.

Or did I? Cloak was dead. There was no evidence of any prisoners that needed to be freed. Why shouldn't I focus my attention on the mystery of the weird alien face instead of the horrors that were all around me? Try to lower my therapy bill in advance.

I decided to keep looking. See what other souvenirs he had lying around. I knew, for example, that one of the hands nailed to the wall was Abigail's, because it was still wearing the sapphire ring that her grandmother, my mother-in-law, had given her last Christmas. So if he'd really stabbed an alien to death and taken its face and other parts back to the cabin, I'd find the other parts.

Another shelf had two large glass jars, side by side, filled with colorless liquid. And eyeballs.

Along with their faces, all of his victims were missing their eyes when the bodies were discovered. The eyeballs in the jar on the right all looked as normal as they could when no longer in their sockets. But in the jar on the left, mixed in with the normal eyes, were two much larger ones. They were shaped like eggs, though about twice that size. No pupils. Completely black.

If a pair of eyeballs had indeed been cut out of an alien head, they would look just like these.

They weren't real. No way were they real.

And even if I were inclined to unscrew the lid and plunge my hand into a jar full of eyeballs, as a police officer at a crime scene I couldn't be tampering with evidence. I really shouldn't have even touched the alien face.

A *disgraced* police officer.

On suspension.

Yes, I'd be a hero for bringing down the Lakeside Mangler, and I was sure I'd be completely reinstated, but the department had thrown me under the bus when our first attempt to capture him went bad. Somebody had to take the fall. It was me.

I continued looking around and quickly found a pair of alien hands nailed to the wall. They had long, grey, slender fingers.

I wished Cloak were still alive so I could ask him about this.

Where the hands had been severed, I could see a couple of exposed bones. The tissue was red. Apparently aliens bled the same color as humans, rather than black or green. Good to know. If this was phony, the attention to detail was remarkable. Maybe not *accurate*, but remarkable.

Screw it. Nobody could fault me for touching alien parts. When backup got here, they'd be whisked away and I might never get another chance. I didn't want to be lying on my deathbed, regretting that I didn't do my own little scientific investigation.

I ran my index finger down the length of one of the hands. It sure felt like a hand. Special effects artists could do amazing things, but their work wasn't typically meant to be examined up-close like this.

If only Cloak kept more of the bodies. Heads, torsos, arms, legs; the things that would be more difficult to convince me were real. I wanted to see the internal organs, touch them, find something that was clearly made out of foam latex.

I searched some more. There was a small television in the corner, and a shelf of videos. In addition to a surprising selection of romantic comedies and inspirational dramas, there was a row of VHS tapes labeled with names. *Heather. Laurie. Nicole B. Nicole M. Abigail.* (I clenched my fists and took a couple of long deep breaths to compose myself.) And, yes, one labeled *Alien.*

I picked up the tape and popped open the case. The front label, in Cloak's perfect, tiny writing, also said *Alien.*

This probably wasn't a bootleg copy of the 1979 classic.

Why did he use VHS? Had he always recorded his killings in this format and wasn't willing to break from it? Was it because a VHS camcorder couldn't get hacked? Was the Lakeland Mangler a hipster?

It didn't matter. I was going to watch that alien tape. Hell yeah, I was. The reason Cloak could have all of his souvenirs out on display was because this cabin was a bitch to get to, and I had plenty of time to myself before anybody else arrived.

I turned on the television, popped the cassette into the VCR, and pressed play.

A shot of a two-story house. The camera zoomed in on a second-floor window. The image went in and out of focus, but it seemed to be a teenaged girl in her bedroom, dancing. It was energetic, uncoordinated dancing, exactly what people meant when they said "Dance like nobody's watching!" Dance like a serial killer isn't recording you through your bedroom window.

I watched for a moment, then fast-forwarded. It went on for quite a while. When the bedroom light went out, he kept taping.

The scene switched to daylight: the girl walking down the sidewalk, wearing a backpack.

Back to night. Behind a strip mall or something. Even on fast-forward, this shot lasted for at least a minute, until a door opened. I resumed normal speed as the girl, in a dirty apron, walked outside with a garbage bag, which she heaved into a dumpster.

Then a park. Still night, but the girl had a different haircut. She was walking and bopping her head to whatever music she was listening to through her headphones, but frowned as she seemed to notice Cloak recording her. The camera swung away from her. The shot went blurry, though I'm pretty sure I was just watching the ground as he hurriedly walked away.

I fast-forwarded until the camera spun around. Cloak pointed it at his own face, then ran his hand over his forehead, doing an exaggerated "wiping off sweat" gesture.

"Whew, that was close!" he whispered. He winked.

Then there was a bright blue light.

The camera swung around again. The light, in the middle of a field, was so bright that I couldn't quite see the source of it.

"What the hell?" Cloak asked.

The light shot up into the sky. The camera tilted upward to follow it, but there was just darkness. The camera moved around in a motion sickness-inducing manner for a while, with Cloak clearly trying to locate the UFO.

Finally, he swung it back down to where the light had originated.

The camera jolted. There was an alien *right freaking there*. Cloak could've reached out and touched it.

There were no surprises in its appearance. It looked just like the alien I imagined from seeing the face, hands, and eyeballs. It held up its hand, as if to convey the classic message: *We come in peace.*

Cloak stabbed it in the chest.

He kept filming as it fell to the ground.

Then the scene switched to a new location. Cloak's cabin. The alien was tied to a bed, still alive.

And then I was watching a goddamn alien snuff movie. Torture porn.

I was fascinated for a couple of minutes, but then I had to fast-forward. Cloak, who took frequent breaks to mug for the camera, slashed away at the thrashing alien as if it were one of his human victims. It was alive throughout the process of mangling its arms and legs, not going still until most of its torso was skinless.

When he went at its eyeballs, I turned off the tape.

Holy shit.

Aliens were real.

I just sat there for a long moment, trying to process this knowledge. Though I very much doubted that alien spaceships were regularly landing on farms, probing butts left and right, *somebody* had been telling the truth.

I'd touched an alien face.

Unbelievable.

I stood up. This was *my* discovery. Nobody else's. I wasn't going to let the government spooks take this away from me.

I ejected the cassette and put it back in its case. I walked over to the sink and opened the cabinet underneath it. Nothing there but cleaning supplies, but after opening a couple of drawers I found a roll of garbage bags.

I tore off a bag and put the tape in it. Then I tossed in the head with the alien face. I pulled the alien hands off the wall and put them in the bag as well. I looked around until I found the alien feet, which I added to my collection.

Obviously, I couldn't reach into the jar for the alien eyes without potentially leaving DNA behind. Even if I put on a pair of rubber gloves, it was a bad idea. I was just going to have to take the whole jar of eyeballs. I felt terrible about that, but the victims could be identified from the other parts. It wasn't as if their families would experience less heartbreak if they knew their daughters' eyeballs had been recovered.

I did a careful sweep of the cabin, making certain I hadn't missed any evidence of visitors from other worlds. Then I took the bag outside and put it in the trunk of my car. Not a great hiding spot, but it wasn't like anybody was going to search my vehicle. If Abigail's hand was still displayed on the wall, ring on the finger, it was safe to say that nobody would accuse me of swiping any body parts.

Backup finally arrived. If any of my fellow cops thought I was acting strange, well, I'd just shot a serial killer dead and found parts of my niece in his cabin of horrors. Hell, after walking in there, they were all acting kind of strange, too. There was zero suspicion.

As expected, I was a hero. I mean, I did get chewed out for some violations of protocol, but Cloak was dead; it wasn't as if he was going to get off on a technicality.

I hid the bag of alien parts under my bed.

Then I bought a VCR from a pawn shop so I could rewatch the video.

I watch it every once in a while. Not the gory parts; just the moment where the alien appears. I freeze-frame it and sit there, studying my television screen.

I look at the alien face, hands, and feet. And, yes, the eyeballs. I threw up twice during the process of scooping out the human ones, blending them up, and flushing them down the toilet, but now I only have the alien eyes in the jar. When I stare at them I like to think that they're staring back at me.

Should I share this with somebody else? Maybe. And maybe someday I will. Until then, I love the idea that I may be the only one who knows the truth beyond any shadow of a doubt. I'm the only one who can prove it. It's not like I'm God or anything, but it does feel like I'm at a higher level than everybody else.

I could be rich and famous someday. But I'm in no hurry.

The only thing that concerns me? The alien probably wasn't here alone. What if the others saw Cloak stab it? What if that's how they see humanity? What if their entire perception of our kind is based on a psychopathic thrill-killer?

I lose sleep over that.

This whole thing might end *really* badly.

But for now, it's just me and my alien.

To Suit the Crime
Jack Ketchum

"I think you've done a remarkable job," said Dugas. "Really."

Morgan leaned back on the red leather-studded sofa and lit a Camel, unfiltered, enjoying the first passage of smoke over his pallet and up through his nose. It was wonderful to him that these old appetites were back in favor.

"Thank you," he said. "But it's hardly my doing. Not even that of the court, entirely." He smiled. "We have all those Republican Presidents to thank- Regan, Bush, Quayle-"

"Not Quayle," said Dugas. "Dear God. Not Quayle."

Morgan laughed. "Alright. Not Quayle. His man, Beavers, never did amount to much. But Denninger, certainly. And Harpe. All the nominations were theirs."

"True."

"Obviously, we were abetted by history. The will of the people. It only remained for a single Democratic judge to fix upon the people and understand their will as it applied here. And we've always been best at that."

Dugas watched him raise his cigarette to his lips and draw smoke into his lungs. It occurred to Dugas that the lips were too thin to be attractive to anyone other than a public figure- for some reason the American people like their politicians lipless- the hands too perfectly manicured and delicate. There was not an ounce of sensuality to the man. Though by reputation he was no less debauched than anyone in Washington.

No less than himself, perhaps.

Dugas thought, though, that had they not both been members of the same Club- empty, now, but for the two of them- he'd never have wasted his time sitting here talking to Morgan. Despite Morgan's power, despite his undeniable accomplishments, and despite their political and career affiliations, there was something smug and distasteful about him. But here, courtesy demanded his attention.

"It was a feeling I'd maintained since law school," said Morgan. "That the punishment, very simply should suit the crime. That something fundamental had been overlooked in the very structure of our adversarial system- *that* being suffering of the victim. The *condition* of the victim at the time of his or her victimization."

Dugas watched him warm to his topic. Here we go, he thought. He owned a television set, after all. He'd heard this dozens of times. Still…

He nursed his single-malt whiskey and listened.

"You, as a lawyer, understand, I'm sure. Take a boy, for instance, struck down by a drunken driver. The boy is in the prime of his life, struck unexpectedly. One moment he's alive, perhaps Happy-the next he's dead. Is it wise and correct to sentence the driver to a given number of years in prison, to allow him the luxury of counting the days toward his release from prison, feed him, clothe him, allow him time in the yard for exercise and time in the day room for television, and then, finally, release him? When, over the intervening years, the bars have not disappeared, the liquor stores have not disappeared? He can even apply for a driver's license again."

He doesn't like me, Morgan thought. But he's reasonably attentive. That will do.

He went on. He had a point to make here, so that Dugas would thoroughly understand what followed.

"Many years ago, when I was still on the State Court, I had a case I will never forget. A man had walked in to a college dormitory, shot the aged house mother in the forehead with a .45 caliber Smith and Wesson, fitted with a silencer, and then stalked upstairs and picked a room at random. Inside were two students, young women, very pretty. The man forced them to strip at gun point, then forced one of the girls to tie the other to the bed and gag her. Then he tied and gagged the second girl, pushed her down on the same bed- and forced her roommate to watch while he *ate her friend alive."*

"He began, I believe, with her buttocks."

"The law being what it was back then, the usual jury of his peers sentenced him to life imprisonment in a State facility for the criminally insane. While, of course, he should have died."

Morgan stubbed out his cigarette.

"Died horribly."

"Excuse me, gentlemen."

It was the waiter, Woolbourne, carrying a tray and picking up Morgan's empty wine glass.

"Will you be wanting another? The workmen, I'm afraid..." Impertinent bastard, Dugas thought. Woolbourne has addressed them both but only looked at Morgan- as though he, Dugas, didn't matter.

Dugas glanced toward the workmen, two large muscular types, laying down a plastic tarp across the far corner of the library. Apparently renovations were in order, though he couldn't see the need of any.

"What are they doing, Woolbourne?" he asked.

"The wallpaper, I believe, sir. They're replacing a section." The man still didn't look at him. Merely picked up his glass, which was not even quite empty.

He'd've liked to smash that glass against Woolbourne's well-bred patrician face.

A goddamn waiter, for God's sake.

"Another," Dugas said. "One more."

"Yes," said Morgan. "One more would be fine."

"Very good, gentlemen."

Dugas lit a Camel and ran his gaze over the gold and red fleur-de-lis wallpaper near the window. Perhaps the damaged section lay behind the heavy Utrecht velvet curtains.

Morgan sighed.

"It changed my life, that case. From that point on I knew what I wanted to do what needed to be done. And, thank God, times have come exactly 'round to that."

"Yes."

The toady in Dugas could easily have said, yes and *you've* brought them 'round to that. Career-wise it was the intelligent thing to do. It would even have been true. But shop talk with this old magistrate was boring him. His career was fine as it stood. He wasn't even sure he cared about a career anymore. He had other interests. He said nothing.

Insolent or not, at least Woolbourne was efficient. He brought their drinks. Sherry for Morgan, another single-malt for Dugas.

Morgan raised his glass.

"To the law," he said smiling.

"To the law."

They touched glasses. Then the old bird was off again.

"I've had a case culminate just recently," he said. "An interesting one, actually. An excellent problem in...appropriateness. The accused was a young adoptive mother who had murdered her three-and-a-half-year-old son, whom she had adopted when he was only one year old. Somehow her systematic abuse of the child had gotten by the welfare people for over two years."

"It happens."

"Yes, unfortunately it does. Her explanation was that the child had fallen down a flight of stairs. Said he was generally a clumsy child. But that was patently false. For one thing, the bruises, some of them, were months old. For another, there were burn marks all over him."

He held up a cigarette.

"These, no doubt. There was evidence of severe malnutrition. Neighbors reported that she had, on at least one occasion, fed the child his own feces. Finally, the rectal passage was severely scarred and lacerated and abnormally distended."

"As usual, we accepted her explanation and then investigated, charged her and convicted her of murder. Her husband, by the way, was also charged and convicted- of negligent homicide. We had no evidence he'd ever touched the boy. And probably he hadn't. But he watched."

"For two years the wife was burned, beaten, neglected, starved, and upon occasion, fed her own bodily wastes, and abused with the broomstick from her own home- I believe they found it in the basement- while the husband of course, was forced to watch. I'm told he is quite insane by now, by the way."

"Then only last week she was pushed down the stairs. She died, as did the child, of a broken neck. We were really quite pleased with it. Rarely, in my experience, has a punishment so closely fit the crime. Nearly a duplication of it."

Dugas smiled. "Ah," he said. "But the boy was just a child. An innocent, so to speak. What about that?"

Morgan shrugged. "After a few months or so of deprivation and abuse, so was the woman. For all practical purposes."

Dugas thought about it, then nodded.

"Elegant," he said. "Quite elegant."

"We thought so," said Morgan. "The only thing missing," he added, "was possibly some of the element of surprise."

"Surprise?"

The workmen went by the window, had unfolded their plastic tarp and were taking a break, standing there smoking, occasionally glancing in their direction. Dugas thought it typical of the lower classes these days. From secretaries to waiters to craftsman.

"Of course," said Morgan. "Go back to our boy on the bike, run down by a drunken driver. Well, he's *surprised*, isn't he? Shocked! One moment he's fine, riding along, and the very next moment filled with some *sudden* blinding agony. Or the two young girls I mentioned, sitting in their dormitory, chatting over boyfriends or schoolmates or family or whatnot, when, suddenly, life becomes an utter horror, a nightmare, all pain and death and helplessness. Unthinkable. Unimaginable. And quite surprising."

Morgan saw he had Dugas' full attention now. Better late than never.

He sipped his sherry.

"The element of surprise. Is the entire reason we investigate, try, and sentence completely out of the public eye these days. Why those early experiments in televised and print-medium reporting, and even with juries in open courtrooms, are over. Because most, if not all, violent crimes definitely include that element. The sudden shock. So, to be fair to the victim, to come as closely as possible to the *experience* of the victim, any punishment which hopes to suit the nature of the crime must come as a shock to its perpetrator, as it did to his or her victim at the time."

"And here this last case, *on the surface*, falls slightly short of our idea. Since her punishment lasted over such an extended time- two years- one must assume that this woman realized, at some point, how it all would end. But look deeper and it's really not so far off the mark. Her initial arrest surprises her. The nature of the punishment- so closely mirroring her adopted son's- *that* must have surprised her, and on an absolutely fundamental level. That it can *hurt*, for instance, be forced to eat your own shit."

Morgan's use of the word "shit" was enough surprise for Dugas so that he choked on his single-malt whiskey.

"Sorry," Morgan said.

And then went on.

"Then look at the end. Isn't death always something of a surprise? Doesn't it always come as something of a shock? Maybe not the how- but certainly the when? Heart patients, cancer patients, even patients in daily, agonizing pain who *pray* for death, must finally be somewhat surprised when it actually comes. Even if it comes...as a relief."

"And who is to say that even a three-and-a-half-year-old cannot realize his own mortality, his grown frailty, his own approaching death?"

He settled back slowly and finished his wine.

"Your mirror may have been a very good one, then," said Dugas.

"Yes," said Morgan, smiling. "I think we've all been doing our jobs quite adequately. Even on that one."

My God. You *are* a smug sonovabitch, thought Dugas.

"Even on you," said Morgan. He stood up, straightening his dinner jacket.

Dugas saw that it was a signal. The two burly workmen approached from the corner of the room and stood close by. Woolbourne appeared in the mahogany paneled doorway, blocking his exit.

"Emil Dugas," said Morgan. "You stand accused, tried, and convicted by this Court of the murder of Lynette Janice Hoffman, aged 23 years old, your one-time lover and one-time secretary, on January 23 of the year 2021, one year, one month and three days previous. Your sentence to be carried out immediately, and your punishment to suit the crime."

Dugas' brain reeled. It was impossible. *Literally* impossible. All this talk. All this hypocrisy. All this crap about punishment to "suit the crime," this tedious prefatory lecture, when in fact they were going to kill him in some fucking phony novel way and that was all they could possibly do. Because the rest was impossible.

He almost laughed. Instead he exploded.

"You're a fool, Morgan! A buffoon! Or a goddamn lying hypocrite. Or all three. How are you going to make this punishment 'suit the crime?' You know damn well you can't *begin* to. If you know what I did to that girl, then you must know *how* I did it. It is not something you can mirror. So what am I going to get here? Some *approximation*?"

He spat the word out in disgust.

Morgan smiled. Dugas still didn't understand. Well, he expected he wouldn't.

He nodded to the workmen. They took Dugas' arms and led him to the plastic drop cloth. Dugas struggled, but it was like struggling with someone three times as strong as he was and three times his size. Which, he guessed, these two were. *Exactly as he'd been three times as strong and nearly three times as heavy as Lynette when he'd....*

And now he was laughing, hysterically as they stripped off his clothes. Laughter mixed with fury.

"You can do it!" He screamed. "You can't fucking do it because I've got no *hole* there! You see? No fucking orifice you dumb goddamn asshole! She saw me when I did it to her, do you understand that? You know what that means? You see the goddamn difference? To see the face of your murderer? To see his *pleasure*? What are you going to do, stick it up my ass, you goddamn hypocrite? You, fucking *loser*! You can't even begin to know how I made that little bitch suffer! Right up to the moment I decided to wring her fucking neck! That entire goddamn time she was looking right at me, right into my *face*!"

"We understand that," said Morgan. "Perfectly."

He nodded again and one of the workmen drew an object out of his clean white overalls. To Dugas it looked like a combination garden trowel and apple-corer. Made of surgical steel. With a two-inch diameter. And a sharp serrated edge.

When the man applied it to his groin, sunk it deep and twisted, and then withdrew, Dugas screamed and screamed.

"Will *my* face do?" Woolbourne asked politely.

Through blinding pain, Dugas watched the waiters trousers fall down around his ankles.

Almost as Dugas' own had been, Woolbourne's was quite an erection.

That's Not My Cat
Michael Bray

They would never believe her even if she told them the truth, and why should they? She sat in the interview room, white paper forensic suit crisp as she put her head in her hands. Across the desk, Detective Gibbs watched her, blue eyes sharp and reading her. He ran a hand through his blonde hair and folded his hands on the desk.

'Okay, Miss Christian Lourenco, thirty-nine. Born in France but residing here in the United Kingdom, correct?'

'Yes, but I haven't done anything wrong.'

'It's in your best interest to talk to us, Miss Lourenco. To tell the truth so I can do my job. As things look right now, you're in a lot of trouble and I can't help you unless you talk to me.'

'I don't know what to say. I'm not even sure what happened myself. It makes no sense.'

'Let us worry about making sense of it. All you need to do is tell me what happened. To you and Daniel.'

She shook her head, eyes streaked with makeup where she had been crying. 'You won't believe me.'

'Neither of us can know that unless you talk to me. We have our people in your home and the report from forensics are due in any moment now. We *will* find out what happened one way or the other. If you talk to me I can help you.'

'You don't understand,' she said as more tears came. 'Even as I sit here and think about how it happened it doesn't make sense. You won't believe it because it can't be true.'

Gibbs leaned closer, sensing he was close to a breakthrough. 'We won't know until you try. Tell me it from the start. I won't interrupt or judge you until I've heard it all.'

She exhaled, realising just how exhausted she was. She felt as if her mind was close to fracturing, exploding into a billion shards of memory she would never get back. 'I'm not crazy.' She said as Gibbs passed her a box of tissues across the table. She took one and dabbed her eyes.

'Nobody said you were crazy.'

'That's the thing,' she replied, managing a half smile. 'I know it's going to sound that way. And I know what you're going to think of me.'

'We won't know until you talk.'

All the fight left her then. Crazy as she knew it sounded and regardless of the fact she wasn't even sure what had happened she decided there was no option but to do as he asked and tell her side of it. After all, it was the only one she knew and it might help to say it out in the open and have it somewhere other than inside her brain.

'Okay,' she said, dabbing her eyes again. 'I'll tell you what happened. Shall I just begin?'

'In your own time.' Gibbs said. 'We're still recording

this conversation.'

She nodded and tried to organise what had happened into some coherent order.

'It started a few weeks ago with a cat called Henry.'

II

The ginger cat was rubbing itself against the window when Christian first saw it. It paced on the window ledge, walking back and forth demanding attention. She ran a hand through her red hair and looked at it, grinning at the unexpected visit. She had always liked cats, and she and Dan had talked about getting one in the past but hadn't made the commitment yet. She crossed to the window, sliding it open and hoping the cat wouldn't get spooked and run away. To her surprise, it entered the house, hopping on the floor and sauntering to the middle of the room, where it sat and looked at her, whiskers twitching.

'Well aren't you a bold one?' she said, leaving the window open should the cat want to leave again. 'Do you have a name?'

The cat stared at her, and she felt silly for talking to it. 'How about some milk? I bet you'll like that, won't you?' she said, walking past the cat towards the kitchen. It followed her, sitting just outside the kitchen door as she put some milk in a bowl and set it on the floor. The cat padded over and started to drink. She remained crouched, stroking its head.

'You don't have a collar but you look too clean and too well mannered to be a stray. I hope your owners aren't looking for you.'

The cat ignored her and drank its milk.

'I wonder if you have a name. What could I call you?'

She stroked the cat on the head and it started to purr. 'You look like a Henry to me. Henry the cat.'

The cat finished its drink and looked at her, licking its paw and wiping its face as it cleaned itself. She watched it, happy to see it so comfortable. Without warning the cat walked back to the sitting room and hopped up on the window ledge, where it sat and stared at her.

'You're going already?'

She watched it as it hopped down and trotted through the garden, jumping over the fence and out of sight. She stood by the window for a while, happy with the unexpected encounter, then closed the window and went back to her day.

III

Henry's visits became a regular thing. Both she and Dan found it amusing the way he would come through the window as if he owned the place. They had unofficially adopted him and bought him toys and his own bowls and added cat food to their shopping list. It was as if he was their cat without ever actually owning him. They often speculated about his owners and what his real name was. They joked about following him one day to see where he went, but for the most part, they were happy with the arrangement. The cat became part of their lives, coming and going as it saw fit. There was no foreshadowing of any problem until that Tuesday afternoon when Christian was alone in the house and Henry came to visit.

IV

Christian looked up from her book as Henry hopped from the window ledge and sat in front of her as he always did.

'Hi, Henry,' she said, putting her book down and

getting out of the chair. 'I take it you've come for some food as usual?' She walked to the kitchen, the cat following her and waiting by the door. She took the bowl from the cupboard and started to open the can of food.

'Tuna flavour today. We do look after you, don't we?' she said as she scooped the meat into the bowl. She set it on the floor, watching as Henry trotted to the bowl and started to eat, then she turned to the sink and poured herself a glass of water.

'I don't know how you can eat that stuff, Henry. It doesn't smell very nice.'

'It's not bad.'

She dropped the glass and spun around, staring at the cat. It was eating with its back to her, and she wondered if she had imagined hearing it answer back. The house suddenly felt very empty, and she felt cold wash over her.

'Did you just talk?' she said, realising how ridiculous it sounded even to say it. She waited for a response, but the cat continued to eat its food, completely disregarding her in the way cats did. Even so, she stared at it, convinced what had happened wasn't a figment of her imagination. Henry finished his food, pausing for a moment to clean himself. Christian looked for anything that could be seen as wrong or out the ordinary, but the cat was just that. Nothing supernatural, nothing unusual. She followed it as it returned to the sitting room and flopped onto the floor where it started to paw at one of the fluffy imitation mouse toys they had bought for it. She sat in the chair, trying to make sense of what she was sure had happened. It was reminiscent of a dream in that as the moments passed it seemed less real. The cat continued to play, oblivious to her concerns. She forced a nervous sound intended to break the silence and wished Daniel was with her. She watched as Henry got up and left the way he had come, away over the fence to wherever it went, leaving Christian alone to ponder what had happened.

V

By the time Daniel returned home that evening, she had dismissed it, convinced it was a trick of her imagination. Even so, the situation still bothered her enough to put her off her food.

'You okay?' Daniel asked, watching her from across the table.

'I'm fine, just tired.'

'You sure there's nothing else wrong?'

She shook her head, knowing how stupid it would sound if she told him what had happened earlier. 'I'm fine. Just not hungry.'

Daniel didn't push it, and she was grateful for it.

VI

'Hey look who's here.' Dan said, crossing the room to open the window. Christian looked at the cat waiting outside and almost shouted to Dan not to let it in, but he had already slid open the window.

'We've not seen him for a few days, have we?' he said, smiling as the cat waited by the kitchen for its food. 'Shall I feed him?'

She shook her head. 'No, I'll do it.' she said, determined to prove to herself that nothing had happened. She walked past the cat, looking at it as she did, then went to the kitchen and repeated the routine of getting the bowl and preparing the food, all the time aware of the cat staring at her.

'You can't tell him.'

She spun around, staring at the cat, empty can of

meat clutched in her hand. The cat was sitting by the door, tail twitching in agitation.

'You talked. I definitely heard you this time.' She said, realizing she had never been more afraid than in that moment. She waited for the cat to say something else and prove her right, but it just sat staring at her, waiting for something to happen the same way she was. They could have stood there forever if Daniel hadn't walked in.

'I hope you two are behaving.' He said, going to the fridge and taking out a bottle of orange juice.

'He's waiting for that, I think.' He said, nodding to the bowl of food on the side.

She blinked and looked away, acting on autopilot. 'Yeah, I was just giving him it now.'

She put the bowl on the floor and Henry walked to it and started to eat, the soft, wet sounds of his chewing for a second the only noise.

'I don't know where that cat puts it.' Daniel said, walking back towards the other room. 'He'll be the size of a house in no time.'

She nodded, still dazed and unable to figure out what had just happened. She half opened her mouth, intending to tell Daniel what had happened but he had already gone back to the sitting room. Instead, she glared at the cat hunched over its bowl and considered the possibility she might be losing her mind then took the empty can to the bin.

'He'd never believe you anyway.'

She spun round again, a yelp escaping her throat. Henry was sitting by his bowl staring back at her, green eyes betraying nothing. Animal and human stared at each other, then the cat walked past her towards the sitting room. She pushed herself against the doorframe as it went by wanting to keep as far away from it as possible. Trembling and knowing Dan would see something was wrong, she went to the bathroom, locking the door and doing all she could to compose herself. She was either experiencing something otherworldly which had no rational explanation or she was losing her mind. Either outcome was one she didn't want to face. She composed herself, staring at her reflection in the mirror and willing herself to be normal, then she returned to the sitting room, tense and anxious as she looked for the cat.

'He's gone,' Daniel said from the sofa. 'I swear that thing only uses us when it's hungry.'

She didn't answer, couldn't even if she wanted to. Instead, she walked to the open window and looked out at the street, wondering where it had gone.

VII

Dan had gone out and she knew this was the best chance to get the cat to speak to her. It had been in the house for ten minutes, but instead of following the usual routine of feeding it, Christian was sitting in the chair, staring at it, lips pursed together. Her phone was on the arm of the chair and recording audio.

'So go ahead, talk.' She said, knowing how crazy it would sound when she played it back if no reply came.

The cat looked at her, tail twitching, eyes trained on her.

'I'm not feeding you until you talk.'

As if in direct response, the cat lay on its side, never taking its eyes off her.

In that moment, she was a combination of things. Angry, frustrated, confused. Most of all she was afraid. Sanity, she had come to realize was a much more fragile thing than she ever imagined and it would only take one little thing to tip her over the edge.

'Talk, you little shit.' She snapped.

The cat stood and walked down the hall towards the kitchen where it stopped and sat, staring at her across the length of the room.

'No. No food until you talk.' She said, then almost laughed at how absurd it was that she was in some kind of a bizarre stalemate with a cat which may or may not have the ability to speak. Daniel always said she was stubborn but it appeared she had met her match. The cat continued to stare at her.

'Fine,' she said, getting out of her chair and heading to the kitchen. 'But only because I don't like to think of you going hungry.'

She put out the food, aware she as being watched as she went through the motions and set the dish on the floor.

'There. Food. Now talk to me.'

The cat looked at her and walked towards the dish, but it didn't eat. She knew this was going to be it and the cat was going to talk to her, but it simply put one of its rear legs in the air where it sat and started to bite at its fur.

'You better not have fleas. Stop that, you hear me?' she said, wringing her hands, unable to rid herself of the anxiety that was close to taking over. She crouched by the cat, speaking in a near whisper.

'You have to help me. If this isn't happening then I'm losing my mind.'

The cat finished cleaning itself then moved to the bowl. She watched as it ate, frustrated and enduring the mixture of fear and stupidity that was becoming the norm.

'There must be some reason this is happening.'

'I won't talk unless you stop trying to record it.'

She lurched back, landing hard on the floor and slamming her spine into the cupboard door. The cat stopped eating and looked at her in disgust at being disturbed, then returned to its food.

'Why do I never see your mouth move? Why do you always have your back to me when you talk?' she whispered to the otherwise silent room.

Maybe he's not talking.

That idea scared her more in a way because it all seemed so real. This wasn't like in the horror movies where weird shit happened in big Victorian houses draped in cobwebs and heavy with shadows. This was happening in suburbia in the middle of the day with sunlight streaming through the windows leaving nowhere for any evil things to hide and grab at her from the dark. She waited for an answer, mind reeling from what was going on.

Why did it choose me? What reason could it have to want to talk to me?

She glared at the cat as if just thinking it would present an answer, but the feline she had christened as Henry simply ate his food. She made a decision then for the sake of her sanity. She would get to the bottom of what was going on even if it meant opening that door in her mind that most people kept locked and bolted behind which the dark and madness lay. She got to her feet and skirted around the room, not taking her eyes from the cat then hurried to the sitting room and grabbed her phone. She played the recording back, skipping through in the hope it had picked up the impossible conversation, but from such a distance, all it had managed to record were a few cars passing by outside. Frustrated, she tossed the phone into the chair.

'You'll never get me on tape. It's pointless to try.'

She spun around and almost let out a scream but managed to swallow it back down.

The cat was sitting at the entrance to the room, watching her.

'God, I'm losing my mind.' she muttered.

'No, you're not.'

'I didn't see your mouth move. Are you real?'

'We're talking, even if you don't see my mouth move.'

'Prove it. I have to know this isn't just me losing my mind.'

'You hear me, don't you? We're interacting.'

'You're a fucking cat.' She said through gritted teeth. 'This makes no sense.'

'It will. And there is no need to be so rude.'

She wished the cat's mouth moved when it talked instead of it just sitting there motionless. It made it even harder to figure out if she was losing her mind or not. It was apparent to her that if the cat's mouth wasn't moving and nobody else was there to hear it speak, then she could well be imagining the whole thing.

'Relax. I'll prove I'm real soon enough. I'm here for a reason.'

'What do you want with me?'

The cat walked across the room and hopped up on the sofa. It lay down, turning its back to her as it curled itself against the cushion.

'Is this better? You don't seem comfortable looking at me when we talk. That's why I first started when you couldn't see my face.'

She gave no answer. Couldn't even if she wanted to. Her tongue was so much useless muscle sitting on the floor of her mouth.

'Anyway,' the cat said, 'On to why I'm here. I need your help.'

Christian sat in the chair. There was a certain detachment as if she were watching the conversation externally or hearing it through a wall or at a distance. She supposed it might be some kind of coping mechanism.

'I live at number 72. I need you to call the police and

get them there. Bad people live there.'

'I've not seen anything out of the ordinary. This is a nice area.' She mumbled.

'No, you wouldn't. It's what happens behind closed doors that is the problem.'

'You need to tell me more.' She replied, frightened at just how quickly this was becoming something her brain was accepting. Not normal, not even close, but acceptable which could mean she was one step closer to whatever lurked behind that locked door in her brain.

'There are bad people who do bad things to other people in the basement. I see it all the time. It's a death house.'

'I can't handle this right now. I don't know what's real.'

The cat stretched half turning towards her as it yawned. 'I'm real. And you need to help before anyone else dies. You don't need to get directly involved, just make a phone call.'

'And say what? A talking cat that may or may not be a figment of my imagination tipped me off to a potential murder house? They'll lock me up and throw away the key.'

'Maybe. But at least nobody else will die.'

'I can't deal with this alone. I need to talk to Daniel about it. He-'

'No.' The cat turned towards her as it said it, eyes now locked on hers. 'I already told you, nobody else can be involved. Only you.'

'Why just me? If you can talk to me you can talk to him. He'll know how to fix this.'

'Because human men are stupid. They try to be all macho and get directly involved and that means more people will die or get hurt. Just do the right thing and make the call.'

'Not without proof. You have to understand I'll need

some kind of evidence.'

The cat got to its feet and stretched, then hopped onto the window ledge. 'Fine. I'll get you your proof. You just make sure you keep this to yourself, for now, understood?'

She nodded, then realising the cat had its back to her and couldn't see her, said yes.

'Good. I'll be back in a day or so once I figure out how I can prove it to you. Hopefully, nobody else will get hurt before then.'

'What do I do in the meantime?'

The cat glanced at her then looked out into the street. 'Sit tight and keep quiet. Whatever you do, don't attempt to go over there. When I say bad people, I mean it.'

She was going to say more, perhaps choose one of the countless questions that were spinning around in her head to the point she was sure it was going to explode, but the cat had gone.

VIII

The house at number 72 was ordinary. There was nothing to suggest anything sinister was going on inside. The walls were painted white, and a car was parked in the driveway. The grass in the front garden was a little long but certainly not overgrown. Christian stood across the street, hands in pockets as she stared at the house. It had been a day since her encounter with the cat and although he knew something was wrong and she wanted to tell him, she hadn't said anything to Dan. The idea she was losing her mind had kept her awake most of the night, and now she wasn't even sure why she was standing across the street and staring at what appeared to be a perfectly normal residence. She had read on the internet about schizophrenia and other mental illnesses which could explain her encounters with the cat that was speaking to her, yet she was struggling to believe her imagination could work in such a way to make it so real. The longer she kept it from Dan the harder she knew it would be to eventually tell him. She felt bad keeping it from him but wasn't in a position where she even understood it herself. Telling someone else about it was, for now, out of the question.

Without realising she had done it, Christian found herself standing at the front door to number 72. She stared at the blue painted wood and knocked, her inner voice screaming at her to think about what she was doing and how, if what the cat said was true, she was putting herself in a massive amount of danger. She waited, frightened and curious and glad that the street was busy. There was a dog walker a few hundred yards away and she could see a learner driver and their instructor struggle through the process of parallel parking. She was safe enough or at least hoped so. She heard the key turn in the lock and waited for the door to open.

'Can I help you?' the man who answered said, giving her that look reserved for strangers who knock on house doors in the middle of the day. She had no idea what to expect when the door was opened but this wasn't it. The homeowner looked to be in his seventies and was bald. His eyebrows were wild and pure white and were the only hair on his heavily lined face. He looked at her from beneath them with blue eyes which were untrusting. He leaned on a walking stick and was wearing crème pants and a shirt open at the neck. She realised he had asked a question and was waiting for a response.

'Yes, hello, I'm sorry, I just… I live down the street from you and what I think is your cat has been coming to visit our house, the ginger tom? I just wanted to come and talk to you to let you know.'

It was a flimsy but plausible excuse to knock on the door, but under the circumstances, it would suffice.

'A cat?' the man said, frowning and looking past her for a second. 'I think you've made a mistake. No cat here, just me and my wife.'

'Oh, I just…are you certain?'

'Young lady, I think I would know if we owned a cat. Dreadful creatures full of fleas. You've made a mistake. Your cat isn't here.'

Or doesn't exist at all.

The thought seemed plausible, then she remembered Daniel had seen and interacted with it too. Even so, without going inside, she was certain this was no house of death.

You don't know that. Look at Fritzel. Look at Fred and Rose West. Not everything is always as it seems.

'Was there something else? I was just about to eat lunch.' The man said.

'No, nothing at all. Apologies for the inconvenience and the mistake I made.'

'It's quite alright,' the old man said, softening a little now he knew she wasn't trying to sell him something. 'There are lots of those things in this area. Strays breeding and ripping up the rubbish bags. Perhaps it belongs to one of the neighbours?'

'Yes, it's possible. Have you seen one in the area by chance? Ginger?'

The old man shook his head. 'Sorry. I can't help you I'm afraid. I've not seen it.'

'No problem, thank you for your time and sorry again for disturbing you.'

The old man shut the door and she stood there for a moment, confused and a little embarrassed.

Maybe I am losing my mind.

That seemed the most likely scenario now. The time for keeping things from Daniel was long gone. She needed his help and advice and couldn't take the pressure of dealing with it on her own. On the way back to the house she composed a text message, then for a while couldn't force herself to press send until she realised the alternative was more confusion and misery. She sent the message asking him to come home as they needed to talk, knowing now things were in motion and for better or worse, it was all going to come out in the open.

IX

Daniel didn't say anything at first. He sat on the edge of the sofa, hands clasped in front of him. She waited, giving him the space he needed to process it. She had told him everything right up to the visit to number seventy-two earlier in the day. Instead of feeling better for getting it off her chest, she felt worse for spreading the burden. Speaking about it had made her realise how insane it sounded and she hated herself a little bit for putting it on him.

'Am I losing my mind?' she said, dabbing the tears from her cheeks with a tissue.

'No, we'll work this out. You're not going mad.'

'A cat was talking to me. I just… how else do you explain it?'

'I don't know, but we'll do it together.' He went to her and sat on the arm of the chair, holding her hands in his and making her feel better.

'I'm so scared. I don't know what's real anymore and it frightens me.'

'I think we need to look at options, maybe get some kind of professional advice.'

'No, they'll take me away and lock me up. I can't do that. I'd never cope.'

'Relax and calm down, okay? I won't let anyone take

you anywhere or hurt you. I was thinking we start with some research online. See what we're dealing with here.'

She nodded, wiping her eyes again. 'I hate feeling like this. It feels so real. When it talks…'

'I understand. Try not to think about it. We can-'

She followed his line of sight to the window where the cat was pacing, rubbing itself on the glass and waiting to be let in.

'I'll shoo it away,' he said, starting to stand.

Christian grabbed his hands. 'No. Let it in. Now that you know it has no reason to hide. If it's true it can talk, it won't need to hide it and then we'll know, won't we?'

'I don't think this is a good idea. You don't need this.'

'I think I do,' she replied. 'I think this is exactly what I need right now. Please. Let it in.'

Daniel walked to the window and slid it open, watching as the cat came in and took up its usual pre feeding position in the middle of the room. Daniel returned to where he was sitting on the arm of her chair, and they both looked at the cat.

'Go ahead, you can talk,' she said, hating how crazy she sounded. 'I've told him everything. There was no death house. No bad things going on. You lied and I want to know why.'

The cat looked at them, a blank expression on its face.

'Talk to me, I know you can,' she said crying again.

Still, the cat sat there and stared.

'Calm down,' Daniel said, putting an arm around her.

'It can talk, I know it can and it's not and now I look like I'm crazy.'

'You're not crazy, we can fix this, we can.' Daniel was hugging her now, unsure what else to do.

'No, that's not the point. It can talk and it's doing this on purpose to make me look like I'm losing my mind.' She lurched out of the chair, screaming at the cat. 'Talk, you little shit. Talk to me. I know you can. Talk to me so

I know I'm not mad.'

Not liking the sudden movement or the change in volume, the cat scrambled to its feet and ran, leaping out of the window then over the gate. Dan followed and closed the window, wondering what they were supposed to do now. He watched the cat disappear down the street then turned back towards Christian, who was sitting in the chair crying. He knew no matter what, the road ahead was going to be a long one.

X

Two days had passed.

The atmosphere in the house had been difficult, to say the least. On a couple of occasions, Daniel had tried to raise the idea of them seeking help, but Christian had been too upset to even discuss it. The little research he had done into it himself had led down some paths he wasn't looking forward to them facing together, but he would do it without question if it meant getting her to the point where she was well enough to function. He had left her sleeping in bed, her nights now spent lying awake and crying, meaning the daytime naps were necessary so her body could rest. The cat had not been back and he was glad. Its presence was only ever going to cause problems until she could get the kind of help she needed. It was only when he went to the window by chance he saw it. It was sitting in front of the gate, staring at the house rather than pressing itself to the window like usual. Daniel was suddenly angry at it and didn't want to risk Christian becoming even more upset if she saw it. He waved his hand, trying to shoo it away, but the cat didn't move. It sat and looked at him the way it always did.

'Little shit,' he grunted, then went to the front door and opened it, hoping the sound would scare it off.

Again, though, it simply sat there and looked at him.

'Go on, get out of here, you hear? Go.'

The cat remained motionless.

'I said go.' He took a few steps towards it and this time the cat moved. It hopped onto the gate, balancing in the way felines did and watched him.

'You're a brave one, aren't you? Go on, go home. Get out of here.' He took another step towards the gate and this time the cat did move. It leapt onto the pavement and started to walk up the street away from the house. Daniel was about to go back inside the house when an idea came to him. He ducked back into the house and grabbed his keys, then closed it behind him. He then followed the cat as it made its way down the street. He realized he had to know for himself, he had to go to number seventy-two and follow the cat there. When they opened the door to let it in, he would confront them about why they had lied about owning it and perhaps get some answers that would help Christian in what was to come. He kept his distance, the cat hugging the side of the pavement nearest to the walls and hedges. Daniel counted the house numbers as he got closer to his destination.

62.

64.

66.

68.

70.

Here.

Number 72. Only, the cat didn't stop. It walked on. Daniel glanced at number 72 as he passed then carried on walking. The cat crossed the road and Daniel followed. It came to a garden and hopped up onto the fence then went inside. Daniel followed and stood outside, looking at the house. It was a detached property, the red brick old and tired. The windows were grubby and the grass in the garden yellow and overgrown. A trampoline with ripped netting sat forgotten in one corner. In the other, a rusty shell of an old freezer. Mounds of dog excrement littered the garden and the smell was enough to make Daniel's eyes water. The cat was waiting by the door to be let in and Daniel approached it, curiosity taking over. He stood behind the cat, looking at the object that had caught his eye. Outside, leaning against the wall was an old steel sign peppered with rust. It looked like the kind that used to hang in petrol stations to advertise motor oils. In it, was an old style formula one car, a green painted Lotus cresting a hill, driver wrestling for control as it left its rivals in its wake. Above it, in faded red paint the slogan said:

Unleash the spirit of the Lotus 72, only with Texaco motor oils.

His eyes were drawn to the number.

72.

It was then the door opened to let the cat in. Daniel and the homeowner made eye contact. Then Dan saw the hammer in the man's hand still covered in bloody human hair. There was no time to run, no time to call for help, no time to do anything before he was dragged inside and the door closed behind him as the world went on without his knowledge.

XI

She had slept for five hours and felt better for it. To her surprise, the house was in darkness when she woke and she wondered if Daniel had fallen asleep too. She walked into the sitting room, rubbing her eyes and looking around, surprised not to see him.

'Daniel?'

The house was silent, no reply coming back. She

went to the kitchen and poured a glass of water, then opened the cupboard to see what there was to eat.

'You need to get out of here.'

She spun around and saw the cat sitting by the kitchen door. 'How did you get in here?'

'They left the door open when they brought him back. You have to go. Run before they come for you.'

'Before who comes back? What are you saying? You're not even real.'

'He struggled. They got it out of him in the end though. Your address. He had his keys. There's no time. You have to go, now.'

'You lied to me. This isn't real.'

'I told you the truth. He found it. Number 72. He found it and they got him.'

'I went there. There's nothing bad there.'

The cat leaned past the outer edge of the doorframe and grabbed something in its mouth, then dropped it on the kitchen floor, blood spattering out of the end of it.

'You wanted evidence, there it is. I snatched that just after they cut it off.'

She dropped the glass, hardly aware of it smashing around her feet.

On the floor was a severed index finger. The cat sat behind it, looking at her and waiting for her to do something. Even though it was impossible to make a positive identification, she knew without a doubt it was Daniel's. Something in her gut told her it was. The fragile sanity she was hanging onto received another blow, sending more cracks shearing out towards the eventual shatter point.

'Now do you believe me? Get out of here. Tell the police to go to 72. Don't you realise what they've done? They've been here when you were sleeping. They've set you up for this. Run. Go, now and call the police. They've put him in the bedroom.'

Crying and hysterical, she ran past the cat and down the hall to the spare room, throwing the door open and going inside, slipping on the blood and falling in a heap on the floor.

The scream.

The one she had swallowed back a couple of times now over the last few weeks came in force when she saw what was scattered around the room. Amid the chaos and the panic in her broken mind, a rational thought came to her, one so calm and clear it was, in a way, the worst one of all.

There are only small pieces left.

Nausea surged in her gut and she screamed again, scrambling to her feet and covering herself in the blood all over the floor. She ran outside into the street, bloody and screaming, knowing whatever had happened to Daniel was on her. She fell to the knees in the street as they came to comfort her. The police were on their way, they assured her and asked her where she was injured so they could stop the bleeding.

She didn't hear them. She looked at her garden fence and the cat sat there watching her. It was all too much. She started to laugh, a cackle that frightened even her as her neighbours began to shout about what they had discovered in the bedroom.

Christian watched as the cat walked away down the street, the sight of it bringing more laughter.

She didn't think she would ever stop.

XII

'See? I told you. It sounds crazy.'

Detective Gibbs leaned back in his chair and folded his hands. He seemed much more at ease and confident now and she wondered if that was because he felt he had enough to convict her with.

'And you're adamant that's how it went down?'

'It's the truth.'

Gibbs exhaled and sipped his coffee. 'Alright, let's put all the cards on the table. You've told me your version of events, now let me tell you ours.'

'There is no version of events. Everything is exactly as I told you.' She said, feeling the tears well up again. Gibbs held up a hand to silence her.

'Just admit you killed him and we can help you. Tell us what you used and where you the murder weapon and I promise you I'll do all I can to help you. It's clear you need some kind of psychological evaluation.'

'I already told you. Just check out number 72 and you'll see I'm telling the truth.'

'That's just it. We already did. The homeowner was good enough to let us in without a warrant. There was nothing there.'

'What about the basement? The cat said it was in the basement.'

'They don't even have a basement. Look, let's cut the crap for a second. Here's what I think happened. You and Daniel had an argument, you lashed out and killed him. Maybe not by intention but killed him regardless. You needed a way out so you concocted this cat story to try and cover your tracks so you could plead insanity if it came to it.'

'No,' she said, crying again. 'I'd never do that.'

'Problem is, we checked the search history on your computer. You were actively looking into this. Schizophrenia. Looking for the right way to behave.'

'No, we were looking for ways to help me. Those people at number 72 killed Daniel and then brought him back to the house to frame me. The cat tried to warn me.'

'Explain how there was no sign of forced entry? The only DNA or fingerprints we found were yours and his. No murder people. No imaginary cat. Nothing.'

'I don't know, maybe they wore gloves or got him to open the door for them. You're the police, not me. I didn't do this. The cat is real. We bought him food, he has his own dishes.'

'Alright, I've heard enough of this. I've done all I can.' Gibbs said, standing and putting his hands in his pockets. 'If you're unwilling to help us then I can't help you. We'll let the courts decide, but I'm telling you now straight. I've dealt with a lot of cases that have led to convictions for a lot less than this. When we get your psych evaluations back and they say you're of sound mind, then you're looking at life in prison.'

'I know I'm not mad, I've been saying that all along. If anything, that proves I was telling the truth. Please, you have to believe me.'

Gibbs shook his head. 'There's nothing I can do for you now. It's up to the courts to decide.'

'Please, you have to believe me. Find the cat. It can talk, I swear it. Get it to tell you what happened, please…'

Gibbs heard no more. He left the interview room, confident they would get the conviction and another murderer would find themselves behind bars.

EPILOGUE

It had been a hell of a long day for Gibbs. He was finally on his way home but was unable to get the Lourenco case out of his head. Over the years, he had heard some outlandish stories used by people to try and get themselves off the hook, but talking cats was a new one. Even so, he always thought he had a good bullshit detector when it came to interviewing suspects and in this case, as absurd as it was, it seemed Lourenco was utterly convinced in her version of events. Gibbs pulled the car to a stop opposite number 72 and got out. There was no reason to go back there, as the case was as good as closed. Even so, he couldn't shake the nagging feeling he was missing something and it was starting to bother him. He leaned on the front of the car and lit a cigarette, letting the breeze carry away the smoke so his wife wouldn't know he'd had one on his way home. She'd been on him to stop smoking but with a job so stressful it was proving difficult to kick the habit. From his vantage point, he could see the old man in the house and his wife watching TV.

No.

There was no way they were capable of murder. It was stupid. The same instinct that told him Lourenco was, in her own mind at least, telling the truth was also telling him that these people were squeaky clean and guilty of nothing.

'Screw this,' he said, tossing the cigarette into the gutter.

He was tired and wanted to go home and get a few hours rest. He got back into the car and started the engine, and was about to set off when something landed on the front of his car, scaring him half to death.

'Son of a bitch,' he said, not liking the prickly feeling on his skin or the slow rumble in his gut.

The ginger cat was sitting on the bonnet of the car looking right at him. Gibbs looked into its eyes, unsure why he suddenly felt so afraid.

'Come on cat, move.' He said, tapping on the window.

The cat's tail twitched but it stayed where it was.

Gibbs had learned not to believe in coincidence over the years, but also wouldn't allow himself to be led down the road where craziness lay.

'Come on, move,' he said, tooting the horn to try and frighten it off. Still, the cat stayed where it was, staring at him. Gibbs got out of the car and was about to swat at the cat when it jumped down onto the path and stared at him.

Could it be a coincidence? This animal definitely fit based on Lourenco's descriptions, but if that was the case then maybe...

No.

Gibbs forced himself not to think about it. He wouldn't risk his career like that. He watched as the cat walked a little way down the street then stopped and looked back at him as if…

'You're waiting for me,' Gibbs muttered under his breath. 'You're actually waiting for me.'

Gibbs walked around the car and started to follow the cat, trying not to think of that old saying, the one about what curiosity did to the four legged feline. That was the last thing he wanted.

The ginger tomcat led the way and Gibbs followed, unsure where he was going or what would happen when he got there.

They Die Easy
Chad Lutzke

"It won't stay down for long," my Gramps once said, as he handed me the bag of sand. I was eight years old. My parents had long since passed, leaving me with Gramps and every skeleton that came with him. He'd felt bad that I had a long, parentless future ahead of me. He'd seen me interact with kids my age, and it never ended well. I'm not sure why. Gramps used to tell me it was because I was smarter than them and thought deeper than the rest. Eventually Gramps pulled me out of public school and homeschooled me. He taught me everything I know. He'd tell me that I knew more than any of those kids, that I'd always be smarter than them.

Gramps did everything he could to give me a good life as a young boy. But it broke his heart to see me alone with no one to call friend. No one to share a soda with. No one on the receiving end of a fast pitch, other than himself. So he did what any old man with the power to summon would do. He gave me a Djinn.

I suppose at first glance you might call it an imp, but Gramps said sometimes they look different. Mine had deep blue/green skin like a peacock's feather. All four extremities were humanoid and perfectly intact. My Djinn wasn't a legless demigod that poofed in and out of a bottle when rubbed. For the most part, it was expressionless, voiceless, and about the size of a toddler—small enough to stuff into a duffle bag when dead.

It always died easily. The first time it died was within an hour of being summoned. I had asked it to bring my parents back from the dead. There was smoke and a split ran from its shin to the top of its forehead. Blue blood seeped from the wound, and the skin fell off like an unzipped one-piece suit. It keeled over dead, right at my feet. That's when Gramps gave me the sand—a rather large pouch of it. I think he knew I'd need it frequently. Gramps told me that sometimes the Djinn couldn't handle my imagination, or any requests to raise the dead, and as a result it would die. I often asked for my parents to be alive. I was convinced that one day the Djinn would hold the power to make it happen.

I hated the texture of the sand. It was too gritty and reeked strong of death. Like a sweet, wet cardboard. Every time I opened the bag I thought of the mouse that had died within the house walls of the house one hot summer.

Gramps taught me to sprinkle the sand in the mouth of the dead Djinn, cover the body with red velvet, and bury it in a shallow grave in the back woods behind our house. The first rainfall after each burial, the Djinn would rise up after midnight the following day, then be along my side like it never left, with no memory of its temporary demise.

Fortunately for me, we lived in the northwest where it rained often. Over time, I could accurately calculate what days I should ask for my parents without being away from my Djinn for too long. Nearly every time I asked, it would rain that night. So I was never without my Djinn for more than a day or two. Gramps said I should be a weatherman.

Gramps explained that the Djinn couldn't talk but that it did understand everything I said and will obey accordingly, though he stressed the importance of never using the Djinn for bad deeds or selfish gain. He said if I ever made such demands that the Djinn would die and never come back.

So, while the wishes weren't limited in number, they were in degree. Raising the dead was certainly beyond its ability, so I stuck to only minor wishes—those of a more entertaining or helpful nature. One year I couldn't get the walls in my tree house to stand up. The Djinn strengthened the nails, and that old mess still stands today with the nails shining bright silver. Another time, there was a neighbor kid who bullied me to no end. I asked for help with that, and the boy's dad lost his job and they had to move away. I never saw the kid again. I can't be for sure that was my Djinn's doing, but I'd like to think so.

Gramps knew what he was doing when he gave me this one. While he did tell me the Djinn would have no memory of our previous times together, nor of its own death, I speculated the Djinn's memory was better than Gramps had let on. In particular each time I asked for my parents back. Granted, the wish would always result in the Djinn becoming a pile of blue-hued flesh, I began to sense deeper consideration for my request, as though the Djinn were trying harder each time to make it work. A few times, the Djinn outright exploded, leaving a bloody mess behind for me to clean up and bury. These were the times I felt he tried the hardest.

But I was wrong.

One day I headed to the back woods, looking for an ideal spot to dig yet another grave for my Djinn. It was the one hundred and eighty-seventh grave I'd dug in the last six years; all deaths related to asking for my parents back from the dead. I often wondered if my parents somehow had an idea how much I missed them or if they were able to watch over me like some people believed.

While in the woods, as though drawn to it, I stumbled across a large rock covered in blue-tinted moss. I chose the ground under it as the area for the grave and began to dig. Before too long, my shovel hit a hardened surface. I dug around it, and after much sweat revealed a three-foot long wooden box, much like a small coffin.

I sat with an uneasy feeling next to the hole I'd dug, scared to open the box. Had my Djinn been with me, I would have pried the lid open and peeked inside. Instead, I dug another hole next to the one that held the box, and buried my Djinn's remains—sand in mouth and covered with velvet. It was due to rain that night so I would wait to open the box until the morning, when I'd have my Djinn with me. Before leaving for the house, I shoveled a layer of dirt back over the box.

I woke the next morning with the Djinn sitting quietly on my nightstand. I dressed, did some of my homework, and headed for the woods while Gramps was in town. I had dreamt of the box all night. I had two dreams. In one dream, the mysterious box was filled with gold from an ancient sunken ship, and Gramps and I became rich. We bought everything we ever wanted, including a giant new house. In the other dream, the box contained a jar of gas that changed my perception of things when opened. Colors changed, things that used to seem big were now small, and even Gramps looked different. He stood tall and muscular instead of hunched and frail, yet he was sill an old man.

I headed to the burial site from the night before and easily found it. Normally I don't visit the most recent plots. They're disturbing. The ground is caved in where the Djinn had climbed out, and the first ten feet or so from the temporary graves are covered in a transparent film, like what a slug leaves behind. I took the shovel and dug away the shallow bit of dirt I'd put back onto the box. I looked at my Djinn and requested that he have my back.

Once the dirt was cleared, I pried the lid of the box open with the shovel. The nails in the lid easily gave and revealed a dirty cloth sack cinched up tight. I thought of my dream about the gold, and like many times before, I was tempted to wish for riches. But like Gramps had warned, selfish gain would cost the life of my only friend. So, like every other time, the temptation left as quickly as it came.

Once I'd opened the box, the air filled with the heavy scent of mint; though strong to the point of being unpleasant. I poked at the sack with the shovel. There was no jingling of coins. It was a solid mass that rocked when poked.

Finally, I pulled the sack from the box and set it on the ground. I slowly pulled the drawstring and opened it. It was the remains of another Djinn. It was preserved and intact like a mummy. The head had another sack on it that was wrapped tight around its neck. I removed it and found the Djinn's mouth to be covered with twine that wrapped several times around its head. It was as though precautions were taken to ensure the Djinn would never rise again.

From behind me, my Djinn jumped at the sack and helped me pull it off. I'd never seen it make such movements before. Its eyes widened; not with horror, but positively with hope. Other than when it would struggle through the wishes regarding my parents, I'd never seen any hint of emotion on its face, until now. Curious as to what had gotten my Djinn so excited, I ran back to the house and got my bag of sand and red velvet. I wanted to resurrect the dead Djinn. I removed the twine and filled its mouth with sand. I wasn't sure it would make any difference, but I put more in than usual. The sky was overcast and I knew it would rain again that day.

I filled the grave that held the box and dug a fresh one, placing the Djinn inside, then covered it with dirt. That night, as usual, Gramps slept in his chair. I, however, could not sleep at all. As midnight approached I lay in bed staring at my ceiling, wondering about the Djinn I had buried. I contemplated any possible danger I may have put myself or Gramps in. Maybe I should have told him what I'd found. I had no doubt he buried it himself and that there was reason for it. But the excitement of my own Djinn–such joy in its eyes, and the look of anticipation as it watched me perform the burial–after all these years I could not deny it whatever hope had stirring within.

Just before midnight, I snuck out. It had rained, but the clouds had parted and the night was clear and bright with the moon's glow. As I made my way to the grave, the walk of my Djinn wasn't the usual somber trudge, but almost a skip. I sat next to the grave and waited. Nothing happened for several minutes, until around half past midnight, the earth above the gravesite moved and a single, small hand poked through, followed by another. The Djinn pulled itself free from the grave. It glistened under the moonlight with a brilliance that wasn't there before, in hues of purple.

My Djinn spoke up and called the other by name. One I could not even begin to pronounce. They both interacted in front of me, using several different languages with bits of English mixed in. They'd often look at me, making it clear I was part of their discussion, then at last they spoke in only English and directed all speech toward me.

My life forever changed as a result of that conversation. And I walked under the moon, wet with tears, with years of deep reflection ahead of me. I learned that Djinns can only speak while in the presence of another, and that the Djinn I had resurrected was purposely buried by Gramps in order to keep a dark secret: that my parents were not dead at all. They were very much alive but had left me. In ways I could not understand, they had deemed me a handicap in their life. My understanding of a parent/child relationship was different than theirs. The Djinns used words like "autism" and "disorder" and "abnormality" in attempting to describe who I was and why my parents considered me a hindrance in the plans they had for their own future.

Gramps had put the burden on himself and spared me the anguish of knowing why. So much began to make sense. I now understood the struggle in my Djinn's face when I would ask, through tear-flooded eyes, for my parents to be with me once again.

I owed Gramps. He had offered to give up what others were not willing to. After speculating that Gramps created fictional rules to help keep the secret forever–as well as the rules concerning wishes based on selfish gain and bad deeds–the Djinns assured me that those wishes were indeed well within their capabilities and that no ill will would be had by any, including themselves, as a result.

Before returning home, and after much contemplation, I requested one wish that Gramps would likely regard as a bad deed. For years I'd believed my parents were dead while they lived their life without me. Dead is how they wanted to be remembered. Quietly, I spoke my wish to the Djinns, to which they replied with a grin:

"We've waited years for the opportunity to grant you this wish, Master."

Welcome to Anderson
Eddie Generous

It was the first time all night that he enjoyed any sense of peace. An ache appeared hours earlier and grew steadily. It was as if an invisible meat-grinder worked through his grey matter. Throbbing and pulsing pain traveled his slimy sinus, into his ears, and behind his eyes.

Despite the agony, there was momentary peace.

They were on day two of what proved to be a royal mistake. Driving saved them approximately three hundred bucks. Time is not money until the new jobs begin. Saving cash by driving did not save sanity.

The sun lowered into a pink crack before the aging Nissan Xterra. It was almost time to stop. The signs for Ogden seemed to stretch farther than the miles.

Ogden was the plan. Ogden had a Holiday Inn. At Ogden, according to the map printed from Google, they were exactly three quarters of the way to their new home in Fort Smith.

"Ah hell," Jerry whispered as he passed a sign for Ogden: ninety miles.

In shotgun, Rachael Jacobs shifted. Her eyes remained closed.

Small favors, Jerry thought and looked into his rearview. Billy, nine, and Kyla, seven, slept, both leaning toward the vacant center seat.

Sleep for ninety more miles?

Good luck.

To save money was an embarrassing excuse. When asked by folks they'd left behind, it was that they wanted to see more the country. The kids were getting old enough that they ought to know something about the world. Not that there was much to see from the interstate: grassy shoulders, overflowing trash bins, and asphalt. *Ooh la la!*

The sun drifted further. It was thirty minutes since the last sign and Jerry couldn't help himself upon reading the next sign: Eighty miles. He glanced at the speedometer, he was lingering right around seventy-seven.

"Impossible," he said. "Goddamned impossible."

"Tell me we're close," Rachael said, eyes still closed.

"Eighty miles yet."

She opened her eyes then. "How slow have you been driving? Map said we should've finished the day at eight. It's eight now!"

"Shh."

"Mom, I gotta pee," Kayla said.

The demon on the meat-grinder laughed maniacally and threw the handle into overdrive. Jerry imagined pulling over and dropping his family off in a ditch, leaving them for the mountain lions, or the coyotes, or the cannibals, or whatever the hell lived out in the middle of that lifeless stretch of county highway.

"Hey, look!" Rachael said. "Food and sleep, next exit."

The way she described pictures on signs made Jerry wish he turned tail at the altar to live a bachelor's existence until something better came along. There were a million little aggravations he hadn't noticed before that blew trumpets in chorus lately.

Stopping early screwed up the plan for the next day. Jerry nearly screamed this. They had a plan and wasn't it *just like her to screw with the plans?*

"Dad, I'm hungry," Billy said.

"I gotta pee!" Kyla screeched.

Jerry's left index finger made circles on his left temple. Another sign danced into view, EXIT .5MI. Jerry blinkered his way across the lanes while the volume within the vehicle continued to rise. Everybody wanted something and he wanted peace.

The sign at a T suggested a right for food and shelter and a left for fuel. Jerry turned right and saw the first sign for Anderson. *2 MI.* Onward, Jerry and Rachael ignored the constant harmonious whine from the backseat.

Two miles, two miles, Jerry increased the pressure against his temple uncertain if it really helped. The Nissan pulled to another T. Anderson was to the left and Jerry rolled thinking he'd done his two miles, *so where are you, you sonofabitch?*

It was eerily dark away from the interstate. Tall trees on either side of asphalt blocked out any moonshine. Jerry rolled down his window and took a deep breath. The air was good. Surely at any second they'd find a McDonald's or Dunkin's, then a Super 8 or a Holiday Inn. He closed his eyes again, taking in cooling, fresh air.

The wheels bumped and crunched. Jerry's weary eyes opened onto the gravel road. Two more miles along.

"Mom, I gotta pee!" Kyla shouted louder than earlier and Jerry slammed on the brakes.

"Rachael, take her to the ditch if she's got to piss so damned bad that she can't shut up a minute!"

"Don't you yell at me because you're a shit driver," Rachael seethed.

"I'm not kidding… mind me, for once!" Jerry shouted until something cracked at the back of his throat. "Go, now," he rasped.

Rachael sneered but unbuckled and pulled Kyla out of the back.

"Dad, we gonna get something to eat soon?"

Jerry wished his son older. Wished him all the way to adulthood so he could drag him out of the vehicle and pummel his smart mouth. *God, it would be good to punch something.*

"Real soon, give me a break, huh?" Jerry begged with a frog's whisper.

"Dad, how come we're still driving, you said…"

The words melted away and that bastard fixing hamburger of his brain ran the whole mess through a blender. Jerry closed his eyes again and tried to imagine a soft bed. Nope. Jackhammers, lawnmowers, motorcycles, racecars, rocket ships.

Doors opened and closed. Jerry slid the shifter into gear and rolled on. One mile. Two miles. Three miles. Four miles and there was another T. The hand carved sign directed him right to Anderson. In seconds, the gentle light invaded the dark landscape and relief began a slow wash. The gravel bumped to mostly smooth asphalt and a sign welcomed the Jacobs family to the town.

Tall bulb lamps lined the street like something out of Dickens, but electrified in the modern terms. Homes had white picket fences, or elm trees with tire swings, or flagpoles with stilled patriotic symbols, and then some had it all. There appeared no Golden Arches. A diner came into view and in many ways that was better.

"Under the Umbrella," Rachael said, reading the sign above the diner windows.

Jerry parked the Nissan in next to an older Ford truck and two recent model Chevy sedans. The kids raced for the doors, Rachael behind them a step, and Jerry bringing up the rear. A silver bell jangled on the doorframe and a middle-aged woman in a peach shirt and a white apron waved.

The floor was checkerboard grey and white, the booths were brown vinyl and the tables were worn faux-stony Formica with tarnished stainless steel ribbon bolted around the edges. The bench seating wheezed under the weight of the family.

The waitress moved at a steady pace across the floor. "Hey'a folks. Fryer's cooling, but the grill's on and we've got pie. Just so ya know."

"So no fries," Rachael explained to the kids.

"But I want fries," Billy sulked.

"Well that's too bad, kid," the waitress said, never losing her smile, or her charm.

Jerry laughed.

Rachael scowled.

"You need time or you want me to lay it out for you?"

"Excuse you," Rachael said, expecting the woman in the apron to kiss ass right up to tip time. "I don't know where you think you get off with such an attitude…"

Jerry sighed and then said, "Four burgers, three with the works, one with only cheese. Three Cokes, one iced tea, and four glasses of water. Please."

The waitress patted his shoulder and smiled. "Right away, sir."

"What a bitch," Rachael said under her breath.

Jerry watched the woman through the cook's window and thought the opposite. That woman gave him the first hint of respect he'd had all day, hell, since the damned trip began.

"I've got to pee," Jerry said and slid from the bench.

Uncertain of direction, he walked toward a dim corner, sure enough there was a door featuring the universal sign for toilet. Another door opened down the hall before Jerry entered the can and the waitress popped out.

"Thought you looked like you could use a smile," the woman said as she approached.

Jerry, curious, waited by the open door. The waitress reached into her apron and withdrew a pill bottle. Tylenol. She popped the lid and held out the bottle.

"Thanks," Jerry floated his hand palm up.

Without looking at the pills, Jerry popped three into his mouth and dry-swallowed. The waitress smiled and he entered the can. Standing before the toilet, out and flowing, the door behind him opened.

"Occupied," he said and shook off. "Two seconds."

Before he flushed hands came around his hips and a body pressed tight behind him.

"Pills aren't a smile," a whispered voice said into his ear.

Fingers worked faster than he could've imagined. Jerry closed his eyes and in seconds, the headache drained out as those hands stroked and cradled and rubbed. He exploded. It was all gone, but for the sense of guilt.

"Jesus, what am I...?" he started to say as he turned to find the room empty.

Quickly he washed his hands and charged back out to his family. If he was fast then maybe they'd never know and maybe he tell himself it never happened, and eventually, maybe, he'd believe it. The waitress stood at the table with his family, she had laid out four plates as well as the drinks. Much more than a single trip's payload and he was gone for *what, three, four minutes?*

The waitress was in view or in presence for most of it.

Jerry took the smile the waitress offered, even tried to bat one back. Suddenly, he knew he had nothing to feel guilty over because he hallucinated the whole thing. The road can play tricks on a traveller, whether riding between the lines or stopped for a bite.

The burgers were fine. The price was right. The tired Jacobs' asked directions to a motel. The waitress laughed. The motel in town was two doors down.

Jerry turned the key twice before the engine caught. It had never done that before. He rolled to the motel, Rainy Days Inn, and parked again. That jogging start was a new worry, one he'd try to push aside until morning. He needed rest.

Rachael went in to pay and came out with the first smile she'd worn all day. They'd gotten to Anderson at eight-fifty-five and it was minutes after ten when they finally settled into the two queen beds of the rented room.

At first light, Jerry showered. Rachael followed and then the kids begrudgingly each took a turn. Rather than drive back the short distance, the family paraded along the clean sidewalk to the diner.

Jerry's heart fluttered at the memory that was or was not. Unable to help it, he excused himself after the waitress–a different one–came by the table with menus. Forcing a frown, he made noise in the hall leading to the washroom. Nobody came out and he shrugged it off. Once inside he waited a moment, not actually having to go. He stared at his reflection in the smoky mirror and heard the door open behind him.

"Occupied!" he called out.

"Oh you do like to say so," a whisper said.

It was no hallucination and Jerry lifted his eyes to the tile drop ceiling while he let those knowing hands do their work. Wonderful.

Gobs clung to the porcelain and he rinsed out the sink before he stepped through the door into the hallway. No guilt this time. None at all.

Rachael had ordered his usual, almost. As was her style, she ordered one item slightly off and then pretended that she hadn't meant to do so. It was a game as old as time. The war of the sexes.

Smiling in spite, he munched down his semi-running eggs, taters, crispy bacon, and brown toast. Liquid egg yolk made him think of aborted chicken fetuses.

Rachael's eyes wandered about the diner. Billy held Jerry's cellphone, playing something, and Kyla held Rachael's doing the same.

"Everything good for you folks?" the waitress asked.

Never getting much of a look at the face matching the friendly hands in the washroom, he wondered if this was the woman. As much as he figured it had to be the woman from the night before, it didn't seem to fit. The timing was askew. Not that that mattered, in a few short minutes they'd be gone from Anderson forever.

Jerry and the kids cleared the room while Rachael went to check out. They'd loaded the Nissan fully by the time a blushing, grinning Rachael stepped through the office door.

"What are you so smiley about?" Jerry asked under his breath and turned the key. It didn't kick. It didn't click. It didn't buzz. "What now?"

He pulled the hood latch as Rachael got in the vehicle.

"Won't start?" she asked, her voice was higher than normal.

"Battery, I think."

The cell service was great and it took only a few seconds for Jerry to locate the number of a tow service that could give him a boost.

"You're at the motel? In that Nissan?" a gruff voice asked.

"Uh, yeah. How'd you know?"

"I'm looking at you out my window. Be there in a couple minutes."

Jerry looked around the quaint world of Anderson. Sure enough, there was a gas and service station further down the road: Sunshine Automotive.

Traffic was limited and only a few people strode up the sidewalks of the village. The man that came by to boost the vehicle looked as if pulled from a fifties' Esso advertisement, sans captain's cap.

"Try it," he said.

Jerry turned the key and the silence reigned.

"Nothing!"

The man jiggled the clamps and demanded Jerry try again, and again. It was lifeless. The reliable Nissan was suddenly a mass of metals and plastic, and ass pain.

"For shit sakes," Jerry said slamming the driver's door.

"Don't get excited. I can have a look, but we need to get it to the shop. Hey boy, you look about old enough to drive," the mechanic said.

Billy's eyes glowed. "Me?"

"Sure, you hop up in behind the wheel."

Jerry started to protest and Rachael waved him off. The family and a middle-aged mechanic in blue overalls pushed the stalled SUV a quarter-mile to the service station. Billy did a fine job steering.

"Worse places to get stuck, I figure," the mechanic said.

Jerry grimaced slightly and Rachael gathered what they might need to entertain the kids for a morning. As a family, they strode off the main drag of Anderson and came upon a small park. It was drab and rusty, but a fine spot to stretch out.

A little before noon, Jerry called the mechanic and the mechanic offered a summation. Battery shot and fuel pump on its last legs, a combination that would keep the Jacobs family waiting until parts arrived. It was a lost day.

Instead of getting mad, Jerry shrugged.

The shipping container with all their stuff was long awaiting them in the driveway of their new home and his job didn't start for a week. Rachael's didn't start for two. There was no school and damned if he'd turn down free smiles at Under the Umbrella.

Rachael offered to find the grocery to gather the goods for a picnic. According to her phone, it was two blocks away. Jerry shrugged again. He was all right with parking it while the kids watched videos saved to the tablet.

They ate and three o'clock became four. Jerry wondered if that meant they'd spend another night in Anderson. He dialed the mechanic and got no answer.

"We'd better go see. I guess we'll likely need to take a room again," Jerry said.

At this, Rachael's eyes sparkled.

Billy and Kyla were bored and began to argue. Jerry told them to shut up. Rachael told them to shut up. They continued bickering and pinching and punching.

They found the service station vacant, but with every door open. It was strange and off-putting. Their luggage was there in the Nissan and the mechanic left it unlocked for any thieves in the area. Not that Anderson seemed a hotbed for much of anything unruly.

Things needed gathered, Rachael used the secondary fob to lock the vehicle and they started back toward the motel. She wondered how she'd word it so that she could shoot inside unattended–catch a quick smile from behind while she filled out the paperwork–when Jerry offered to take the kids for pie and ice cream at the diner. She agreed. Both had agendas and ways of dealing with the stress of the road. Anderson was so nice to offer.

The motel was empty.

The diner was empty.

The children sat at the same booth they'd used at both the initial visits while Jerry stood outside. The breeze had picked up and storm clouds began gathering overhead. A single fat drop landed on Jerry's face. It was cool and nice. He peered down the parking lot outside the diner windows. The old Ford truck was there, as were the two Chevs.

Beyond the vehicles in the lot, Rachael stepped toward him on the sidewalk. She wasn't smiling. Jerry walked toward the road and looked north and then south. Empty of life.

Glancing back, he registered the plates on the vehicle for the first time. The truck was from Wyoming. One Chev was from New York and the other was from Alberta.

"The guy wasn't there," Rachael said.

"These cars were here last night too. They're from out of state."

"So what?"

Jerry shook his head. "No idea, but the whole damn town seems gone and there's something strange about out of state vehicles parked here when there's no drivers here to accompany them."

"That is strange," Rachael said. "You know, Jerry, I've been thinking. Maybe this move wasn't such a good idea, maybe we're just running from the real problem."

"Now's not the time. I think we ought to get the kids and figure…"

Rain began to fall in a torrent. Rachael and Jerry both sprinted into the diner where they could watch the downpour from assumed relative safety.

"Where is everyone?" Rachael demanded, flustered, staring at a business card pinned to the wall just inside the doorway. A man named Morgan Ryerson worked for a travelling insurance company called Pribine. The card had curled some in the atmosphere. Seeing the phone numbers typed along the bottom third, Rachael pulled her phone from her purse.

"No bars."

Great service all day and suddenly no bars, no residents, no vehicle, no bonus smiles, and no supper.

Jerry stomped into the diner. His children stared at him. They'd made a pyramid of napkin dispensers and had done so at another table, *wisely*, so they saw it. Using a different table gave them the benefit of doubt, even if there was not another soul to take blame. To their surprise, Jerry stormed past the towering pyramid of shining stainless steel and white paper.

"Hello! Is anybody back there?" Jerry shouted and looked into the kitchen, over the clean aged equipment toward a screen door. His body followed his gaze. "Anybody out there?"

Rain thumped like hail. In the distance, beyond a line of houses, were rows of shadowy trees. Other than the road through town, the place was a forest. If it were like the rest of the state, he guessed eventually those forests butted against either farmland or mountains.

Suddenly the pleasant, welcoming town of Anderson was ominous. It was almost as if someone or something had zapped the life out of the place.

"Something? Jerry, you're losing your marbles."

There was a crack and a bolt of lightning slashed the dim sky. For that bright second, Jerry thought he saw figures standing in the street behind the diner, on yards, amid the trees. He shivered and then as if someone flipped a switch, the rain ceased.

He peered for long seconds and then jumped.

"Hey'a, can I get ya something?" the waitress from his first visit asked.

Jerry spun and the diner was alive with life. A tubby cook in a stained apron and yellowed undershirt smiled a gap-toothed grin while he stood next to the fryer. There was a disconnect happening somewhere and Jerry drank in the world about him. The grill sizzled, the air reeked of hot oils, and Rachael was crying out. Something like a landed fish, Jerry felt his jaw working as his addled brain attempted sense of it all.

"Go on out and we'll fix you up something nice," the waitress said and then leaned forward, "and if you're still stressed, someone can meet you in the toilet, no extra charge." She jerked off the air and made a squishy sound with her tongue and inner cheek.

"I'm… no, I'm ok… for now," Jerry mumbled and rushed out of the kitchen in the direction of his family who had huddled in their usual booth. "Let's go!"

Rachael corralled the quiet and frightened children without trouble and passed three smiling women in puffy Sunday dresses. The women remarked on the cuteness of the children and one leaned down to pinch at Kyla's cheek.

Jerry's cellphone rang in his pocket as he stood in wait. "Hello?"

"This is Bernie over at Sunshine."

Jerry blanked only a moment before replying. "Tell me it's ready! We're leaving as soon as it's ready!"

"Oh, umm, I guess I can do a little overtime. Swing by at about seven, it'll cost ya though."

"Fine. Fine."

Rachael reached Jerry outside the door. The sun was high and the parking lot was dry and dusty. In fact, the only dampness remaining from the torrent downpour was on the backs of a husband and wife momentarily stranded.

"Nissan's ready at seven, then we're gone."

"Yeah, until then?"

"I don't know, not the diner. What about the motel?"

Rachael gulped thinking about her easy smiles and wanted nothing to do with the skilled man the snuck out from behind the desk ever again. Those smiles had soured.

"You have to go in though, to book. I can't."

Jerry frowned. "Come on kids, back to the room for a couple hours."

A couple hours. A lifetime. Little difference.

Jerry stared at his watch, the hands refused to increase pace. At six, the children forgot the fear and began to complain about hunger.

"You're monsters, you know that?" Jerry asked his children seriously, candidly.

Billy whined, "Mom, I'm hungry and Dad said…"

"Market, let's go to the market. It will kill time then we'll get the car, grab our bags and go. Sound good?" Rachael asked, speaking only to her husband.

Jerry agreed and they set off. Most of the life that had arisen after the storm had again departed. It was a lot of walking for the modernized children and they moaned constantly. The front of the grocery came into view and clouds began to gather once again. Three fat drops landed on Jerry's head. He glanced skyward. Rachael saw the trepidation and when the heavens opened, the children burst towards the grocery in a sprint.

"Wait!" Rachael screeched.

Soaked instantly, Jerry gathered more storm into his clothing before recognizing that he ought to follow Rachael. Through the window, he saw mostly as he expected. A wind chime tingled as the door opened.

Rachael was calling out for the children, walking up and down the front of the room behind the till, gazing along vacant aisles.

"Where'd they go?"

Rachael spun. "How the fuck do I know?"

"There's no need to yell, just a question!"

Jerry stomped up the center aisle and toward an EMPLOYEES ONLY door. Rachael trailed him, shouting out names. Lightning flashed and this time Jerry saw no figures in the glow. His eyes remained hardened on the door at the back of the store.

Thunder rolled.

More lightning flashed.

"In the restaurant, I saw things outside. I saw people," Rachael said, jogging up to Jerry.

The thunder began a constant drum and the lightning danced to the beat.

Jerry reached the door and yanked it open. Lightning cast a strobe and as if peering through a poorly constructed penny viewer, the Jacobs watched a weightless man charge at them wielding a sickle.

The only sound came from the atmospheric disturbances. The charging man was silent despite an open mouth. Jerry slammed the door and fell back. Rachael jumped sideways and the man blew through the swinging door on the light of the storm.

Jerry rolled onto his side. Rachael screamed and stumbled against a rack of potato chips. The man stood over Jerry, smiling and cocking back his arm before slamming down with a practiced arc.

A blink before the rounded blade slashed into flesh, the lightning ceased and the activity of the grocery snapped to life. There were four customers perusing goods and one at the till. A woman with a giant mole and thick glasses smiled at Jerry and Rachael.

Scared and confused, Jerry climbed upright and tried the door again. Rachael wanted to tell him no, but the children had to be somewhere. Had to be and that door was the only option he wanted to consider.

Through the door, a man poked his head from around a corner. He held a box cutter and a cut piece of skid banding. It was the same man that charged from the light of the storm. But not.

Jerry backed up three steps and ran through the door, shouting over his shoulder, "Get the Nissan, pay whatever, and wait on the road! I'm gonna find the kids!"

Rachael nodded and turned heel.

"Can I help you buddy?" the sturdy man with box cutter asked.

Jerry pivoted once close to the man and drove his shoulder into the man's stomach. Unready, the man fell backwards, the air whooshing from his lungs via goofily pursed lips.

"Where are my kids?"

The man's surprise quickly melted. He put a hand down and began pushing himself up. The difference in size and strength was obvious. Jerry ran through the damp, cool area to a loading dock. He cried out for the children, slowing to a jog. The man from the grocery leaned against the loading dock door and watched Jerry tear away, unconcerned.

Where would they go?

It was like any small town. Nothing enthralling, nothing to pull attention.

There was a wall of homes ahead of him and one vast greyed shed. Stupid, the children hadn't run out of the grocery. Someone took them somewhere.

The breeze picked up and the clouds gathered overhead as if plucked from a time-lapsed video. A damn burst and rain battered the dry world of Anderson.

Thunder crashed and Jerry jumped. Ball lightning swirled and jerked, shining unreal figures over the street.

Jerry screamed and broke for a home. The sickle-wielding grocer chased, children and the elderly chased, all nuts and all *electric*. The street was suddenly full of flimsy blue life. The universe wanted a piece of Jerry Jacobs.

Jerry broke through the door of a shed.

It was darker inside. The lightning glowed constant through the windows and quick on his heels were the blue figures. It took only seconds before he understood that he'd cornered himself.

"Billy? Kyla?" he shouted, huffing for air.

Thunder cracked god-like reports amid a continuous roll. Into the dim wooden shed, the murderous figures followed him. Creeping. Closer. He closed his eyes and ran. His lungs pounded. His head ached amid the aches, the exhaustion, and the fear. Pain struck. His face found the end of the building amid an enveloping shadow. Upon impact, he tumbled.

Jerry spun and reeled his legs tight to his chest. "Go away!"

There were figures pouring in through the door. The grocer led the charge. Each carried tools of destruction. All wore masks of fate.

"Please, I want my kids and…!"

As the figures passed the spots where the lightning did not touch, they disappeared, reappearing once the glow resumed. Closer and closer. Jerry screeched helplessly, begging the universe for intervention. The grocer swung a wide arc and as the blade disappeared as it reached the heavy shadow cloaking Jerry.

"Daddy!" a voice cried somewhere out the window.

The figure looked around, stalled and waiting for Jerry to crawl within reach.

"Daddy!"

"Hold tight baby, I'm coming!" Jerry cried back and reached from the shadow for an oil can leaning against the wall.

A knife cut through the light and Jerry jerked his arm as if stabbed with a razor-edged cattle prod. Blood dripped and an old man clutching a butcher's knife grinned. Jerry scrunched tight and waited.

The children continued to scream beyond the wall. Jerry's heart ached and not for a second did he recall fantasizing about leaving them in the ditch or boxing his son bloody. He had to save them. Had to rescue them. Had to…

The storm ceased suddenly. The blue figures evaporated. Jerry shot to his feet with a limited understanding of survival.

"Billy! Kyla!"

At the backend of the shed was a tree. Tied to that tree were the children. Unthinking of how much the situation appeared an obvious trap, the man ran to his children. Once there, the skies opened and rain began to fall again. He tugged and slipped the knots in the skinny yellow ropes.

The storm surged and the voiceless figures appeared all around them.

"Shadows! Get out of the light!" Jerry screeched and took a hand of each of his children.

They raced, screaming. Behind them and next to them on either side, the blue things surged, closing the gap, but never coming too close.

"The dumpster!"

The steel dumpster was mostly empty and had no lid. Jerry lifted Kyla in first and then Billy. He felt a shocking fist jab into the back of his head while he climbed, forcing him to tumble down on top of his kids. They screamed into the garbage, but were safe for a time.

The blue things were outside the dumpster, shaking and slamming the steel.

"What do you want?"

"Where's Mommy?" Billy asked.

"Yeah, I want Mommy!"

"Shh, ok?" Jerry cooed, hoping to God that Rachael had figured out the protection of shadows and that the Nissan was ready and rolling.

Again, the storm ceased and the sneering blue faces Jerry peered at through the cracks disappeared.

"Quick now!" Jerry shouted, dropping the children outside the grimy steel bin.

The headache returned and was in full bloom. The hair on the back of his neck had singed and the cut on his hand hardly trickled from the cauterizing effect of the electric slash. The wind sped and the clouds rolled.

"We have to run all the way, ok?" Jerry tugged his children toward the main street. The Nissan was not there. The wind pushed them on. "Come on. Come on."

Kyla wailed and Billy cried, followed their father.

They reached the service station and peered at the dismantled SUV. Wheels, panels, gas tank, someone had gone to work and they were not about to leave in the vehicle.

"Jerry!" Rachael screeched and popped up out of the service pit beneath the Nissan. Grease coated her and her hair was slick with oil. "There's monster people! Ghosts are everywhere!"

"I know! I know!" Jerry shouted, holding his wife and kids.

The wind picked up and the clouds began to gather.

"Holy crow, you can't be out there in the storm!" a waitress shouted from the doorway of a tall house across the street. "Come on! Come on, before they come back!"

Jerry scooped up Billy and Rachael took Kyla. Again, they ran as hard as possible. The rain dropped and the thunder pounded. It came slower this time. The lightning slashed bolts and the waitress disappeared into the home.

Rachael and Kyla stepped through the open door first, then Jerry and Billy.

"Up here," the waitress said.

There were shadows leading the way up a set of stairs. It was black mid-way up and that was good, black was safety, black was hope.

"Come on!" the waitress said from the top step.

There was a glowing strip rounding a door. Rachael reached it first and felt for a handle.

"Jerry, I cheated on you. I'm sorry. It was the man from the motel. I had to tell you."

"What?" Jerry screeched, cradling his son, following his wife and daughter through a door.

"It meant nothing and I didn't really do anything… like a really, really good massage."

"Oh," he said and thought, *I took smiles too, they got us both… but why?*

The door slammed behind him and voices chanted in the silent darkness. *"Rain, rain go away. Accept blood sacrifice on this day."*

The ceiling opened and the lightning emblazoned an iron altar. The townsfolk shined in amalgamated forms, flesh and light together in grotesque harmony. Hands jerked Billy from Jerry's grasp.

"No!"

Dancing blue blades sliced into Rachael. Her blood steaming on the heat of the current before running down onto the altar, attracting a bolt of searing white light from above.

"You motherfu…!" Jerry gargled on the word as blood sprung up his throat.

The children screamed once more each before they joined their parents as fleshy sacrifices upon this horrid platform. Meat and fluids dripped and rolled.

The lightning danced and the electric storm accepted the sacrifices. The rain slowed, the thunder quieted and the lightning ceased.

The townsfolk swayed, hand-in-hand, eyes closed, faces turned to the clear skies above.

~

In a Chrysler minivan, the Tootoo family had begun the immense trip from Winnipeg to San Francisco at three AM. Neither Todd nor Brenda could drive another hour. They took an exit that promised food and shelter.

"Gees, where is this Anderson place, huh?" Brenda asked.

"Don't ask me, I'm just the driver," Todd joked, exhausted, hungry, and in need of a toilet.

They turned right at the second T since the interstate and saw the evening lights of a quaint village.

"Look't, the diner's still open," Brenda said. "What do you kids say to some hot eats?"

The four Tootoo children in the back two rows of the van peeled their eyes from the screens and shouted in agreement. Todd parked the van between a Nissan Xterra and a Chevy Cruze. A dust cloud climbed from beneath the Chrysler's wheels.

"Sure is dry here, huh?" Todd asked.

The Damned
Wade H. Garrett

The Damned

Tim Murray opened his eyes and glanced at the clock. It was 3 AM. He eased his head up to see if his wife was asleep. When he noticed she was snoring, he became aroused. He softly spoke in her ear. "You awake?" Excitement overcame him when she didn't answer—he was hoping she was asleep. He eased his blanket off, then slowly got out of bed, being as careful as possible not to awaken her.

Something caught his eye as he stood next to the bed; the moonlight was shining through a window, illuminating his reflection in a mirror that was hanging on the wall. He wasn't happy with the person he was looking at, and it seemed as if he was staring at a stranger. He was now in his early thirties, his red hair receding and his face showing signs of aging. It seemed like it was only yesterday when he was in his twenties and full of life; now he was getting old, and that sucked. He smiled as he admired his new mustache, thinking how he should have grown it a long time ago, then he frowned when he noticed his medium-sized beer belly.

His penis began to harden with anticipation, causing him to lose interest in his reflection. He looked at his wife and quietly asked, "You awake?" When she didn't answer, he could feel his penis growing larger in his pajama bottoms from the lust that was building up inside of him. He asked again, "Are you awake?" Still no response. She seemed to be in a deep sleep, indicating that she had taken a sleeping pill. He was now fully aroused.

He tiptoed to the bedroom door and eased it open, then closed it quietly behind him. He slipped through the darkness like a thief in the night. He could feel the butterflies building in his stomach as he stood at another bedroom door. He knew deep inside what he was planning was a crime against God and nature, but he had done it for so long that he was now numb to it—his desires had overtaken his humanity. The door squeaked as it closed behind him.

Fifteen minutes later he slipped back into bed. His heart was racing as he laid next to his wife, worrying that if she ever found out about his transgressions, his life would be over. Fuck it, he thought, it would be my word against theirs. And it's who I am, so why am I feeling guilty? It's not my fault I was born this way. Relief overcame him as he comforted himself. His eyes became heavy and within no time he fell asleep.

Tim awoke abruptly, feeling nauseous and lightheaded. The sun was up and it seemed exceptionally intense, causing him to squint. He must have overslept, he thought. Everything was blurry and he could only see shadows. A strange feeling overcame him. Something wasn't right. He was cold and his legs felt numb. When he sat up, he noticed he was nude and his body felt stiff. He rubbed his eyes to clear up his vision. What the hell, he thought, I didn't drink last night. Suddenly, the numbness in his legs changed to a burning sensation. He became confused when he found himself on a stainless-steel table. His lower body was covered with a blood-stained sheet. He jerked it away, revealing a horrifying sight; rows of fishhooks lined the insides and outsides of his legs. Each hook was connected to a steel wire, and the wires on the insides of his legs entered holes that were running down the center of the table. The wires on the outsides of his legs ran off the sides of the table. The wires were very tight, causing his skin to be stretched outwards in a gruesome manner.

He was still light headed, but his vision was quickly clearing up, allowing him to see further. Horror overcame him when he realized he wasn't in his bedroom. He looked up and noticed the bright light wasn't from the sun but from some lights above. When he looked to his right, he noticed there were six more stainless-steel tables with people on them. The tables were lined up side by side with about three feet of space between them. Four men were awake and sitting up. They had already removed their sheets, and their legs were bound in the same gruesome manner. A woman on the far end was starting to come around and she seemed as dazed as he was. One man was lying down, possibly still asleep, or maybe dead, he wasn't sure. He reached out to the men who were sitting up and yelled out in a raspy voice, "I need some help!"

An older, heavy-set man that was next to him spoke. "Just stay calm. The effects will wear off shortly."

Tim could barely hold his head steady. He felt like he had just gotten off a merry-go-round. "Effects of what? What are you talking about?"

"We were given some type of drug."

"Given what? Why? I don't understand."

"Just try to remain calm."

"Who are you?"

"My name is Henry. I woke up in here just like you did."

"I feel strange… I can't think straight."

"You're still lightheaded, but it will wear off in a little bit."

He leaned over the side of the table and vomited. He wiped his mouth with the back of his arm, then looked at Henry. "Where am I?"

"Not sure. Like I said, I just awoke shortly before you did."

He noticed Henry was nude and around sixty years old. He was also big, around three-hundred pounds. He was bald on top, but the rest of his hair was very long and unkempt. He had a long gray beard and his body was covered in gray hair. He looked like a sasquatch. Tim looked around for a moment, then back at Henry. "I don't recognize this place. Where are we?"

"I've already told you I don't know."

"You must know something."

"I'm sorry, son, I don't. Like I said, I awoke myself just before you did. About an hour ago."

Tim noticed the other three men were sitting up and talking to each other. They were on the other side of Henry and the man that was still lying down. He pointed towards them. "What about them? Do they know what's going on?"

"No. None of us do."

Tim started panicking. He needed answers. He started shouting, "I need help! Anyone here? Please come help me!"

One of the other men yelled out, "Hey! Calm down. It's no use yelling for help."

Tim was desperate. "Someone must know something. I need some help."

Henry seemed aggravated. "I told you to keep calm. You're upsetting the others."

"I'm sorry, but how can everyone just sit and do nothing?"

"We haven't just been sitting with our thumbs in our asses. We've all yelled for help. No one is here except for us."

Tim leaned forward to grab his sheet so he could cover his privates, but something jerked him back. He noticed there were metal bands around his wrists. Chains ran from the bands to his neck. He grasped his neck, finding a leather collar; it felt thick and tall. He felt around it to see if he could remove it, but it was secured with a pad lock. He looked at Henry and noticed he had one too. The collar looked beefy and covered most of his neck. It reminded him of the bondage style collars he'd seen in pornos. He noticed a chain was secured to the back of his collar, and the other end was connected to the end of the table behind him. "Why are we chained?"

"I don't know." Henry grabbed his collar. "But the damn thing is too tight."

Tim noticed the room seemed very large. In fact, he couldn't see any walls or the ceiling due to the darkness. Only the area around the tables was lit with high bay lights. "We seem to be in a large building of some sort." He looked at Henry. "Do you at least have a speculation as to what is going on?"

A fearful expression overcame him. "All I know is, I want to get the fuck out of here before something bad happens."

Tim looked confused. "Bad?" He looked at his legs. "How much worse can it get?"

"Have you not looked around?" Henry pointed to a machine that was sitting on a track system. "I don't want to stick around to see what that's going to be used for."

Tim noticed the machine had a large saw blade, around three feet in diameter. "We must be in an old saw mill or something."

"I don't think so. I've worked in one before. This equipment is different, and the way everything is laid out, I think it's intended for us."

"Why would someone want to do such a thing? There's got to be another explanation." Tim noticed some ducts. Each person had the open end of a two-inch pipe right above them. The seven pipes ran to a steel junction box that was mounted up high. From there, a single pipe ran to a large glass hopper that was on the other side of the tracks. He pointed to the piping. "Check out the pipes. It looks like a dust collection system." He noticed numbered signs were hanging above each table. He was number one, Henry was number two and so on. "This equipment isn't meant for us; it's used for some type of production. There were probably some type of hoppers or containers under these pipes. Someone just happened to put these tables here. We just have to figure out why."

Henry shook his head. "I'm glad you're optimistic, son, but I'm afraid you're wrong."

"Stop calling me son. My name is Tim."

"Listen, I'm not the bad guy here. No need to be snappy with me."

"Sorry. I'm just scared. Something bad must have happened and I need to find out what." Tim thought for a moment, then his eyes got big. "I know. Maybe there was some kind of disaster that has happened, like a terrorist attack or something, and the government had to use any buildings that weren't damaged for makeshift hospitals."

"That wouldn't explain our legs."

"Maybe we all have the same type of injuries and they grouped us together for treatment."

"Those kinds of thoughts have run through my mind as well, but there is no medical reason to do this to our legs. It's barbaric. And the collars around our necks, being chained; that tells me we're being held captive, possibly for some type of torture."

Tim started getting upset. "That's not true. You're mistaken. We're just here for treatment or something. No one would want to harm me."

"You're just in denial."

"No, I'm not. This is all explainable. This is just a makeshift hospital or something. Someone will come around eventually and explain what's going on."

"If this is a makeshift hospital, then why are we all on top of stainless steel tables? That alone points more to my theory of being held captive."

"Maybe it's all they had."

"Do you think these tables already came equipped with these knives?"

"What?"

Henry pointed to the side of Tim's table. "You have a knife hanging beside your table. We all do."

Tim noticed there was a knife hanging by a cable. The other end of the cable was secured to the top of his table. He pulled it up, then stared at it. "What the hell is this?"

"It's a skinning knife with a gut hook."

"I know that. It's just weird that it's hanging off the side of my table."

"Exactly. Now look what's hanging off the other side."

Tim pulled up a pair of pruning shears. They were the single-hand operated type. He closed and opened them a few times, then he noticed his name was engraved on the handle. "What the hell?" He looked at Henry with a confused look. "My name is written on these."

"Maybe it's a different Tim." Henry was just being sarcastic.

"It's my full fucking name. Timothy Ray Murray."

"Still think we're in a makeshift hospital?"

"I don't know what to think, but there has to be a rational explanation for all of this."

A stocky black man with a bald head on table four had been listening to Tim's conversation with Henry. He spoke up as he held his hands over his genitals. "Listen, dude, we've all tried to come up with an explanation. Unfortunately, this place is bad. We need to find a way to get the fuck out of here before whoever did this returns, so you need to listen to the fat guy and stop thinking everything is peachy."

Tim shook his head. "I can't accept that someone is planning on harming me. There is a rational explanation for this."

"You're just in denial, like the fat man said. I went through it too when I first woke up. We all did. The fact is, we're all in deep shit."

Henry became a little aggravated. He glared at the black man. "Screw you, Charles."

"Why you say that fo'?"

"Stop referring to me as the fat man. I've already told you my name is Henry."

Charles smiled. "Yo man, don't get yo' panties in a wad."

Tim noticed Charles had a gold grill. It was glimmering from the bright lights above. He was muscled up and covered in tattoos. He looked like a gangbanger. "Hey, back to what you were saying. I think you are just trying to fuck with me."

Charles laughed. "You just can't grasp the fact that some crazy motherfucker, and probably a crazy white motherfucker at that, has yo' ass bound on that table so he can fuck you up some mo'. He's probably gonna cut off yo' dick with them snips, then he gonna do some real fucked up shit to ya."

Henry shook his head. "There's no need in scaring him any further. None of us are sure what's going to happen or why we're here."

Tim had a worried look as he stared at Charles. "Why do you think someone wants to harm us?"

"First off, look at our fuckin' legs. And don't tell me it's medically needed. No fuckin' doctor would do such a thing. And no sane motherfucker would secure us with rusted chains and these creepy-ass collars. The fat man is right; this shit is barbaric. Some sick bastard has done this. And that equipment over there is fo' us, so you better get yo' head out of yo' ass and start tryin' to figure out a way to get the fuck out of here."

"You don't know if that machine is for us. You're just jumping to conclusions."

Charles pointed. "Then what's all those bags of blood fo'?"

Tim noticed everyone had a rack behind them. The racks held numerous bags filled with a red substance. He looked over his shoulder and noticed there was a rack behind him as well. "Why is that a bad thing? We probably lost a little blood during our procedure or something."

"Are you bleeding now?"

Tim looked at his legs. "No."

"Do you see a lot of blood around your table?"

"Not really. Just some dry blood on my legs and some on the sheet I was covered with."

"Does it look like you bled a lot?"

Tim shrugged his shoulders. "Not really."

Charles sarcastically popped off, "Then why in the fuck do we each need ten large bags of blood?"

Tim looked scared. "Uh… I don't know."

"I do. Some crazy motherfucker is planning on cutting our asses up with that saw. And that blood is going to keep us alive longer so we have to endure more pain."

"You watch too many movies."

Charles shook his head. "And you're just another clueless white boy that grew up in a sheltered neighborhood."

"You're an ignorant hood rat."

"Hood rat? Fuck you, cracker!"

"No, fuck you, you… you fucking…."

"Come on, say it, if you got the fuckin' balls!"

"You… You fucking black piece of shit."

"That's what I thought; just another punk ass white bitch."

Henry interrupted. "Hold up! Arguing and calling each other names isn't going to help any of us. None of us know for sure what's going on, but I also think this is something bad. Something real bad, and we need to get out of here as soon as possible."

Tim didn't want to accept that as a possibility. He frantically looked around for some kind of answer. Relief overcame him when he noticed that the plastic hoses coming from the bags disappeared under the tables. "I don't think the bags are connected to us. The hoses run under our tables."

Charles leaned over as far as he could to see where they were going. "Maybe your white ass is right. They do disappear under the tables."

Tim looked over his shoulder, then looked at Henry to see if he had a hose connected to him. "I don't see any hoses. I don't think they connect to us. Maybe the bags are filled with something else, like hydraulic fluid or something. You know, maybe for the tables. They could be hydraulic."

An older Spanish man on table five spoke up. He looked like Edward James Olmos. "Those aren't hydraulic lines. And unfortunately, they are connected to us."

Tim looked at him. "How do you know?"

"Because I know the difference between hydraulic hoses and plastic tubing. And besides, I know how the hoses are connected to us."

"And?"

"The tubing comes out of the tables where our chains are connected. Then it's intertwined with our chains up to our collars." He felt inside his collar. It was loose enough where he could slip in two fingers. "I can feel the hose. I think it's connected to a catheter in my neck. I can also see part of the hose hanging out from under Jason's collar."

Jason was on table six. He was a lot younger, bald with a long goatee and covered in tattoos. He had been sitting forward with his head down while crying quietly to himself. He looked at the Spanish man. "What did you say?" He quickly found the hose, then he tried to reach between his collar and neck, but it was too tight. "Oh shit! Is there a needle in my neck?" He began to panic. "Can someone get it out? Oh my God! I can't stand needles."

The Spanish man shook his head. "You fucking serious? You're worried about a needle when you're covered in tats."

Jason glared at him. "Fuck you, Joe. This shit ain't funny."

"No shit, Sherlock, so stop acting like a bitch."

"You're an asshole."

Tim became upset. He glared at Joe. "Why in the fuck are you just now telling us this? How much more are you holding back?"

"I'm not holding back anything. I just figured it out when y'all started talking about it."

"You've been awful quiet over there, like you're guilty of something."

"I've been meditating, dickhead." He pointed to his legs. "And how in the fuck could I be guilty of something when I'm bound just like you?"

"I think you're a fucking liar."

"You need to watch your mouth, boy."

The woman started crying hysterically and making a lot of noise. She was on the last table. Table seven. She was very normal looking; mid-thirties, average build, long blond hair and fair skin. Henry yelled at Jason. "Calm her down."

Jason turned to her. "Ma'am, please stay calm."

She raised her hand, palm out, as she covered her breast with her other arm. "Leave me alone."

"It'll be okay, ma'am."

"Stop calling me ma'am, asshole. My name is Beth."

The person on table three was just waking up. He looked like a heroin addict; skinny, unkempt, sores on his face and needle marks down his arms. He immediately started screaming at the top of his lungs when he noticed his legs. Joe and Charles were yelling at him to calm down. It was becoming chaotic.

Tim became frightened and started cutting at the wires with the knife that was attached to the cable in an attempt to free himself. The violent jerking was causing the hooks to tear his skin. Henry yelled out. "It's no use! The wires are made of stainless steel."

Tim looked at him. "What?"

"They're stainless steel. You're not going to cut them with that knife, or the shears. All you're doing is causing yourself pain."

He stared at his legs as he was panicking. "Then I will cut out the hooks."

"It's no use. Even if you could overcome the pain, your chains will prevent you from reaching all of them. Your knees are about the farthest you'll be able to reach."

His eyes opened wide. "Oh my God! That's why we're chained. Someone doesn't want us cutting ourselves loose. We are being held captive."

Charles started laughing sarcastically. "You finally caught on, you dumb ass peckerwood." He started clapping. "Congratulations."

Tim became angry. "Screw you, spook."

Charles laughed again. "There we have it folks. The racist finally showed his true colors."

"I ain't a fucking racist! You called me a peckerwood and a cracker first, so you're the racist."

Henry got everyone's attention. "Listen up! If we're going to get out of this, we need to work together."

Joe agreed. He seemed to be very calm and rational. "He's right. We need to ask each other questions to see if there's a connection. I'm Joe, by the way." He nodded towards Jason. "Jason and I were the first to awaken, then Charles. We had already discussed the possibility of what's going on before the rest of y'all woke up."

Tim looked over at him. "And?"

"Possibly a ransom thing."

"That's stupid—I don't have any money. And if that was the case, why would anyone do this to my legs?"

Joe shrugged his shoulders. "I don't know. It was just a thought." He looked at Henry. "Do you have any ideas?"

"It can't be a ransom thing—I'm on a fixed income. Outside of that, I don't know. I haven't done anything to deserve this."

Joe looked at the drug addict. "What's your name?"

He could barely speak. "Ryan. And I don't know shit."

Tim was getting upset. "This is bullshit! Someone must know something."

Beth looked distraught. "I know why I am in here."

Tim looked at her. "Don't just fucking sit there. Speak up."

She had a solemn expression as she looked at everyone. "You must have all done something. Every one of you. This is karma. It's payback for our sins."

Jason was shaking his head. "That's bullshit lady. You don't know me."

Charles got defensive. "I haven't done a fuckin' thing to anyone, especially to deserve this shit."

Ryan's hands were trembling. "I haven't done anything either."

Tim glared at Ryan. "Then why you acting so nervous, shaking and all? You must have done something. Maybe we're all in here because of you."

"It's withdrawals, asshole. Don't blame me for this shit. Maybe you've done something. You just look guilty."

Tim thought about what he had been doing, knowing there was no way anyone knew. "You're wrong. You don't know shit."

"I know that you look like a fucking rapist. You must have raped someone."

"Screw you!" Tim had a pit in his stomach. He looked at the others. "I'm a good person. I've never hurt anyone."

Beth laughed sarcastically. "You're so full of shit, dude. You know why you're in here. You've done something bad to someone. Real bad." She looked at the group with a solemn expression. "We're all damned."

Everyone became disorderly, blaming each other for their own predicament.

The Vigilante's Bitch

A man came walking up from out of the dark as everyone was arguing. "Hey, y'all fuckers need to calm down and be quiet."

It became so quiet you could hear a pin drop. Everyone was staring at him with confusion. He was a normal looking man, around forty years old, around five seven in height, medium sized belly and a round face with chubby cheeks. He was wearing a blue hospital gown, gray sweatpants and white high-top shoes. A red beer hat was on top of his head, but instead of it holding cans of beer, it held IV bags filled with a greenish liquid. Hoses ran from the bags to each side of his neck where they connected to catheters.

"What the fuck is this shit!" shouted Tim.

The man pointed at him. "I said shut the fuck up! I'm here to…."

"You need to let me fucking go!"

Everyone became unruly, shouting and screaming at him. The man could barely walk as he went over to Tim.

He held up a pair of pruning shears. "Interrupt me again and I will start snipping off your toes, you fucking loudmouth prick."

Tim noticed the pruner was the same as the one hanging on the side of his table. At that moment, he knew the man was responsible for everything. He remained quiet, not wanting to upset him further.

Ryan shook his fist. "What the fuck, dude!"

The man walked over to him. "I said be quiet, jerkwad."

Ryan looked at the beer hat. "Is this some kind of fucking joke?"

"I'm not in the mood to listen to your shit." He quickly moved the pruner to Ryan's left foot and snipped off two toes. He had done it in such a half-ass way, it appeared that he didn't care how many he cut off. The amputations were even done on an angle.

Ryan was shocked when he noticed his pinky and forth toe were missing. "What the fuck!"

"I said shut up!" Again, being sloppy with the tool, he carelessly snipped off two more toes and severed half of his big toe.

Ryan started screaming at the top of his lungs. "Oh my God! Stop cutting off my fucking toes!"

The man grabbed Ryan's big toe and bent it in the opposite direction of the cut. As soon as the bone made a loud snapping sound, he started twisting it. Within seconds the remaining skin tore, then he pulled back, stretching ligaments until they popped like rubber bands.

Ryan had foam running out of his mouth as he screamed out, "You sorry motherfucker! Get the fuck away from me!"

The man threw the severed toe, striking Ryan in the face. "Stop yelling!"

"Fuck you, asshole! You cut off all my toes!"

"No, I didn't." He pointed to his other foot with the pruner. "You still have those."

"Get the fuck away from me, you sick son of a bitch!"

He moved the pruner to his other foot. "Not another peep, or bye-bye big toe."

Ryan was desperately trying to reach him, but the chains held him back. "You sorry fucker! You're going to pay for this!"

The man cut off his big toe and index toe in one motion. "I said shut the fuck up!"

Ryan couldn't believe his eyes. His anger changed to panic. "Please don't cut off anymore! I beg you!"

When two more toes fell into the pile of toes on the floor, the man moved the pruner to his last toe. "One little pinky left. Open your mouth again and it's gone."

"Okay, okay. I'll be quiet."

After his pinky toe fell to the floor, he moved the pruner next to his crotch. "Your dick is next. I dare you to say something again, you hardheaded prick. Please, please say something. I really want to cut it off."

Ryan remained silent outside of his muffled whimpering. Everyone had quieted down. In fact, they weren't making a sound. The man tossed the pruner on the table by Ryan's feet, then asked, "If it was, would it be funny?"

Ryan just sat staring at him while tears ran down his cheeks.

"Now you can speak, fuckhead."

He looked confused. "I… I don't understand what you're asking?"

"You asked if this was some kind of joke. So, if it was, would it be funny?"

"I… Uh… Not sure what you mean."

"Never mind."

Joe raised his hand. "Sir. We'll cooperate with you. You don't have to do that kind of stuff." He nodded towards Ryan's feet.

"Listen, fuckers, I just want to get this shit over with so I can go home. I was…."

Tim blurted out, "Get what over with?"

He shook his head. "I was in the process of telling you, dipshit. Do you need a pedicure too?"

"I'm sorry. I'm just upset. Please continue."

"Upset about what?"

Tim motioned to his legs.

"Oh, that. I'd be pissed too."

"Why did you do this to me?"

"I didn't."

"Then who did?"

Everyone else was staying quiet as they stared at the psychopath. The man flipped over a five-gallon bucket that was sitting next to the tables, then eased down on top of it. He seemed to be in a lot of pain. Joe was the most level-headed out of the group. He knew he needed to establish a positive relationship with him. "Sir. You look to be hurt. Is there anything I can do?"

"Yeah. Don't be a suck-ass. Your cop bullshit isn't going to work in here."

Everyone looked at Joe. Jason glared at him. "You're a fucking cop? Why didn't you say that earlier?"

Joe snapped back. "What the fuck does that have to do with anything?"

"It makes a big…."

Charles interrupted. "Y'all fuckin' chill out!" He looked at the man. "Dude, why the fuck am I in here?"

"First off, don't call me dude."

"Sorry, dog."

"Dog?" You better talk to me like you got some sense."

"Yes, sir."

"And don't call me sir—I'm not your fucking daddy."

"Then what do you want me to call you?"

The man gritted his teeth as he softly said, "Elmer Fudd."

Tim leaned forward until his chain stopped him. "What was that? I wasn't able to hear you."

The man seemed angry as he shouted. "Elmer Fudd, asshole!"

"Okay, okay. You don't have to get upset."

Joe knew they were at the mercy of a crazy man. He needed to gain his trust. "Sorry if we upset you. And yes, I am a cop, but you're the one in charge. We will do whatever you ask."

"Listen. This isn't of my doing. I'm just here to explain what's going on. And stop fucking patronizing me—I'm not an idiot!"

Beth laughed. "Then stop acting like one, Elmerrrrr."

He glared at her. "What did you say to me, you crazy bitch?"

"Screw you, asshole! You're the one wearing a silly ass beer hat and going by the name Elmer Fudd."

He stood up. "Have you lost your fucking mind?"

Joe couldn't believe what Beth had said. He glared at her. "Shut the fuck up, bitch. You're going to get us killed." He looked at Elmer. "Don't pay any attention to her. She's not rational."

"Oh, I'm plenty rational." She looked at the men. "Y'all need to grow some fucking balls and stop sniveling like a bunch of little bitches. Look what this piece of shit did to us."

Everyone started freaking out in one way or another; Jason, Joe and Charles were arguing with Beth, Ryan was crying hysterically, Henry looked as if he was going to have a heart attack and Tim was cutting at his wires.

Elmer walked over to a control cabinet and pressed a button. Everyone became quiet when the large blade on the saw started turning. At first, the electric motor made a deep humming sound as it slowly spun the blade, and as it picked up speed, the room began to fill with an ear-piercing whirling sound as the saw blade cut through the air.

A few seconds later Elmer shut off the saw. When the blade stopped, he looked at the group and laughed. "That definitely got y'all's attention." He pointed at Beth. "And if you say another word, I will cut out your fucking tongue." He looked at Tim. "Look what you've done, dumbass. The fat man already told you it's stainless steel wire."

Tim had ripped out several hooks from his legs, causing large gashes in his flesh. He had a troubled look as he stared at the open wounds—there was very little blood, and it was thicker than normal, almost like molasses. "Why aren't my legs bleeding?" He looked up at Elmer. "What have you done to me?"

"You've been given a clotting agent. All of you have."

Tim was scared. It seemed his legs were dead, but he had feeling in them. "That can't be it. Clotting agents don't work like that. They help clot once there's bleeding. I'm only oozing thick blood, like it's old or something. You must have done something to my legs."

"It's not just you." Elmer pointed at Ryan's stubs. "He didn't bleed much either. Didn't you notice that when I cut off his toes?"

Charles looked scared as he stared at Ryan's feet. "What the hell? How is that possible?" He didn't understand why there wasn't blood everywhere. It should have gushed out of his stubs, but there were just a few thin trails of dried blood. His open wounds had somehow quickly clotted. He could even see the dark red clots that had formed over the open ends of the stubs.

Ryan was horrified. "Oh my God! I noticed that too, but thought it was due to the wires stretching my skin. You know, like slowing down the blood flow or something."

Joe shook his head. "That's impossible." He looked at Ryan's legs. "You must have tourniquets around them."

Elmer became aggravated. "He doesn't have tourniquets. I've already said it was because of the clotting agent."

"Tim is right. Clotting agents don't work like that."

"It's not the same shit like at the hospital. It's a homemade blend. And y'all have been pumped full of it. And I mean full to the brim."

Tim was worried. "Is that safe?"

"I doubt it. I'm surprised none of y'all haven't already died from a blood clot or a heart attack."

Tim looked as if he was going to cry. "Oh my God! Why would you do something like that?"

"Stop blaming me. I've already told you I didn't do this shit."

"Then who did?"

He looked at the group. "Have y'all heard of the Angel of Death?"

Tim nodded. "Yes."

"He's the one that did this."

Joe knew Elmer was referring to Seth Coker, also known as The Angel of Death. He had been a notorious vigilante that the cops and FBI had been after for decades. Two years ago, the FBI had tracked him down to a house in Oregon. The house exploded and burned to the ground with Seth inside. They recovered a body and ruled the remains were that of Seth Coker. Joe knew Elmer was lying and possibly a copycat killer, or just plain psychotic. "That's not true. He was killed two years ago by the FBI."

Elmer pointed at him. "Say another word and I will cut out your fucking eyes!"

Joe looked down.

"Now back to what I was saying. He's the one that did this to you fuckers. I'm just here to babysit."

Charles raised his hand.

"What the fuck do you want?"

"Who is this Angel of Death person? I've never heard of him."

"I take it that gangstas don't watch the news, read the paper, or even communicate with people that have a brain."

Charles glared at him. "Naw, dog, it ain't like that. I'm street smart."

"You're fucking retarded."

"Whatever! It is what it is. Just 'cause I ain't heard of this fool don't mean I'm a fuckin' retard."

Ryan looked confused. "I haven't heard of him either."

"I'm sure. You spend all of your time shooting up and jacking off."

"You don't know shit."

"I know you like to blow your load into a sock while spanking it to cartoons."

Ryan turned red from embarrassment. "I… Uh…."

"Cat got your tongue, you sock rapist?"

"I don't know what you're talking about."

"Sure, you don't." Elmer looked at the group. "For the dumbasses that have kept their heads in their asses, the Angel of Death is a really cool dude who goes around and punishes scumbags and lowlifes. From here on out, we'll refer to this great and exemplary man simply as Seth, even though that doesn't do him justice."

Tim looked confused. "Hold up! I'm not a fucking scumbag." He looked at Ryan and Charles. "I work my ass off, own a home and pay taxes."

Charles flipped him off. "Screw you, white boy! You don't know shit!"

Tim looked at Elmer. "This Seth dude must be mistaken."

"He never makes mistakes—he's perfect."

Ryan was upset that Elmer knew he jacked off to cartoons. "How do you know so much about me if you didn't do this shit?"

"I was forced to watch all of y'all to get information about your habits and routines. Seth made me do it. I had no choice."

Ryan became angry. "Are you some type of fucking pervert? You had no right to do that. You invaded my privacy. And look what you did to my fucking toes. You're a piece of shit. You're going to get what's coming to you."

Tim was furious as well. "You said you didn't have anything to do with this, but now you just said you spied on us. I think you did this shit to my legs and put this fucking collar on me."

"Seth is the one that set this place up and did that to you. I only brought you here."

Tim's eyes got big. "What? Now you're telling me that you abducted me also? Wow! You are more a part of this than you led us to believe. It just keeps getting better and better, doesn't it? Maybe you just need to stop talking."

"What does that mean?"

"It means you keep telling on yourself every time you open your mouth. In fact, I don't think anyone is making you do shit."

Joe whistled to get Tim's attention. He didn't want to speak since Elmer threatened to cut out his eyes if he did.

Tim looked at him. "What?"

Joe covered his mouth, indicating for Tim to be quiet.

"Fuck that. He's just jerking us around."

Elmer was getting upset. "I'm telling the truth. I only spied on you and brought you here. Seth did everything else. I'm not a bad person."

Ryan's jaw dropped. "Hold up! What do you mean you're not a bad person? You cut off my fucking toes!"

"Shit happens."

"What the fuck? All you can say is shit happens? What kind of fucking response is that?"

"Hey, I've gone through some fucked up shit myself, so don't get me started."

"You're no saint. You're just as bad as that Seth character. That is, if he exists."

Tim thought for a moment. He glared at Elmer. "Wait a minute. You made all this up. There is no person named Seth. You must be the one the cops are looking for. You're that Angel of Death dude."

Elmer was getting angry. "I'm not a fucking liar!"

"Then why didn't you go to the police when he asked you to do this?"

"I can't."

"Bullshit! No one is forcing you to do shit."

Elmer raised his hospital gown and showed the group a fresh wound. It ran across the width of his abdomen and was stitched with large, black thread. "He did this to me. He implanted an exploding canister filled with acid in my abdomen that's activated by remote control. He said he will burn me from the inside out if I go to the police or don't do what he says."

Tim shook his head. "Oh shit. That's fucked up."

Charles' eyes got big. "I got an idea. If you call the cops, they will take you to the hospital. They can remove it. And I'm sure you will get some type of reward for helping us."

"I can't. He booby-trapped it. They can't even x-ray it without causing it to go off."

Ryan was still angry about his toes. "Why did he do that to you? Did you fuck someone in the ass or something?"

Elmer glared at him. "Screw you. You don't know shit."

Ryan laughed in a sarcastic way. "Fuck you and your power trip, Elmer fucking Fudd. You're probably getting off on this. I bet you like staring at our nude bodies, you fucking queer!"

Elmer's face turned red with anger. "You just signed your death warrant, punk."

Charles intervened. "Hold up you two. We're all in this together." He looked at Elmer. "Why is Seth forcing you to do this?"

Elmer looked sad. "A few years ago, I blamed him for something I did. He…."

Tim interrupted. "What did you do?"

"It's none of your fucking business. But anyway, he made me do some things. Some real bad things to teach me a lesson. Then he let me go. He told me not to go to the police, but I did. So now I'm being punished for ratting on him after he gave me a second chance."

Tim's eyes got big. "That's good news that he gave you a second chance. That means he's a rational person. If I can talk to him and explain that I haven't done anything, he will let me go."

"I don't think so. He has it in for you."

"If he gave you a second chance, he can do that for me."

Elmer looked down. "He is forgiving, I suppose—he could have done something worse to me." He looked at Tim. "But for you, you're fucked."

"What? Why can't he give me a chance, too? What makes you so special?"

"The shit he made me do was some disturbing shit. After that, I became mentally unstable. I wasn't in my right mind when I went to the police. That's a lot different than the shit y'all have done."

Charles held his hands out, palms up. "I haven't done shit, so I don't know why you keep sayin' I have."

Tim got an idea. "You can go tell the cops that we're here, then take off. Seth can't set off the device if he doesn't know where you are."

Elmer looked as if he was going to cry. "It has an internal clock mechanism. I have to check in with him so he can reset it or it will explode."

"How often do you have to check in?"

"Depends on how he sets it up. He can adjust the amount of time. He does it with this wireless thingamajig. Right now, it's set for every forty-eight hours."

"You can kill the bastard."

"I can't do that either. He made it clear that if something happened to him I would die too since no one else would be able to stop it from exploding." Elmer pulled the front of his sweatpants down, revealing another freshly-stitched wound across his lower abdomen. "He also put this thing in me that shocks my innards. It has numerous wires scattered throughout my stomach. He even dropped two down inside my ball sack from the inside. It's so fucking gross. I can feel them moving around and poking my testicles." He sat back down on his bucket and started crying. He could barely talk as he cried hysterically. "I have to do whatever he asks or he will shock me. If I go to the police or tell anyone about him, he will make me suffer. My real name is Barry, but he makes me go by Elmer Fudd because of my fat cheeks." He covered his face with his hands. "I'm his fucking slave... his fucking bitch."

Tim couldn't believe what he was hearing. "Then you're in the same boat we're all in. Cut us loose and we'll find a way to help you."

"It's too late for you. I can't risk him punishing me anymore, so stop trying to talk me into letting you go."

Tim was getting desperate. "He won't punish you if...."

Elmer became enraged. "The last time I went against him, he cut off my fucking dick. What the hell do you think he will do if I let you go?"

Charles grabbed his genitals. "Oh my God! Why would he cut off your dick?" He started to panic. "Is he going to do that to me?"

"I'm sure dick play is in the cards. He likes doing that kind of shit to assholes like yourselves."

Tim, Charles and Ryan became upset and started shouting at Elmer after the dick comment. Joe and Beth were being quiet, as they had been told. Jason and Henry hadn't said a word since Elmer walked up. In fact, they had been staring downwards the entire time.

A Dickless MF

Everyone was still freaking out. Elmer raised his hand. "Hush! Yelling isn't going to change anything. It's only going to make things worse."

Tim looked as if he wanted to cry. "At least tell me why I am here."

"Because you've done something bad. Each of you have. Your time has come. The hour of retribution is upon you. Just like Beth said earlier, you are all damned."

Tim was terrified. "Oh my God! You can't let anything happen to us. You will get in trouble too. There must be something you can do."

Elmer shook his head. "Even if I wanted to, it's no use. He's been listening to what we're saying."

Charles was looking around. "How? Is he here?"

Elmer pulled the neck of his gown downwards, revealing a device sewn to his upper chest. "He sewed a transmitter to me."

Joe was shaking his head. He was fed up with the lies. "This is all bullshit. No one is listening. The Angel of Death was killed in Oregon during a standoff with the FBI. This is your doing."

Elmer became aggravated. "I told you not to say anything."

"I know. I'm sorry."

"Yes, you are. And you're also fucking clueless." He stood up and glared at him. "And I have no use for cops, especially crooked ones."

Joe's eyes got big. "Crooked? I haven't done anything."

"Crooked and a liar."

"You're mistaken."

"So, it wasn't you that's been going around raping people?"

Joe was caught off guard. "I... I haven't raped anyone."

"Oh, then it must be some other lowlife cop named Jose Alberto Del Castillo the third that's been sticking his dick in underprivileged women that live on the streets of Houston... my bad."

Tim became angry and blurted out. "Am I being punished because of that piece of shit?"

"No. You're being punished because you've been sticking your dick in your eight-year-old daughter."

Tim's eyes opened wide. He felt like he had been caught with his hand in the cookie jar. At first, he didn't know how to respond. He was now in the spotlight and everyone was staring at him. "That's not true. You're making that up. I would never do that to my daughter."

Ryan glared at Tim. "I knew it. You are a fucking rapist. What a piece of shit."

Elmer shook his head. "And that folks, is an example of the pot calling the kettle black."

Ryan looked confused. "What does that mean?"

"It means, when you're not raping a sock, you're raping your son."

Ryan looked down. "That's not true."

"Sure, it is, asshole. That's why you're looking away." Elmer looked at Henry. "You've sure been quiet. But I guess I would be too if I had been having sex with my disabled daughter for the last thirty-three years."

Henry was holding his head down. He didn't respond.

Charles had a strange expression. "Hold up! Sounds like these assholes are in here for sexual crimes. I haven't raped or molested anyone."

"True. You just murdered a few people. And speaking of killing…" Elmer looked at Jason. "This sorry bastard killed his own mother."

Jason didn't say a word as he stared at his lap.

Elmer looked at Beth. "And worst saved for last. Do you want to tell everyone why you're here?"

She quickly responded while looking down. "I drowned my baby in the bath tub."

Elmer started clapping. "That takes balls to admit to such a heinous act." He looked at the others. "And for the rest of you lying sacks of shit, each one of you will face your sins in one way or another."

Henry started crying. "What are you going to do?"

"The fat man can speak. Congratulations." Elmer walked over to the saw. "Before I get to that, I need to explain what all of this equipment is." He laid his hand on the saw. "This is an industrial radial arm saw; modified of course for just such a special occasion. It's mounted on a track system so it can travel back and forth from table one to table seven, and it can boom out over the tables. The blade is set an eighth of an inch higher than the table tops and the blade can reach all the way to each of your heads. It's controlled by a computer and…."

Tim looked confused. "Hold up! What are you saying?" He looked at the saw, then his expression changed to a grimace of terror. "Oh my God! You're planning on cutting us in half."

Everyone started panicking. Elmer shouted, "Hush! I'm not done explaining how this all works!"

Jason started screaming like a little girl while rocking back and forth. Elmer walked over to him. "Stop acting like that."

He kept rocking as he made high-pitched screams.

"Stop it! You're acting like a retard."

"Get the fuck away from me, you fucking psycho!"

Elmer grabbed his penis and started pulling on it as hard as he could. Jason screamed at the top of his lungs as he held onto Elmer's wrists, pulling them back towards him to relieve the tension. They looked like two kids fighting over a Stretch Armstrong toy, and as they fought with each other, Jason's penis was being gruesomely stretched. Jason's eyes were huge as he fought with Elmer. "Please stop! You're fucking killing me! Oh my God, you're going to tear it! I beg…." Suddenly, Elmer fell on his backside.

Jason immediately started shouting, "Oh my God! You ripped off my dick! Someone please help me!"

Elmer stood up and tossed the organ onto Jason's lap. "At least you're not going to bleed to death thanks to the clotting agent. Now shut the fuck up or I will rip off your balls next."

Jason glared at him with hate as he shouted, "Fuck you! I'm going to kill you for this!"

"I told you to shut up." Elmer pulled out an ice pick and poked Jason in the throat.

Jason covered the hole with his hand. He could feel air coming out of it as he exhaled. When he tried to speak, a sharp pain shot through his neck and his voice sounded raspy. "Oh shit! You fucked up my vocal cords, you motherfucker."

"Speaking of motherfucker, I heard you fucked yours after you killed her. Is that true?"

Jason looked away. "Leave me alone."

"Hey, sicko, do you like fucking dead mothers?"

"Get the fuck away from me."

Elmer laughed. "A dickless motherfucker. That's what we have here, folks."

Jason reached out and grabbed Elmer as he shouted muffled screams. Elmer took the ice pick and started thrusting it into Jason's body like a crazed maniac. At first, Jason tried to block the blows, but Elmer jabbed holes in his hands and arms until they fell limp from trauma. He didn't miss a beat as he continued pounding holes in Jason's body. After two hundred plus punctures, Jason fell to his back and became lethargic. Elmer jabbed the ice pick into his chest, leaving it in place. "Now I bet you will keep your fucking mouth shut."

Jason could barely speak. "Please kill me."

Elmer laughed. "All in due time, you fucking prick." He looked at the rest of the group who were staring in horror. "Anyone else want a pokin'?"

No one responded.

"That's what I thought."

Elmer walked over to the saw. "Now back to what I was saying. This thing is automated. It's programmed to cut each of you down the center of your legs, from your feet to your hips. It might only cut a short distance, or to your knee. It might even cut all the way to your hip. It's unpredictable. The saw will start at table one. After it cuts into one of Tim's legs, it will move to Henry, then Ryan and so on. Once it's done with Beth, it will start back over with Tim. The blade might go back into the same cut, cutting more of his leg, or it might start on his other leg. It's also programmed to cut into the crotch after the legs have been cut."

Several of the men made an "ohhh" sound.

"Oh yeah, baby. And if you fuckers think you will bleed out before that happens, I have bad news for ya." He pointed to a torch head that was mounted by the blade. "This is a propane torch. The blade will be red-hot when it's cutting into you, and between the cauterizing and clotting agent, you will keep ticking like a fucking Timex. Seth has even added a little adrenaline in your IV bags to keep you from passing out too soon." Elmer lowered his head so he could speak clearly into his mic. "He is such a thoughtful person. Such a great inspiration and a ray of hope. I aspire to be more like him one day."

Tim shouted at Elmer, "You're fucking crazy. You're just a sadistic piece of shit!"

"Really? You have the audacity to call me that after the shit you've done."

"I didn't touch my daughter."

"You keep telling yourself that, pervert."

"You have no right to do this."

"And you didn't have any right sticking your dick in her."

"I've already told you I didn't."

Charles wasn't sure if he wanted to speak after seeing what happened to Jason. He slightly raised his hand as he covered his penis with his other hand. "Mr. Fudd."

"What the fuck do you want?"

"Is there anything I can do to keep this from happening? I will do anything you or Seth ask. I'll fuck up anyone for you." He nodded towards Ryan, Henry and Tim. "I'll even fuck up these perverts for you. I have the skills. I've been on the streets my whole life. Please Mr. Fudd. Please have mercy. I will…."

"Hush! He's not going to let some scumbag work for him."

Charles looked down.

"But for what it's worth, there is a chance for one of you assholes to make it out of here alive."

Everyone looked up.

"That's right. The last person alive gets to live. They will also receive a really cool prize. And if you play the game right, the blade will never touch you."

"Game?" Tim had an aggravated look, but he was also relieved there was a chance for him to get free. "So, this is just some twisted game?"

"If you don't want to play, I can go ahead and fuck you up." He nodded towards Jason. "You can join dickless over there."

Tim held his hands out, gesturing for Elmer to stop. "Hold up. That's not what I meant. I'm appreciative. Please finish what you were saying."

Charles raised his hand.

Elmer glared at him. "Now what?"

"How can I stop the blade from touching me?"

"See the pipe above you?"

"Yeah."

"You just have to put something in there that the sensor will detect."

"Huh?"

Tim also looked confused. "What are you talking about?"

"Oh yeah. I hadn't told you fuckers how this thing works." Elmer went to a control panel and flipped a switch. Within seconds, the ends of the pipes above each person started making a suction sound. He walked closer to the tables so everyone could hear him. "All y'all have to do is stick something in the end of your pipe." He pointed to a digital read out that was mounted next to the junction box where the seven pipes joined.

"The computer keeps track of who has put something in their pipe. Each pipe has its own sensor. You also have to make sure the item is big enough—the proximity sensor will not see smaller items, and each time the saw starts back at the beginning, which is Tim, the items have to get bigger." He pointed to a set of lights that were mounted above the tables. They looked like a smaller version of a traffic signal with red, amber and green lights. "Each of you have a set of lights. If the red light is illuminated, that means you're going to get cut, the green means the item was big enough and the saw is going to pass you by, the amber light means the item was too small. When the saw gets to the end, which is where Beth is at, it will start back over with Tim, and you will have to put something else in your pipe if you want the saw to miss you again."

Tim was more confused than before. "That's kind of weird that I have to do that, but if it gets me out of here, I'll play along. So, what am I supposed to put in there?"

"Anything you want. That's the beauty of it."

Charles was looking around. "Like what?"

Beth shook her head. "Body parts. The sick bastards want us to cut ourselves apart."

Tim had a horrified expression. "Oh my God! That's why we have the knives and pruning shears connected to our tables."

Everyone was speechless.

Elmer turned off the vacuum system, then flipped a switch and turned on some heart monitors that were mounted behind everyone. "I have good and bad news. The good news is, the monitoring system will know if you pass out, and if you do, the saw will skip over your legs until you have regained consciousness. The bad news is, you will be punished for passing out."

Tim popped off. "How? It can't get any worse."

"Sure, it can. If you pass out, the saw will slice into your ball sack, and possibly into your dick, depending on how it's hanging at the time." He looked at Beth. "Of course, you're exempt; perks of being a woman, I reckon."

Tim was angry. "That's fucking sorry!"

"What is? That she's exempt?"

"I don't give a fuck about her. I don't want that fucking blade to touch my dick or balls."

"Well, that's part of the game. It makes sure you will try to stay conscious."

"This is fucking sick. You have no right to do this."

"Look at the bright side. At least the saw won't cut you into pieces while you're asleep. That wouldn't be fair—you wouldn't have a chance to win the game."

Henry's body was trembling. He was terrified. "I feel like I'm going to have a heart attack from the anxiety. I don't want to go through this anymore. Please just end it."

"You're probably just feeling the clotting agent. I'm sure it's starting to gum up your innards."

"Please just kill me and get it over with."

"We don't want to rob your daughter of retribution, do we? You must have some remorse over what you did."

Henry started crying. "I didn't do anything. Please make all this stop. I beg you."

Tim became angry. "Don't you have any fucking mercy?"

"Not for molesters and rapists. And you need to worry about yourself and not the fat man."

"You ain't no fucking better."

"Yeah, maybe not, but at least I'm not lying on one of these tables, you fucking smart mouth."

"Screw you, dude."

Elmer pointed at him. "You say another word, I'm going to end you right here and now!"

Tim shook his head as he looked down.

Elmer opened a box and pulled out a syringe. He held it up so everyone could see it. "Here's some extra adrenaline. You already have some in your IV bags, but these will give you a little extra kick to help keep you from passing out. I'm going to give each of you three of these." He started laying three syringes on everyone's table, starting with Beth. When he got to Tim, he handed him five. "There's your mercy, asshole. You get two extra."

Tim grabbed Elmer by the shirt. "You sorry motherfucker! I'm going to…."

Elmer backhanded him, knocking him to his back, then he started choking him with both hands as he yelled, "I've had enough of your mouth, you fucking prick!"

Tim was fighting with all he had to catch a breath. He could feel his heart pounding and his body going numb. What a terrible way to die, he thought, as his vision slowly faded to black.

The Angel of Death

The sound of a door opening, then slamming shut, echoed throughout the building. Footsteps could be heard and they were getting louder with each passing second. Finally, a man came walking out of the dark while smoking a cigarette. He pointed at Elmer. "Don't kill the bastard—he's the star of the show."

Elmer released Tim's throat. "Sorry boss. The fucker just rubs me the wrong way."

"I'm sure—he's a fucking molester."

Everyone was staring at the man. He was tall with a stocky build and looked to be in his mid to late forties. He was wearing a black, long sleeve shirt tucked into a pair of blue jeans, brown square toe western boots and a black cowboy hat. He had a neatly trimmed brown and gray goatee.

Tim sat up while holding his throat. He completely forgot about his struggle with Elmer and that he almost died—he was now focused on this man. He was standing at the edge of the darkness, but he could still see him clearly. All kinds of thoughts were running through his mind; was he the Angel of Death that Elmer talked about? He didn't look like the villain he was portrayed to be. Maybe this was someone else. Elmer did call him boss. Does he work for this man? Could Elmer really be the crazy one, and now his boss busted him in the act? Tim started to get excited, thinking he was going to be rescued, then he remembered the man called him a molester. A fucking molester at that. He now felt nauseated, knowing they were in cahoots.

He watched Elmer as he was pointing to the group. He appeared to be explaining what happened to Ryan's toes and Jason's penis. Tim wanted to speak, but felt intimidated by the man's presence—he looked serious, unlike Elmer, who was more of a joke. Could this man be reasoned with, he wondered? He looked to his right and noticed everyone else was staring at the man as well, except for Jason. He was still lying down. The puncture holes must have done some serious damage, or he was simply upset about his penis being ripped off.

Tim started to speak until Elmer pointed at him. He had a sick feeling when he noticed the man was staring. His eyes were strange looking. It seemed he was staring at his soul. Tim's mind was running a hundred miles an hour, trying to process everything at once. All kinds of things were bouncing around inside his head; could the man really know what he had been doing behind closed doors? No way, he thought, he's just a man. Then he remembered that he referred to him as the star of the show. What show? Was he referring to the horrifying game Elmer has been talking about? That would mean he knew about his transgressions. The man was still staring. Fear overcame him. He could sense that he knew all his secrets. For the first time in years he felt ashamed, knowing the man knew what he had been doing. At that moment, he realized his destiny; he was going to join the ranks of the ones who had already crossed this man's path. He lowered his head as he thought about the horror and suffering that lay ahead. Hopefully it wouldn't last long, he thought. Maybe he will be merciful and make it quick. He looked back up, noticing he was still staring. He wasn't sure what to do. He wanted to speak, but his throat tightened up. He became emotional, then teary eyed. Before he knew it, he was crying.

"I'll be damned!" yelled Elmer, followed by someone laughing.

Tim noticed the man was the one laughing and Elmer seemed upset. He wasn't sure what was going on. Shortly after, Elmer starting walking towards him. Tim raised his arms in defense. "Please don't hurt me."

Elmer was gritting his teeth. "You cost me a hundred bucks, asshole."

Tim looked over his arms. "What?"

"Seth bet me he could make you cry just by staring at you. You've been the biggest loud mouth in here. That should have been money in the bank. What the fuck got into you?"

"I... I'm sorry."

"I was going to bet on you to win the game, but not now. In fact, I'm going to bet you go first." Elmer laughed. "I hope the saw blade snags one of your arteries in your legs and rips the aorta off your heart."

Tim was horrified. "Oh my God! Can that really happen?"

"All kinds of shit can happen like that. You're fixing to be fucked up way beyond anything imaginable. The pain. The horror. The gruesomeness. You're going to experience suffering like you've never imagined."

Tim was horrified. He was crying hysterically. "Please don't do this. I will do anything you ask."

Seth motioned to Elmer. "When you're done terrifying the fucker, you need to get this party started. Unfortunately, I can't stick around—I have a date."

Elmer walked over to Seth. "With Missy?"

"Yep, she's waiting in the truck."

Elmer handed Seth a hundred dollars. "Here's your money." He looked at Tim and mumbled under his breath. "Fucking punk."

Seth laughed as he put the money in his wallet. "Winner winner chicken dinner."

"Yeah yeah. I'll make it up with the next one."

Seth nodded towards Tim. "Five-hundred on him."

"I'll take that bet."

"And don't cheat. I know you have an issue with the bastard."

"I wouldn't do that, boss."

"You better not if you know what's good for you. And did you explain everything to everyone?"

"Yep, and they're all excited about it."

"You've been dragging ass and doing a lot of jawing. I was expecting it to almost be over by the time I got here."

"Sorry, boss, they've been an unruly bunch, especially Tim. He's a real troublemaker."

Everyone had been quiet, unsure if they should speak, but Tim was outraged. He had listened to Elmer whine and cry about how Seth was making him do all of this. Now he was over there acting like Seth was his best friend. He couldn't hold his tongue any longer as he blurted out, "You're a fucking backstabbing liar!"

After that comment, no way in hell was anyone going to make a peep. Seth patted Elmer on the shoulder. "Sounds like you're being called out, pal."

"Fuck that little bastard. I'll deal with him later."

"Stop fucking around and get this done. There should have already been guts, blood and ass everywhere."

"I know, I know. I'll get it up and running as soon as you leave."

"Let me know who makes it to the end. I have something special saved up for them."

"Sure thing, boss."

Seth handed Elmer a piece of paper. "That's your next assignment. After you gather them up, take them to that address."

"Will do, boss."

Seth pointed at Tim, then ran his thumb across his throat, indicating he was dead. Tim was horrified. He was hoping to have a conversation with him, but not now.

Seth looked at Elmer. "I'm outta here."

"Later, boss. I'll call you when I have all the scumbags in the warehouse."

When Seth started walking off, Joe yelled out, "Sir! Can I talk to you?"

Charles yelled out right after Joe. "Mr. Seth, don't leave! I have a proposition for you! Please come back!"

Ryan was trying to yell over Charles. "I need to talk to you! You have me pegged all wrong!"

Elmer pointed at them. "Don't waste your time—he doesn't care what you fuckers have to say."

The sound of a door opening, then slamming closed, echoed out in the distance. Charles looked aggravated. "Don't tell me he left."

"Yep, the king has left the building."

"He didn't even give me a chance to explain."

"He doesn't give a fuck what you have to say. He won't even listen to me."

Henry looked up. "Why are you moving us to a warehouse?"

"No one said anything about that."

"You told Seth you were going to let him know when we were moved over there."

Elmer laughed. "I'm glad you're starting to see yourself for what you are, but that's a different group of scumbags."

Henry looked down. "I didn't do anything."

"Sure, pal, you're innocent right along with the rest of these assholes."

Joe was disturbed. "I can't believe he's going to do this to me and not even have the decency to face me."

"He's got more important shit to do."

"You fucking serious? We're going to be butchered like animals while he's going out on a date. That's fucked up."

"He wouldn't do this to an animal."

"What?"

"You heard me. You're less than an animal in his book."

Ryan was pissed. "This is bullshit. He could have at least been man enough to hear what I have to say."

"He's too good to do his own dirty work; that's what I'm for. I'm just his little bitch."

Joe glared at Elmer. "So now what? You going to actually do this? You going to do his dirty work, as you call it? Murder all of us in cold blood? Do you think you can live with that?"

"I don't have a choice. I wish I did."

Tim was irate. "You're a fucking coward! You fucking swing on his dick when he's around, then talk trash when he's not. You ain't no better than he is. Hell, you're worse."

"Fuck you! I can't wait until the saw is cutting your ass up."

Tim quickly realized upsetting Elmer wasn't going to help his situation. "I'm sorry. I shouldn't have said that. I know you're under a lot of stress. We're all in this together."

"Don't patronize me, you fucking prick."

"I'm just trying to…."

"Shut the fuck up."

Tim looked down. "I'm sorry."

"You ready to get this shit started?"

"Please don't do this."

"I'll take that as a yes." Elmer looked at Henry. He was sitting motionless with his head down. "Hey, fat man, you ready?"

He didn't respond.

"I'm going to cut off your fucking dick if you don't say something."

"Please just kill me."

"In due time, fuck stick." Elmer looked at Joe and Charles. "You two ready?"

They both started begging and pleading.

"I didn't ask you fuckers to ramble on. A yes or no would have sufficed."

Elmer went over to Jason. He was lying on his back while staring up at the lights. "How's it hanging, pal?"

"Leave me alone."

"Come on, don't pout. You still have your balls."

"Fuck you! I'm not playing your fucking game. You might as well go ahead and kill me."

"I don't care if you just lie there and get cut up. I'm rooting for Charles anyway." Elmer looked over at Beth. "You ready to play?"

She glared at him. "Why don't you shut the fuck up and go flip the switch, you sawed off piece of shit. I'm tired of hearing your lips flap."

"You need to chill out, darlin.'"

"Screw you, you nasty little bastard."

"Screw me? Listen here, you fucking…" Elmer thought for a moment. "You know what, I think I'm going to take you up on that. I might even fuck you in the ass. What do you think about that, bitch?"

"You better stay the fuck away from me, asshole!"

"There ain't a damn thing you can do to stop me. I'm going to…." Elmer's phone rang. He noticed it was Seth. "Yes, sir… Uh, I was just joking… No, sir, I would never rape anyone… I understand… Sure… Okay… Do I really have to do that?... Okay… I will soon as we hang up... Talk to you later… Hello, are you still there?" Elmer put his phone back in his pocket, then looked at Beth. "I'm sorry for threatening you. I couldn't have raped you anyway because I'm not a man. Even though my penis was sewn back on, it doesn't work because I'm a bitch."

She looked irritated. "I don't give a shit about you or your dick."

Elmer looked worried. "Seth is angry at me for the rape threat, regardless if it was a joke or not. He said there is no excuse in sexual aggression, even if it's towards a child murdering bitch like yourself."

"I just want you to get the fuck away from me."

"He wants you to punch me in the nuts a whole bunch of times."

"I'm not touching you, you creepy little bastard."

"If you don't, I have to do it myself."

"I don't give a shit."

"I'll give you another adrenaline shot."

"I told you…" She thought for a moment. "Let me go and I will."

"I can't do that."

"Then get the fuck away from me."

Elmer started pacing back and forth in front of the tables. He finally came to a stop, then started punching himself in the nuts as hard as he could. He hit himself about ten times. Afterwards, he just knelt on one knee so he could recuperate.

Tim looked at Joe and shrugged his shoulders. Joe made a circular motion with his finger next to his head, indicating Elmer was crazy.

Elmer noticed what Joe was doing. He became upset. "Seth made me do that. He said if I didn't he would make me pay later." He became upset. "He overheard what I was saying. Now he's mad at me."

Tim blurted out. "Why would he be mad at you? I thought y'all were such great pals."

Elmer glared at him. "Don't be sarcastic. I'm in a fucked-up predicament myself."

Charles was shaking his head. "You don't have to be his fucking puppet. Get some balls and stand up to him. You can start by calling the police."

Beth laughed. "Like he said, he's a bitch with a broke dick."

Elmer stood up and shouted. "I'm fucking sick of all of y'all! It's time to die, motherfuckers!" Elmer took off towards the main control panel, yelling, "Die motherfuckers die!"

The Suffering

Everyone was freaking out as Elmer energized the main control panel. Joe and Ryan were shouting at him not to do it. Tim and Charles were apologizing for their comments.   Henry was on the verge of a nervous breakdown. Jason was still pouting over his penis and Beth was calling Elmer names and telling him he didn't have the balls to throw the switch.

When Elmer got to the control panel he pressed a button. Everyone looked up when the pipes above them started making a suction sound. "I hope you fuckers all burn in hell." He pressed another button, activating the saw blade. "And speaking of hell." He turned on the propane, then pressed a button, igniting the gas. The torch heads lit, engulfing the blade with flames. He pointed at Tim. "And fuck you, asshole, this is for you." He pressed another button, activating the automated system.

Tim was horrified as the saw began slowly moving down the tracks towards his table. Everyone was sitting up, staring in terror, including Jason and Henry, as the machine passed by their table. The sight and sound of the blade spinning while covered in flames was horrifying. Tim was panic stricken. He was chaotically jerking at the fishhooks in his legs and at his collar while shouting at Elmer. His heart felt like it was going to explode as the machine slowly moved along the tracks, getting closer and closer. He had never faced such fear. He was terrified. Suddenly, his bowels released and he started urinating.

Everyone was petrified as they watched Tim. He was violently jerking around while screaming at the top of his lungs as feces and urine dripped off the sides of his table.

When the machine was even with the end of his bed, a loud ear-piercing buzzer sounded for a few seconds, then the blade started moving outwards on a horizontal arm. Tim was frantically trying to tear his legs loose and screaming as the blade approached his left foot.

Everyone else had a different set of emotions: Joe and Charles were shouting at Tim, telling him to cut off one of his fingers and stick it in his pipe, Henry was covering his face, Ryan was talking to himself, Jason was hitting his head with his fists and Beth was laughing as if she had gone mad. It was pure chaos.

Tim was panic-stricken. His body was frozen and he was having a difficult time bringing himself to cut off one of his fingers. His hands were shaking as he held the pruning shears around his left pinky finger. About the time, he got the courage and snipped it off, the saw was inches away. His hands were trembling so much that he dropped his finger on the floor before he could get it into the pipe. To his horror, the blade cut into his foot. He screamed with all he had as blood and pieces of flesh slung all over him. The heated blade coming into contact with his body fluids was creating a lot of smoke. The rancid cloud of burnt flesh was burning his eyes, and as he inhaled between screams, the smoke would enter his lungs, causing him to violently cough. The blade moved slowly as it cut through his foot, and when it got to his ankle, he began to feel pieces of shredded bone fragments hitting him all over the front of his nude body. He was horrified when the blade passed his ankle and continued cutting up his leg. He could feel the vibration of his tibia and fibula being cut. Everything seemed to be in slow motion. His mind was flooded with terrifying thoughts: How much more pain could he take? What if the blade didn't stop? He remembered what Elmer said about the blade snagging an artery. He started feeling weak, as if he was going to pass out. He had screamed so hard that his voice was now raspy and he could barely make a sound. Finally, the blade stopped progressing when it got to his knee, then it quickly retracted. Tim stared in dismay—not only had his leg been cut down the center, but the fishhooks were pulling the two halves apart. He leaned over the side of his table and vomited.

Everyone was horrified as they looked at Tim. He was covered in blood and sprinkled in tiny pieces of white bone. Some of the larger bone fragments had penetrated his skin. Tim knew he was on the verge of passing out. He remembered what would happen if he did, so he grabbed one of the syringes and injected himself with adrenaline. The sudden rush of alertness caused him to become aggressive. He glared at Elmer and shouted in a raspy voice. "You motherfucker, you're going to pay for this!"

Elmer was sitting on a five-gallon bucket next to the control panel while smoking a cigarette. He looked like a carnival worker manning the controls of a carnival ride— he had a don't-give-a-shit expression and not a care in the world.

Tim couldn't believe Elmer was ignoring him. "Hey, I'm talking to you, fucker! Look what you did to my leg!" Tim held up his hand. "And my finger. This is bullshit!"

Elmer ignored him as he blew smoke rings.

The machine was now moving towards Henry's table. He seemed dazed. Joe and Charles were yelling at him, telling him to cut off one of his fingers, but he just sat dumbfounded. Joe shouted, "Ryan! Ryan!"

Ryan was about to have a nervous breakdown himself. He slowly looked at Joe. "What?"

"Henry isn't coherent. Try to snap him out of it. He needs to cut off part of a finger and get it into the pipe."

Ryan leaned over towards Henry as far as he could and yelled, "Cut off your finger and stick it in the pipe."

He didn't respond.

"Henry! Cut off your finger before it's too late."

A buzzer sounded, indicating the machine was lined up and the blade was ready to extend out. Joe knew Henry didn't have long. He shouted out, "You need to hurry!"

Henry turned and looked at the group as the blade approached his right foot. He had a solemn expression. "I did it… I've been raping my handicapped daughter. I deserve to die." To everyone's surprise, he just laid there and let the saw cut into him. Everyone stared in absolute horror as the blade slowly cut all the way up to his knee. Blood, bone fragments, pieces of tendons, cartilage and flesh were being spewed out from the machine like a wood chipper. Henry was lying back while arching his back as much as possible. His arms were stretched upwards while making tight fists. It looked as if he was having a seizure, but he was having to endure the pain due to the adrenaline in his IV bag. The machine was very loud, but his screams could be clearly heard. As the blade progressed past his knee, the fishhooks were pulling the two halves apart. The air was filled with a putrid odor of burnt flesh, and Henry's entire body was completely covered in blood and fragmented body parts. When the blade reached halfway up his thigh, he lunged forward, and for no logical reason, he tried to grab the blade with both hands. As quick as he had reached out, the blade had severed most of his fingers on one hand and cut his other hand in half.

When the blade reached his hip, it quickly retracted. Henry's body gave out, causing him to fall back onto the table. His arms flopped off the sides, then he let out an agonizing moan as the last bit of air left his lungs. Seconds later he died.

Everyone was taken aback. They had witnessed something very violent and sadistic. Up to this point, each person still had hope, thinking they would be saved from this nightmare. After witnessing what happened to Tim and Henry, they now realized the horrifying reality they were in.

Ryan was next. He was petrified as the saw started moving down the tracks towards him. He didn't give it a second thought as he cut off his left pinky finger with the pruning shears. The fear combined with the adrenaline rush completely masked the pain. He didn't hesitate to stick the severed appendage into the pipe. The suction almost sucked it out of his hand. A bell chimed, his red light turned off and the green one came on. A few seconds later he saw his finger fall into the glass hopper on the other side of the tracks. The machine didn't even pause as it passed him by, heading for Charles.

Charles' hands were shaking as he held the shears to one of his fingers. "I can't do it! Oh my God! Someone please make this stop."

Joe was yelling at him. "Do it, Charles! Do it now!"

The machine stopped at the end of his table, the loud buzzer went off, then the saw blade began extending out. Charles got the courage and snipped off his pinky finger at the middle joint. He quickly stuck it in the end of the pipe. To his horror, the amber light came on and the blade was still progressing towards his left foot. He was panic-stricken. "Oh my God! It didn't work!"

Joe shouted over the sound of the machine. "It's too small. You have to put something bigger in there."

Charles quickly cut off the remaining stub and tossed it in the pipe, but nothing changed. "It's fucking broke!" He started violently jerking around, trying to tear his legs loose.

Joe shouted again, "Cut off another finger. The whole thing."

Charles' eyes were huge as he started at Joe. "What?"

"Cut off an entire finger."

Charles snipped off his ring finger and tossed it into the pipe. When he noticed his green light came on and the machine stopped, he took a deep breath, then shouted, "Fuck yeah!" Suddenly, flames came blowing out of the machine, engulfing him. His screams echoed throughout the building as he was being burned alive.

Joe was shouting at Elmer to help. Elmer was still sitting on the bucket like he didn't give a shit, but this time he was playing on his phone. Around twenty seconds later, the flames dissipated and the machine started moving back down the tracks. Joe didn't think twice as he snipped off his left pinky finger and threw it into the pipe. As soon as he saw his green light come on, he leaned over towards Charles to check on him. His hair was still smoking and he had been severely burned, but he was still alive. "How you doing, buddy?"

Charles' body was shaking. He could barely talk. "I'm cold."

"Just stay calm and rest. It will be a while before the machine gets back to you."

Joe leaned towards Jason. "You need to cut off a finger before the machine gets to you."

Jason was lying on his back staring up at the lights. "Leave me alone."

"Don't just lie there—the machine is approaching."

"I don't care."

"You can survive this."

"Why would I want to? I don't have a penis." He rolled his head over to face Joe, then held the knife to his neck. "Sorry, Joe. I would rather go out on my own terms."

"Listen to me, son, you don't have to…."

Within seconds, the machine had quickly moved down the tracks and extended the blade into Jason's crotch. Joe was in shock. One moment he was trying to talk Jason out of cutting his neck, then the next moment he was watching as Jason was being mutilated by the machine. Joe stared in horror as the blade slowly cut Jason through his abdomen. Blood, feces and pieces of intestines were being slung everywhere. The heated blade was creating a huge amount of smoke as it ripped through his insides. He screamed at the top of his lungs for the last few moments of his life. When the blade reached his ribcage, it stopped, then quickly retracted, dragging pieces of intestines with it.

Joe was speechless as he looked at Jason. His abdominal cavity lay wide open and most of his ravaged intestines had slid out onto the floor, and a few pieces were hanging out like spaghetti. Joe thought about how the machine had quickly moved, not giving Jason a chance. He shouted at Elmer. "What the fuck happened? Your fucking machine is broken. What kind of bullshit is this?"

Elmer just sat dumbfounded, as he had been doing.

The machine was now heading back towards Tim. He became hysterical as he looked at Elmer. "Why is it coming back towards me?" He pointed at Beth. "What the fuck about her?"

She held her hand up, showing that she was missing a pinky, then she flipped him off with the same hand. About halfway down the tracks, the machine stopped and the blade started slowing down. Elmer came walking up with a frown as he looked at Jason. "Look at this fucking mess. I ain't cleaning this shit up, pun intended." He fanned the air. "And it smells like burnt ass."

Tears were running down Joe's cheeks. "You're a fucking insensitive asshole. He didn't deserve that."

"That's what he gets for trying to kill himself. He knew the rule."

"What are you talking about? What rule?"

"Seth told me if someone tries to kill themselves to engage the execution mode. He wanted to make sure they would suffer before they died, even if it was for a short bit of time."

Joe became angry. "You sorry motherfucker! He wasn't trying to kill himself. It was just the way he was dealing with the stress."

"Then I guess it was his lucky day."

"Fuck you, pendejo! You had no right to do that!"

"And you had no right doing what you did, so get off your high horse."

"Who made you God? You ain't no better than any of us."

"Does it really fucking matter? There's only going to be one survivor. The rest of you fucks are going to be dead soon anyway." Elmer looked at Jason. "At least he didn't suffer long."

Joe nodded towards Charles. "What about him? He's still suffering."

"I'm sure—his fucking skin is peeling off and half of his dick is charred."

Charles had been lying motionless until Elmer mentioned his dick being charred. He could barely move his arms as he reached for his penis. His hands were trembling as he felt around his crotch. "Oh my God! Is it really burnt? I can't feel it."

Joe looked at him. "It's okay, Charles. Your penis is fine. Just try to relax."

Elmer laughed. "Your dick is fucking toast, pal."

Charles started crying. "Oh no! This can't be happening. Please call an ambulance."

Joe glared at Elmer. "Leave him alone, asshole. You've already done enough to him."

"I didn't do shit to him."

"Yeah you did. You burned him."

"He waited too long to feed the pipe. Being burned is the punishment. That part is automated. In fact, everything is automated except for the execution mode, and that's the only reason I'm fucking stuck here with y'all assholes. Seth didn't want any of you fuckers getting off too easy and he couldn't figure out how to make that part automated."

"You could have told us that, you fucking prick."

"I thought I did."

"No, you didn't."

"Oh well, I guess I forgot."

"You forgot? That was kind of fucking important, don't ya think?"

"I got a lot of shit on my mind. Plus, I have my own problems to worry about."

"You're going to burn in hell for this."

"Whatever." He walked over to Tim and picked up his finger off the floor. "Nice souvenir, fucktard."

"You're fucking sorry."

"Actually, you're gonna be." Elmer pulled out a pair of pliers from his back pocket. "You owe me a hundred bucks."

"No problem. I'll give you everything I own if you let me go."

"You know I can't do that. But I can give you two options to pay me back. First, Seth bet me five-hundred bucks that you will be the last one alive. Just make sure that doesn't happen, then I'll actually make four hundred bucks on this gig."

"Seriously? You want me to die so you can make four-hundred bucks? You're fucking crazy."

"I didn't think you would go for that." He tossed the pliers on Tim's lap. "The other option is you can give me five of your front teeth."

Tim looked confused. "What?"

"I didn't stutter, asshole. I want six of your teeth for payment. I'm going to make a necklace out of them."

"You said five."

"See, you are listening, but every time I have to tell you, the number is going to go up."

"You're fucking nuts."

"I'd pull 'em out myself, but I don't want to tear my stitches fighting with you."

"Seth will get mad at you if you do this."

"Don't patronize me. And besides, he's the one that told me he would give me my money back if I made him a tooth necklace out of your teeth."

"Bullshit."

Elmer showed Tim a text message from Seth that verified his story. "See, I told you. He likes necklaces made of teeth. And now you owe me eight. Get them fuckers out so I can start the saw back up."

"Please don't do this. I was serious about giving you everything I own if you let me go: my house, cars, money, everything. And I won't say anything about what happened here.

"Stop trying to get out of this—we've already been over that."

Joe got Elmer's attention. "Hey! I have about twenty-five thousand in the bank. I also have a house, two cars, gold and some guns. It's all yours if you let me go."

Ryan was being quiet—he didn't have a pot to piss in.

Beth laughed. "I'd take them up on that offer. Maybe then you can go buy yourself some balls."

Elmer glared at her. "Fuck you, bitch. You'll be getting yours soon."

"I'm in charge of my destiny, you fucking prick, not you."

"You're awful cocky for someone in your predicament."

"Go to hell, asshole."

"You first, bitch." Elmer looked back at Tim. "Get to pulling your teeth."

"You're fucking…."

Elmer grabbed a hold of Tim's penis. "Pull out your fucking teeth before I rip off your cock."

Tim started hitting Elmer's hands with the pliers. "Get the fuck away from me!"

Elmer jerked his hands away. "I'll get 'em one way or another." He started walking towards the control panel.

Tim started panicking. "Okay, okay. I'll do it if you don't start the saw again."

Elmer stopped next to the control panel. "Fuck you! I'll pull 'em myself as you're letting out your last breath of air." He looked at the group. "And by the way, one finger isn't going to greenlight ya this go around, so you better get ready to start cutting yourself into pieces."

Tim was horrified when the saw started back up. He was mentally exhausted. He had been on an emotional roller coaster ride. He had never experienced so many emotions in such a short period of time. He had flip-flopped between being confused, angry, horrified, scared, timid, aggressive and submissive. He felt numb inside. He had to make a choice; lie down and die, or fight to survive. Now he was experiencing a new emotion; he wasn't going to give Elmer the satisfaction of seeing him beg anymore. He took the pruning shears and snipped off his ring and middle fingers. He smiled at Elmer as he stuck them in the pipe.

Elmer laughed when Tim's amber light came on. "It's gonna take more than that, you fuckin' punk."

Tim didn't expect that. He started to panic, not knowing how many fingers he was going to have to cut off. He started to snip off his index finger, then thought about what he would do after that. He only had so many appendages. That realization scared the shit out of him, knowing he was going to have to start cutting off other body parts. Mentally he went into a downward spiral. He began jerking at his collar and legs again, as he had done the first time. He had to get control of himself and come up with something before the saw sounded its buzzer. There was no way he could bear that much pain again, and he didn't want to be burned like Charles. Without thinking, he sliced off his right ear with the knife, then quickly stuck it in the pipe. His heart seemed to stop when the amber light stayed on. He began to freak out.

Joe had been watching to see if the system would accept separate pieces, combining them for the required amount, or if it would need one large item at a time. He shouted at Tim. "You have to add something larger. Small pieces spaced out don't count."

Tim was horrified. That meant he had wasted two fingers and an ear. He shouted at Elmer. "This isn't fair! What the fuck am I supposed to do now?"

Elmer was leaning against the control panel. He grabbed his crotch and shook it."

Tim was devastated. There was no way in hell he was going to cut off his dick and balls. By now the machine was approaching his table. He had only seconds to make a decision. Without giving it another thought, he jabbed the knife into his thigh and began violently cutting. The pain was almost too much to bear as he cut a hockey puck sized circle. When completed, he tried to pull out the piece of flesh, but it was stuck. He quickly realized he should have angled the knife to the inside of the circle as he was cutting to sever the bottom of the plug. In a state of panic, he started prying at the plug with his knife while working it around. When he got most of it cut loose, he gripped it with both hands and ripped it out. He held on to it for dear life, making sure not to drop it as he stuck the piece of meat into the pipe. Relief overcame him when his green light came on.

Even though he was relieved, he knew he was going to have to do it all again. And to make it worse, there were less people, meaning the saw would be returning more quickly. He wasn't sure how much more he could take. He became nauseated as he looked at his mutilated body. It was bad enough that his leg had been cut in half up to his knee, but the halves were being pulled apart. He could see the inside of his leg: white bones, ligaments, cartilage, veins and muscles. The cuts were smooth and kind of shiny. His leg reminded him of a science prop designed to show the inner working of the body. It was very disturbing. Then he looked at his left hand; that pissed him off. He thought he looked like a freak sporting only a thumb and index finger. Then he looked at the hole in his thigh. He quickly looked away—the tendons and veins hanging out of it grossed him out.

Suddenly, he heard an ear-piercing scream. When he looked, he noticed the saw was sitting in the center of Ryan's crotch. Oh my God, he thought, Ryan's getting it bad. He had been too preoccupied with himself and didn't see what caused it. Then Ryan made the same mistake Henry did; he grabbed at the blade in a desperate attempt to stop the pain. The blade mutilated the majority of his hands. There wasn't much left except for the palms and a couple of fingers dangling by tendons. Then Ryan did the unexpected; he shoved his head into the blade, instantly killing himself. When the saw backed away, he remained in the sitting position. The chain was holding him where he was leaning slightly forward. His head was hanging downwards and oozing brain matter.

Tim was horrified. Henry, Jason and Ryan were already dead, and Charles was on the verge of death. He knew from the beginning that the game was going to be bad, but never dreamed it was going to be this barbaric and sadistic. He thought about killing himself and getting it over with. Waiting until the saw was on the furthest end would be the best, he thought. That way it wouldn't have time to get to him and cut him like it did Jason. He looked at Elmer. He wasn't paying attention as he played on his phone. What a fucking prick, he thought. People were being tortured and dying and this asshole was goofing off. Wait a minute, he thought, Elmer was supposed to be on suicide watch. This might be his chance. He took his knife and started to cut his wrist while keeping an eye on Elmer.

About that time, he heard Charles screaming. He looked over and noticed the saw was cutting up one of his legs. He was just lying there, screaming. It appeared he didn't even try to feed the pipe. His body must be in shock from being burned, or he must have simply given up, he thought. The blade didn't stop until it reached his hip. Tim knew there was no way Charles was going to survive much longer. He only had two competitors left, Joe and Beth. Elmer had referred to this as a game, but it seemed more like some twisted way just to mentally fuck with them. Just like with the hooks pulling his leg apart. The hooks weren't done to prevent anyone from escaping. They were done for psychological torture. He looked at his leg that was cut in half. Who wouldn't be grossed out by that, he thought. Now that he had an understanding of how Elmer and Seth operated, he had to decide if it was worth the extra pain to win this so-called game. They would probably kill him anyway if he somehow managed to outlast everyone else. Either way, he decided to see what the others were going to do first. He could probably handle a few more rounds, if need be.

Tim hadn't been paying much attention to what Joe and Beth had been doing. It had been pretty much chaos for everyone since the saw had started. But now he was focused on them. He couldn't believe his eyes. Joe had cut off his left hand. What a dumbass, he thought, now he only had one hand. That was going to make it difficult for him to cut something else off. He wasn't sure what Beth was up to. She was frantically cutting at one of her legs as the saw approached her. Was she cutting off a kneecap, he wondered. That was actually a good idea, especially for him since his left leg was already mutilated. Right before the saw got to her, she rolled off the table.

Tim yelled out to Joe. "How did she get loose?"

"She cut her legs off at the knees."

Tim was confused. "How did she get through the bone?"

"She probably cut through the tendons."

"Where is she?"

"Sitting next to the table on the floor. She can't go anywhere because of her chain. But it looks like she's trying to pick the lock with the knife."

Elmer heard what was being said. He stood up. "Well I be damned. I didn't see that coming." He looked at Tim. "Looks like I might win the bet after all."

Tim knew he had to do the same thing. He had plenty of time—the saw was at the other end. He grabbed his knife and started to cut into his knee.

Elmer yelled at him. "Hold up! Are you trying to kill yourself?"

Tim shook his head. "No. I'm going to cut off my legs."

"You can't do that. That would be considered a suicide attempt and I will have to engage the execution mode."

"Chill out, dude, I'm not trying to kill myself."

Elmer shut off the saw, then walked over. "Don't call me dude. And it will be if you cut into an artery."

"I'm not going to."

"Apparently, you didn't take anatomy in high school. You can't cut off your fucking leg without cutting arteries, dumbass."

Tim was confused. "You didn't have a problem with Beth doing it."

"I didn't catch her in the act."

"I think you're trying to cheat. Seth has already warned you about that."

Elmer looked guilty. "I, uh… You know what, just do what the fuck you want to do."

Tim injected himself with another adrenaline shot so he wouldn't pass out from the pain. Right before he started to cut into his leg, Joe yelled out, "She's dead! Don't do it, Tim."

He looked at Joe. "What?"

"She bled out."

Tim looked at Elmer. "Did she not have the clotting agent?"

"Of course, she did."

"Then why in the fuck did she bleed out?"

He shrugged his shoulders. "I guess 'cause she was a stupid cunt."

"Can you be serious for once?"

Joe had an idea. "Maybe the clotting agent couldn't stop the larger arteries from bleeding."

"My leg is cut all the way to my knee and I'm not bleeding that much." He thought for a moment. "Fuck, I know why. My leg was cauterized by the blade." Tim was glad he didn't cut off his legs. He would have bled out too.

Elmer pointed at Tim. "See, you were trying to kill yourself. Prepare to die, asshole."

Tim's eyes opened wide. "Hold up! I'm not doing it."

"Rules are rules, you fuck. I have to execute your ass."

Tim was horrified. "Please don't. I beg you."

Elmer was smiling like a possum eating shit. As soon as he turned to head for the control panel he tripped on the tracks, causing him to fall. His head slammed into the concrete, causing him to lose consciousness.

Mind Incarceration

Elmer could feel his head pounding as he woke. The impact had knocked off his beer hat and his IV bags fell out of the hat's holder. He grabbed his neck as he laid on the floor. The IV lines had jerked the shit out of his catheters. When he caught his composure, he sat up, put his IV bags back in the holders, then put the hat back on. He tried to stand up, but a sharp pain shot through his stomach. The fall had jarred his guts and stitches. He took a knee, worried that he had torn something.

Tim could tell Elmer was hurt. He felt showing concern could work to his benefit. "You alright? Is there anything I can do?"

Elmer was holding his stomach. "Fuck you, you little bastard. You're really gonna get it now."

"Hold up! I didn't cause you to fall."

"Fuck you anyway. I'm going to make sure the saw cuts you into pieces, starting with your fucking dick. You're going to be in so much pain that…." Elmer's phone rang. He noticed it was Seth again. He answered it. "Hold up, boss." He stood up and eased off to the side so no one could hear him. "Yes sir… Sorry, I didn't mean to put you on hold… I know, I'm your bitch. It won't happen again… I was just messing with him… I'm not trying to cheat you out of your money… I'm not lying… I'm sorry… I know… Oh! Okay… I will… Sorry, boss… Hello, you still there? Boss?" Elmer put his phone in his pocket. "Fuck me runnin'!" Under his breath, he said, "I hate this fucking transmitter. Fucker can hear everything I say." He looked at Tim. "Now Seth is mad at me again, asshole. He said I deserved to bust my head on the concrete. He said if he was here he would have done it himself. You got me in trouble, you little prick."

Tim was still scared shitless, but was glad Seth had called. Now he didn't have to cut off his legs. All he had to do was outlast Joe. Charles was on his way out, so he wasn't concerned about him.

Elmer was angry. "I know what you're thinking, so fuck you. You're still going to have to cut yourself apart, and I get to watch." He took off towards the control panel.

Tim needed to get something in the pipe. He remembered the kneecap idea. It was obvious to take the one on his leg that had already been cut.

"Fuck you, bitch," shouted Elmer as he started the saw.

Without hesitating, Tim sliced the skin across the top of his knee. He started gagging as he pulled the skin apart, exposing the white bone. He tightly grasped his kneecap and pulled back on it. How is this damn thing attached, he thought? After cutting away more skin, he noticed there were tendons connected to it. Big tendons. He wasn't expecting that. He started to cut them, then paused. His stomach was nauseated and his hands were trembling. He wasn't sure if he could do it. Then he heard Elmer heckling in the background. That pissed him off. He shouted, "Fuck you, asshole!" then he started cutting at the tendons with the knife. Within seconds he was holding his kneecap in the air. He was absolutely sick of Elmer. He stuck the bone into the pipe, then shouted, "How you like them apples, you piece of shit?"

As soon as the saw reversed, he decided to have the next item ready. Even though his leg was split from his foot almost to his knee, the upper portion of his tibia, the epiphysis, was still in one piece. He jammed his knife into the top of his tibia, then wiggled it, snapping the epiphysis in half. Now his tibia was in two complete pieces. He started prying on the bone on the inner side of his split leg, but it was still connected. After he severed all the tendons and ligaments on the upper portion, he started twisting the bone to tear the tendons at the other end that were attached to his ankle. When it pulled loose, his eyes opened wide. Dangling from the end of his tibia were other bones and their attached ligaments. He looked down at his foot and noticed half of the bones had been pulled out. At that moment, he knew he was going to outlast the other two. Not only did he have several more rounds in his hand, he had the other bones in the other half of his leg to go if he needed them. His leg being cut in half turned out to be a big advantage. Not only had it provided him with plenty of items for the pipe, but it was also numb, or at least partially numb, reducing the pain.

He glared at Elmer, then raised the split bone into the air as the smaller bones hung from the end of it. He waved it like a flag. "How do you like me now, dickhead?" He looked at Joe. "You're fucked, pal. You might as well go ahead and cut your throat." He looked at Charles as he was barely breathing. "And you, you black piece of shit, you can go to hell." He looked back at Elmer. "This is what you get for betting against me."

Elmer shook his head. "That's fine—it's only money. And besides, after getting to spend this quality time with you and seeing who you really are, I'm glad that you're going to win this and the prize. You really deserve to live for a very long time. Seth was smart picking you."

Tim felt like he was on top of the world. He started laughing in his head, thinking how messed up it was that he was getting excited after all the shit he had gone through. My God, I'm holding my freakin' leg bone, he thought as he chuckled under his breath.

Charles didn't even scream when the saw cut into him. He died before the blade was fully retracted. Joe was crying and appeared to have given up. Elmer stopped the saw, then walked over to him. Tim couldn't hear what was being said. "Hey, what the fuck are you two talking about?"

Elmer glared at him. "Don't fucking worry about it, you fucking prick. Mind your own business."

"You need to get that fucking saw started and finish this shit." He pointed at Joe. "That motherfucker needs to die."

Elmer shook his head. "Listen here, you cocky piece of shit, you need to show some fucking respect. Joe hasn't done shit to you. In fact, he's been trying to help you."

"Whatever, dude."

"He could have let you cut off your legs and bleed out, you ungrateful bastard."

"I don't give a shit about him or you. And I don't know what you two are fucking scheming, but Seth isn't going to like it."

"Seth already knows. He told me what your prize is going to be, and I'm just telling Joe what it is."

Tim grinned. "You should be telling me, not that fuckhead."

Joe had a solemn expression as he looked at Tim. "You don't have to act like an asshole. We were all in this together."

"Whatever. You're just jealous you lost."

Joe looked at Elmer. "At least give me the satisfaction of telling that arrogant fucker what his prize is before I go."

Elmer nodded. "I think that's a great idea."

Tim had a cocky look. "Well, let's hear it, Joe."

"They're going to incarcerate your mind."

Tim looked confused. "What the fuck does that mean?"

"When this is over, they're going to cut off all your appendages, including your dick and balls. Then they're going to cut out your tongue, remove your voice box, bust your ear drums and rip out your eyes. You'll get to live the rest of your life in some nursing home in total silence and darkness, forced to think about how much of a sorry piece of shit you are."

Tim had a grimace of terror as he looked at Elmer. "Is he telling the truth?"

"For the most part."

Tim started to panic. "Hold up. I won. The deal was I get to live. You can't do that."

Elmer laughed. "You are going to live, numb-nuts."

"But you didn't say anything about doing that to the winner."

"You knew there was a surprise that went along with winning."

"You sick son of a bitch! You had this planned from the beginning. You played all of us."

"Just remember this was your fault for molesting your daughter when you're nothing more than a breathing bag of thoughts. Keep that flowing through your head as the years go by. And maybe you will get lucky and live to a ripe old age, you fucking child molester."

Tim started thinking of the reality of living in total silence and darkness without arms and legs. How horrifying would it be to have to live like that, not being able to communicate, only being stuck with his thoughts. Horrible thoughts at that. He desperately wanted to live, but not like that. He knew what he needed to do. He had the courage now to take his own life. He looked at Elmer as he pointed at Joe. "I haven't won yet. He's still alive. I want to keep playing."

Elmer put Joe in a headlock, then shoved a long screwdriver into his eye, sinking it all the way to the back of his skull. Joe's lifeless body fell back onto the table as the handle of the screwdriver stuck out of his eye socket. Elmer looked at Tim. "Game over, pal."

Tim grabbed his knife, and before he could cut himself, Elmer ran over to him and injected him with a tranquilizer. The last thing Tim saw was Elmer's smiling face as his vision faded into darkness.

Solitary of Horror

Tim Murray woke up. He felt dazed. He was having a hard time thinking. It was dark. So dark he couldn't see anything. He had never experienced such darkness. And it was very quiet. He had never experienced so much quietness. He went to move his arm, but something was wrong. He couldn't feel his limbs. *What the heck is wrong*, he thought. Am I paralyzed or something? Did I have a stroke? Suddenly he remembered everything: Elmer, the saw, the tables, the duct system. The entire horrifying experience flashed before him. Terror overcame him when he remembered what Seth and Elmer were going to do to him. He screamed, or at least he thought he did. He couldn't tell. Someone, or something, was touching his chest. It felt like a hand patting him. Or maybe more than one hand. Was it Seth? Elmer? Who was it? Was he in the hospital? It could be a doctor or nurse touching him. He tried to speak, but his throat felt strange. Oh my God, he thought, they cut out my vocal cords. He started to panic. How was he going to communicate with this person or persons?

He became angry. They had no right to do this, he thought. He had to find a way to tell on them. Then he remembered why they had done it. He tried to block that out. He desperately fought to keep those thoughts out of his head, but they kept coming back. All kinds of flashbacks of what he had done were running through his mind. He didn't want to see them, but they kept coming, one after another. He tried to convince himself that he hadn't done anything wrong. It wasn't his fault—he was born that way. For some reason that excuse wasn't working anymore. Would it help if he admitted to what he did? He didn't want to think it, but the thought of him being a child molester ran through his mind. I did it, he screamed in his head, I molested my daughter. He felt ashamed. Almost deserving of his punishment.

Between the silence, darkness and the horrible thoughts, he was in mental agony. He needed to stop thinking. It was going to drive him crazy. He needed to find a way to kill himself. But how? He had no hands. Banging his head against something crossed his mind. He tried to move, but it felt like he was bound by something. Was he tied? Was he in a bed with railings? He tried to hold his breath, but that didn't work. He tried again and again with the same results. It was hopeless. He wasn't going to be able to end it. He didn't even have a tongue that he could bite in hopes he would bleed to death. How much time had already passed, he thought? Was it days, or just minutes? How was he going to live like this, with all these horrible thoughts and the guilt that came with them? Horror overcame him when he realized he could live for another fifty to sixty years.

gone
CEMETERY DANCE PRODUCTIONS PRESENTS
A CHIZMAR FILM
BILLY CHIZMAR JACOB WARREN ANDREW MORGAN
SPECIAL APPEARANCE BY STEPHEN KING
"GONE"
PRODUCED BY RICHARD CHIZMAR CO-PRODUCED BY KARA & NOAH CHIZMAR
DIRECTOR OF PHOTOGRAPHY JEFF ZINGER ART BY FRANCOIS VAILLANCOURT
SCREENPLAY BY BILLY & RICHARD CHIZMAR ORIGINAL SCORE JIM TAYLOR
DIRECTED BY BILLY CHIZMAR

GONE

An Original Short Film
by
Richard & Billy Chizmar
Guest Cameo Appearance by Stephen King

EXT. WOODS – DUSK

We see various shots of the wilderness. Tall trees. Heavy brush. Running creek. Secluded pond. Abandoned shack. Tiny waterfall. Muddy puddles on a trail.

Three teenagers crossing a creek on a fallen log. The same three teenagers fishing in a creek.

TITLE SEQUENCE

EXT. WOODS – CREEK - DUSK

Three teenagers fishing in a creek. BILLY is the serious one. JACOB, the sarcastic smart ass. ANDY, the class clown.

Andy tries to set the hook. Misses another one.

ANDY
Dammit!

Billy gets a bite and pulls in a fish. He holds it up proudly for his friends to see.

> JACOB
> My dick is bigger than that fish.

Andy LAUGHS.

> BILLY (releasing the fish)
> You wish.

> ANDY (reeling in his line)
> Anyone else hungry?

> JACOB
> I mention my dick and you get hungry.

> BILLY (shaking his head)
> Let's go. I'm starving.

EXT. WOODS – NIGHT

From across the creek, we see the three boys sitting around a blazing campfire.

EXT. CAMPFIRE – NIGHT

We watch the three boys around the fire. Talking. Laughing. Eating hot dogs and drinking out of red solo cups. The fishing poles lean against a nearby tree. The glow of the fire shines on their mostly happy faces. Billy is the only one that doesn't look like he's having a great time. He looks thoughtful.

EXT. CAMP FIRE – NIGHT

Andy takes a big swig from his red solo cup. Belches.

ANDY
So what do you guys think the big emergency was?

JACOB
Who cares? It got us out of school early, that's all I care about.

BILLY (looking serious)
I wouldn't count on us having school tomorrow either.

Andy and Jacob both jerk their heads around to stare at Billy. Surprised.

ANDY
No shit?

JACOB (eager)
Your dad tell you that? He finally answer you?

BILLY (shakes his head)
My dad says the only time the base sounds the siren is if something bad happens. Really bad. They close the gates and no one can get in or out until the situation is under control.

ANDY
Sounds like something from The Stand.
(newscaster voice)
An airborne biological warfare agent has escaped from Edgewood Arsenal and entered the general population…

BILLY
We better hope not.

JACOB
Jesus, chill out, man. You sound like Mikey. He was
going on and on today about monsters escaping from
one of your dad's labs.

ANDY (points at Jacob)
The Mist! Now that was a cool movie.

We hear a RUSTLING in the woods nearby. All
three boys turn and look and listen.

EXT. WOODS – NIGHT

We see the boys sitting around the fire through a veil
of tree branches. One of the boys is looking right at us.

EXT. CAMPFIRE – NIGHT

BILLY
All I know is my dad hasn't answered any of my
calls or texts. That's something to worry about.

JACOB
C'mon, your old man's like a mad scientist, he's
spacy as shit.

ANDY
I swear I think he smokes up. He can't even
remember my name half the time.

BILLY (ignoring them)
Did you guys notice all those Army trucks in town today? And helicopters? I saw like a dozen of them flying around on my way here.

JACOB
Dude, you need to have another drink and stop worrying.

BILLY
And what about Mikey and Doug? They were supposed to be here three hours ago. Why aren't they answering their texts? Where the hell are they?

JACOB
Probably at your house...banging your mom.

Andy spits out a mouthful of beer, cracks up laughing. Billy flips Jacob the bird.

We hear a LOUD KNOCKING in the woods. In the distance. The boys all look out into the darkness.

ANDY
(redneck voice)
There's a sasquatch lurking in these here woods.

Billy ignores him.

BILLY
I'd just feel better if I heard something from my dad.

Jacob drains his cup and tosses it on the ground.

JACOB

And I'd feel better if I drained my dragon.

Jacob stands up. Takes a pack of cigs from his pocket. Slides one into his mouth. Sparks up a lighter and heads off into the woods.

Andy pulls out the knife from his belt. Starts tossing the point into the ground.

ANDY
You see what Katy Parker was wearing today?

BILLY
That red dress?

ANDY (nods)
And those shoes, man, she looked like a stripper.
God, I love her so much.

BILLY
So ask her out.

ANDY (gives him a look)
I think I'll avoid that level of embarrassment until
after we graduate.

A RUSTLING from the nearby bushes. Both boys look in that direction expecting to see Jacob. When they don't...

BILLY
What's taking Jacob so long?

ANDY (same redneck voice)
Maybe a sasquatch got him.

Billy gets to his feet. Starts walking toward the area where Jacob disappeared. Andy looks around. Doesn't want to be left alone by the fire. He grabs a flashlight, hurries to his feet and follows.

ANDY
Hey, wait up!

EXT. NEARBY WOODS – NIGHT

Billy is slowly making his way into the woods – when Andy BUMPS into his from behind, startling him.

BILLY
Christ.

ANDY (looking around, eyes wide)
Sorry.

They keep walking. Andy close on Billy's shoulder.

ANDY
Where'd he go?

Billy doesn't answer. Keeps walking. He's about to turn around when he sees the glowing red tip of a cigarette ahead in the distance.

BILLY
Jacob?

They walk around a tree – and there on the ground is the still glowing cigarette. And right next to it, JACOB'S EMPTY CLOTHES. Billy looks around.

BILLY
What the hell?

ANDY (breaking into a nervous smile)
He's messing with us.

He looks around. Starts yelling.

ANDY
Hey, loser! Come out, come out, wherever you are!

Billy isn't so sure. He bends to a knee. Picks up the cigarette and stubs it out in the mud. Then he picks up Jacob's sweatshirt.

BILLY (quickly dropping the sweatshirt)
Damn.

ANDY (O.S.)
Jacob!

He picks it up again. Really examines it. Rubs his fingertips together. Reaches it up to Andy. Andy takes it and examines it.

ANDY
It's freezing.

BILLY (nods)
Smell it.

Andy smells the sweatshirt. Wrinkles his nose.

ANDY
Stinks. What is it?

BILLY (shrugs)
It's like a burnt smell.

Andy drops the sweatshirt to the ground. Looks into the woods and cups his hands around his mouth. He's starting to look and sound a little panicked.

ANDY
This isn't funny anymore, asshole! Come on out!

BILLY (looking around)
I think we should go back to the fire.

EXT. CAMPFIRE – NIGHT

Billy is sitting by the fire, really examining Jacob's clothes. He checks the pockets. Pulls out a wallet. Turns the socks inside out. Looks inside the boots.

Andy can't sit still. He gets to his feet. Paces for a few seconds, then sits down again.

ANDY
Why would he take off all his clothes? That's weird even for Jacob.

Billy looks up at him. Doesn't answer.

ANDY
You think he's okay?

Billy doesn't answer.

ANDY

You think this has something to do with the
emergency today, don't you?

BILLY
I don't know, man.

EXT. WOODS – NIGHT

A quick glimpse of the two boys through a veil of
trees.

EXT. CAMP FIRE – NIGHT

ANDY
What're we gonna do?

Billy picks up Jacob's wallet, starts stuffing it into
his pocket.

BILLY
We're gonna go look for him.

ANDY
Are you sure that's a good idea?

BILLY
Do you have a better one?

Andy doesn't respond. Billy looks over at him – but
he's gone. His EMPTY CLOTHES lay heaped on the
ground where he was sitting. The flashlight resting
beside them.

BILLY (getting to his feet)
Andy?

Billy picks up the flashlight. Touches Andy's shirt. It's freezing. He looks around – and we see panic spreading on his face. Something RUSTLES in the nearby trees. Billy's had enough – he takes off running.

EXT. TRAIL – NIGHT

Billy's POV as he runs into the night. We hear his HEAVY BREATHING. We feel his panic.

EXT. TRAIL – NIGHT

We watch as Billy, just a dark figure in the night, comes running toward us.

EXT. TRAIL – NIGHT

Billy climbs a steep hill, scrambling as fast as he can.

EXT. HILL – NIGHT

Billy's POV with heavy, ragged BREATHING.

EXT. TREELINE – NIGHT

Billy scrambles up the hill. Using his hands to claw his way up.

EXT. TREELINE – NIGHT

Billy bursts from the trees and enters his truck.

INT. TRUCK – NIGHT

Billy climbs into his truck. Fumbles with his keys and starts the engine. Starts to drive away.

EXT. ROAD – NIGHT

The truck drives a short distance. The brake lights blink a couple times. Then, the truck veers off, hops the curb, and drifts to a stop.

We slowly PAN closer to the truck and right inside the driver's side window...

...where we find BILLY'S EMPTY CLOTHES heaped on the front seat.

A CELL PHONE RINGS.

The camera goes CLOSE on Billy's RINGING cell phone on the floor of the truck.

The Caller ID reads: **DAD**

Voice mail picks up and we hear:

                    BILLY'S DAD'S VOICE

Listen to me, Billy. You have to get out of here before they close the roads. You have to get far away. I'll try to find you, but I don't know if—

CUT TO BLACK

END CREDITS ROLL

(SHOTS OF EMPTY CLOTHES AT VARIOUS LOCATIONS)

Playground.
Gas station pump.
Playground.
Floating in empty swimming pool.
Suburban road next to an empty dog collar.

The Silverado Springs
Memory Care Posse
James H Longmore

There was a sign on Smiler's door that read '*No Entrey – Wildcat Lose*'. It was written with a bright red sharpie in what was unmistakably Juanita's childish scrawl – as nice a care assistant as that girl was, she really wasn't the brightest button on any shirt; and spelling certainly wasn't her strong point. There was no wildcat in the room, of course, but everyone at the home was afraid of wildcats so it gave them the privacy they needed to clean up the mess. Besides which, had they written '*murderous, slimy monster at large*', it was likely no one would have believed it, or the residents would have been tempted to poke their noses in for a look-see.

As Lewis Jones ambled by Smiler's room on his way down to the breakfast room, he snuck a peek in through the gap afforded by the slightly ajar door and saw Juanita and her supervisor, Karl cleaning up Smiler's room. Mopping, scrubbing, tidying, they buzzed around in there like white-clad industrious insects, seemingly oblivious to the fact that Smiler's body was still in his bed.

It was early yet, far too early for the good folks of Carpenter's Funeral Services to come collect Smiler. Silverado Springs Memory Care was their farthest point of call and they'd most likely be there around lunchtime. Still, there really was no rush; it wasn't as if poor old Smiler was going anywhere any time soon – especially considering the state he was in.

"Ain't no wildcat did that to Smiler." Lewis – *Louie* to his handful of close friends – mumbled to Bones, the small care center dog that scampered around his feet as he walked by; they had a trio of small dogs around because it was supposed to cheer up the patients and keep them calm, but all the damned things seemed to do was crap everywhere and yip at nothing. Ignoring the dog, Lewis allowed himself to be lured away from the gruesome scene in Smiler's room by the delectable smell of cooked bacon that wafted up from the kitchen.

Or was it sausage?

Damned if he could remember.

And by the time Lewis had reached the stairs, the memory of the horror he'd seen in the room had already faded to little more than fuzz.

***

"Good morning," Lewis greeted the two strangers – one of each sex, he noted – who sat at his table. Lewis knew it was his table because there was a place setting with his name and the picture of the same face he had printed on his ID badge in his pocket. "Thank you, Stacey," Lewis said to the morbidly overweight lady who helped him to his seat. Stacey was your salt of the earth, single mom type who more often than not worked double shifts at the Center just to make ends meet and pay the rental on her double-wide. She always had a broad smile on her face, as if she were playing a long and elaborate joke on everyone and she always had a kind word for the residents.

In the center of the breakfast table sat a small, red vase of fake daisies that sported a thin veneer of old dust. Sticking up from the midst of the flowers was a tall, wooden place holder at the top of which was glued a picture of a Monarch butterfly on a milkweed flower, its gaudy wings spread as if it were about to take flight. Each one of the half dozen or so tables in the room were similarly laid out, each with a different creature on its placeholder. This was so that the elderly residents could better remember their designated seat should they forget that their ID was in their pocket – colorful animals are apparently easier for dementia sufferers to recall than numbers or letters – and although Lewis had nothing against the Monarch as such, he would have preferred to have been seated at the baboon table.

The strategy did work, somewhere in the hazy recesses of Lewis's Alzheimic brain he did remember the butterfly, and could actually relate it to where he was supposed to be – yet had it not been for the fat woman's large-lettered name badge, he'd have been lost as to her damn name.

Lewis sat down and scrutinized the two people with whom he was to eat breakfast and he had a feeling in the back of his foggy mind that he was supposed to know who they were. Likewise the light gray notebook that lay adjacent to the white plastic cutlery in front of him.

"Say, where did your friend go?" Stacey asked with that broad smile of hers. The woman at Lewis's table stared blankly up at the big woman. "The guy with the hat? He was here a minute ago." Stacey continued, but was met by nothing more than puzzled looks from all three patients at the table. "I'll go get your breakfast," she said to Lewis with an exasperated snort and waddled off towards the kitchen.

"I do remember a man," the woman said quietly. "Do you?"

Lewis shook his head, as did his other breakfast companion.

"He was tall," the woman carried on, as if trying to convince herself. "Or was he short? Definitely one of the two," she said with conviction. "Will you look at me, I spend all day around you dementia patients and my memory starts to go – are you sure it's not contagious?"

"Enjoy your bacon, Louie." Stacey reappeared and with a smile she plonked a white, plastic plate in front of him.

"Bacon?" Lewis said as he examined the plate's greasy passengers. "That's sausage."

"No, it's definitely bacon, three strips to go with your egg and hash brown."

"What is?" Lewis asked.

Stacey chuckled and gave Lewis a pat on the shoulder as if the exchange was nothing more than a private joke between them. She then waddled off in the direction of a sad-faced old lady who had barely a handful of white wisps of cotton candy hair clinging to her head. The old lady shuffled in to the breakfast room behind her aluminum walker, it was one of those with slit open tennis balls on the front legs to save the thing from scraping the laminate floors.

"Good morning, Louie," the woman at Lewis's table said. "I trust that you slept well?"

"I did, thank you." Lewis forced a smile and reached deep into the back of his mind to try to recall the woman with the jet black hair (dyed? wig? – he figured it best not to ask) and who's fashion sense appeared to have stalled the year Buddy Holley died.

"It's Constance," the woman's voice was patient; this being a ritual they'd performed every morning for the past three years.

"Ah, yes, Constance." At the sound of the name, something vague formed on the edges of Lewis's crumbling brain. It felt like a long lost lover walking towards him, arms spread wide through a thick, swirling mist. "Connie," Lewis said with a triumphant smile.

Constance hated having her name abbreviated so; in her book it was a sure fire sign of laziness. Still, she was prepared to set that minor irritation aside for the time being, at least until poor old Louis regained his bearings – a task that seemed to take a little longer each morning.

At just sixty-seven, Constance was very much the baby of their rapidly dwindling group, and since that Janey Whatsherface had passed not all that long ago, she was also the only female. Constance was – always had been – a proud, vain lady; she kept her petite figure trim with a diet as good as she could get at the memory care center, daily exercise and formidable undergarments that supported her not inconsiderable breasts. She awoke at five-thirty sharp each morning to apply her make up (the memory of *how* was thankfully stored in her long-term vaults and thus far had remained untouched by the ravages of the disease she still tried to deny) so as to face each and every day looking her absolute best.

Dementia had crept up on Constance in the last year of her fifties, shortly after her husband's accident (some had speculated at the time that it had been God's retribution, since the justice system had failed) and had begun to eat away at her brain like some ravenous, malevolent parasite. She'd been dumped at Silverado Springs by her daughter who Constance maintained simply didn't want to have to deal with the inconvenience of an ailing mother. Although, the incident in which Constance had popped her daughter's family dog in the oven for a few minutes to dry off after its walk one rainy day may have had more to do with Janice's decision than pure selfishness. The kids – Constance's trio of adorable grandchildren – had been there to witness the full horror as their beloved Yorkshire terrier screamed like a banshee as it spun around in slow, tortuous circles. The dog had still been squealing when the microwave had finally pinged and Constance's grand children had shortly thereafter embarked upon an expensive round of intensive therapy.

They visited from time to time, but Constance would see the look of fear in the children's eyes and sense the trepidation in Janice and her husband; and she knew in her heart that things would never be the same again.

"Welcome back, Louie." Constance reached for Lewis's hand and gave it a fond squeeze.

"Yeah, welcome back, buddy." Lewis's other dining companion – a tall, lanky black guy – said through a mouthful of bacon. "How you doin'?"

Lewis wasn't sure exactly how he should answer the man's question, nor did he feel that he was back from anything; although he did find that dim thoughts swirled into his comprehension – such as his memory of Connie – and if he grasped them before they floated away back into the fog, he could actually retain snippets of the memories they represented. It was a slow and frustrating process, but it was pretty much all Lewis had.

There were fat, gaping holes in Lewis's memory which he imagined mirrored the fat, gaping holes in his inexorably deteriorating brain. And those holes just kept on expanding, like the sinkholes that open up beneath small mining towns to swallow large chunks of his mind and leave fewer and fewer places for new memories to stick. In some ways, Lewis considered himself lucky insomuch he still enjoyed more lucid moments than most, even if they did require a kick-start to get them moving every morning.

Lewis's short term memory – once he brushed off that morning daze – actually retained a great deal. Sadly though, because of the Alzheimer's that had been systematically destroying his gray matter for the latter twelve years of his seventy-nine, that ephemeral part of his mind was wiped clean every night as he slept, much as a teacher wipes clean the class whiteboard at the end of each school day. The brain function responsible for shunting information to the vaults of his more secure long term memory had almost completely disintegrated – on some days, if he concentrated really hard, Lewis imagined he could feel the break in the virtual cable. Ask Lewis Jones what he had for dinner the previous day he'd be clueless, but he could tell you what color pants he was wearing the day after Regan was shot.

"I'm doing okay – Maroon, isn't it?" Lewis replied to the black guy after some pondering.

"Muldoon," the black guy corrected with a fond smile. "Still, that's closer than you got yesterday, my old friend." He shovelled a gelatinous glob of scrambled eggs into his mouth, choosing to ignore the bits that fell from his spoon and became entangled in the straggled gray hairs of his sparse beard.

"Of course." Lewis smiled back as clumsy memories of the guy swam into view like the fake ghosts in a carnival horror house. "How the devil are you, Whitey?" Lewis's grin was a broad one; he was delighted with the flash of clarity his friend's prompt had afforded.

Whitey Muldoon was a musician, played jazz in the Big Easy under the moniker Sticky Fingers Muldoon back in the day – he'd even had a record deal with someone who claimed to have worked with Bunny Berigan sometime before the trumpet player had gone the way of most jazz musicians in the early part of the century and drank himself to death.

Muldoon had thin, gaunt features that sat uneasy with his lanky six-two frame, and he had huge, skinny hands with impossibly long fingers. And in those rare moments of lucidity his own advanced dementia afforded and in which Muldoon's rotting mind remembered the notes, those fingers could pick out a tune on the rec' room piano that would bring the residents to tears.

Lewis had first met Muldoon at his wife's funeral; Muldoon was there because he'd been Bethany Jones's lover for the better part of twenty years.

"I don't want to appear rude on such an occasion," Lewis had approached the tall, shiny-faced guy who was skulking at the rear of the church before the service. "But just who the fuck are you?" He'd long suspected Beth of being less than entirely faithful throughout their forty-five years together, and had been guilty of the odd dalliance himself whilst away on the many business trips and sales conferences his job had demanded. So, as the man said – glass houses, stones and all that – and of all the things Lewis Jones considered himself to be, a hypocrite wasn't one of them.

"I knew Bethany." Muldoon had at first been coy, embarrassed even. "She was a remarkable woman."

What else could Lewis do but agree?

He'd invited Muldoon down to the front line of pews for the service and afterwards to his home. That night, long after they'd lowered the woman they'd both loved into the cold, hard ground, they'd spent the night on Lewis's porch cracking cold ones and reminiscing about just how remarkable a woman Bethany had been, and some of the weird shit she liked to get up to in the sack.

The two had thus become firm friends and the universe had once more woven its perverse magic when they'd both been diagnosed with early-onset

Alzheimer's within the same month and drafted into Silverado Springs together.

"Ya hear what happened to Smiler?" Muldoon broke Lewis's splintered reverie.

"No," Lewis replied. "I'm guessing he passed on?" Death was a regular visitor to Silverado Springs Memory Care, more so than the relatives of the majority of the residents. It was a safe guess.

"I heard he was murdered," Constance chipped in, a glint in her eye at the thought. "We should ask Karl."

"Ask me what?" Karl's ears pricked up at the mention of his name. He was making his way through the breakfast area to change since he'd gotten a smudge or two of blood on his scrubs whilst cleaning out the old man's room and he wanted it off of him *tout suite*.

"Is it true they killed Smiler?" Constance was as direct as ever; no point beating about the bush when there's a good chance she'd forget the question before it was answered.

"Nobody killed anybody, Connie," Karl patronized her. "Mr. Deakins passed over peacefully in his sleep." A strained smile. "You know he'd been sick for quite some time, and he *was* eighty-five, you know."

"If there's someone running around killing the inmates, you would tell us, wouldn't you, Karl?" Muldoon asked.

"You'd be the first to know, Mr. Muldoon; and you're *guests* here, not inmates." Karl deflected.

"So we are able to leave the facility whenever we like?" Muldoon's voice was his typical deadpan.

"Not on your own, and not until Activity Day," Karl told him. "You know that full well, Mr. Muldoon. And it's not a *facility*, its –"

"Case, rested." Muldoon cracked a grin and spread his arms wide in a well-there-you-are-then gesture. He plucked a cold, stiff strip of bacon from his plate and crunched on it loudly as if that further underlined his point.

"Leave the poor man alone," Lewis admonished his friend. There was something in a dingy corner of his mind that advised him that perhaps Karl was not in the mood for banter this morning. He also eyed the three empty chairs at the Monarch table and wondered if there perhaps was something in Muldoon's suggestion of someone other than Death bumping their fellow inmates off after all.

Karl sped off towards the kitchen and disappeared behind the door with the brass *Staff Only* plaque screwed to it, leaving Lewis, Muldoon and Constance alone with their cold breakfast and stilted conversation that sounded as if the three were meeting for the very first time.

***

Lewis chewed on the last of his bacon. It was satisfying enough although it felt rough and salty in his mouth and split into slivers like shards of rubbery glass. As he munched, he contemplated the notebook that sat by his left hand. It was a pleasant, light gray Moleskine; half letter sized and with a broad strip of black elastic to hold it shut. The elastic reminded him of the suspenders his Grandfather used to wear to keep his pants up.

"I think it's yours." Constance told him.

"Why's that?" Lewis said.

"Because it's by your place at the table." Constance replied before cottoning on to Lewis's joke.

"He got ya good there, Connie, old girl!" Muldoon guffawed and almost choked on his slurp of tea.

Lewis winked at Constance and she pursed her lips at him to pretend that she was disgruntled. He picked up the notebook and was surprised that its covers felt velvety beneath his fingers, much as he would have imagined an actual mole's would feel. Perhaps, he couldn't help but wonder, they actually made the things from *real* moles?

Upon opening the book, Lewis discovered that there was a name written in neat, black ink on the inside cover. The handwriting and the name looked surprisingly familiar, but it took a minute or two for it to filter through his muddled brain cells that both belonged to him.

"It *is* mine," Lewis informed his breakfast companions with a grin. "Look, it says *Lewis Jones* right here." He lifted the book up and turned it around to show them his name and the writing below it that was in an altogether different hand.

Happy Birthday Grandpa.

A tear formed in Lewis's eye and a sick lump rose up in the back of his throat. He was a grandfather, and therefore by default, a father too. He had family out there in the world and he couldn't remember a damned thing and at that particular moment, Lewis would have given anything to have had even the faintest glimmer of a memory of them.

Constance reached for Lewis's hand and held it whilst he struggled with his emotions. It had been this same way every morning for as long as she could recall – Lewis discovering as if for the first time that he had a family. For Constance, the saddest thing of all – other than to watch the man she cared for deeply facing the same pain anew every single day – was that Lewis's loving son, daughter-in-law and three beautiful granddaughters visited him every week and he was always so incredibly happy in their company.

And Lewis's cruel brain, in common with hers and Muldoon's deteriorating gray matter, would misplace those precious memories overnight whilst he slept.

Which is why things were written down in that book,

otherwise everything would have been forgotten.

Lewis flicked through the notebook, his eyes darting to and fro across the tightly written handwriting that filled almost two-thirds of the silken pages. His brow would furrow in a quizzical expression when he happened upon places where the occasional page or two had been torn out.

Muldoon peered across the breakfast table, slurping on his cold tea with all the finesse of a buffalo at the watering hole. "So?" he enquired. "What's in the book, Lewis?" He strained his eyes to try reading the neatly printed words upside down. "And what's that supposed to mean?" He jabbed a long, bony finger towards the book, to what he guessed was the title written in block capital lettering at the top of each and every page.

"*The Silverado Springs Memory Care Posse*," Lewis read out loud the neatly printed words.

"What the hell is that supposed to mean?" Muldoon wrinkled up his nose as if he'd caught a whiff of something particularly disgusting.

"I think it's us." Lewis looked his old friend straight in the eye. "Yeah, it's us alright – look." He spun the book around on the stained cotton tablecloth and pointed at one of its pages.

Muldoon and Constance leaned in to catch a better look. Constance had to lift up her chin to see through the bottom part of her narrow spectacles.

"Chuck Rifkin?" Muldoon looked perplexed. "Who the heck is Chuck Rifkin?" He nodded at a list of names in the center of the right hand page.

"Janey Martinez, now that does ring a vague bell," Constance mused and closed her eyes in order to search for the memory that she simply *knew* was skulking in some far corner of her head somewhere.

"Smiler's name is on the list, too." Lewis ran his finger down the half dozen names that were all written in meticulous cursive. "Whitey Muldoon – that's you, I guess?" he said to Muldoon. "And this one is me." Lewis appeared pleased to have recognized his own name for the first time, although he'd only just seen it a minute or so ago at the front of the book.

"And that one is me." Constance was back with them, the fuzzy image of her erstwhile friend Janey Martinez still loitering on the periphery of her mind; pretty much all she could recall was that Janey had died, although that could have been years ago.

Or yesterday.

"So, why are those ones crossed out?" Muldoon reached over the table and poked a finger at the first three names on the list.

There were thin, straight pencil lines through the names 'Chuck', 'Janey' and 'Smiler' which looked as if they had been drawn with the aid of a ruler.

＊＊＊

Lewis flicked through the notebook, the pages rustling softly as he turned them, as if they were whispering their secrets to him with quiet, impatient voices.

"This has happened before," he announced and the suddenness of his voice startled the others. Muldoon almost dropped his tea – his fourth of the morning – and Constance jumped from the muddle of her thoughts, which were almost instantly forgotten.

"Hm?" Muldoon grunted.

"Smiler," Lewis said. "What happened to Smiler has happened before – I think to each of these people." He flicked back to the list of crossed-out names for emphasis.

"*What* happened?"

Lewis fought to recall what he'd seen earlier that morning, and something that Constance had asked the care assistant guy. But it was like peering through a thick, black curtain into impenetrable darkness. "I looked into Smiler's room, and there was –" The word just refused to form; it felt to Lewis as if there was just a deep, dark hole in his brain where the word he wanted ought to be. "– that red stuff that comes out when you shave," he compensated.

"Foam?" Muldoon was genuinely confused by this concept.

"You have red shaving foam?" Constance asked him.

"Who does?" Muldoon slurped at his cooling tea.

"Hm?" Lewis joined in.

"Karl did say that he'd passed," Constance tried her best to be helpful, although she was having difficulty remembering exactly who the care assistant was.

"And according to this, so did Chuck and Janey." Lewis scanned the notebook, increasingly frustrated by the missing pages – something niggled at the back of his mind that there must have been very important things written on them.

"We're in an elderly care facility," Muldoon added with a wry smile and a twinkle in his rheumy old eyes. "Of course the inmates die – it's what us old folk do best at." A smile.

"I think there's more to it than that." Lewis glanced up at his old friend. "And I think that we were investigating it, quite possibly even trying to put a stop to it."

"You talking 'bout murder, Lewis?" There was a glint in Muldoon's eyes that Lewis didn't much care for. "Isn't that what the police are for?" he drew out the word as if he were relishing its caress upon his tongue; it came out as *po-leece*.

"I don't know – perhaps, maybe," Lewis struggled.

According to the notes he'd made in the notebook, whatever had happened to the owners of the three struck out names had happened overnight, and whilst he, Constance and Muldoon had quite clearly pooled their memories and theories to write down in the Moleskine, their recollection had been nebulous to say the least.

"Then it looks like I'm next." Muldoon pointed a shaking finger at his name on the page. "So, what are we gonna do about that?"

Lewis turned over a page or two, more to be away from that ominous list of names – that did contain his own, remember – than in the vague hope of finding an answer hidden amidst the disjointed prose. He was going to need more time to read and inwardly digest his forgotten writings before anything close to answers presented themselves. Suffice to say though, the three on the list prior to Muldoon were deceased *and* crossed out, so perhaps it was safe for them to assume –

"Dammit." Lewis growled as once more his brain drew a complete blank and his thoughts tumbled into a bottomless black hole.

"Hm?" Muldoon queried.

"What if Lewis and I were to keep watch over you?" Constance filled the silence.

"All night?" Muldoon raised a sceptical eyebrow.

"Well, I don't seem to need all that much sleep these days." Constance smiled at the two men. "And Lewis only forgets things when he sleeps, so I'd say it was doable."

"Yeah, that's what I suggested here." Lewis drew a finger along several lines of his own writing. "We sit with you from midnight 'til the sun comes up. That's it."

"That's what?" Constance said.

"Hm?" Muldoon grunted.

"It would help if we didn't all have memories like that blue fish in *Finding* – something," Lewis declared, his frustration bubbling to the fore.

"Wasn't it a red fish?" Muldoon asked.

"Finding Red?" Constance threw in.

"No, that's not it," Lewis said as he wracked his brain, the image of the fish tantalisingly out of reach in there. "I think it was definitely blue."

"What was blue?" Constance asked.

"Hm?" Muldoon grunted and took a slurp at his tea.

Lewis sighed a loud, rattling sigh; it really was going to be a long wait until midnight

***

It got dark early at Silverado Springs. Lewis figured that was because they closed the heavy blinds tight shut and moved the hands forward on the clocks to fool the inmates into retiring early. However, since he couldn't exactly remember what had occurred on previous nights, he really couldn't say for sure.

He'd spent much of the day reading through the Moleskine. He'd read and re-read those parts of it that made little sense to him yet made him think that they should. The majority of the notebook's contents seemed to be disjointed conjecture and odd ramblings about what they *thought* was happening to their fellow residents; there were even mentions of contributions from Janey and Smiler – whatever was going on had started with Chuck because there was not one word of his written down from the clandestine meetings that Lewis had obviously so diligently minuted.

The popular conspiracy theory amongst the dwindling members of the Silverado Springs Memory Care Posse was that the facility was killing off the inmates and continuing to collect their resident's fees. Pouring through the notes, Lewis couldn't see how that theory got around the one, simple fact of the deceased resident's families; surely they'd notice their loved ones' absence on visiting days? Unless, of course they only selected those whose families never visited – this upset Lewis since he'd only just learned (*re*-learned!) that he had a family; and now he had to deal with the fact that they never damn well visited him.

"I'm not sure how a man's supposed to sleep with you sitting there thinking all freakin' night," Muldoon moaned from his bed and then tossed around nosily to emphasise his point. "And that goddamned nightlight is killing me too; what am I, five?"

Lewis glanced at the small, dim light that sat in his lap; the LED bulb in the thing emitted a faint, bluish light that was barely adequate enough for him to read the notebook by, let alone disturb his complaining friend's sleep.

Lewis was sitting mouse-quiet inside the cramped closet in Muldoon's room, his back twinging and his dickey hip throbbing like a bastard. He peered out through the thin gap he'd left in the door at his friend who was supposed to be fast asleep by now. "You can't hear me *thinking*, you dumb old coot," he whispered loudly to Muldoon. "Go to sleep already."

"I can't, it's kinda weird knowing that you're in there watching me sleep."

"At the moment, all I'm doing is watching you fidget and complain, Muldoon," Lewis growled. "You'll not be worth crap in the morning if you don't get your full eight hours, you know that." He really couldn't believe the man; they'd shared the same woman for near-on two decades and here he was, bleating because Lewis was hiding in his closet.

"Well I just can't," Muldoon grumbled and thrashed around some more beneath his crisp, white sheets to further make his point.

Lewis checked his watch and grunted. He'd been in

Muldoon's closet for almost an hour now, upon relieving Constance of her watch at midnight; the old fart had managed to sleep like a baby when she'd been watching over him, although Lewis suspected that she'd not actually spent her watch in amongst Muldoon's clothes. There'd been a definite dent in the bed where a small, feminine frame had laid and Lewis was convinced that had he touched said dent when he'd arrived, it would still have been warm.

Reading through the notebook had stirred up a whole plethora of blurred memories in Lewis's deteriorating mind; images of people he thought he should know, nebulous faces that swam tantalizingly out of reach, conversations that he felt sure he'd be able to remember if only he could think deep enough – it felt as if by reading the notebook he was sifting through the collective mush of what remained of his and his fellow Posse's neurons.

Hey, didn't that used to be a rock group?

Finally, Muldoon was asleep. At first, Lewis thought he was just pretending, but once the rhythmic buzz-saw of the man's resonant snoring split through the darkness, it became clear that he wasn't faking. Lewis smiled to himself at this; Bethany used to hate snoring and she would actually banish him to the sofa whenever he had a cold and with help from his blocked sinuses he would rattle the bedroom windows. And Lewis couldn't help but wonder if she did the same with Muldoon on the nights she'd spent in his bed.

Lewis sat there in the dark and discomfort and listened as his friend snored. He stretched his legs out across the full length of the closet – just enough room – and absently stroked his fingertips over the notebook's soft cover. The book rested on Lewis's knees, along with a cheap Bic pen and Constance's thin, penlight torch; they had considered taking pictures but since none of them had a camera or a cell phone with a camera (Silverado Springs' policy – too many residents used smart phones to create home-grown pornography, which was also banned in all of its many and wondrous forms) it would have meant stealing one. Also, it was detailed in the notebook from a previous meeting that using a flash would be foolish, as it would give the observer away. All he was there to do was to record what he saw in the notebook – in lieu of being able to remember, of course – and alert the staff should anything untoward happen.

It didn't once occur to Lewis that if they'd followed this procedure with Janey and Smiler, then how come they had still wound up in the back of Carpenter's grubby old hearse?

The door opened.

At first, it was just a crack that let in a sliver of the subdued lights from the hallway beyond. It seemed to Lewis's overactive imagination that someone was checking out Muldoon's room to make sure he was asleep.

And perhaps to see if someone was hiding in the closet?

Lewis held his breath, fearful that whoever it was at Muldoon's door would be able to hear him breathing. He squinted through the thin gap of the closet door, his heart pounding so hard that he feared that Muldoon's visitor would actually be able to hear that, if not his labored breath.

Slowly, carefully Muldoon's door eased open. If this had been a movie, Lewis thought, it would have creaked loudly on complaining hinges to the strains of tense violin music. This not being a movie though, the door remained silent as it swung open.

Then the unmistakable shape of Karl's head appeared between the white lacquered door and its frame.

Doesn't that guy ever sleep? Lewis thought to himself and let go of the stale breath in his lungs, relieved beyond belief to see Karl's familiar face, even though come the morning, he'd have to read the man's name badge to remember who the hell he was. Of course the staff checked in on the inmates; between twelve and three in the morning was the most popular time for old folk to shuffle off their mortal coil, so it made perfect sense.

Lewis watched as Karl's head retreated back into the hallway, no doubt satisfied that Muldoon's nasal reverberations were a sure sign that he hadn't passed on to the Great Beyond. The slit of light grew thinner, then thinner still until Lewis heard the faint click of the latch as Muldoon's door closed and all was dark once again.

Before long, Lewis's eyes began to close. His eyelids felt almost preternaturally heavy, and Lewis began to regret not having brought along one of those energy drinks Constance had tried foisting upon him - one of those in a tiny bottle that promise five hours of uninterrupted energy and tasted like stale cat pee.

And the more he fought it, the more sleep crept up on Lewis, overwhelming him like Dorothy's sea of poppies. And before he knew what was happening, Lewis Jones was sound asleep in his cramped boudoir.

Beyond the closet door, the outlined shape of a man appeared from the shadows. Neither tall nor short, fat nor thin, the shape congealed within the ink black of the shadows to step out into Muldoon's room, its nebulous shape becoming ever more solid.

The shadowy man wore a plain, darkish gray suit, white shirt, black shoes – the only detail of note was that he wore a hat atop his neatly coiffured head. The hat itself was of an unremarkable style, gray and squat like those worn on a hundred thousand heads day in, day out. In fact, there was absolutely nothing remarkable about the man who strode with purpose towards where Whitey Muldoon slumbered peacefully; he was precisely the kind of guy who was instantly forgettable, even outside of an Alzheimer's care facility. Stick him in front of one hundred people in broad daylight and you'd get a hundred different descriptions, not one of them accurate. He was exactly the guy one could pass on the street a dozen times and not once register that you'd crossed paths before and if you looked away for a second or two, you'd look back at him as if for the very first time.

Yet as ordinary as the man appeared, his purpose was most decidedly extraordinary.

Lewis awoke as the dark of the man's shadow passed by the narrow chink in the closet door, for that fraction of a moment swallowing the view of Muldoon's sleeping form. Lewis grunted himself awake. Immediately he clamped a hand over his mouth as he peeped out and saw the stranger standing over his friend's bed.

As the man contemplated the sleeping Muldoon, Lewis attempted to stand within the confines of the closet, only to find that his hip had locked up and he was unable to shift himself off of his bony ass. Panicking and decidedly frustrated with his own body's failings, Lewis gripped the notebook and pencil tight in his hand and eased his weight over to his other hip; there really was nothing else to do than wait for his errant joint to right itself.

Squinting through the gap in the door and using the feeble sliver of light that oozed from his penlight, Lewis jotted down a note or two, although he found it difficult to find the words – *any* words – to describe the inordinately plain stranger in Muldoon's bedroom.

The guy in the hat bent over Muldoon and appeared to whisper something in to the sleeping man's ear. Lewis thought he saw the faintest glimmer of a smile on his friend's face, and more than anything he'd witnessed thus far, that smile chilled Lewis down to his aching old bones.

Lewis rocked his butt side to side; sometimes that would help his hip along some, whilst other times it served only to make the rusted old joint a whole hell of a lot worse – but he had to do something. Finally, and with a pop so loud Lewis was amazed it hadn't woken Muldoon, his hip ground back into place and Lewis found himself mobile once more.

But by the time Lewis had struggled to his feet and had plucked up enough courage to leave the sanctuary of the closet, the strange, plain looking man had his decidedly ordinary looking hand rested gently on Whitey Muldoon's head.

"What the hell are you doing?" Lewis burst through the closet door and hissed loudly at the stranger. He was keen to keep his voice low so as not to attract Karl's attention, but was unsure as to why; there was a peaceful serenity about the stranger – and a niggle at the back of his mind – that prevented him from screaming the place down.

The stranger was obviously doing *something* to Muldoon, as was evident by the sleeping man's low, breathy mumbling and the frantic darting of his eyes beneath their firmly closed lids, so why could he not bring himself to call out?

Lewis pondered this dilemma as he crossed the short distance between the closet and the bed, all the while not daring to take his eyes off of the man in the hat.

The man looked up from his contemplation of Muldoon, all the while keeping his hand placed firmly on the man's head as if it were glued there. He gazed into Lewis's eyes with a blank, unemotional expression, as if waiting for him to say something.

There was a spark of familiarity there, although

Lewis would swear to his dying day that he'd never met the man before in his life.

"I'm going to call the orderly," Lewis broke the cloying silence between them. "You shouldn't be in here."

There was something akin to the faintest of twinkles in the man's gray, empty eyes as he brought up his free hand and pressed the index finger lightly to his own lips.

"Don't do that, Lewis," Muldoon murmured and his eyes flickered open. "Please."

The sound of his friend's voice took Lewis aback, even more so the wide, vacant stare of Muldoon's deep, brown eyes; the man looked for all the world as if he was viewing something quite mesmerizing. And although he had spoken his name, Lewis had the inescapable feeling that so far as Muldoon was concerned, he simply wasn't there.

The stranger returned his gaze to Muldoon, as if not in the least bit concerned about Lewis's threat to cause a ruckus and bring Karl and his night shift compatriots running.

"I can remember," Muldoon said and his eyes fixed on Lewis's and in them Lewis saw such wakefulness and such intense clarity that the breath caught in his throat.

"What can you remember, old friend?" Lewis whispered as his knees brushed against the side of Muldoon's bed.

"Everything," Muldoon's lips trembled as he spoke, "I can remember *everything*." A smile played across those lips and for the first time in a great many years, Muldoon looked completely happy. "Come sit with me," Muldoon asked Lewis and patted the side of the bed.

Unquestioning, Lewis lowered his complaining hip onto the edge of the doughy, welcoming bed, relieved to have taken his weight off of the aching joint, even though this whole situation had turned most decidedly odd.

"They all came back." Muldoon beamed up at Lewis, his eyes fixed firmly on his friend's, but still distant.

"Who came back?" Lewis asked. He tried his level best to ignore the strange man's hand that rested – not too hard, not too lightly – on Muldoon's sweat-slicked head.

"They *all* did," Muldoon told him and Lewis wished the old fart would quit being so goddamned cryptic. "My daughter, my grandkids, the guys in the band –"

"You remember them?" Lewis stared at his friend in disbelief; it had been more years than he cared to recall since Muldoon had shown even the smallest signs of remembering his family, let alone the boys in Sticky Fingers Muldoon's Ragtime Band – all had been lost to the ravages of the dementia that was slowly but surely consuming his brain.

"Beth," Muldoon whispered with a serene smile playing around his lips. "I remember Beth."

It was a shock for Lewis to hear his beloved wife's name, again, especially from the mouth of her long-time lover. It had been a good many years since he and Muldoon had last talked about her, his own memories of the woman they'd unknowingly shared having faded into nebulous, gray clouds as surely as Muldoon's had disappeared completely.

"She was beautiful, Lewis," Muldoon sighed. "The most beautiful gal in the West." Again he smiled.

"Yes she was, Muldoon." Lewis choked back the tears that ran thick and salty along the back of his dry throat.

"Too much love for just the one man –" Muldoon repeated the mantra they'd so often shared over the years following Beth's burial.

"– that's precisely why there were the two of us, my

old friend," Lewis finished his friend's words and forced a wry smile.

"She had the most perfect skin, and it smelled of honey," Muldoon reminisced, his eyes brimming with fat, salty tears. "And that booty, oh Lordy, I remember that behind of hers so well, Lewis!"

Lewis patted his friend's hand; even after all of these years, and the trips down memory lane he and Muldoon had shared on those long, beer-soaked nights, it still tugged at his heart some to hear Muldoon talking about Beth. *His* Beth. But yes, Lewis was the first to admit that his wife had been blessed with the most extraordinary rear end.

"I remember her hair, the way it always smelled of daisies, and how she would glow when she made love; it was like there was a small, delicate fire burnin' deep inside of her." Muldoon smiled and his eyes looked directly into Lewis's, but still he was not really seeing him.

"I'm happy for you," Lewis told his friend as he fought back the acid pang of jealousy that rose up inside of him; not for his wife's infidelity with Muldoon, but for his friend's memories of the woman they had both loved so completely – it had been a long, long time since he'd been able to recall just how sweet Beth's hair had smelled.

"You should write all of this down in our notebook, Lewis," Muldoon told him, "so *you* don't forget."

Lewis nodded and looked down at the Moleskine in his hand, quite surprised to see it there. He flipped the thing open, dug the pencil from his pocket and scribbled frantically at the thick, luxurious pages, all the while keeping half an eye on the strange man who had his most ordinary looking hand rested upon Muldoon's head.

"They're all with me now, Lewis," Muldoon murmured.

"Who's with you?"

"Beth, my family, my old friends, the whole goddamned band."

"That's just great." Lewis glanced up from his notebook just in time to see the whites of Muldoon's eyes as they rolled up into his head.

"Yeah, and we're living our last days together, you and I," Muldoon said with a contented sigh. "We're sitting on that porch, knockin' back the cold 'uns and putting this whole messed up world to rights."

"That sounds just perfect to me, my old friend," Lewis said.

"And we're reminiscing, Lewis." Muldoon's eyes once again burned deep into Lewis's. "We *can* reminisce, we remember everything; it all came back." He reached out a trembling, fevered hand and grasped Lewis's and in that instant Lewis remembered too.

He recalled with startling clarity that he *had* seen the strangely ordinary man before, and that the man did indeed have a purpose. He remembered being there for Chuck, Janey and Smiler as they'd similarly played out the remainder of their days in minds unfettered by dementia and surrounded by the resurrected memories of ones they loved – all thanks to the hands of the average looking guy in the hat.

A swift, unexpected movement, the stranger's free hand nothing more than a blur as the man slit Muldoon's throat and a thick spray of blood shot out.

"What the–?!" Lewis cried out, his shocked scream strangled into silence in his own throat. He tried to move from the bed, away from the thick wash of blood that poured from his friend's lacerated throat and soaked into the pristine white bed sheets. But Lewis found that he simply couldn't; by a cruel combination of his locked hip and terrified shock, he was rooted to the spot.

The stranger shushed Lewis once more, the finger to

those terribly nondescript lips now sporting what appeared to Lewis to be a long, curved claw of sorts. The man in the hat offered up a flicker of a smile and licked the thin line of blood from the claw with a thin, flat tongue. All the while, he kept his other hand planted firmly on the old man's head.

Muldoon's eyes rolled upwards once more, as if venturing away to marvel at the countless returning memories deep within his decaying brain. And this time, they stayed there.

Lewis scribbled frantically in the Moleskine and it was a moment or two before he realized that his friend had finally passed. Only when Muldoon's relaxing body let out a long, rattling sigh from one end, and the pent-up gas from the other did Lewis look up from his notes to see his friend's peaceful, smiling face and half closed and unmoving, glassy eyes.

"Oh no," Lewis groaned. "No, no, no." The tears flowed thick and fast from his eyes which served to make Muldoon's slack face appear blurry around its edges.

"Don't cry for him, Lewis," the stranger said, his voice hushed. "Your friend died happy, he died *remembering*." There was no trace of emotion, nor any accent to the man's tone; it was most decidedly blank.

"Y-you did that?" Lewis's voice shook with emotion. He sniffled up a thick gobbet of mucus and swallowed it down with an audible gulp. He looked the stranger directly in the eye, but still his befogged brain refused to register any of the man's features other than those cold, gray eyes.

"It's why I came here," the strange man told him, "it's why you all invited me during one of your moments of forgotten lucidity – I have to have my presence requested, as you may – or may not – recall."

Lewis stared at the man, and honestly he couldn't

recall a damned thing.

"Whilst it can't cure you of your most unfortunate affliction, I can give them back all of your memories for one final, glorious time before –"

"You kill us?"

"Before I *release* you," the stranger said with that calm, level tone. "I give you the opportunity to live out your last moments with the comfort of the memories that you have so sadly lost through the ravages of this most unpleasant disease."

"You killed him," Lewis mouthed as he looked down at Muldoon and the spreading scarlet mess that soaked into the bed.

"All part of the bargain for my kindness," the stranger said, and still Lewis could not detect an accent. "And now it is time for me to take my payment."

So saying, the strangely average looking guy in the hat drew that grotesque, elongated claw of his around Muldoon's face.

Lewis winced as he watched the obscenely sharp finger nail sink deep into the edges of his friend's face and as the wrinkled old skin peppered with white stubble parted, he could see that the claw had sunk deep into the shining bone of Muldoon's skull.

"You really don't need to see this," the stranger told Lewis as he began to prize away Muldoon's face.

"I don't see why not," Lewis was defiant; he wanted to stay with his friend, no matter what. He simply couldn't bear to leave the man he'd shared so much of his life with. "It's not as if I'll remember a goddamned thing tomorrow, is it?" Lewis knew all too well that if he fell asleep – although after this, sleep no longer seemed likely to Lewis ever again – he would forget absolutely everything he'd witnessed. "Although I do have my notes," he said, absently.

"Ah yes, the book," the stranger said. "Thank you so

much for reminding me." He gave Lewis a faint, wry smile as if they were sharing a secret and very personal reminiscence. He then reached across the bed, over Muldoon's leaking body and plucked the notebook and pencil from Lewis's hands.

Lewis looked on helplessly as the Moleskine was taken from him, and his hands simply refused to resist.

The man tore out the couple of pages upon which Lewis had so meticulously made notes of the night's happenings. He screwed them up with one hand and secreted the crumpled paper in the outside pocket of his drab, gray jacket. Then he flicked through the book with that long, terrible claw of his, and came to rest upon a page close to the beginning.

As Lewis watched, the stranger took the pencil to the names listed there in neat, girlish handwriting in the middle of that page and crossed out Whitey Muldoon with one firm, decisive stroke. Coldness spread through Lewis's body that had nothing to do with the ambient temperature in Muldoon's room, and everything to do with the realization that it was his own moniker that was next on that ominous list. And below that, Constance's name. Lewis hoped that when his time with the strange, ordinary looking man with the hat came along, the old girl would be there for him and to hold his hand whilst his memories returned to him.

The stranger placed the notebook carefully on the bed, away from the blood and went back to working at Muldoon's face with his claw.

Lewis fought the feel of his leaden eyelids as sleep began to creep up on him, determined to stay awake and remember everything that had happened – was happening – to his old friend. Perhaps then he'd be able to reverse whatever process he and the others had set into motion to summon the stranger and save him and Constance from the same fate as Muldoon? But, something resonated deep inside his psyche, something far beyond the reaches of the dementia that was slowly but surely destroying the person that was Lewis Jones; and he wasn't entirely certain that was really what he wanted, given Muldoon's revelation of returned memories right before death spirited him away.

Eventually, inevitably and despite his very best intentions, Lewis succumbed to the seductive siren call of a deep, untroubled sleep. He slumped down on the bed next to his old friend and drifted back to 1956 where the Presley kid is storming the charts and his father was up in arms and banning him from the music stores on account of the fact that it was nigger music.

And whilst Lewis slept, the strange man in the hat tore away Whitey Muldoon's face with a wet, crackling *slurp* and upon conjuring a small, golden spoon from an inside pocket of his dull, gray jacket he began to feast upon the old man's diseased brain. And since there was no one to see, he allowed his façade to slip, revealing to the cool night his true appearance; and in that repulsive, inhuman form, even his empty eye sockets, set in raw, bloodied, shifting flesh, had small, sharp teeth.

***

It was just the two of them at breakfast this morning – Lewis and Constance – and they sat in silent contemplation of their untouched breakfasts of sausage and eggs that congealed in fat before them.

"Ain't no wildcat did that to Muldoon," Lewis broke the quiet between them, his voice pulling Constance out from her foggy wool-gathering with a start. "I saw the poor bastard's face and I'm telling you, whatever did that wasn't a freakin' wildcat."

Already the mental images of what he'd seen on his way past Muldoon's room not five minutes before were fading fast. He'd seen a couple of cops in there, along with Karl and someone else in the center's uniform that he couldn't quite place, and he knew that sometime before lunch the nice men from the funeral service would be along to bag up the sorry looking remains of Muldoon and cart him off to wherever they took the deceased inmates of Silverado Springs to. And for the life of him, Lewis couldn't remember anything about the poor old bastard – perhaps he'd been one of the new ones?

"You have a visitor, Mr. Jones," Stacey blustered as she usher a man in a grey suit in to the dining area. The facility chihuahua that had been hiding under the Monarch table – rich pickings to be had beneath the old folks, them being such messy eaters – scooted away with a loud yelp as if someone had kicked it.

Lewis watched the dog scamper away with its tail tucked tight between its scrawny little legs and thought it strange that it seemed to be terrified of the stranger; any other day and Chiquo would be over and humping a visitor's leg before Stacey had time to shoo him away.

"Thank you, Stacey" the man said to the fat care assistant with the slightest of smiles dancing about the corners of his mouth. "Mr. Jones, Miss Constance," he greeted the two seniors at the table as he sat down next to them.

"Do we know you?" Lewis grumbled. He hated having his meals interrupted and he'd meant to ask Stacey something about something he'd seen upstairs earlier when she happened by, but now he'd forgotten what. He watched with growing frustration at his failing mind as Stacey waddled away. She turned around every few steps or so to glare at the new arrival, each time shaking her head as if there was something about him that troubled her.

"Lewis!" Constance admonished. "I am so sorry for

my friend's brusqueness, Mr. –?"

"Ah, please forgive my lack of manners," the man said. With a broad, toothy grin he fished out a crisp, white business card from his pocket. He placed it on the table by Constance's tea cup.

"So, Mr. – Ordnryman," Constance read from the card with its sharp, precise corners. "To what do we owe this pleasure?"

"Nothing too exciting, I'm afraid, I just wanted to return this – I do believe it's yours," the man addressed both Constance and Lewis. He produced a gray Moleskine notebook from his inside jacket pocket and laid it gently on the table between the two old friends.

"Thank you," Constance said. She peered down at the notebook as if it were something altogether alien to her, although she was too polite to say so.

"My pleasure, Constance," the man smiled, "I'll bid you both a good morning now, and leave you to your breakfast." He stood up from the table and made to leave. "I'll see you both later."

Lewis glowered at the man; something lurked at the distant and murky reaches of his deteriorating mind. It chattered quietly to Lewis and he couldn't help but think he'd seen this dull looking man somewhere before, and just how rude it was that he hadn't taken off his hat at the breakfast table.

The Sorrow of the Hunter
Jaap Boekestein

The prey was standing in the middle of the dungeon, her arms raised high and her wrists connected to the hooks on the ceiling with padded leather cuffs and thick chains.

Helena walked up to Jess. She touched the cheek of the naked girl.

"Do you trust me, Jess?"

The girl, wide eyed, her hair up, answered with a whisper: "Yes Mistress."

They had met at a munch, in the evening of course. Jess was new to the bdsm-scene, exquisite, lovely and very impressed with the fact that Helena was a professional Dominatrix. Helena liked the girl. She was smart, in a quiet kind of way, and innocent as a puppy.

They talked, exchanged numbers and talked a lot more during the next few weeks.

"I work at nights, so don't expect an answer during the daytime," Helena said.

Jess obeyed.

It wasn't long that the girl told about her feelings, doubts and those dark desires that haunted her since early childhood. Pain, being tied up, forced, dominated. She had felt shame, thought she was sick in her mind. Until she found out there were so many people sharing the same feelings. For years she had read and watched everything that she could find, but always from the sidelines, never ever telling anyone about her desires. Never making contact, never doing something for real with it.

That munch was the first time she dared to go somewhere.

"I am glad you did," Helena said.

"So am I."

And now she was naked and chained up in Helena's dungeon.

Prey.

Slowly Helena walked to her closet with equipment, at the wall behind Jess' back. Deep inside her she felt the blood hunger shimmer. She didn't need to feed, she had fed yesternight on one of her clients, but Jess was such a sweet thing. Helena wanted to hug her, bite her and fuck her all at the same time. The Dominatrix grinned. Playing with Jess would be pretty close to doing those three things at once.

Let's start slowly. Helena selected a flogger with suede straps, excellent for warming up.

She approached Jess from behind. "Eyes front, chin up."

Jess looked straight ahead. The tension in her arms and back and buttocks betrayed she was nervous as hell.

Helena suppressed a giggle. *Oh, she is such a sweet thing!* She held the flogger up high and let the hanging straps lightly caress the skin of Jess' back.

The girl almost jumped up, not expecting the soft touch.

Now Helena laughed and she showed Jess the flogger. "I am going to use this one. I will start gently and hit you a little bit harder every time. Indicate when its gets too painful. Just be honest, you are new to this and you don't have to be all tough."

"O... Okay."

Playfully Helena pinched one of Jess' nipples, which made the girl actually jump. "What?" the Dominatrix asked.

"I... Oh... Uh, yes, Mistress!"

"Good girl!" Helena slapped the new sub's behind. *Hm, nice little ass!*

With her excellent vampire ears Helena heard Jess breathing quicker, the girl was getting excited, which triggered a deep rooted instinct in Helena herself. *Panting prey! Scared and running! Catch, fight, drink!*

Down! Not yet.

The vampire started to whip the sweet little mortal who was at her mercy.

Flogger, floggers on shoulders, back and behind, on hips and legs and on breasts and belly and pussy. The impact on Jess was enormous. With her eyes closed the girl hung in her chains, moaning with every lash she received. Sweat ran down her face.

The prey was wet between her legs, Helena smelled it. It triggered some very different instincts. *I want her, I want her,* singsonged through her head.

She stopped whipping Jess, took her in her arms and kissed her.

Warm, sweet body, the smell of sweat and excitement, hot blood throbbing in her veins, tongue against tongue, lips on lips.

Jess moaned some more, she was far, far away.

Subspace. Helena had seen it a thousand times before: the blood of the sub was flooded with natural drugs produced by the brain to cope with the pain and fear. This was when the blood was at its richest and sweetest.

Helena clicked open the cuffs and caught the limp body of Jess. She carried the girl to the big leather couch at one side of the room.

"You are doing great, love."

"Uhumm." Jess threw her arms around Helena's neck and buried her face in her Mistress' throat.

Helena almost let the girl drop while her fangs and claws extended instinctively. Feeling a face, a mouth, at her throat was so... so threatening. *How dare she!* The animal-vampire part of her hissed. *Attack! Throw her down, rip out her throat!*

With shaking arms Helena put the still dazed girl down on the black leather of the couch. She stepped back and took a few deep breaths.

Slowly her fangs and claws receded again.

Drink when you are in control of yourself. Never give in to the beast. Safe and sound, don't hurt the prey. She had lived by those words for a very long time, but somehow the sweet mortal girl had awakened those old, wild desires.

Strange. Helena looked at Jess. So innocent and yet somehow so provocative.

Finally she was back in control. The vampire woman sat down beside Jess and started to kiss the girl again. The mortal responded with a goofy smile and kissed back.

Lower and lower Helena's lips went, down Jess' throat – that vulnerable, tempting, throbbing throat – ending up at the perky little breasts.

She bit them, a little. Jess whimpered but pushed Helena's head back down when the Dominatrix lifted her head to see Jess' face.

So you like a little pain, do you?

Helena's mouth closed around one of Jess' nipples and she hardened the little bud with her lips, tongue and teeth. When the flesh was stiff enough she sucked the nipple a little, so that the very top was resting against the outside of her teeth.

Carefully, oh so carefully, Helena started to scrape the topmost skin layers of the nipple with the end of her incisors. One hand held Jess down, her other hand landed on the *very* wet pussy of her willing victim. Both the middle and ring finger slipped inside, the other fingers massaged the vulva. The palm of her hand rubbed against the hood of Jess' clitoris.

Under her hands the mortal woman moaned and wriggled but without mercy Helena held on to the delicious breast and that hot, filthy wet, delightful slutty cunt.

Scrape, scrape: teeth rupturing skin, touching hundreds of nerve ends, sending sweet, sweet, sweet pain signals to a receptive brain.

Suddenly an all too familiar taste filled Helena's mouth.

Blood.

Blood!

Apparently one of the veins in Jess' nipple was pretty close under the skin. Blood poured out in a steady trickle, right in Helena's sucking mouth.

The taste was so unexpected, Helena had no defense against it.

Noooo!

The red blood hunger overwhelmed her.

In the blink of an eye Helena, the night time Dominatrix didn't exist anymore. Now there was only the vampire. The old, hungry beast; the hunter, the devourer, the fanged terror.

Claws dug deep in the shoulder of the mortal girl, scraped the soft flesh *inside* her.

Knife sharp fangs bit into her breast, hungry for more blood.

Startled Jess cried out, eyes wide open. She tried to fight, but her body almost immediately succumbed to the potent paralyzing toxins in the vampire's saliva. Completely limp the girl fell back while the woman on her drank her blood.

Finally Helena got enough of control over herself to let go of the prey.

What have I done? Is she...?

Jess still breathed, but her pale skin was cold and clammy and her breathing rapid and shallow.

I drank too much. Helena was a vampire, she knew the signs of hypovolemic shock by heart. Every stupid vampire had seen prey die this way.

Shit, shit, shit!

She jumped up, hurrying to the special fridge in another part of her house. Three plastic bags of yellow fluid rested beside a dozen dark bags of blood.

Great Maker, don't let her be allergic to blood plasma.

Helena put the needle in Jess arm. It had been a long while, but she still knew how to find a vein. Of course she knew how, she was a vampire.

Slowly Jess' breath calmed down and her cheeks regained some color. Helena kept the girl warm and checked her wounds.

The bite marks on her breast had almost healed, thanks to the restorative powers of vampire saliva. Very carefully she also checked the vagina. To her immense relief there was no bleeding. Her claws didn't seem to have hit anything mayor.

She will live. Helena felt little relief, because it also meant: *She could have died. Because of me. Because I was stupid, because I let myself go. Because... Because...*

***

After a few hours of sleep Jess opened her eyes.

Helena was immediately on full alert. She had dragged some pillows, sheets and blankets down in the dungeon, turned up the heat and was now spooning Jess under the blankets. She had removed the transfusion patches and had made the wound on Jess' arm disappear with a few licks.

Sleepily the girl moved around, pushing her delightful behind against Helena's naked body. It took a few moments before Jess realized where she was. Slowly she turned around and looked Helena in the eye.

"Hi, pet. How are you feeling?" the vampire woman asked.

"Hi, Mi... Mistress." Jess turned her whole body so she was facing Helena. "I feel... Like, wow. I... It is..."

"A bit overwhelming?" Helena combed Jess' hair with her fingers.

Jess nodded, timidly.

"You are okay, sweetheart?"

"I am *hungry*," Jess confessed. "And I really need to pee."

"Both can be helped. But first tell me, how are you feeling right now? Do you remember anything?"

Jess blushed and smiled. "It was so *wonderful*! It felt so... Like I... All these feelings! I finally could feel it, experience it. I was *free*."

"You remember us on the couch, here?"

The blush deepened. Jess cast her eyes down, but then looked Helena back in her eyes. "Yes. You and I... I liked that. I can't remember everything, but I liked it."

"No bad feelings? No regrets?"

Now Jess' eyes widened. "No! Not at all! Did I... Did I do all right? Did I do something wrong?"

Helena kissed Jess full on the mouth, before answering, after ten, twenty prolonged heartbeats. "You did nothing wrong, pet." *Not you.* "You were great. I am proud of you. And now let's get you to the bathroom and the kitchen."

"Yeah!" Jess tried to jump up but fell back on the couch. "Ow, I am a bit woozy."

"That is normal after subspace, your body is still processing all those nice drugs it produced. Just take it easy. I have some slippers and a nice terrycloth robe. Maybe they are a bit too large, but I bet you look adorable in baby blue."

"Uh... Yeah, Mistress." Doubtful Jess looked at the old robe and the big fluffy panda slippers.

Helena laughed. "Get dressed, you wench! Don't make me say it twice, or I will put you over my knee."

"Would you?" Jess looked over her shoulder, considering her options.

"Not if you try to manipulate me into it. Now, *avanti*!"

***

"How are you feeling, sweet? Everything alright?" Helena messaged the next evening.

"Wonderful! I want more!"

":-) That is how you ask your Mistress? You are a wicked girl."

"Sorry! Mistress. :o I'm wicked. Please Mistress, I want some more. :p Pleeeeeease!"

You are not the only one, kitten, Helena thought. *But is it the wise thing to do?*

After a few seconds the vampire messaged back: "Patience, dear Oliver. Coming evenings I have to work, and you have your day job. Be here Friday evening at seven. And wear those sexy boots and dress you wore to the munch."

"Yeah! :) :) :) Yes, Mistress. Thank you, Mistress. I will obey, Mistress."

Oh, you are a real handful, dear Jess. I got myself a brat. We will have so much fun together!

If you can trust yourself with her, a voice in the back of her mind whispered.

Helena nodded. She really had to address that issue. Without trust there was nothing, but could she trust herself?

A plan started to form in Helena's mind. *There is only one way to find out.*

At her feet a male voice said: "Mistress, I have finished cleaning the floor."

Helena looked down. *O yes, I forgot all about you.*

The chubby man in the French maid uniform, was kneeling on the floor and submissively offered Helena a half filled dustpan.

"You call that clean?" Helena kicked the dustpan over and the collected dirt flew through the dungeon. "Do it again, and better this time. *Much* better or I will punish you!"

"Yes Mistress, of course Mistress," groveled the client.

"You have ten minutes!" It was impossible to clean the dungeon all over again in ten minutes, but that was not the point. The client wanted to be spanked and actually Helena could use a good workout. She had a nice new cane which needed breaking in.

But first she could spend ten minutes more with Jess. She started to text again. "How far are you with the report about last night? As discussed, I am expecting at least a thousand words." *Grin, that will keep her busy tonight, and give her an opportunity to process things.*

***

Jess squealed when Helena yanked the handle and the motorcycle jumped to 140 mph. The girl hung on for dear life. She had borrowed a helmet and a leather jacket from Helena, but was still wearing the knee high boots and the flapping thin silk dress.

Helena wore her black leather motor suit and her mat black helmet with dark visor. Yes, she knew she looked like a badass motor-assassin from a 1980's flick, but she had a weak spot for *some* of the styles of that decade. *But definitely* not *the hair.*

Fifteen minutes later Helena drove through an industrial area with abandoned factories and gutted office buildings. Twenty years ago this had been a bustling place with trucks and night shifts, now looters had taken away anything of value. Only ruins and memories were left.

She parked the bike out of sight and took off her helmet.

Jess followed her example. She looked flustered but her eyes shone.

"This used to be a concrete factory," Helena explained, "Nobody will disturb us here."

"Is it safe?" Jess wanted to know. She looked at the walls that were covered with old graffiti. The headlight of the bike drew a sharp circle of light in the looming darkness.

"It is safe," Helena assured her. With her sharpened vampire senses she didn't notice anything out of the ordinary. Lots of small animals, but there were none of the annoying two legged variant near. "You will always be safe when you are with me."

Jess looked at the ground. "I know. I still can't believe it. You are so wonderful. You are everything I've dreamed of."

"Thank you, Jess. I think you are very special too."

Jess looked up and beamed.

Helena beckoned and they kissed. The sweet taste of Jess filled Helena's mouth.

After an eternity they broke away. "Follow me, pet. And be careful, there is some debris, but everything is safe."

For Jess' sake Helena lit a camping lantern. She took the small rucksack, filled with some clothes and a medical kit, and showed Jess the spiraling stairs they were to descend.

Round and round, down and down. They ended in a concrete silo which was filled with some fine white sand and little else. The place was dry and lacked the weeds that attracted vermin. Helena had discovered the spot years ago and used it every now and then.

A bit unsure, Jess looked around.

Helena watched her. *Now you realize you are all alone here with me. Nobody knows you are here, you don't even know exactly where* here *is. Nobody can hear you scream, little one.*

Prey, prey, prey.

Jess looked at Helena and discovered she was being watched.

"What now, Mistress?" she asked after a few moments of silence.

"Lose the helmet and the jacket." Helena pointed at a spot at her feet where she had dropped the rucksack. She had hung the lantern on a rusty bolt sticking out off the door frame.

The girl folded the leather jacket and put it down with the red colored helmet. Red like blood.

Prey, prey, prey.

"Stand against the wall, facing me."

She licked her lips, the muscles in her shoulders, arms and legs were tense. Without knowing it, Jess was in full fight or flee modus, like some old and half forgotten instinct told her she was in the presence of a predator. Still she obeyed. Of course she obeyed.

She leaned against the wall, her hands flat against the concrete. The thin silk dress clung to her body. There was a defiant look in her eyes. *I am not scared and I can handle anything you can do to me.*

Prey, prey, prey.

From a hidden sheath in her motor boot Helena drew the 4 inch fixed blade hunting knife.

In stunned silence Jess watched the gleaming steel blade. Cutting and stabbing, that was what the knife was for. Cutting and stabbing.

Helena stepped towards Jess, holding the knife loosely in her right hand, like she was ready to make an upwards stab. "Do you trust me?"

The girl against the wall had to swallow before she could answer. "Yes, Mistress."

The vampire woman did not answer, she walked up to her prey, all stern face, black leather and deadly steel.

Unconsciously Jess tried to move backwards, but there was nowhere to go. She was prey and she knew she was prey. Delicious fear glowed deep inside her.

With one hand Helena grabbed Jess' hair, forcing her head backwards and exposing her throat.

"Stay up!" the vampire said when the mortal girl started to buckle.

Pushing with her hands and ass against the rough concrete Jess managed to obey. Her body was arched pushing her breasts forward.

Helena threw the knife upwards and caught it again mid flight, now with the blade pointing down.

In one perfect slash she cut open Jess' silk dress, from the cleavage all the way down to the hem.

"Wuhh?!" Jess was in shock, but didn't get the time to formulate a protest.

Now the blade rested against her throat, Helena was still pulling the girl's head backwards.

Jess didn't dare to utter a sound, her eyes bulged, desperately trying to catch a glimpse of the sharp steel. Her heart beat a billion times per second.

Helena didn't say a word. Wet and slowly she licked upwards Jess' throat and cheek, to end up at her earlobe. The sweet taste of fear, and something else. Oh yes, this girl was so slutty. She was scared to death, and still getting excited.

My sweet pet. Welcome to the grown up games.

The vampire let go of the mortal woman's hair. The girl didn't move, the steel rested still against her throat. Helena looked at her prey. Under her now shredded silk dress Jess wore a demure white laced bra and panties.

My little maiden.

The knife moved. Slowly, lightly, but *very* present it made its way down: throat, chest, left breast.

Still Jess didn't move. She had closed her eyes, her breathing was now deep and slow, like an animal waiting its chance to escape.

The point of the knife reached the lace edge of the bra.

Without mercy the clean steel cut the thin fabric, the woven threads only able to put up a pitiful and utterly futile resistance.

On and on the steel cut, like a wolf in a flock of sheep, leaving in its wake a trail of naked skin.

The little dark nipple was hard. The knife ran over it, on its way down.

A soft moan escaped from Jess' lips.

Helena smiled, her fangs half bare. *Prey, prey, prey.* Yes, prey but mixed with desire to give the girl what she yearned for: domination, pain, lust.

The left breast was bare now. Delicious.

With one quick cut Helena severed the right boob's strap, not even leaving a scratch behind on the girl's soft skin.

The little slut moaned again after a quick intake of breath.

The Dominatrix pushed her body against that of her slave girl. Mouths locked, Helena took and took and took while her free hand and sharp nails roughly caressed the girl's breasts.

Bite her! Feed on her! Drink! The vampire-beast inside Helena's head demanded.

No, not yet.

Helena broke away from Jess' willing lips. She grabbed the neck of her prey and forcefully threw the mortal girl on the ground.

With a startled cry Jess landed on all fours on the soft white sand.

Immediately the leather clad demon was on her, forcing Jess' head down and slicing her white panties to shreds in three quick moves.

With her hair hanging down in a tangled mess, Jess panted, shivering all over. She was a lamb ready to slaughter, she had surrendered completely. She was nothing.

Sweet nothing.

Such an ecstatic feeling.

"You want more?" Helena asked. They were her first words since she had drawn the knife.

One moment of silence, then: "Yes, please, Mistress."

The Dominatrix knelt at Jess's side. Sharp nails ran over her back, other nails dug into her breast.

Pain! Nasty pain, violating her, undeserved, unwanted.

She was a liar. In her heart Jess knew that. Oh, how she wanted it! She felt and felt.

A hand slammed against her ass, sending flames all through her body. And again and again, raining fire.

Jess cried out, cursed.

Her Mistress didn't stop, but Jess didn't want her to stop.

Helena pulled the little slut's hair, face slapped her.

"Tha... Thank you, Mistress," Jess cried out, tears ran down her face, snot ran from her nose. She was so happy.

More pain, other tortures. Helena forced Jess' legs apart, spanking her pussy. Hot flames echoing through her loins, setting her afire even more.

Pinches, bites, beatings, fingers, knuckles, nails.

Jess swayed on all fours, not knowing where she was, who she was, what she was.

She fell down in the sand, not able to trust her knees and arms anymore. With her eyes closed, she felt the fine dust stick to her wet face and body. Her head swam, but she was safe. Safe, underwater in a warm, red sea. She was safe.

Helena clenched her teeth, fighting the hot, horny lust roaring inside her. Damn, she was excited herself. Lust and blood hunger clashed and vied for control.

Time to test myself.

This was it, whatever side would win, she had to know.

She hoped the mortal girl would survive.

Gently she pried open Jess' mouth and forced the heavy leather motor glove partly in the girl's mouth.

"Bite on this when you need to."

Jess didn't reply. She was far away.

Helena arranged Jess' arms straight along her sides. She sat on Jess' naked lower back, with her knees pinning down the girl's wrists and hands. Helena picked up the knife which she had thrown down in the sand.

She didn't take time to focus, to calm herself. It needed to be raw and real. She needed to feel the full force of temptation without artificial defenses.

With one hand she grabbed the mortal girl's neck. The hand with the knife sliced down along the spine.

The steel didn't cut deep. Not deep enough the hit any muscles anyway. But deep enough to cut through veins.

The girl in the dirt only moaned, but didn't move. Her clouded brain ignored all the pain and danger signals.

A slithering canal of blood appeared on her back.

Hot, sweet blood. Food, life.

Helena's fangs extended in less than a second, as did her claws.

Blood! Feed!

She threw herself at the feast. Almost.

Instead she waited and watched, subduing the red hunger inside her.

I am Helena, I am not a beast.

I am stronger then my hunger.

I am Helena, I am not a beast.

I am stronger then my hunger.

She was.

The red hunger slowly receded.

Only when Helena was completely sure she was in control, she bowed forward and fed on Jess' blood.

Afterwards, when she was satisfied, Helena closed the gash and healed the wound with her saliva. Jess hadn't lost that much blood and Helena had been careful not to cut anything vital. The girl would be fine.

Jess moaned a little, but there was a smile on her face. She was asleep.

Sitting next to her, watching and stroking her, the vampire woman smiled and silently cried from pure relief.

Yes, they had a future together.

The Eagle and The Wolf
Iain Rob Wright

Chapter 1

Manius Furia set down his sword and scabbard, placing it with his *scutum*. He propped the entire bundle against the thick bark of an elderly oak tree. Dawn crawled towards them, a few hours distant, and his scouts needed rest. The thick forests of Northern Gaul had fought Manius's men every step of the way since leaving their brothers of Legio IV Gallica back at the main camp outside Vesontio.

Manius's *optiones*, second-in-command, came strolling over in the heavy-footed way that betrayed his Remi heritage. Members of the Remi tribe were notoriously 'big boned,' yet despite his girth, Carigo was a woodsman down to his marrow. Manius relied on the big man all too much. Their *centuria* was named the Cloaked Eagles, but only Manius was born of Rome.

The only man shaven and clean amongst six-dozen wild men.

"Centurion, would you have us camp?"

"I would, Optiones. Four sentries in three rotations. We shall break camp in exactly six hours."

Carigo stomped away to see it done. The *optiones* organised his men with ruthless efficiency, whacking any man dawdling in the head with the flat of his *hasta*. That he used spear over sword gave away his Remi preferences. The other scouts were Gabali, loyal to Rome as a Gaul could be, but still Gauls. Manius had commanded the auxiliary *centuria* for eight weeks now, and so far, the tribesmen impressed him. Hailing from the mountains, the Gabali were strong and hearty, and complained little, but then few in Caesar's legions had cause to complain. The Great Man treated his soldiers well, even named them his son.

Manius loved Caesar no less than any other. The Great Man was truly a father as much as a general.

That didn't mean Manius enjoyed the task he'd been given. Scouting the unkempt lands of the Belgae was an awkwardly achieved task. The forests grew thick, and it rained without end. Manius's men carried their armour rather than wear it, preferring the freedom of loose fitting shirts and short trousers. The only thing in the Cloaked Eagles favour was the abundance of wildlife in the forest through which they travelled. The men filled their bellies to bursting every night, boding well for Carigo who ate twice as much as most men.

In absence of a proper camp—they had neither the space or equipment to lay stakes—they spent most nights and early mornings beneath cow-hide tents disguised with branches and leaves. Sentries hid in the treetops, but the scouting party's encounters thus far had been few. That could change at any moment.

Carigo approached again, palming a handful of berries into the space inside his scraggly brown beard. He grinned with bright red lips. "Tar berries. A good find. Would you like some, Centurion?"

"Perhaps later. I would wish to go over our route for tomorrow's journey."

"As you are, Centurion. We're nearing the river Sambre, and should be able to cross if we look for a place narrow enough. The Bellovaci dwell nearby," he spat berry juice on the ground. "A bunch of unclean brutes, but not to be trifled with. Your man Caesar is right to worry. Last village we travelled through gave me a feeling we were most unwelcome there. Our presence is only going to get less wanted."

"Did you hear anything about the Bellovaci's disposition towards Rome?"

"Not fond." Carigo wiped his wet mouth with the back of a meaty fist. "If Gaul gives your man problems, it will be amongst the Nervii and the neighbouring tribes. We're treading into hot water."

Manius grunted. "Caesar is not my man, he is our man. You have pledged allegiance to Rome."

"Aye, but that don't mean I have to love it. You Romans are decent enough, I suppose, but you can't change a man's heart by enslaving him."

Manius felt a shiver and tried to disguise it by folding his arms. "Can I count on your loyalty, *Optiones*?"

Carigo grinned. "Don't worry, Centurion, I won't put my spear in your back. You should be more worried about the Bellovaci doing it."

"We are only here to observe. Caesar wants an accounting for every tribe in the region not yet allied with Rome. When we spot the Bellovaci, we observe, and then we move on."

"To the Nervii," said Carigo. "About as fierce as they come. They've never had a man turn his back on a fight."

Manius nodded. "Again, we are not here to fight, Optiones. Each man here was picked and trained to stay hidden, to disappear into the landscape itself if pursued. I am not a blood-lusting fool seeking glory."

Carigo lifted the corner of his mouth, as if amused, but after a moment's thought he nodded. "Good to know. Worst men are the men out to prove themselves."

"I shall be brave when bravery is required, as I would expect of us all."

Carigo smirked again, but turned and trotted off. Commanding auxiliaries was difficult. No way of knowing their little quirks and habits. What looked like rudeness to a Roman might be something else entirely to the Remi. While he trusted Carigo enough to sleep at night, an unassailable palisade existed between them. They were different species of the same animal.

A pair of Gabali prepared Manius's tent, and he crawled beneath it. Already stripped of armour, he stayed as he was in shirt and trousers. There would be a chance to undress and wash at the river. With no horses in their party, the only sound was the quiet chit chat of the Gabali settling down to bed. Their tongue was foreign, but the tone light-hearted and relaxed. When soldiers stopped laughing, that was the time for an officer to worry. Manius closed his eyes and thought of home. Did Aemilia miss him as much as he did her? Was their new daughter well? That he had not yet laid eyes on little Tarentia burdened him so. If he died in battle, he would never see her even once. What would become of her then? No name or dowry to speak of, she would be married off to some socially stagnant knight or worse.

Damn you, Sulla, and your proscriptions.

Manius's father, Titus Furia, had been one of Gaius Marius's men and, as such, took the Marian side in the civil war against Cornelius Sulla. When Marius lost his mind, and then the war, Sulla took great offence at the Marian supporters. The Proscriptions had been dark days. Days when men such as Titus Manius could wake up one morning and see their names pinned up against the *Rostra*, marked for death. The rewards for proscribing were so high that two of Titus's very own slaves had bludgeoned him to death in the street. Titus's full wealth was seized by the state, and the two murderous slaves received their freedom. Dark days indeed. But what made Sulla's revenge viler was a caveat that all descendants of the proscribed be stripped of their birth-right and status. Manius was the son of Titus, a wealthy patrician, but by the time he donned the Toga Viriis at fifteen, he stood lower than a pauper with a name meaning nothing.

At least Caesar's ascendancy put Sulla's memory in the past where it belonged. Caesar was not a petty man like Sulla had been. He would sooner see an enemy toss aside their enmity than die on his sword. It was Caesar who recognised Manius's name in the roll calls and immediately elevated him to Centurion, with promise of one day fully restoring his name and station. If Manius retained The Great Man's favour, little Tarentia would grow into a woman of wealth and means. It was because of her, his daughter, that Manius vowed to make it back home to Rome, and become a senator.

With thoughts of his baby girl drifting through his head Manius fell sound asleep.

Chapter 2

Manius awoke to shouts. That they sounded more angry than afraid, eased his mind. But the sudden shock from sleep still left him reeling in the dark. Carigo appeared and steadied him, the man's spear equipped but held casually by his side.

"What is it, *Optiones*?"

"Bloody wolves. Got into our supplies and took all the venison. Tell your man that once he takes Gaul, he needs to take care of the pests once and for all."

Manius blinked and adjusted to the dark. Most of the eighty Gabali were up and about, but only a handful were active. The panic was over before it had begun. "How did a pack of wild mongrels get past our sentries, Carigo?"

"The sentries were watching for men, not creatures of the night. A wolf can crawl up through the bushes until it's right on top of a man. And forget the 'mongrel' talk. The wolves around here can grow bigger than a man. In fact, some Bellovaci pray to the Great White Wolf of the Ancient Groves."

"Jupiter's cock! You *cunni* will believe in anything. In Rome, wolves are to be kicked and shunned, not feared."

"And in Rome, you stay indoors whenever an eagle takes a shit on the forum. We all believe different things, Centurion."

Manius realised he had belittled the Remi man's beliefs, and so chose not to take offence at the man's counter-remark against Rome. He dropped his shoulders and allowed himself a laugh. "I suppose Rome's auspices might seem odd to an outsider, as fear of wolves seems odd to me. Nonetheless, the sentries failed in their duties. Have them on half-rations for three days."

Carigo nodded. "Long as you don't include me in that, fair enough. Can I have their rations?"

Manius realised the man was joking. "Let's hope we encounter nothing as dangerous as your wit. How long have we been encamped?"

"About five hours, I'd say. Sun will be up before you can take a shit and wipe your arse."

"Then there's no point going back to sleep. Assemble the centuria."

"Aye, Centurion."

Ten minutes later, they were once again on the move. Just as Carigo had said, the sun came up to meet them almost immediately. Their camp had been near the edge of the woods so they soon broke free onto a grassy plain. The river shone ahead of them like a slow-moving snake of the brightest silver. Gaul had moments of splendour when it wasn't raining.

Being so close to the river, the area made prime farming land, which presented them with a grave problem. A young Gaul was leading a steer across a paddock beside a small homestead. When the farmer saw the line of scouts approaching, he panicked. It looked like he would run, but fear made him freeze and he stood there in place, eyes brimming with tears. The Gaul saw his own death approach.

"We must slaughter him," said Carigo, although he did so without relish.

Manius said nothing, for he knew the obvious thing to do. If they did not kill this young farmer, he would run and tell the Bellovaci of their presence. "Seize him."

A group of Gabali broke from the group and grabbed the startled Gaul. He kicked out at them and begged, but he did not dishonour himself by screaming.

"What is he saying?" Manius asked Carigo.

"He says, 'Love Rome. Love Rome. No hurt.' Should I kill him now?"

Manius put a hand up to keep his *optiones* from doing anything. "Hold on. First ask this man what he knows about the Bellovaci."

Carigo nodded, then spoke in that uncouth language all the men shared. After chatting with the farmer for a minute, the Remi man turned to Manius and said, "He says there's a Bellovaci village called Carlei right across the river, but you can't cross here."

"Why not?"

Carigo asked the man and relayed the reply. "The mud in this section of river will suck a man down and drown him. The only safe place to cross is further North-East, but that would take us right into the heart of the Nervii."

"What about taking the river further West?" asked Manius.

Carigo relayed the message. The farmer went pale and glanced around sheepishly. When he spoke, he did so rapidly and alarmed.

"What did the man say?" Manius asked.

Carigo shrugged, as if he didn't quite understand it. "He said no one crosses the river West."

"Why not?"

"It is a sacred place, he says. Only the Lacuscii can go there and any who trespass in their groves will meet a bloody end."

Manius rolled his eyes again. He needed the Gabali on board with whatever he decided, and now he worried. Would they share the Bellovaci farmer's delusions? "What do you make of this, *Optiones*?"

Carigo chewed at the side of his mouth as if desperately hungry. He let out a laboured breath and then threw his arms out in a shrug. "The Lacuscii are a myth even I don't believe. Most Remi men probably haven't even heard the tales, they're so old. The Lacuscii are a tribe of men who mated with the creatures of the forest when history first began. Over time, they became as much beast as man, and their druids gained power over nature itself. It's a children's tale. Truth is, this unwashed bugger is trying to divert us north where his bastard Nervii will cut us to ribbons."

Manius tapped on the wooden pommel of his Gladius—the one thing of his father he had managed to retain. "I'm inclined to agree. The man's expression when I suggested going West was untrustworthy. He'd hiding something"

Carigo sighed, then pulled the spear off his back and placed the tip under the farmer's trembling chin. "I'll kill the bugger."

"No wait!" Manius held his hand up again, but wasn't sure why. Why did it pain him to slaughter this tribesman? One day, he would likely take up arms against Rome. Letting him live was a betrayal against Rome. If he let the Gaul go, and he made it to the tribal leaders, he would give up the Cloaked Eagle's location.

But killing the farmer seemed unjust. Not like something Caesar would do at all.

Then Manius saw the woman and child. They stood near the homestead, anxiously looking on. The little boy in the mother's arms was pointing and cooing at the Gabali. The mother tried to shush he child.

"He comes with us," said Manius.

Carigo frowned. "He's Bellovaci scum, and you want to bring him along, feed him, guard him? What about his woman and child? You want a squawking infant along?"

"We'll butcher the man's steer for extra meat, and once we're out of Bellovaci territory, we'll release him. Tell his woman that if the enemy finds us, we shall slay her husband the moment we unsheathe our swords. If she remains at her home, and alerts nobody, she will see her man return safe and sound."

Carigo glanced at the Gabali who seemed as little enamoured by the idea as he was. While they were not natural enemies of the Bellovaci, like Carigo's Remi were, they were still not friendly. Carigo couldn't wipe the frown off his face. "I don't understand your thinking, Centurion. We are a scouting party. Having a prisoner will compromise us. How will we stay silent if this lad cries out to the nearest enemy we see?"

"If he makes one sound intended to give us away, you may kill him, *Optiones*. Until then, he has done nothing deserving of his death."

"Being Bellovaci is enough," Carigo muttered.

Manius locked his jaw and stared daggers at his second-in-command. "*Optiones!*"

"Yes, okay, all right. Your will, my hand, and all that. I'll inform the lad he is now an honoured prisoner of Rome. Best tell his woman too."

After receiving the news, the young Gaul bowed and muttered enthusiastically.

"He says 'thanks,'" said Carigo.

"I gathered, thank you. Okay, men, form up. We're heading West."

The men butchered the steer and collected the choicest meat, leaving the rest to the woman and her child. Then they resumed their journey across the plain. Reaching the river, they headed West. That was when the young Gaul started hopping, long blond locks flapping in the breeze. "Ester ester!"

Carigo translated, not that it was necessary. "He means East."

"Tell him we are going East, and that we will cross away from the Nervii realm."

Carigo said so, but the Gaul kept arguing, on the edge of panic. "Ester ester!"

Manius groaned. Thank Jupiter there were no other tribesmen in the area to hear them. "Tell that man we are a scouting party and that no harm will come to him or his kin so long as he shuts his damned mouth, right this instant."

Carigo seemed at a loss, not something the big man wore well. "He knows that, Centurion. The bugger keeps insisting we're heading into danger. I think he truly believes it."

Manius stopped marching and approached the troublesome prisoner. The Bellovaci farmer begged him in foreign tongue, waving his arms madly. He was making it very difficult to justify not killing him. With a sigh, Manius threw a stiff punch. The Gaul slumped to the silty mud beside the river. "Pick him up. We shall carry him the rest of the way."

Carigo grunted. "Still think we should kill him."

"Such actions are growing more favourable, Optiones."

Despite his argument, Carigo was the one to carry the young farmer. As the strongest amongst them, he still managed to keep pace, as if carrying nothing more than a sackful of figs. The Cloaked Eagles made good time and soon stopped amongst the nearby hills to wash in a stream running toward the river.

Manius waded up to his knees, but the water ran no deeper. It felt good to rinse the stink off him, and he sat down in the current and allowed the stream to rush around his torso. He'd lost a little weight, despite eating well, but these were the best years of his life physically. He was strong and lean, with stamina to march a whole day through. While scouting duty lacked the finer pleasures of Roman life, like wine and whores, it hardened a man's body better than being at camp. He hated it out here in the wild most times, but he knew he would miss it when it was over. Few Romans got to explore beyond the main roads laid by their forefathers.

Carigo, however, looked a man who would spend the rest of his days away from civilisation. The Remi were a well-fed sedentary people, but his *Optiones* had a nomad's spirit, more Germanic than Gaul. But the Gabali making up the bulk of the party were most adaptable of all. Wiry men with vulpine eyes, they saw everything and hid themselves with preternatural ease. Manius had learned much during the short time he had commingled with them. Far more enlightening than being surrounded by a bunch of bickering legionaries. Romans had too many opinions. These Gabali men got on with the job at hand.

As Manius continued washing himself in the stream, laying back on his elbows so that his entire body sunk beneath the surface, he thought once again about his daughter. That Tarentia was black of hair like he, was understood from his wife's letters, but he knew not yet of her eye colour and complexion. Was she pale, like her mother? Did her eyes shine green as finest jewels? Or smoulder like burnt, brown mahogany? He could not wait to see her, yet the prospect of arriving home was daunting. So much time and distance to draw in, and all while surrounded by Gauls.

Something bumped against Manius's tricep, but he kept his gaze on the grey-blue sky above him. One of the men had merely struck him as they waded by. But then something else bumped against his other arm, causing him to lower his gaze upstream. He frowned at what he did not understand. Dark shapes moved in the water, floating past on their way downhill towards the river.

Some of the Gabali in the water chattered, calling out to one another.

Men splashed. Others on the riverbank cried out.

Manius leapt to his feet. His stomach clenched. Objects bumped against his shins.

Corpses.

The stream was full of corpses. Nothing too large—rats, squirrels, and maybe a half-dozen fox cubs—but the bloody flotsam came in an endless wave. The water was red with animal blood.

Manius rushed to the water's edge and climbed the bank, almost slipping in the silt. A dozen Gabali did the same, a tide of shouting men.

Once on dry land, Manius demanded an explanation. "What could cause such an ungodly thing?"

Carigo held a hand against his chin, watching the stream as more corpses floated by. It didn't seem shocking to the Remi man, but instead profoundly interesting. While others screwed their faces in disgust, Carigo seemed only thoughtful. Manius approached his *optiones* and demanded answers again, even though it was not his fault. The big man gave no reply, kept on standing there with a thoughtful expression.

The Bellovaci farmer roused from his unconsciousness at the water's edge, now fully awake. He muttered and mumbled at first, his fear slowly rising in the tone of his voice. The last thing Manius needed. "Quiet that man before I gut him myself. I will have no more noise from him."

One of the Gabali grabbed the young Gaul by the scruff of the neck and shoved him away from the stream. The roughness was enough to shut him up for now.

Finally having enough of Carigo's silence, Manius demanded his input a final time. Carigo moved his hand away from his chin and looked at the Centurion. "If you were to ask the Bellovaci lad, he'd tell you this was the work of the Ancient Grove. A warning that we step into a land not ours. But we are all servants of Rome now, ay? And Romans tread wherever they please."

Manius frowned. "Do you hold stock in the farmer's warnings?"

"Do I believe in gods and monsters? No, Centurion, I do not. The only monsters I know are men, and the only Gods are kings. Both commit foul deeds."

"Glad to hear you have sense. We continue onwards then, but what of this odd occurrence? It is a poor omen surely?"

Carigo gave his characteristic half-smirk. "Omens are for Rome. This is not Rome. The only thing here is the known and the unknown. Do I know what would cause a stream to carry corpses of a hundred dead animals? No, I do not. But if we continue onwards, then perhaps we shall learn."

Manius studied the Gabali men. They were unnerved by the occurrence, but it left them pugnacious rather than afraid. These were men who did not tolerate the bizarre. In that way, they were as Romans. Rome also did not tolerate ignorance.

"Let's move, Optiones. I want to cross the river as soon as possible so we may find safe camp on the other side."

So, the Cloaked Eagles marched on, ascending the largest hill that would lead them back towards the river on the other side.

Chapter 3

Atop the hill, Manius watched the sun slip behind the clouds. A light drizzle had started, which he feared would turn ferocious. The river lay North-West, two miles distant, and a mile further than that, it narrowed by two-thirds. That was the place to cross. But to make camp early here and cross tomorrow, or try to make it across the river first... which was wisest?

Manius decided to make camp on this side of the river. They could sleep knowing their backs were safe whereas on the other side of the river they could be attacked and pinned against the water's edge. Better to have a full day's march on the other side so they could take time to scout a safe spot. They'd lose time overall, but keeping to this side of the river until tomorrow made most sense.

"*Optiones*, we will descend the hill, and camp in that forest beside the river. We shall cross tomorrow."

The young Bellovaci acted up again, and this time tried to make a run for it. A Gabali kicked his legs from under him and sent him sprawling into jagged rocks. Carigo winced and then laughed.

Manius, however, did not laugh. "What is that *cunni* shouting about now?"

"Says that there forest is the sacred grove he spoke of. The hunting grounds of the Lacuscii."

"You mean the tribe you say is a myth and most have never heard of? A tribe that has no reason to oppose a centuria of Roman scouts just passing through?"

Carigo shrugged his wide shoulders. "Even if they are real, we should have enough men for them to keep their distance. No point picking a fight for the thrill of it. If they do exist, they are surely a shy people, more likely to hide than confront. If I'm wrong, then at least we'll have a good fight on our hands. I'm not a fan of dying, but killing… well, that thickens the blood. Makes me hungry."

"Everything makes you hungry, Carigo."

"Aye, which is why I'm all for making camp early. The forest will shield us from any Bellovaci on the other side of the river, so the Gabali can use the extra hours to hunt and relax. Nothing better to settle a tribesman's nerves than a big hunt."

Manius cleared his throat and briefly watched the men. "You think the Gabali are anxious?"

"In a way, Centurion, yes. They think the scene back at the stream was some kind of threat. Set their minds to a useful task and they will relax themselves ready for bed."

"So be it, Optiones. Have the men strike camp inside the forest first, then they may hunt until two hours past nightfall. I wish to cross the river as early as possible come the new day."

"Ay, Centurion."

Manius remained on the hill's summit as the Gabali filtered down its side. He wanted to keep his view of the land as long as possible, so not to be caught unawares. Would they truly find a lost tribe inside the forest? The thick expanse of trees went on for miles, so much so they might not even see any tribesmen, even if they existed.

And what of the grove itself? The young Bellovaci seemed to think the place was touched by death, a dangerous place.

Pah, primitive superstition. Even Rome once held unsavoury beliefs, human sacrifice for one. Something intolerable to today's Romans. These Gauls just needed to catch up with the rest of the civilised world.

Once the Gabali disappeared into the woods, Manius went in after them, but he kept his hand on the hilt of his Gladius as he descended the hill.

* * *

Once camp had been struck, in a small clearing between trees, that Carigo informed were Silver Firs, all was peaceful and quiet. Thoughts of unexplained danger went away. Even the young Bellovaci farmer had calmed, sitting cross-legged on the floor and staying quiet. A good thing too, because Manius had reached the conclusion that the man must be killed, but if he remained calm, he might still get to see his woman and child again. Manius would like that very much. The boy deserved a father.

And may the young farmer pass on my clemency to the Bellovaci and show them Rome does not wish to fight. Rome wishes only to uplift the whole of Gaul and bring it into the great tapestry of nations.

Roughly half the Gabali had gone deeper into the forest to hunt deer and rabbit, which left the camp quieter than usual. Manius tried to enjoy it, but hustle and bustle was the background to a soldier's life, and it was unsettling to hear so little. In fact, the forest itself was more silent than he would have expected. Where were the birds, the squirrels, the insects?

Carigo came and sat beside Manius on the ground. He chomped on salted fish and offered a part. Manius took it and thanked him. "No problem, Centurion. Got to enjoy these little moments. Superstition might have kept the Bellovaci away from this place, but it means we get to enjoy it in peace. It's an honour. We are nature's guests here. You may wish to sacrifice a fatted boar to Camulos. Let him know your gratitude."

"If we find a boar, you may do so, yet I see none here."

"Ay. Well, let's see what the Gabali bring back. Those mountain men were made for hunting."

"Living in the mountains leaves little option not to be, I'd expect. Do you never yearn for a permanent home, Carigo? After your campaigning is through, will you take a wife?"

The big Remi man seemed to think on this, as if it were a real consideration. Eventually, he shrugged, as if any answer he gave could not be certain. "Why stick to one place with one woman when the whole world is on offer? Men are like wolves, Centurion. It's in our blood to roam. Your Romans identify yourself by a city, instead of the people you are. You expand throughout the world, yet you always go running home every time. Why? All of your problems lie in Rome—your politics, your wars. Men are not meant to rot in place. Move on and your problems fade to dust. Stay in one place and they gather like flies."

Rather than object, Manius allowed the man's words to gestate. "There's wisdom in which you speak, yet I would not give up my wife or daughter for anything."

"You've been with whores?"

"I… of course."

Carigo chuckled. "Romans want it all. To roam and war, fuck and steal, but return home at the end of the day to the bosoms of your wives and the comfort of your villas. The Germans have it right. They take what they want and never stay in place—they have no illusions of civility like the Romans."

"Careful, *Optiones*. You are a loyal subject of Rome, yet you speak like a traitor."

"Is it treachery to speak one's mind? If I were the great weakling, Cicero, I could slander all and sundry under the guise of satire."

"I hold no great love for Tulius Cicero, for the man holds enough for himself, yet he is a Roman citizen. A Consular."

Carigo smirked. "And so, we get to the crux of the argument. You label me a Roman in ways only that suit you. I am less than you, yet must act even more Roman than a true Roman. I do not love your glorious Republic, Manius Furia, and I never will. If you wish to execute me for that, then do so now."

Manius realised his fists had clenched, yet it felt more instinct than actual offence. As much as the Remi man's words were anathema, he couldn't help but like the man. "I ask only one thing of you, Carigo."

"Yes, Centurion?"

"Do not speak your mind in front of any other Roman but I."

"Long as I can speak my full mind to you, Manius Furia, then I will keep it in your care."

Manius nodded and the two of them grabbed forearms, an ironically Roman gesture.

"It's getting dark, Centurion. I'll have the Gabali still in camp get some rest, so they may keep watch tonight while the hunters sleep."

"I shall join them," said Manius. "I have a feeling tomorrow will ask more of us than days prior."

Carigo patted him on the arm and smiled, fish bits dotting his scraggly brown beard. "Long as the Lacuscii don't come slaughter us in the night, aye?"

Manius swallowed, but felt stupid once Carigo released a belly laugh so loud it shook the leaves from the trees.

Chapter 4

That night, Manius wasn't awoken by shouting, but by the sound of breathing. As soon as he opened his eyes, he sensed a presence right beside him. Hot, fishy air on his face. Before he could cry out an alert, a meaty hand clamped over his mouth. He tried to struggle, but another hand held him down.

"Quiet, Centurion!"

Manius blinked twice and Carigo's face revealed itself in the darkness. He was lying on his belly and leaning over Manius, but his eyes were pointed elsewhere. When he removed his hand from Manius's mouth, he did so slowly.

Manius understood enough to keep quiet and whisper. "What is happening?"

"Something's in the camp. I thought I noticed something in the trees when night first fell, but when I went into the forest, there was nothing there. Whatever it was I saw in the trees, it's back. It's in the camp."

"Then raise the alarm."

Carigo shook his head. "Wait! Let's see what we're up against."

Manius rolled onto his side, looking where Carigo did. Sure enough, a shadow moved through camp, slinking between tents. It made no sound, or so little it was covered by Gabali snores. The shadow belonged to no man, that Manius could imagine, for it was large and low to the ground. A beast.

"It's a wolf," whispered Carigo.

Someone in camp got up in the darkness. They did not scream at the shadow nor alert others in the camp. In fact, Manius didn't think they were even aware of the shadow's presence. Was one of the Gabali getting up to take a piss?

When the man's slender frame finally took shape, it became clear who it was. "It's the Bellovaci farmer," said Manius. "He's planning on making a run for it."

"Blasted imbecile," said Carigo.

"We have to get to him."

Carigo nodded, then started shuffling towards the centre of camp on his belly. Manius grabbed his sword and started after his Optiones, both men in the dirt like slugs. The young Bellovaci crept between sleeping Gabali, careful not to step on any of them and ruin his chance at escape.

The shadow moved towards the unaware farmer.

Faced with the need of urgency, Carigo heaved from his belly into a crouch. He hissed a warning to the young Bellovaci, but it only succeeded in startling him. Realising his silent escape had been foiled, he turned and ran.

Right into the shadow.

The beast leapt up and devoured the young Bellovaci, tearing into him on the ground. His screams woke the camp and eighty Gabali leapt from their bedrolls. Chaos erupted.

Manius leapt up and raced towards the centre of camp. The young Bellovaci's screams ceased, replaced by the shouts of confused Gabali. The shadow flitted between tents, somehow avoiding the reach of the men. Swords swung at empty darkness and Gallic curse words filled the forest. Carigo yelled to the men, trying to keep them from doing anything stupid like stabbing each other. The man had his spear in front of him and used it to slap any man making too much noise. Meanwhile, Manius kept his eyes on the shadow. Slowly, taking each step carefully, he crept towards the beast.

Could it be a mere wolf?

The thing was as large as a man. Larger.

The first Gabali fell. The shadow rose three feet and came down on top of the man as he looked in the opposite direction. His screams lasted seconds. One of his brothers came to aid but became the shadow's next victim. Once both men were dead, the beast dashed between tents, vanishing from the spot where the panicked Gabali converged. Manius still had the shadow in his sights though, and he continued towards it.

He told himself to stay back, to let his men confront this thing, but he could not. Why?

Because these were his men, and they were dying.

He would gut the bloody wolf himself and use its pelt as a coat.

The shadow took down another man, forcing Manius to move faster. He almost tripped over a sinewy rope attached to a tent, and his stumble announced his presence to the enemy. The shadow focused on him.

It slunk towards him, a living part of the darkness.

Mars, help me slay this beast.

Manius gripped his sword tightly and wished he had grabbed his *scutum*.

The shadow rose in front of him, two feet taller than he.

Manius did not flee. To turn his back now would be his end. Instead, he held his sword in front of him.

As the shadow edged closer, its odour filled his nostrils—an earthy stink. Its features came into view.

Pointed ears, bristle of fur, yellow, lupine eyes.

And a human face.

Manius felt his heart stop, and in that instant the beast pounced. It felt like the forest itself was falling down on him, and all he could do was thrust his sword out in front of him. The weight that collided with him was too much to bare. He fell backwards into the mud. The huge beast crushed the life out of him.

Manius lay there in agony, waiting to be torn asunder.

The moment never came.

Hotness covered his chest. Blood, or something else?

Carigo's shouts filled the forest, and the Gabali fell silent. Manius tried to call for help, but he could not breathe, the weight on his chest too great. Seconds passed and the pressure in his lungs grew until he saw stars. His life ebbed away. Oh, Jupiter, take what you will for a single, glorious breath. Just one more breath to fight off the darkness.

Chest threatening to explode, Manius felt lightheaded and then dizzy. Suffocation was not the way he thought to die. Where was the honour? Was this Mars' plan for him?

Then the weight shifted and Manius seized half a breath. When the weight fell away completely, he sucked at the air wildly, gasping and coughing, wailing and choking. A meaty hand clamped his shoulder.

"That's it, Centurion, get your fill. You're all right. Get some air. It's right there."

Manius nodded his head to let his *Optiones* know he was hearing him, but he concentrated only on the glorious air filling his lungs. It took some time before he finally got a hold of himself. He sat there on the ground, covered in blood, and pawed at his shirt while wondering where it had all come from. A wound crossed his belly, a thick scratch, but not enough to account for all of the blood.

"You gutted the bastard," said Carigo, pointing at the shadow on the ground. Manius's sword stuck up out of its middle. "Not bad for a Roman."

Manius was too beaten to laugh. He shook his head in confusion. "That thing. It's not a wolf. It's a man."

"You get a bonk on the head, Centurion. It's a wolf. I told you the things run big in these parts. No wonder there's no game in these woods. I couldn't believe it when the hunters came back empty handed. It nearly made me wake you."

"I'm telling you, Carigo! Look at that wretched thing. I swear it by Jupiter and Mars both."

Carigo tutted and sighed, clearly humouring him, but when he turned his head towards the shadow, he froze.

The Gabali mumbled amongst themselves.

"The stories are true," said Carigo, more to himself than any other. "No!"

Manius had recovered enough to get off his back, yet he didn't try standing. He dragged himself along on his side until he was right beside the beast he had slain.

Yet it was a beast no longer.

Lying in the mud on a bed of broken twigs and leaves was a naked man, the likes of which Manius had never seen. His skin was white as purest marble and he lacked a single hair anywhere on his body. His dead eyes were yellow suns, clear even in darkness, and his ears curled up into points. Inside his open mouth were sharper fangs than a man had any right to own. This creature had been of the forest, a beast as much as a man.

Carigo shook his head in disbelief. "The Lacuscii... The Lacuscii are real."

Manius was shaking his head too. "You didn't tell me everything, did you, *Optiones*? So, tell me now."

Chapter 5

"The stories about the Lacuscii are told to scare children and keep them from wandering too far into the woods," explained Carigo. "Parents warn their sprogs about wolf men in the trees that will eat them. No one believes it's true."

"I believe it," said Manius, the Gabali stood in a huddle behind him. His slaying of the beast had elevated him in their eyes. "Tell me the stories in full."

Carigo looked at the dead tribesman lying on the ground and nodded. "They are changers. Men by day and monsters by night. They descend from a human male named Luscus and the great white she-wolf Vuluptra. For generations, they have preyed on those entering their forests, breeding carefully to keep their numbers down. They are a quiet people, knowing the world would hunt them down if they were deemed a threat. I never believed the stories, Centurion, but I think we may have entered their grove. If that's the case, we need to leave right now. There's a reason no game exists in this forest. The Lucuscii hunt here."

Manius hated to admit it, but he believed it all, Jupiter forgive him. Yet, he was on a mission for Caesar himself. "We are soldiers, *Optiones*. These Lucuscii might have the taint of the wolf in them, but they can be killed. What would you do if we were bested by Bellovaci?"

"I would say give me a sword and a place to stick it."

"Exactly. Men fear the unknown, but with your explanation, the Lacuscii are not unknown. They are a tribe in hiding, but tonight they killed subjects of Rome. It is not something that may go unanswered."

Carigo looked at him through narrowed eyes. "Where's the man who promised not to lead us to pointless deaths in the name of Rome?"

"You would have us flee like children?"

"I would have us live. Rome does not know all, Manius Furia. Some things no civilised man can understand. This grove is of the Gauls, and it does not care about the glory of Rome."

Manius looked at the Gabali. Their fearlessness had evaporated, and they now looked like frail senators surrounded on the steps of the Forum by torch wielding plebs. These men had families they wanted to get back to. That poor Bellovaci farmer had a wife and child waiting for him back at the homestead, trusting in the word of a Roman. Manius's word was already broken, and the glory of Rome had been diminished. Were the losses worth the risk? Was punishing a forgotten tribe for crimes against the Republic more important than completing the mission Caesar gave them?

Manius stood gingerly, ribs aching. With a shaking right hand, he clutched his gladius and yanked it out of the Lacuscii warrior's chest. A gout of blood spewed forth and pattered the leaves on the ground. With a snarl on his face, he turned to his men with the bloody sword raised high. "I am a centurion of Rome, and a son of Caesar. You are the Cloaked Eagles, tough men and servants of Rome. Tonight, we have been beset by a foul enemy. An enemy who attacks sleeping men in the night without warning. Gabali men litter this forest, their lives cut short by abominations born of man and beast. Yet, I would ask no man here to risk his life for something not tasked of him by Rome itself. I lack Imperium, and such cannot speak for Rome. Caesar has asked us to scout the tribes of Gaul, and this is one of them. He did not ask us to fight them. That will come later. Therefore, our report will include the Lacuscii as a tribe hostile to Rome. We will return of a day to raze this wretched forest to the ground, and every beast within it. But not tonight. Tonight, we flee, for not to would be foolhardy. Let us pack up, Eagles. We are leaving."

He had never seen the Gabali move so fast. They swept through the clearing like hunted hares, gathering up their bedrolls and abandoning any belongings that rolled away from them. Carigo studied Manius and, when caught looking, gave a respectful nod. Then he left to gather up his own belongings.

Manius gathered his *scutum* and moved over to the fallen Bellovaci. The young, blond Gaul wore a woven braid around his neck, a thing made with a woman's delicate craft. Manius plucked it free and placed it inside his belt. Little would stem his woman's grief, but she deserved back what was hers. He would also see she received payment from Rome, if she accepted such an offer.

"We lost five men," Carigo reported moments later. "Plus the Bellovaci lad. One Lacuscii did that. You're a wise man, Manius Furia."

Manius nodded, although some part of him still nagged that his 'rational decision' to leave was really cowardice and fear. "We still need to cross the river, Optiones. We still need to scout the Bellovaci and the Nervii. If we return to Caesar without..."

"By day," said Carigo. "Once we're back on the hill we need only wait for daylight. The Lacuscii are only men in the glare of sunlight. We can cross the river at dawn while the beast inside of them sleeps."

Manius nodded.

The Gabali formed up, carrying their dead amongst them. Manius had no intention of keeping them for a single second, so he led the way back out of the forest, sword unsheathed and *scutum* held firm in front of him. The wound on his stomach burned, but the pain only made him move faster, a reminder of what he was leaving behind. The darkness seemed to have blackened further and the trees, both ahead and behind them, swayed with renewed life. Several times, Manius thought he saw shadows move from one place to another. Several times he thought he saw something watching.

"How deep did we travel into the forest?" Manius asked Carigo.

"We came in about half a mile, I'd say, but I'm not positive we're heading in the exact same direction. Either way, we'll be out soon enough. Just keep moving."

Twigs broke as the men hurried through the trees, but when twigs broke up ahead, Manius called a halt.

"What do you hear, Centurion?"

"We're being watched. Something has looped around in front of us. They want to keep us from leaving. But why?"

Carigo readied his spear. "Because we're meat."

Manius groaned as he thought about the lack of game in the forest. "We're the largest prey they've had in years. Men! Form a shield wall. Leave our fallen behind, lest we join them."

Such a manoeuvre was difficult in the cramped forest, but the Gabali did a decent enough job of clumping together and raising their shields. Some wielded spears, like Carigo, but most adopted the gladius given to them by Rome. It made the shield wall unbalanced and awkward. Fighting this way was not why the Cloaked Eagles existed.

Carigo tilted his head and whispered. "Centurion, shadows, up ahead."

Manius nodded. He had already seen the shapes flittering in the darkness, twenty yards ahead. "Men! Forward march, half-time. Those *cunni* want to dash themselves against our shields then we shall let them."

The Gabali moved forward, feet tangling the weeds and roots that tripped them constantly and made the whole formation waver. Shields on the flanks moved forward, pointing towards the enemy.

The shadows remained ahead, multiplying in number.

"I count at least a dozen," said Carigo.

Manius nodded silently, focusing on where he was putting his feet. A man beside him tripped, and he had to reach out and steady him.

Step, step, step.

The formation moved forwards, keeping as tight as it could, shields locked together.

The shadows remained in place, ready to meet them. Within seconds, the two groups would clash.

"Shields forward," Manius shouted.

Any shields still facing the flanks now turned to clink against their neighbours, forming an impenetrable shield in front of them. The Lacuscii could not break through, Manius was sure of it. His men would cut their way out of this forest and gain revenge for their fallen brothers.

"Ready!"

The men breathed heavily, steeling themselves for battle. Swords and spears slid through the gaps in the wall.

Manius locked his jaw. Clenched his sword.

Something caught the corner of his eye.

Shadows to the left, sliding out from between the trees.

The enemy had sprung a trap.

Carigo realised it too. A smirk crossed his face, visible even in the darkness. "Clever boys!"

The shadows leapt out from the forest and attacked on two fronts, one group striking the shield wall and locking the formation in place while the second group pounced upon their undefended left flank. The men there were not unprotected, their shields locked in front of them. They fell quickly, sides torn open by sharp claws glinting in the moonlight.

For the second time that night, Gabali screams pierced the air.

Manius growled. Jupiter fuck this grove.

He wheeled to his left and leapt amongst his men, screaming for them to kill, kill, kill. To their credit, they rallied, and managed to unthread their weapons from the shield wall and turn them on the enemy. Carigo killed the first beast himself, driving his spear right through its groin, so deeply that the weapon was nearly lost to him. He had to place his foot on the creature to yank the hasta back out. The dead beast turned back into a man, pale fleshed and tainted by the wolf.

More beasts fell to spears and sword, but the shield wall broke as men stumbled and tripped in the dark. Each time a man fell, another would try to fill the gap, but slowly the Lacuscii pushed them back and forced them to fall over their own feet. Shields got wrenched away and tossed aside.

More men screamed.

Manius leapt up in the air and plunged his sword into the neck of the nearest beast, grinning as its arterial blood spurted into his face. He felt the blood drip down his face and it sent him wild, made him a force of nature. He twirled, in a most un-Roman fashion, and impaled another foe. Leaping and kicking, he fought like the gladiators of Capua he had watched as a boy. His enemy was primal. So he became primal, and he matched their ferocity.

Carigo bellowed. A creature grappled with him, and bit into his neck. He pulled his spear around and slid it up beneath the beast's ribs. On its back legs, it looked as much a bear as a wolf, and even mortally wounded, it continued to attack. Carigo roared and shouted in Gallic, no doubt cursing the thing biting into his neck.

Manius ducked under a swiping claw and made his way to his struggling *Optiones*. A few steps and he was there, thrusting his sword into the beast's back and pulling it right out again. Then stabbing again. Over and over. Blood was everywhere. He breathed it in the air.

His attacker now dead on its feet, Carigo shoved the beast aside. His spearhead had snapped off and his neck bled profusely. He clamped a hand against the wound and grinned at Manius. "Looks like you led me to my death, after all, Centurion."

Manius took hold of the fading Remi man. "My apologies, *Optiones*."

"Fuck it, I'm not dead yet." He shoved Manius aside and threw himself at the nearest attacker, tackling it to the ground despite it being bigger. He pummelled the creature's head until its skull cracked open then let out a belly laugh as loud as thunder. "Years from now," he shouted, "the Lacuscii will be scaring *their* children with stories about *me*!"

More shadows emerged and fell on top of the Remi man, but before they could envelop him, he grabbed the broken shaft of his spear and rammed it into his own eye socket, killing himself instantly. He remained there on his knees, dead but not fallen.

The Gabali closed ranks. Those still holding shields did their best to form a wall. But it was no use. The shadows filled the forest and surrounded them on all sides. Every second, a beast leapt out to take a man, and the formation grew smaller, tighter. More vulnerable.

Before long, Manius realised, with absolute horror, that only three Gabali still lived. Eighty men slaughtered in a single night.

"I am sorry, Caesar. I have failed you."

Two of the three Gabali men fell, their deaths sickening and painful.

Manius wished he could speak Gallic. Wished he could tell the lone soldier fighting beside him that he was sorry. But it would mean nothing. Within seconds, the Gabali warrior was yanked away into the night, screaming as he died.

So Manius stood there alone, surrounded by an enemy not even the mighty Rome knew existed. A myth made real. Wolf men of the forest.

A children's story.

Jupiter, forgive me. I ask you to look over my daughter. Provide Tarentia with a man greater than I.

Tarentia! Oh, how I wish to gaze upon you before my death.

The shadows moved in, took up space around Manius. But they did not attack. He could hear their breathing, smell their stench, yet they did not tear him apart. "What are you waiting for, you cunnis? You stink of shit and piss, so get it over with."

Still, they did not attack.

Instead, they backed away. Why?

It wasn't until the first thin shaft of light pierced the canopy of the trees that Manius realised the source of their retreat. Jupiter had sent the dawn. True daylight was still an hour away, but its impending arrival was enough to send these creatures back to their nests.

Like a protective mother, the forest seemed to swallow up the Lacuscii until Manius was standing there alone. For a second, he wondered if they had even been there. Perhaps he suffered malaise, and this was all a fever dream. He certainly felt lightheaded. Would he wake up soon? Or die in his sleep?

The sight of six dozen dead Gabali told him he was not dreaming.

Manius staggered over to Carigo, a part of him needing confirmation that the big man could actually be killed. Of course, it was no surprise to find the man dead. The Remi was no Roman, but he had served with honour. Even in the face of his own death, he had fought for his brothers. Bravery was a most Roman virtue. Manius removed the broken spear shaft and lay his Optiones down beside a thick oak tree that matched the man himself. "I am sorry, Carigo, to leave you in such a cursed place. I shall return and find what remains of you, I give my word as a Roman."

With more daylight breaking through the trees, Manius made his way out of the forest. He felt nauseous and dizzy, the wound on his chest burning, but he was able to keep going by stopping at every tree to take a breath. An hour later, the small shafts of sunlight turned to great beams, and he was free.

The grassy hill lay ahead, a place he had recently stood and watched for threats. He had found none, but how wrong he had been. Now the hill mocked him, not least because he lacked the energy to climb it. He ended up dragging himself on his belly, not knowing if he would ever make it to the modest summit. His head spun and his chest burned. Death lay behind him in the forest, but he wasn't so sure it didn't lay ahead of him too. He was a failure to Rome, crawling on his belly like a worm. But one thing kept him going.

Tarentia.

* * *

Manius opened his eyes beneath a wooden roof. That there were no screams to wake him was a comfort, yet his heart beat with fear. His body burned and his mind spun. Death all around him. Monsters. Blood. And shadows. He had taken himself to the underworld and left eighty good men behind.

So where was he now? What Hell greeted him as just deserts?

A familiar face watched over him. A woman.

He spoke the answer the moment it came to him. "The farmer's wife. The Bellovaci."

"No, I am Helvetii. My husband was Bellovaci. The Nervii slaughtered my family when I was a child and I was taken in by the Bellovaci. My husband was a good man, but I was given to him as trade when my village went hungry and was unable to pay for his meat. He was a good man. He is dead?"

Manius nodded. "Not at my hand."

"You went into the forest?"

"I am sorry."

The woman nodded. She seemed upset by the news, but not broken as a good wife should be. "He always said that forest was cursed, that I must never let my boy enter."

"The boy was not his?"

"No. Part of the reason I was traded as chattel. Nobody desires a woman with an unwanted child. Who will provide for him now, I wonder?"

"I shall see that Rome pays its debt to you. Your husband's death was in service to the Republic. How… if I may ask, do you know Latin?"

"I not speak it so well, but I try. My father was a mercenary who fought with Quintus Sertorius in Hispania. He was recruited when great Roman pass across the Alps. My father made it back alive to raise me 'til I was eight, then Helvetii clashed with Nervii and he was slaughtered with the rest. A waste. My father was a good man. A servant of Rome."

Manius kept nodding his head. He realised it was a tremor in his neck and fought to stop it. Shivers wracked his entire body.

"You are ill, Roman. The fever may yet kill you. I have done what I can, the but wound on your chest festers."

He coughed and cleared mucus from his throat. "T-thank you. If I perish, send word to Rome that a centuria lies dead in the forest. They will reward you for your loyalty. Keep my body and they shall pay you handsomely for it too. I am a centurion."

She nodded. "You are lucky I found you, Centurion. Your body was at the top of the hill. The shield you carried caught the sunlight like a beacon. I saw it from a mile away while I was out playing with my boy."

"W-where is your boy now?"

"Asleep. As you should be. It is getting late."

"A whole day has passed?"

She nodded with a little grin. "The sun went down just before you awoke. I shall check on you in the night, but you must sleep again until morning."

Manius tried to agree, but his throat was thick and sore. His body shook harder and his fingertips itched like they were being bitten by ants. His head pounded like a drumbeat.

"Be still," the woman said, a mixture of worry and pity on her pretty face.

Manius coughed, spluttered. His mind whirled with horrifying images. His vision turned red. "The… the… the wolves!"

She frowned at him. "Wolves? Where wolves?"

"The wolves. The wolves."

"Where? Where wolves?"

The itching in his fingertips turned to pain and he felt the nails split open. A tingling in his mouth alerted him to teeth lengthening and his jaw widening. Something was happening to him. He was changing.

He was a changer.

Chest burning, Manius fought for breath. Bolt upright in bed, he turned to the woman and threw out an arm. When he saw the prickly hairs popping up along his forearm he almost gagged. The woman saw them too and her mouth fell open. "L-l-leave," he roared. "Get your boy and run. RUN!"

Eyes still wide, the woman nodded, and, thank Jupiter, she turned and fled. Manius held himself in place as long as he could until he heard her gather her crying child and flee into the night.

The night. It calls to me.

What am I now?

A beast in the night.

A Roman by day.

His body continued changing, but he kept his mind. He knew to show himself as a monster would mean death. Rome did not abide monsters. Yet, he could not abandon his life. He had a home, a wife, a daughter.

Tarentia!

Manius spilled from the homestead and entered the freezing air of the Gallic night. He smelled everything around him and sensed the heartbeat of every creature within a mile. The hunger inside of him was primal, and the strength he felt…

The change in him was glorious. He was more than a mere man now.

Yet he kept his mind. The only way he would ever see his daughter was by being smart. He would travel by day and hunt by night. The enemies of Rome would become his prey as he made his way back to the civilised world.

As he made his way back to his life in Rome. He would live a life of secrecy and shadow, as all of the most powerful men in Rome did. Sulla had had his perversions. Caesar too. This would be his.

Yes, he would make this work. The Lacuscii were primitive Gauls, but he was a Roman. He would use this curse as the gift it was. By day he would live as a man and by night he would be something great and powerful. Nothing would hold him back. Nothing would stop him.

And once he was home, he would pass on this great gift to his wife and child, and future grandchildren. Their bloodline would last until the end of time, purer than the purest patrician. Wolves in sheep's clothing. It was all so clear to him in his animalistic mind. He was a predator now. Smart and strong. Devious and sly. A wolf.

And his only place now was home. Back to his wolfpack.

Back to Rome.

Every night, the streets of the great city would fill with frightened whispers. "Where's the wolf? Where's the wolf?"

Firebug
Michael McBride

Prologue

Twenty Years Ago

"Don't shake it!"

"Why not? It's just a firebug, Amelia. It can't feel anything."

"Yes it can. It feels just like we do. It even has a soul so it can go to heaven."

"That's not true. Who told you that?"

"It's practically a fact, Emma. Look it up in the dictionary."

"Encyclopedia, dummy."

"Mom said not to call me names. And it's a firefly, not a firebug."

"They're beetles, not flies. Besides, Dad says they're 'firebugs.'"

"He also says not to catch them in jars."

"You're not going to tell him, though." The older girl leaned over the edge of the top bunk and glared at her younger sister. "Are you?"

"'Course not. We stick together."

"That's right. Sisters always stick together. Don't forget it."

The older girl shook the jar and set it on the windowsill. A brilliant yellow light flashed from the firefly's rear end as it tapped against the glass.

"What do you think makes it glow, Emma?"

"Probably fire. Why else would people call them firebugs?"

"Fire*flies*. And the color's too pretty for fire. I'll bet that's their souls. All fire does is burn."

I

One Year Ago

Colorado Springs, Colorado
July 22nd

"Damn it, Carol! There's no time to pack!"

She sobbed as she shoved everything of personal value into her suitcase. Jewelry, photo albums, sentimental trinkets. Anything that couldn't be replaced. Her hands shook so badly that most of what she tried to take fell to the floor, which only served to make her cry even harder.

"Listen to me!" Raymond took his wife by the shoulders and turned her to face him. Her eyes were wide and wild. Tears streaked her mascara down her cheeks. He spoke as calmly as he could, carefully enunciating each word. "We need to get out of here right now or we aren't going to make it."

"This is all your fault!" She pounded her fists against his chest, his shoulders. He pulled her close and pinned her against him. Felt the fight drain out of her. "All your…fault…"

"We're going to get through this." He stroked her hair as he whispered into her ear. Struggled to hold her upright. "You and me, Carol. We've made it through hard times and we'll do so again. Right now. Shh. Shh…Right now, though, we have to leave or we won't be able to get out of here at all."

She pushed out of his grasp and grabbed her bag.

He glanced back over his shoulder at the second-story window. Deep black smoke boiled against the sky. He could already see the brilliant glare of the advancing flames, working their way across the valley and up the slope toward his neighbor's house. The fire was chewing through the dry weeds and pines like a runaway thresher.

Raymond turned and ran for the stairs. He caught up with his wife at the bottom. Ushered her toward the door to the garage. Looked back. Everything. Everything for which he had worked so hard. The house. The furniture. The books. The paintings. The pictures of his children. The memories. All of them were going to burn.

Carol opened the door and screamed.

Raymond pulled her away from the garage and slammed the door. He caught a fleeting glimpse of a silhouette in the darkness beside their SUV before it vanished behind the closing door.

It was already too late.

He took his wife by the hand and pulled her toward the sliding glass door in the family room. A carpet of flames swept across the back lawn. He slid the door open and a cloud of smoke billowed into the house. Rushed up the walls. Gathered near the ceiling. He coughed and covered his mouth and nose. Watched the flames race up the posts supporting the balcony above him.

No escape would be found through there.

He heard the wail of sirens in the distance.

Glowing embers gusted into the house, settled upon the carpet, and started to smolder.

Raymond dragged his wife away from the open door.

They ran up the stairs again. Through the living room. Into the foyer and toward the front door. He grasped the knob. Turned. It twisted in his palm but wouldn't open. He put his shoulder into it. Quietly. No give. Harder. A thumping sound that made him cringe. Still no movement. It was somehow sealed from the outside.

The garage door burst inward with the sound of cracking wood. Struck the wall behind it.

Raymond opened the hall closet and shoved Carol inside, down on the floor, below the hanging coats. He ducked down out of the smoke and crawled across the tiled floor. Peeked down the stairs.

The silhouette stood framed in the back door as cinders gusted into its face. It stared through the smoke, the fire reflecting its bulky silver form. He could hear it breathing. Heavy. Labored. Mechanical.

It reached for the handle on the door.

Paused.

Raymond's heart beat so hard in his chest it made his vision tremble.

Slowly, it slid the door closed. A fiery breath of cinders and ashes gusted through the narrowing gap until it latched with a click.

They were going to die in here.

He scurried back to the hall closet. Looked at his wife. So small, crouching there in the shadows. Tears streamed from her closed eyes. Her lips quivered.

Thump.

A heavy boot struck the bottom stair.

Thump.

Another. One step higher.

Raymond ducked into the closet. Pulled the door closed. Softly.

Thump.

Turned the handle until the tongue slid silently into the groove.

Thump.

A creak of the handrail, just on the other side of the wall.

Thump.

He scooted closer to his wife and pulled her into his arms.

Thump.

Smoke crept through the crack beneath the door. Burned his eyes, his throat.

Thump.

He tried not to cough. Kissed his wife's hair.

Thump.

A shadow passed across the gap. The floorboards groaned. Large boots, scored black with carbon. Deep tread. They stopped in front of the door.

Again he heard the mechanical breathing.

Carol whimpered and he pulled her face to his chest. Felt the dampness of her tears. Prayed her death would be quick and merciful.

The shadow passed from beneath the door and Raymond wept in relief.

Maybe they had a chance after all.

The door swung open.

Carol screamed.

II

July 25th

"At times the smoke has been so thick we can't see beyond that ridge over there to the west. Now I want you to look back this way, where you can see the flames rising from the roofs of the houses over the trees. So far, more than a hundred homes have burned and the fire remains zero percent contained..."

"...learned from the National Weather Service that there was no lighting data recorded within the last seven days in this part of Southern Colorado. Priority number one is getting a handle on this fire, but in the backs of their minds, though, they do want to know what started this destructive blaze..."

"...expanded—just within the last few hours—the evacuation zone to include an additional eighteen hundred homes."

"As you can see behind me, these police vehicles racing past—We've just been informed we need to wrap this up and get out of here. Because of these high winds, the fire's moving fast and becoming more and more unpredictable..."

"...investigators suspect arson as now more than one hundred and fifty homes have been consumed by the fire and upwards of thirty-five hundred evacuees remain in shelters around the city. Hotlines have been set up to help..."

"...saddened to report the first confirmed casualties of the blaze as firefighters and relief workers sift through the rubble left in the fire's wake."

III

Four Months Ago

Provo, Utah
March 4th

"You're wasting your time coming all the way down here," the medical examiner said. He was younger than most in his position and much better looking. He applied lip balm with his pinkie while he talked. "There's not a whole lot left to see."

"There's really only one thing I need to see." Special Agent Emma Behrent wore her auburn hair in a ponytail threaded through the back of her FBI ball cap and the customary blue and gold windbreaker and jeans. She carried a Glock 23 .40 caliber in a sling under her left shoulder and a plastic grocery bag in her right hand. "And I should be able to find it regardless of the physical condition of the remains."

"You're the boss. I'm telling you, though, this is by far one of the worst I've seen."

"I appreciate your concern, Dr. Doleman, but you'd be surprised what I've seen in the last eight months."

She followed him down the corridor, past the autopsy suites, and into the morgue. She'd grown accustomed to the smell of formaldehyde and sawed bones, a scent that reminded her of getting a cavity filled as a child, and yet she would never be adequately prepared for the scent that emerged from the locker when the ME opened it and slid the body out on its tray. A cross between thawed, freezer-burnt meat and bloody stool.

Doleman drew back the plastic sheet covering the remains, which came away glistening with greasy, suppurated fluids.

"She's all yours, but don't take too long. I want to get this one done before it gets any riper."

Behrent removed a mini LED Maglite and a stainless steel probe from her jacket pocket and leaned over the body. Carefully, she used the probe to pry the bared teeth apart.

"If you let me know what you're looking for, I'd be happy to help you find it."

She pretended not to hear and directed the beam through the gap she'd created.

"What can you tell me about the physical condition of the decedent?" she asked.

Behrent already knew the woman's name was Cassandra Hopkins and the first responders had arrived at 11:32 p.m. last night to find her horse barn in flames. The neighbor from the adjacent ranch had called 911 eighteen minutes prior, when she first smelled smoke and noticed the orange glow on the horizon. It took less than ten minutes to extinguish the fire and even fewer to find Ms. Hopkins's burnt remains in the wreckage of what remained of one of the rear stables, beneath the charred rubble of the wooden roof. While the fire marshal's report had yet to be released, Behrent had no doubt the fire would be ruled accidental in origin, as she'd seen so many times already.

"Fourth-degree burns over the entirety of her body. Significant eschar on her digits and face. Fixed rigor places her time of death within the last twelve hours. Lack of pustules and hypostasis indicates she was already dead before the fire consumed her. I'd lay odds the cause of death was asphyxiation—the most common cause of fire-related deaths—but until I crack her open, I won't be able to tell you for sure."

"You're saying she was overcome by the smoke?"

"That's how it works. The smoke first makes the victim cough, then, as it intensifies, limits their oxygen intake. As the brain receives less and less oxygen, it passes from dizziness and disorientation to outright loss of consciousness. They're generally dead before the fire reaches them, or at least well on their way."

"Nothing else you can think of that might have caused asphyxiation other than the smoke?"

Behrent pried the teeth as far apart as she could and angled the beam from side to side to better see into the dead woman's blackened throat.

"You can tell by the tissues in her mouth and oropharynx—right there—that she was breathing the smoke. In my field, you quickly learn that the obvious explanation is nearly always the correct one."

"Did you notice the puncture wounds on her wrists and ankles or the ones on her cheeks?"

"Like I said, I have yet to perform a thorough examination."

"Have an obvious explanation for them?"

He made no reply.

"How about the lacerations in the back of the throat?"

She leaned aside so he could see where the light struck the back of the dead woman's throat. The small cuts were barely visible behind the bulge of her desiccated tongue, but were readily apparent as the heat and smoke had caused the edges to darken and peel apart.

"That's not the kind of thing you just *happen* to find. You'd have to know they were there to look for them. What aren't you telling me?"

"Here. You hold her mouth open and I'll show you."

Dr. Doleman took the probe from her and applied traction to the mandible. Behrent opened the plastic bag and removed a canister of whipped cream. Shook it.

Acknowledged the confusion on the ME's face with a half-smile.

Within an hour of Ms. Hopkins's death, Behrent had been on a plane from Las Vegas to Salt Lake City, where a rental car had been ready and waiting to take her down I-15 to Provo. She'd used the time in the air to learn everything she could about Ms. Hopkins, what little there was, anyway. She was a single, twenty-eight year-old horse trainer, who'd never gotten so much as a parking ticket and whose Facebook account was about as uninteresting as they came. She inherited the Whispering Glade Ranch from her grandfather two years earlier and appeared to have no ambition when it came to the business itself. She had been a reasonably attractive woman, in a plain sort of way, with a slender, athletic build, pale white skin, and—most importantly— natural flame-red hair.

"What do you intend to do with that?" the ME asked.

"She may have asphyxiated from the smoke, doctor, but she had a little help."

"What are you talking about?"

"Where are the lights in here?"

"By the door, why…?"

Behrent killed them before he could finish his sentence. A bank of emergency lights on the other side of the morgue remained on, but it was dark enough to see what she'd flown four hundred miles and driven another sixty to see.

She stood beside Doleman, removed the cap from the whipped cream, and inserted the nozzle between the dead woman's teeth.

"Are you familiar with the *Lampyridae* family of beetles?"

"They secrete a toxin called lucibufagin when threatened that can cause hypertension and cardiac symptoms in large quantities, but there've been no reported cases of respiratory symptoms, let alone death, in humans."

"This particular family also has another unique trait. It has a specialized organ in its abdomen called a lantern, in which a combination of enzymes—luciferase and luciferin, specifically—produces a complex chemical reaction that's converted to bioluminescence."

"Fireflies."

"Exactly. And each different species of firefly produces a slightly different reaction so as to create a unique color, but all of them require nitrous oxide to trigger the reaction and oxygen to turn it off. They accomplish this through a specially adapted means of breathing, but it can also be artificially stimulated by other means."

She pressed the nozzle on the canister. Pressurized gas hissed into the victim's mouth and down her throat. The reaction was instantaneous. Green spots glowed from the dead tissue. And faded every bit as quickly.

"What the hell was that?"

"You'll find traces of the lucibufagin toxin in the scratches from the firefly's legs. When it was forced down her throat, it triggered her gag reflex, which made her muscles spasm and start crushing it, squishing out some of the fluid from its abdomen, including its lantern. Just enough for one final glow."

"How does someone force a firefly down another person's throat?"

"He binds their wrists and ankles behind them with barbed wire and wraps it around their jaws so they can't close their mouths."

IV

Yesterday

Colorado Springs, Colorado
July 26th

Behrent sat on the foot of the bed in her room and stared at the patchwork of maps affixed to the wall above the small writing desk. They depicted the American Southwest, from Southern California through New Mexico and Arizona, and north into Nevada, Utah, and Colorado. Dozens of locations were marked with colored pushpins, beside which notes, names, and dates had been scribbled. Once she developed this system, the pattern jumped right out and bit her. Each pin represented an individual death matching her profile: asphyxiation by smoke and fourth-degree burns of a red-haired female in her twenties to early thirties, and each color corresponded to a different season. A blue pin indicated the victim had died during the winter; green during the spring; yellow during the summer; and red during the autumn. Each color was clustered geographically. Blue pins lined the coast from San Diego to Los Angeles. Green pins traced a line from Las Vegas to Salt Lake City. Yellow pins stretched from Denver to Santa Fe and red pins traversed the route from Las Cruces to Phoenix. And each and every one of those pins represented a different year, a single death by fire in each location every year, so few as not to stand out as a statistical anomaly, but more than enough to draw a direct correlation, if you knew what you were looking for.

One victim for each season in an annual cycle that started on the eastern slope of the Rocky Mountains in the summer, headed west through the Sonoran Desert in the fall, followed the Pacific coast in the winter, and completed the circle through the Mojave in the spring.

For six consecutive years.

And no one might ever have made the connection had the man she had come to think of as the Firebug not incinerated a twenty-seven year-old high school teacher in Colorado Springs, Colorado. Her name was Amelia Behrent and her older sister, a Special Agent working out of the field office in Denver, had dismissed her concerns that someone was stalking her three days earlier in what would be the last conversation they ever had.

That was thirteen months ago now, in what would come to be known as the worst summer for wildfires in the history of Colorado after a blaze a month later destroyed more than one hundred and fifty homes, forced the evacuation of more than ten thousand residents, and claimed the lives of a married couple, whose remains were found in a closet where they apparently took refuge in an attempt to flee the smoke.

It was in Amelia's mouth—her little sister's burnt mouth—that the presence of the lucibufagin toxin was first discovered. From the subsequent pathological assays, it was determined that the specific toxin was endemic to one particular species of firefly, *Luciolinae luciola*. A firefly native to Japan. One that had never been encountered on either the North or South American continent. One that could never have found its way into her sister's mouth had someone not forced it inside.

The Japanese firefly averaged approximately an inch in length; however, based on the thin lacerations in the soft tissue, the one that had been inside her sister's oropharynx was closer to two inches, presumably as the result of generations of selective captive breeding. Its lantern glowed an almost fluorescent green, and in traditional Japanese lore, represented the vessel in which the souls of the dead traveled.

The monster who murdered Amelia believed he was capturing the souls of his victims inside the fireflies and then incinerating every trace of evidence.

Or so he thought.

Behrent had discovered his *modus operandi* and had been hunting him ever since, coming closer to him with each passing season. She was slowly getting inside his head, gaining an understanding of how his mind worked, an appreciation for how he selected his victims. She'd studied the final days of each and every one of his victims in as much detail as she could find. They were all single and tended to live a more reclusive lifestyle. They were all routine-oriented, from shopping at the same grocery store on the same day to filling at the same gas station to taking the same routes to and from work at the same times every day. Theirs was a lifestyle of predictability, one that made them easy prey.

That was why Behrent rented this house two months ago, why she'd adopted a fictitious life of her own careful design. She'd gone to great lengths to make herself the most accessible target possible. The house was in an area known as Woodmen Valley, which featured houses on large lots surrounded by a vast wilderness of pines and aspens. The only way in or out of the development by vehicle was through a bottleneck granting ready access to I-25, the main thoroughfare from Denver to Santa Fe, while one could approach nearly invisibly on foot through the dense forest by merely straying from the public recreational trail or the railroad tracks to the east, walking overland from the Air Force Academy to the north, or wending through the newer neighborhoods to the west. She stopped at the same coffee shop at the same time every morning, drove the same stretch of highway across town to the same park where she walked around the same lake before heading to the same ground floor office where she worked at a computer in front of a window through which anyone passing her on the street could see her. She walked to lunch at the same sandwich shop at the same time every day, one clearly visible from two major downtown intersections and the highway, and drove home along the same stretch of highway at the same time, stopping only long enough at the same grocery store to shop for her evening meal, which she made in a kitchen surrounded by windows. As she had every day for the last two months.

The house had a security system that featured views from four exterior cameras she could watch on her laptop day and night, as could the agents posted in another rental house three blocks away. The same agents took turns following her to work in different vehicles and spent their days surveilling her leased office space from another unit on the fourth floor, while she watched the same feeds on her computer and pretended to be an accountant. It was a tedious routine that became more frustrating with the passage of each uneventful day. The only thing keeping her going was the relief from opening the morning paper and discovering that there had been no fire-related fatalities in his summer hunting grounds.

She set her laptop on the nightstand beside her bed and tilted the screen so she could clearly see it with her head on the pillow. Each of the four quadrants showed the same thing they did every night: aspen trees with leaves that shivered in the breeze, pines with swaying boughs, wavering waist-high weeds, clusters of scrub oak, and the seemingly sentient shadows lurking beneath and inside them. She picked up the two-way, battery-powered transceiver from beside it and brought it to her lips.

"Ten o'clock guys," she said. "You know what that means."

"You got everything locked down for sure?" Special Agent Troy Abrams asked from three blocks away, where he watched the same feeds as she did. His partner, SA Warren Young, took the first shift sleeping.

"Crap. I thought you guys were going to lock up."

"That gets funnier every night, Behrent. Anything to report? We're still tracking the same commuter vehicles on this end, but so far they all check out. Just ordinary folks going to and from work at the same time as you. And no one out and about in the neighborhood. You see anything we're missing?"

"Today was the second day in a row there was a jogger at the lake who—"

"Davis Peele. He's a solar engineer for Excel. Nothing about him stands out."

"And the guy at the coffee shop?"

"Neal Alpert. Mortgage broker. Removes his wedding ring in his car every morning before going in. I think he's sweet on you."

"Wonderful. Anything on your end?"

"All's quiet on the western front."

"Do me a favor. See if you can put together a database of car and foot traffic by day of the week. I want to see if there are any patterns there that we might not have recognized."

"We'll see what we can do. You want any company up there tonight?"

"That gets funnier every night, Abrams."

"Get some sleep, princess. Tomorrow promises to be another day like every other."

"One of these days it won't be."

Behrent set the transceiver back on the nightstand. She watched the security cameras around her house and thought about her little sister until sleep finally took her.

V

Nine Months Ago

Tucson, Arizona
October 14th

Behrent clicked on her flashlight and stepped across the threshold where once the front door of the small stucco house had stood. Broken ceramic tiles crunched underfoot. The floorboards were still soft from the sheer quantity of water they'd absorbed. The plaster of the walls had been consumed, exposing the burnt skeletal framework, through which she could see the blackened appliances in the kitchen, the remains of the furniture in the living room, the tiled bathroom, and the nearly unidentifiable furniture in the bedroom. Firefighters had found the victim, a twenty-six year-old leasing agent named Ashley Freeman, in the walk-in closet, where she appeared to have been trapped by a fire that originated in the kitchen.

All that was left of the closet now was a soggy mess of the burnt contents of the fallen shelves toward the rear. She nudged through them with the toe of her shoe. She didn't know what she hoped to accomplish by coming out here. Maybe a part of her hoped she might stumble upon something the firemen and the fire inspector missed. She knew deep down, though, that if anything had ever been here, if the fire hadn't destroyed it, then the high-pressure hoses had. Or maybe she just needed the right setting to put her in the proper frame of mind to contemplate the profile Behavioral had generated for her.

Their unknown subject was a Caucasian male in his mid- to late-thirties. There was nothing extraordinary about his appearance, one way or the other. He would have stood apart from the crowd while stalking them if he was anything other than unexceptional, which excluded his having red hair himself. He was of average height and unthreatening build, and above-average intellect. His was a white-collar job that required significant travel or lengthy periods of relocation. Behrent had initially suspected a trucker or someone in the interstate shipping business as his hunting grounds followed the course of the major highway routes: I-5 up the coast of California, I-15 and I-70 through Nevada and Utah, I-25 from Colorado to New Mexico, and I-10 and I-8 back through Arizona to Los Angeles, each chosen by the season when a death by fire would be least likely to stand out and betray his pattern.

The sadistic nature of the barbed wire bondage suggested both sexual and emotional dysfunction. Binding their wrists and ankles behind their backs was meant to make them feel utterly helpless; his way of demonstrating his control over them when he believed he was in control of so little else in his life. The barbed wire itself was more than a means of ensuring they wouldn't be able to move or close their mouths, it was to deliberately inflict the greatest amount of pain on a category of victim that represented a female in his life who had wronged him in some way. An ex-lover or object of his affections who spurned his advances. A person in a position of trust from his childhood who abused that relationship, possibly a teacher or family friend. Someone who manipulated his emotions and made him feel physically inadequate.

Maybe it was that association that had drawn him subconsciously to fire in the first place, a correlation between the red hair and the flames or its indomitable will and that of the person who imposed hers upon him.

It was that fascination with fire that stood out most. Something about its destructive and irresistible nature spoke to him on a primal level. Perhaps it was the way that fire killed in an almost merciful manner before violently consuming its victims; a dichotomous aspect of its nature that reminded him of himself. He knew it intimately, respected it to a degree that could almost be classified as worship. And he understood its actions under various environmental conditions and how to control it to such a degree as to make its origin appear accidental, how to bend the flames to his will. The profile suggested his affinity dawned at an early age and he'd chosen a career path that allowed him to work with it from a distance, in potentially some form of research or investigatory capacity, some job that allowed him to further develop his relationship with it, to hone his ability to control it, rather than putting him in a position of having to destroy it. On some level he resented and abhorred firefighters, which would make him want to spend as little time in their presence as possible and his interactions with them strained, if not downright hostile.

And then there were the fireflies, which he had somehow romanticized. Theirs was a fire of their own creation that they could turn on and off at will, one that could only be extinguished in death, one that it used to attract its most suitable mate. Perhaps that was what he was trying to do on some level, attempting to win over the woman who rebuked him or to catch the eye of the one who never noticed him. Or maybe he really believed he was capturing the souls of his victims inside their abdominal lanterns. Whatever the case, his use of the Japanese species reflected a westernized, literal interpretation of the mythology that suggested his knowledge came from books rather than from firsthand experience.

Yet none of that knowledge brought Behrent any closer to finding the man who murdered her sister.

She kicked the moldering pile of debris and screamed in frustration.

A light snapped on in the window of the house next door. Its fence was scored with carbon and the bushes lining it were brown and wilted.

She clicked off her flashlight and stared up into the night sky. The stars made her feel even more insignificant than she already felt. She'd discounted her sister's fears and allowed her to be killed and then let another innocent woman die because she couldn't catch the man who did it. At this point, she didn't even know where to begin. He'd been doing this for so long now that he had it down to a science and she had only just figured out that he existed at all.

Behrent stepped out of the scorched wooden framework of the closet, no better off than she'd been when she arrived. She caught movement from the back yard.

Stopped.

Her right hand found the butt of her Glock.

At first she thought she'd seen flashlights at a distance, but that couldn't possibly be the case with the fence less than thirty feet away. She walked across the cracked pavestones and the flooded ornamental rock garden to where a half-dozen blinking golden lights swirled around a bird fountain.

It was the same kind she and her sister used to catch when they were children. They hadn't called them fireflies in Colorado back then.

They'd called them firebugs.

VI

Today

Colorado Springs, Colorado
July 27th

Behrent surreptitiously watched the passersby on the sidewalk over her computer monitor. She recognized the regulars by now, but not well enough to feel confident that one of them wasn't her guy. Even the dogs they walked could be props. In a neighborhood like this, a man fitting the Firebug's profile would blend in just about perfectly. Assuming she'd even done enough to attract his attention. And there was still the chance that after spending so much time stalking her sister he'd recognized her right off the bat. She and Amelia hadn't looked as similar as a lot of sisters she knew, but they did look enough alike that there was no mistaking the resemblance if they stood side-by-side.

Amelia.

There were so many things Behrent wished she'd done differently. So many things she wished she'd had the chance to say. Most of all, she wished she could hear her sister's voice, her laugh, if only one last time. All she could do now was make sure that this monster didn't kill again, and even that was starting to feel like a hopeless proposition.

She'd gone through every case file so many times she could almost recite them by heart. She knew the names of all twenty-three of his victims, knew nearly as much about them as their mothers did. There was nothing to link them together outside of their physical similarities and their geographical locations. She'd pulled on every possible string she could think to pull, from first boyfriends to jilted lovers to coworkers and neighbors with criminal records. She'd looked into nearly every interstate sales and distribution firm and thousands of their employees. She'd beaten her head against every possible wall in hopes of making the breakthrough that eluded her. If she hadn't done enough to attract him, then he was just going to keep on killing until she figured out another way to stop him. And the blame for every death hereafter would fall squarely on her shoulders.

This was her one best chance and she knew it. If he'd seen her here and then saw her three months from now outside of Phoenix, he'd make her in a heartbeat. And if he went to ground, there would be nothing they could do about it until he popped back up on their radar.

If he ever did.

He was nothing if not patient, which in many ways marked him as unique among serial killers. Most enjoyed periods of escalation, during which their bloodlust became so insatiable they accelerated their timetables and took risks they might not ordinarily take. This was when they were most likely to be caught. Yet not once had her unsub given in to his primal urges and broken from his pattern. Not once had he taken a victim out of season. His restraint bordered on superhuman. To think that not once had he slipped...

Behrent tapped her fingernails on her desk as she stared out the window. A woman in spandex jogged past behind a stroller.

What if he *had* slipped and they simply hadn't noticed?

She closed her eyes and tried to follow that elusive line of thought. If he'd taken another victim who fit the profile, she would have caught it right away. She'd searched every fire-related death across the country during the past six years so as not to see only what she wanted to see. Approximately 2,500 people died every year in residential fires, the majority of them children under four and adults over sixty-five. She opened her eyes. What if he only picked off a victim here or there, just enough to keep the demons at bay?

Behrent logged into the U.S. Fire Administration database on her laptop. What if she factored out those age groups, as well as the most common at-risk groups? Smoking was the leading cause of fire-related deaths and alcohol use was the single greatest contributing factor. African and Native Americans represented the greatest cross-section of fatalities, as did people who lived in rural areas and prefabricated homes. She limited it to the previous year, filtered out all of those factors, and initiated a search.

Still more than six hundred deaths.

She broke it down further into just the six southwestern states.

Forty-eight.

January through March. California.

Five deaths. She read the brief summaries. A fifty-six year-old female in Sherman Oaks died after improperly stored linseed oil caught fire. A seventeen year-old male in Sacramento while attempting to make a pipe bomb in his garage. Moira O'Reilly, victim number eighteen. Two twenty-four year-old males in Barstow in a meth lab.

March through June. Nevada and Utah.

Four deaths. A forty-three year-old male and twenty-six year-old female in a one-car accident that resulted in the gas tank exploding. A sixty-three year-old female in Reno who failed to put out a grease fire. Natalie Wilkins, victim number nineteen.

June through September. Colorado and Arizona.

Five deaths. Amelia Behrent—her baby sister— victim number twenty. Four fatalities associated with the

Mountain Vista Fire, which burned more than a hundred and fifty homes and forced the evacuation of nearly ten thousand people: two volunteer firefighters—a fifty-one year-old male from Saguache and a twenty-eight year-old male from Lincoln, Nebraska—and a forty-eight year-old male and forty-seven year-old female, whose remains were discovered in the rubble of their home within the evacuation zone.

She looked out the window again. At the mail carrier walking down the opposite side of the street with his bag over his shoulder. At the teenage girl who managed to juggle a Starbucks cup, a cell phone, and a purse, while carrying a dog that looked more like a rodent. At the lengthening shadows of the trees stretching across the road.

A middle-age couple who stayed in their home even as the fire consumed the houses surrounding them and the air filled with smoke.

The worst summer for wildfires in the history of the state.

She tapped her nails on the desk again.

Opened a new window and initiated a search. Their names were Raymond and Carol Waldon and their remains were found in what was left of their house at 136 Ponderosa Lane, near the theorized source of the fire. All sixteen houses on their street burned to the ground before the first emergency responders arrived on the scene. The majority of their neighbors had been at work, but those who were at home when the flames swept up the slope of dry grass and shrubs claimed to have smelled the smoke with enough time to hurriedly pack and evacuate before they saw the first hint of fire. Even their retired neighbors managed to flee before their houses were gutted. Only Raymond and Carol Waldon remained to watch the fire rise up like a tsunami and crash down upon their home. Only Raymond and Carol, the local franchisee of a national insurance company and his wife, organizer of an annual 5K race to benefit breast cancer research.

Behrent stared at their pictures on the screen. Maybe Raymond was past his prime, but looked like the kind of guy who jogged in the morning and spent his weekends on the links. Carol was obviously a runner and still in the kind of shape she enjoyed flaunting in tennis shorts and spandex. These weren't the kind of people who were generally the first to be overcome by smoke, nor were they the kind who had all of their money tied up in their physical possessions. They were undoubtedly so well insured they could have walked away from their incinerated house better off for it. So what caused them to stay in their house while those around them fled? Why were a businessman and a socialite both home on a weekday anyway?

Behrent pulled her cell phone from her purse and dialed a number she knew by heart.

"We're knocking off early today, boys," she said. "There are a couple of stops I want to make on the way home."

She hung up and stared through the window. A man stood beside the thick trunk of an elm across the street, staring right back at her. The hood of his sweatshirt was drawn down low so she couldn't see his eyes, only the smile that formed on his lips when he caught her looking.

A UPS truck emerged from the corner of her vision.

When it passed, the man was gone.

VII

"I'm telling you," Behrent said. "He was there."

Young flashed through a series of menus on his tablet as they hiked up the steep path between the new growth of aspens and willows and scrub oaks that were barely taller than they were. Only the occasional chunk of blackened wood or scorched earth showed through the grass and weeds as a reminder of the devastation. A year ago, this entire valley, right up through the foothills and into the Rockies, had burned for nearly two weeks straight. She remembered news footage of smoke so thick you could barely see the headlights of cars, policemen in respirators directing traffic with glowing embers settling on their shoulders, firefighters with black faces and goggles chopping down acres of forest in a rushed effort to build a firebreak while the same violent wind that fanned the flames hurled ashes and cinders into their faces, cars lined bumper-to-bumper on all of the roads leading away from a mountain made of flames. It was the kind of nightmare that would have scarred her, were she not already completely overwhelmed by the grief of losing her sister in such a horrific manner only weeks before.

"I can access the security footage from here and you can see for yourself," Young said. He was as broad as he was tall and wore his blond hair buzzed short. He'd left his cap and windbreaker in the car, but his physique and bearing still screamed law enforcement, if his sunglasses didn't give him away first. Abrams waited with the cars at the foot of the trail, simultaneously scrutinizing the traffic wending upward into the neighborhood and filing his report for the day's surveillance. "Right about quarter to one, you say?"

"12:43. I made sure to note the time."

He passed her the tablet and she selected the quadrant that gave her the best chance of seeing the man she positively knew had been there. The camera was positioned in such a way as to focus on the sidewalk in front of the office building and anyone who so much as slowed to look at her through the window. The cars parked at the meters along the curb were clearly visible, as was the asphalt beyond them. Traffic passed in colored blurs. She could read the license plates of the cars parked diagonally across the street and hints of the opposite sidewalk between them. She saw just the thinnest strip of grass at the top of the screen, the very bottoms of the trunks of the elms, and the uneven earth from which their thick roots snaked. She located the tree behind which the man had stood and watched it clear up until the brown blur of the UPS truck eclipsed it.

"I'm sorry, Behrent. If he was there, we didn't get him."

"What do you mean 'if'?"

He held up his hands when she rounded on him.

"No offense. It's just that we've been running through this same routine for so long we're starting to look for things that might not be there, you know? All of us, Behrent. Abrams and I both feel like we're projecting what we want to see rather than observing what we actually do see."

Behrent backed up the recording and played it again. She watched the very top edge of the screen and nothing else. A shadow appeared on the grass. It moved ever so slightly, but not in time with those of the branches of the trees. A brown blur. When it passed, the shadow was gone.

"Watch the very top of the recording." She passed the tablet back to him. "Then tell me I'm seeing things."

"Emma…"

She tried to recreate his image in her mind, but the harder she concentrated, the more elusive he became. All she clearly remembered was the hood of his sweatshirt drawn low over his brow so that his eyes remained in shadow. She remembered a lower face like any other and a smile unlike any she'd ever seen before. It was the kind of smile that belied the expression, the kind that would haunt her until her dying breath.

It was predatory.

Evil.

The trail wound back to the north and granted her a magnificent view of the valley. A dry streambed lined with saplings cut through the bottom. It was clogged with charcoaled chunks of trees that had run downward from the higher country. Grasses that shimmered golden in the afternoon sun lined the northeastern slope. Ripples raced upward toward the houses perched on the crest with each gust of wind.

The fire started somewhere down there and ran uphill through the dry grass, growing taller as it gained momentum. In a matter of minutes, it crowned the knoll, consumed the hedges, and sped across the lawns. By the time all was said and done, one hundred and fifty-three houses had burned to the ground and there was a great black stain upon the mountains large enough to be seen from space. As no source of the fire had been identified, the investigation had turned to arson. The case remained open.

Behrent imagined a man with his hood drawn over his eyes standing downhill in the shadows of the mature pines. He held something silver in his hand. A flick of his wrist and it produced flame. He smiled at her and touched the flame to the crisp mat of dead leaves and pine needles and vanished into the smoke as the wind accelerated the flames up the hillside toward the conspicuous gap amid the new construction.

She broke away from the trail and ascended through the spear grass and yuccas and cacti. The topsoil was crisp with windswept charcoal and crunched underfoot. She stopped in what had once been the back yard of the Waldon house and stared downhill. The way the wind blew, she could almost see the exact path the fire had taken. A total distance of maybe a hundred yards and it would have been visible the entire time. It looked like it would have reached the neighboring house to the north first, then followed the topography right across the back of Raymond and Carol Waldon's.

"Abrams just received the coroner's report," Young said. "He's forwarding it now."

Behrent nodded as she surveyed the neighborhood. The houses to either side of her were brand new and composed of brick and stone with ceramic-tiled roofs. Same with the ones across the street. Only this one lot had yet to be built upon, presumably because the insurance guarantor was tied up in court battling being held to the full payout for an expensive home that was only going to be inherited by the Waldons's children and resold for a profit while the company was stuck with the tab.

The house had been razed, but the foundation remained intact. She could see where the garden level main floor opened onto the yard. There would have been a door and windows giving right onto the yard. The fire would have been clearly visible through any of them. The black nubs of the posts that once supported a balcony framed the patio. There'd been a fireplace off of the family room and a door accessing the three-car garage, now a cracked apron collecting puddles of water. Another concrete pad spread across the leveled hillside where the kitchen and formal living room had once been. She walked around to the front steps and tried to find where the foyer closet in which the Waldons died had been. She stood inside what remained of the frame and turned in a circle.

The fire had rushed uphill toward the back of the house. There would have been no hope if fleeing in that direction. That left the garage door and the front door, both of which opened on the complete opposite side of the house from the flames. Why had they not gone out either, and instead chosen to hide where she stood now? Raymond had underwritten enough insurance policies to know that there was absolutely no percentage in trying to save his physical possessions and that the most important thing for anyone to do in case of a fire was get the hell out of the building.

"Here we go. You want the husband or the wife first?"

"The husband."

"Decedent: Raymond Leonard Waldon. Autopsy: ECCS070113-06C. Autopsy authorized by Dr. William Gustafson for the El Paso County Coroner's Office. Identified by dental records. Rigor: absent. Livor: purple to black. Distribution: left ankle, hip, and shoulder. Age: forty-eight. Race—"

"Skip ahead to the findings."

"External Examination: Fourth-degree burns with significant eschar development cover ninety to ninety-five percent of the surface area. The remaining five to ten percent have second- to third-degree burns and represent the points of contact with the ground. No pustule formation. The third through fifth digits on the right hand and the lateral four digits on each foot are absent. No indication of traumatic amputation."

Bahrent listened as she walked through what was left of the house. She kicked at detritus that had blown into corners and inspected anything left of the original construction, no matter how small or burnt.

"X-rays: Total body x-rays demonstrate heat-induced patina fractures of the calvarium and skull base and transverse fractures of bilateral scapulae and ilia. A fracture of the right ulnar styloid process appears perimortem. As do the penetrating injuries to the cortices and cancellous bony surfaces of the bilateral radii and ulnae, and tibiae and fibulae, and, to a lesser degree, the occipital bones."

"Son of a bitch," Behrent said. "This was our guy, all right. But what made him break his pattern to go after these people?"

"Do you want me to keep going?"

"Skip ahead to cause of death."

"Asphyxiation."

"Manner of death?"

"Accidental."

"Disposition of the remains?"

"Cremation."

"Damn it. Any further mention of the non-heat-induced fractures?"

"They found them buried under the second story of the house, Behrent."

She knelt, brushed through a pile of detritus that had accumulated in a corner of the foundation on the main floor, and extricated a twisted length of rusted metal. Rolled it over in her palm. Wiped it off with her shirt. Held it up to the sun and inspected it. It was maybe an inch long, all told. Coiled twice in the center and sharp on either end. No doubt about it.

It was a barb from a length of barbed wire fencing.

VIII

"I'm Douglas Waldon." The twenty-five year-old broker extended his hand. He was the eldest child of Raymond and Carol and looked like a miniature version of his father. "How can I help you?"

Behrent shook his hand and used it to guide him away from the assistant who'd fetched him from his office.

"Can we talk in private?"

His expression was one of confusion, but he gestured toward the office door and allowed her to lead the way. She was already seated when he closed the door and took his seat on the opposite side of the desk from her.

"What can I do for you, Miss…"

"Behrent." She flashed her badge. "Special Agent Behrent. I have some questions I hope you'll be able to answer for me."

"Sure. If I can."

His face and posture were both open. No sign of deception in either. He was a recent graduate of the business school at the University of Northern Colorado and had been in process of completing his training at the corporate headquarters of the agency franchisor when his parents died. Now he was the inheritor of more than just his father's job.

The office had obviously belonged to his father, as well. While the framed picture of his desk was of an attractive brunette about Douglas's age and his diplomas and certifications adorned the walls, the remaining framed pictures on the wall were of his father with various people Behrent didn't recognize.

She'd learned on the drive over that the fire had nearly crippled Douglas on a personal level. The loss of his parents was compounded by the losses of his clients.

Having to deal with so many families whose entire lives had gone up in smoke inside their burnt homes, all of their tears, and all of their condolences had driven him to the point of discreetly trying to sell the office and seeking psychiatric care.

The last thing she wanted to do was to tell him that she believed his parents' deaths hadn't ben accidental.

"This is a regional office," Behrent said. "Is that right?"

"Yes, this is the base of operations for the southwestern region. We handle the insurance needs of roughly two million people out of offices in six different states, including the southern half of California."

"Who runs those offices?"

"Managing partners who essentially enter into a subcontract agreement. Our overall percentage is relatively small compared to what the parent company makes, especially considering we bear the brunt of the risk." He paused. "Can I ask what this is all about?"

She'd come prepared with a story.

"We're investigating fraud in an industry with a similar organizational structure and we're looking for a better understanding of the overall functionality and accountability." He nodded as though the explanation made a certain amount of sense. "So what I want to know is how you oversee all of these managing partners, how you make sure they toe your line."

"We have weekly managerial meetings via FaceTime and bi-annual organizational retreats."

"That doesn't sound like a whole lot of supervision."

"We invest a lot of time into researching our prospective partners and limit our appointments to only those agencies we've identified as having long-term growth and profit potential. We're not only accountable to our partners and our clients, but to our parent company and its shareholders. As such, we also employ a regional supervisor who serves as our proxy and performs monthly physical and financial audits to ensure that both image and accountability are in compliance with corporate standards."

A tingling sensation passed through Behrent's abdomen.

"This proxy physically travels to each of the individual offices once a month?"

She had to concentrate to regulate her breathing.

"He's on the road two weeks out of the month. It's a good thing we're paying for the car and not the mileage."

"And which states are in your region?"

"Arizona, Southern California, Colorado, Nevada, New Mexico, and Utah."

Her mouth was dry, her palms damp.

"I wonder if it would be possible to talk to this proxy."

"I'm sure Wes would be happy to help you out. He's one of the nicest guys on the planet. He's still on the road, though. You want me to give you his cell phone number?"

"Sure, but I'll probably just wait for him to get back." She attempted a smile. "How long has he been with the company?"

"I don't know for sure. Five, six years? He's been here since before I came on."

The ground tilted underneath her.

"Is he in any of these pictures?"

Her heartbeat.

Thupp-thupp. Thupp-thupp. Thupp-thupp.

"Yeah, that's him up there with my dad and John Elway."

Blood rushing in her ears.

She stood and leaned closer to the picture. Three smiling men in suits in a luxury box at Sports Authority Stadium. Two of them she recognized, but it wasn't until she reached up and covered the upper half of the third man's face that she recognized him, too.

"What did you say his name was again?"

"Wes. Wes Moore."

IX

The ranch-style house was located on five heavily wooded acres northeast of town. It was built in the late seventies and showed its age. The majority of the driveway was gravel, and weeds grew from the cracks in the concrete apron by the garage. There were blackout blinds over every window and it was impossible to tell whether or not there was a car in the garage. Despite the younger Waldon's insistence that Wes Moore was still out of town and the GPS in his company Explorer showed its current location to be in eastern Utah, Behrent knew what she had seen and wasn't prepared to take any chances.

CSPD officers had every road into and out of the area closed off and secured. Moore's immediate neighbors had been evacuated and were currently under federal protection and Young's supervision, although so far none of them used anything other than kind words when asked about Mr. Moore. Snipers had taken up position in the ponderosa pines and SWAT teams were prepared to go through the front and back doors on her mark. She and Abrams wore Kevlar vests beneath their fire-retardant gear and were prepared to follow SWAT through the front door. Behrent knew that her evidence was circumstantial at best and that she wasn't the only person who'd climbed out onto a limb on this takedown, but she'd be the one who took the fall if it failed. Were it not for the fact that Moore had potentially caused the most destructive fire in the history of the state and cost the community more than forty million dollars in firefighter expenses, there was no way any judge would have executed the warrant. That he'd been one of Raymond Waldon's weekend golf buddies probably played a considerable role, too.

This was her one and only shot.

A miss, and Moore likely walked, free and clear.

If he was even the man she'd seen for the briefest of moments across the street.

Her transceiver crackled.

"On your mark, Special Agent Behrent."

From where she knelt roughly a hundred yards away behind a stand of junipers, she could barely see the house, let alone the men with Heckler & Koch MP5 submachine guns and full tactical gear hidden in the bushes, prepared to converge on either door on her go. A single knock and either Moore opened the door or they knocked it down and went in hard and fast through the smoke and blinding glare of a flashbang.

"You sure about this?" Abrams whispered. "We don't get a do-over on this one."

Behrent drew a deep breath and blew it out slowly to steady her nerves. Her hands shook and she could barely think over the thrum of her heartbeat. She rolled her head on her neck. Was she sure? If she was wrong, her sister's murderer would remain on the streets to kill again.

And again.

She stared at the house through the maze of trees.

She'd never been more certain of anything in her life.

She pressed the button on her transceiver.

"I want him taken alive."

A half-dozen men in black materialized from the forest, streaking toward the front door.

She readjusted her grip on her Glock.

One raised his fist and pounded on the door. Stepped back. Paused. Two others moved in front of him, a battering ram held between them. They drew it back, swung it forward—

A blinding light.

Behrent barely had time to raise her arm to shield her eyes. A wall of heated air struck her and tossed her backward onto the ground. She heard a thunderous crack, then nothing over the ringing in her ears.

She opened her eyes and looked up to find the branches above her burning. Pine needles curled and blackened and rained down to the forest floor. She tried to stand. Couldn't. She was on her back, her fire-retardant jacket smoldering on her chest.

The high-pitched tone in her head toyed with her vision. Her balance.

She fought to her feet. Swayed. Stumbled forward. Fell to her knees. Grabbed her two-way from the ground. Shouted into the microphone.

"The place was rigged to blow! Everyone's dead!"

Pushed herself to her feet. Staggered toward the house.

The bushes and weeds all around her were on fire. As were the body parts scattered across the dirt between them. She couldn't hear the crackle of the flames or her own voice as she shouted for survivors. Only the infernal hum.

One of the snipers dangled from a fiery pine by the cord he'd used to secure himself. His entire body still burned. Even his skin.

A hand on her shoulder.

She screamed. Turned around. Thrust her pistol into Abrams's face.

His face was black with soot and blood flowed freely from a gash across his hairline. His nostrils and lips were caked with ash. He pinched his eyes shut tight. Steadied himself against her shoulder. Opened his eyes and pointed at his ear.

She nodded her understanding and made a sweeping gesture toward the ground. Judging by the expression on his face, he obviously hadn't seen what had happened to the SWAT team yet.

Both raised their weapons and advanced toward the house. The smoke grew thicker and the heat intensified. The detritus underfoot served as the perfect fuel for the fire, which raced across the forest floor in every direction.

Behrent struggled with the realization that the front door had been rigged with explosives. She'd never considered the possibility. For her lack of foresight, sixteen men had paid with their lives.

There was a crater where the front door had been and the flaming roof had collapsed onto the living room. Glass from the shattered windows twinkled like rubies. The garage door was buckled outward far enough to see the rear bumper and tires of an SUV inside.

Behrent coughed and buried her mouth and nose in the crook of her left arm, which did little to spare her the smoke. She could barely see her Glock in her extended right hand through the smoke, which obscured the house, save for the flames burning from the impromptu entrance.

The heat was hellacious, like nothing she'd ever experienced before. It singed what little hair had come untucked from beneath her cap and made her eyes water so badly she could hardly keep them open. She choked and coughed and felt the dry smoke invade her lungs. It swirled on the waves of heat, revealing just the hint of a living room full of furniture burned to the bare wooden framework before hiding it once more.

Beneath the ringing she heard the faintest roar of the inferno, so loud in actuality that it reverberated in her chest. She felt Abrams's shoulder against hers and drew strength from his proximity.

The smoke funneled through the back of the kitchen, where she could only assume the back door had once been. The doors must have been rigged to blow together. The appliances were crumpled, and smoldering and melted glass had fused to the linoleum.

There was a hallway to the right, past the stairs leading down through the smoke and into the basement. She shouted directly into Abrams's ear for him to guard them while she cleared a guest bedroom that had been converted into a home office and a master bedroom that looked like something out of a catalogue. Only actively burning. Wherever he slept, it wasn't in there.

"Watch the smoke!" Abrams shouted into her ear when she returned to the head of the stairs.

It took her a moment to see what he meant. The smoke neither moved up nor down the staircase; it merely filled the space between the walls on the landing below.

There was no airflow.

The fires burning all around them were drawing air through the blast holes, through the broken windows, down the flue from the chimney. She could positively feel it rushing past her, feeding the flames that would soon consume this entire structure.

The basement was sealed.

Behrent nodded to Abrams and started down. One step at a time. Holding her breath in an effort not to cough, which made her chest lurch. She followed her pistol down to the landing, then around to the flight leading into the basement.

The door at the bottom and the surrounding wall were covered with blown insulation secured by a layer of foil. The door itself had a pressurized seal and a wide handle and reminded her of the kind they manufactured for industrial coolers. It made a popping sound when she pulled it open.

The air screamed around the seal and past her face, sending her cap bounding up the stairs. She braced her feet and lowered her shoulder to absorb the impact with the door, which nearly knocked her to the ground.

She stepped out of the way and it slammed into the wall hard enough to embed the handle in the drywall.

Behrent stared into the unblemished darkness with cool air that smelled of damp earth buffeting her in the face.

Sighted down the barrel of her Glock.

Swallowed hard to stifle a cough.

And advanced into the pitch black.

X

The rushing sound of blood in her ears metered the high-pitched ringing.

She swiveled from left to right, praying to see anything at all. Her sense of hearing was shot and she couldn't see a blasted—

A beam of light streaked across the basement from the mini-Maglite in Abrams's hand as he pulled the door shut behind them, sealing off the smoke and the flames. He flashed it quickly from one side of the basement to the other, then more slowly back again.

Insulation that had to be several feet thick covered the walls and the only windows were sealed with metal sheets screwed into the frames. Skeletal framework cast long, thin shadows across the floor leading up to what she at first mistook for an indoor garden.

Carefully tended bonsai trees and ferns grew from a rich medium of black soil and sphagnum moss. Running water flowed along the ground between them in a wide, winding oval shape, in the center of which was a small pond with stagnant water and lily pads. Abrams shined his beam down into it and inch-long nymphs wriggled down under the rocks.

Behrent took him by the wrist and raised his arm so the beam pointed into the trees. There were large beetles everywhere. Crawling up the trunks and on the branches, on the undersides of the leaves and all over one another. She leaned over and touched one with her index finger.

Its hind end emitted a greenish glow as it took to flight.

The response spread through the startled fireflies until the entire room lit up like it had been strung with Christmas lights.

She shuddered at the thought of what Moore intended to do with them.

There was a lone egress behind the habitat. Another freezer door set into the insulated wall. Abrams's beam focused on the handle as they worked their way around the habitat and the banks of lights and filters that serviced it. Behrent reached it first and closed her hand around it.

Cool to the touch.

Abrams shined the beam around the seams. No indication of tripwires or other rigging. They could easily be on the other side, though.

Along with her sister's murderer.

Behrent pantomimed for Abrams to step to the opposite side of the door while she swung it outward toward her. He'd go through low while she came high around the open door.

She held up five fingers.

Four fingers.

Three.

She finished the count silently while Abrams watched her lips.

Two.

Adjusted her grip on the handle with her left. The Glock with her right.

One.

Pulled the handle. Fought the suction. Felt the release. Swung the door wide open.

A blur of darkness as Abrams ducked around the wall and across the threshold.

Behrent shouldered past the rebounding door and registered a flickering reflection from the wall of glass at the back of the room. Smelled a petrochemical accelerant. Raised her Glock. Shouted for Abrams.

He turned to his right. Brought his pistol around.

Too slowly.

She saw another reflection on what she recognized as a trophy case, the reflection of a man in shimmering silver. He stepped forward from around the corner and the nozzle of a flamethrower appeared, a tongue of fire protruding it. Mere inches from Abrams's head.

The expulsion of flames was blinding. A molten liquid wrapped around his skull and filled the doorway. He screamed and threw himself to the ground. Covered his head with his arms, which only started to burn, too.

Deep black smoke billowed through the doorway as Behrent shoved through, bringing her weapon to bear on the golden face shield of the silver fire entry suit. She saw her distorted reflection in it. The flames burning up the wall behind her. Her wild eyes. The barrel of her Glock.

Searing heat encircled her abdomen. Her skin blistered and her clothes ignited.

She screamed and pulled the trigger.

The pistol bucked.

A black hole appeared in the golden mask. Cracks spread away from it.

A starburst of blood spattered the wall behind the silver hood.

The report was deafening.

The impact lifted the man from his feet. Slammed him against the wall. He lost his grip on the flamethrower and the molten rainbow splashed across the floor toward the glass case. He toppled to the ground with the clanking sound of the tanks on his back striking the concrete.

Behrent fell to her hands and knees in front of him, her entire midsection engulfed in fire.

She screamed as the pain took root beneath her skin.

Fell to her chest. Rolled over and over. Smothered the flames. Ignited the nerve endings.

Struggled to all fours. Crawled toward the man slumped against the wall in his silver fire entry suit. Pulled off the hood. Looked into his eyes. One was bloody and misshapen and fringed with bone shards; the other barely acknowledged her before rolling upward under the lid. Blood ran down his cheek and dripped from his chin.

"Not yet!" she screamed and crawled back out through the doorway. Every muscle in her abdomen and lower back sang in pain. Fluid dripped from burns that felt as though they'd eaten clear through her. An icy sensation crept upward from her toes. "You don't get to die yet!"

She found what she needed and dragged herself back to where the liquid fire spread across the floor toward the trophy case. Crawled into the murderer's lap. Felt his legs tremble. Pulled herself up his chest. Opened his one good eye as wide as it would go. The iris slowly rolled down until she saw the pupil and the fading light in its depths.

Behrent held up the object so he could see it. Watched its reflection as revelation dawned, before being eclipsed by sheer terror.

Epilogue

Colorado Springs, Colorado
August 3rd

Behrent sat on the back porch of her rented house, watching the shadows of the trees lengthen across the mat of brown needles and leaves. The first stars twinkled through the upper canopy of the pines even as the crimson sun set behind the Rockies on the other side of her house. The night air felt divine in her lungs, and even better against the skin underneath her T-shirt. For a while she thought she might never feel anything other than pain again. The doctors assured her the skin grafts were healing nicely, although they still had a patchwork look to them. Not that she was complaining. Abrams had gotten the worst of it and it would be months before what was left of his face would be healed enough to even attempt a graft. Longer still before he'd be released from the plastic isolation chamber in the burn unit. He served as a daily reminder of just how lucky she'd been.

Weston Franklyn Moore wasn't quite as fortunate. He hadn't been able to reach the escape tunnel from the back room in the basement, which would have allowed him to pop up outside of the police cordon and vanish forever. No one was entirely certain whether he'd stuck around to finish off his pursuit or to protect his case full of trophies. Likely, no one ever would. As it was, the teams from Behavioral had their hands full trying to make sense of everything they found down there, including an altar of sorts to his father—a firefighter who died in the line of duty—he'd built back in the trees surrounding the small pond, and the decomposed remains unearthed from the fertile soil filled with firefly cocoons. The working theory was that they belonged to Moore's stepmother, who'd married his father after his mother's death, when he was a child. While the results of DNA analysis were still pending, the pictures of her they were able to find showed a woman of the same approximate height and bone structure, natural red hair, and a string of Japanese characters tattooed above her left breast. It took a matter of minutes to translate the word "Firefly," but the implications would forever be the subject of speculation. As would his reasons for killing Carol and Raymond Waldon—his longtime friend and employer—who could easily have stumbled upon a picture and an insect in the glove compartment or a fire entry suit in the trunk of the company-leased vehicle and innocently enough asked why they were there.

The trophies in the case, however, were self-explanatory. There were more than fifty pictures, dating back to the early-nineties, pinned to a giant sheet of corkboard behind the glass. Pictures of red-haired women from all across the country. Pictures taken from a distance and enlarged so that their faces were clearly visible as they struck a specific pose, one in which they were photographed looking back over their left shoulders at the camera.

And pinned in the center of each one was a firefly.

There was no doubt that the DNA collected from the microscopic bits of human tissue excised from the sharp tips of their feet would match that of the victims whose mouths they had been inside, even if it was impossible to compare them to the lacerations.

No one even thought to look for the cuts in the back of Moore's throat, however. Nor did they compare the crescent-shaped wounds on the backs of her fingers to his teeth. They hadn't thought twice about the non-functioning flashlight Behrent had commandeered from her partner or connected it to the melted batteries fused to the concrete. They'd even kept it safe for her in the

ER with the rest of her belongings. By the time she transferred its lone contents—the firefly she'd crawled to the habitat to collect, even as she burned—into a jar, it was barely still alive.

Now, its abdomen glowed fluorescent green as it repeatedly tested its confines.

While darkness descended, Behrent thought about two young redheaded girls and contemplated what made the lantern of the firefly in the jar glow.

When she finally stood, it was with tears in her eyes. She set the jar on the barbecue grill, lit the charcoal, and watched the flames lick the glass before engulfing it. The firefly darted from one side to the other, faster and faster, until the jar turned black and she could see it no more.

She watched until the glass shattered and the flames chased the smoke high into the air, where glowing embers danced like fireflies.

The Sea-Slop Thing
Edward Lee

When the going gets tough, June reflected with a wince, *the tough hijack a sausage from the deli counter.* Indeed, it had been a hectic day at the deli, taking orders, running the slicer, tabulating the scale, etc., yet never–even during peak store hours–did Zefowitz, her boss, ever see fit to give her help. *I can't do it all myself,* June often complained. *Nobody in this fuckin' shit-hole grocery store works but me!* which was true. But even the worst job in the world was better than no job.

When there was finally no line at the deli, June put up the BE BACK IN TEN MINUTES sign, secreted the aforementioned sausage under her apron, and scurried to the employee's restrooms. *Shit, I'm horny as fuck!* In a moment's time, the stall door was locked, her pants and panties were down, and the foot-long sausage was sliding quite vigorously in and out of her already-drenched womanhood. These moods hit her more often now that she'd hit 40–hormone changes, she'd read in *Cosmo,* the ultimate peak of the woman's sex drive–and being stuck in the deli 12 hours a day (and with no over-time since she was "on salary") left her little time or energy to pursue intercourse of a variety more normal than sticking sausages in herself, and even if she *had* the time and energy, there was not one single member of the male population of this redneck sinkhole of a town who June would touch with a 10-foot pole. Ex-con, drunks, life-long pot heads, guys with a dozen kids from a dozen different redneck tramps, guys who hadn't had jobs for most of their adult life, and guys with cars but who couldn't drive due to multiple DUI's. *No, thanks!* was June's resolve. *I'll stick to sausage!*

She'd previously been fantasizing of being taken hard and rough by some faceless man who was football-player-sized: 6'8", 350 pounds, all muscle, just hot and heavy right there on the deli floor. His rippled body would squash her mercilessly into the tiles as his hips hammered her loins with the endurance of a gas-powered sod-pounder. June, close to smothering, would quiver through one bomb-burst orgasm after another while the faceless muscle-rack greedily pounded on, until at last the reward of his lust arrived. Given that this phantom lover was much larger than the average man in physical stature, he too was much larger than average in genital dimensions–10 inches, 12 or thereabouts, with the girth of a brawny wrist; and the volume and number of spurts of his ejaculation shared this "much-larger-than-average" trait. To be eloquent, the purse of June's womanly pleasures was flooded with one warm, adoring gust of seed after another. To be less than eloquent, the massive phantom cock and balls filled her squirming pussy up with so much spunk, he could've been pumping it into her with a fireplace bellows.

Hence, it was the recollection of this fantasy that June now summoned: standing spread-legged into the grocery store toilet stall, pants and panties at the ankles, apron jacked up, and banging a prodigious sausage fervidly in and out of her sex. The sausage was still shrink-wrapped, of course, and for those interested in minutiae, it was specifically a Dietz & Watson Chorizo Sweet Sausage, 12 inches long. It would be appropriate to mention that June, at 5'1" tall and 95 pounds, very much qualified as "petite," but her vaginal depth did not correspond to this qualification. She knew she could take more than 12 inches but she'd never met a man close that size. Once she'd used a 14 inch zucchini, and even *that* had not reached "rock bottom." As for width, 2 inches barely cut it but would do in a pinch; 2 and a half (about the girth of a beer bottle) was better. She'd tried 3 inches once (a Boar's Head Genoa Salami) but that had been a wee bit too much. But this Dietz & Watson? At precisely 2 and five-eighths, it seemed *made* for her. *Now I know the PERFECT width for me!* she celebrated.

And so horny was she that moment, and so stuffed was her head with the fantasy of being used as a fuck-dummy by a faceless giant, that on the tenth penetration of the Chorizo, she came so hard she nearly fell over in the stall, and nearly shouted out loud.

Holy motherfucking SHIT! she thought, panting, and then she hissed through her teeth, standing on tiptoes, at the delicious post-orgasmic sensation of slowly withdrawing that big honker of a sausage.

It was just what she needed to take the edge off a tiring, thankless, and very tedious day. *Much better now!* She collected herself quickly, kept an ear out for the door when she washed off the sausage, then put it under her apron, and whisked back to the deli where, thankfully, no customers were waiting. She had just put the Dietz & Watson back in the front display case when she turned around–

–and froze.

Mr. Zefowitz was standing behind her, arms crossed over the bulbous belly that stretched his white dress shirt nearly to the point of popping its buttons.

"Uh, hi, Mr. Zefowitz," June said.

"You're fired," Mr. Zefowitz said.

June, not a passive personality, replied, "You can't fire me! Everyone else in this store is too STUPID to run this deli!"

"That's true, but I *can* fire you and I just have."

"What for!" June bellowed.

"For masturbating with store inventory," and then he walked to the case, removed the culprit sausage, and patted one end of it into his open hand. He smiled.

Embarrassment turned June's face beet red but it only took a moment for that embarrassment to transform to stark-raving rage. "You fat fuckin' pervert! You have a camera in the ladies room!"

"Not *a* camera, several," her boss remarked. "Security cameras, for your safety. Any old psycho could come in off the street, walk into there, and rape someone. Then we'd get sued, and we can't have that, can we?"

"Well you're sure as shit gonna get sued now! I'm takin' this shit to Channel 9!"

He put the sausage back (why not? It was shrink wrapped) curled an index finger at her, and beckoned her into the back room. "Come in here to see why that will *never* happen."

Veins beat at June's temples. She was grinding her teeth she was so mad. She followed him into the back room, then he closed the door, and when he turned back around...

...his penis was out of his pants.

"Why is your dick out of your pants?" she asked, seething.

"Well, it *has* to be for you to suck it," he said. He pulled on in a bit, then scooped out his testicles. "And you *will* suck it and you'll swallow *everything* that comes out of it, otherwise that security tape will be on the internet five minutes from now."

June stared. She was shaking, she was vibrating. Then–

Then–

She sighed long and despondently, got on her knees, and began to suck.

* * *

Fuck! Shit! Piss! This was the character of June's reflections once she got hope. *No fuckin' job! How can I pay the rent!* Her useless, tits-on-a-bull, dead-beat of an ex-husband would be bringing the kids home from summer camp in a week, and with the piss-ant child support he paid, she couldn't even get a decent amount of groceries.

She plopped down in the ancient arm chair, and would've cried if she'd been so mad. Perhaps some TV would take her mind off things.

But no.

The TV was broken.

I am so screwed, and all because I just HAD to stick that sausage in my cooter...

At least it had been a good orgasm.

The taste of Mr. Zefowitz's sperm still buzzed in her mouth. *It's funny how sperm tastes worse when it comes out of the dick of someone you hate. Yeck!* She should've bitten it off, not that there was much to bite. Everything seemed to go wrong for June. *Just once,* she thought, *just ONCE, why can't something go right?*

Her cellphone rang, and before she answered it, she saw the text message saying that her pay-as-you-go card would expire in one day. *No job, and no money to renew my card. The hits just keep on coming.*

Then she answered the phone, expecting a bill collector. "Hello?"

"Hey, sweetheart!" a sly male voice answered. It was Fishy, probably her only friend in town. "How's the love of my life doing today?"

"I don't know, Fishy. What's his name?"

Fishy barked laughter. Everybody called him Fishy because, well, he worked the docks and smelled like fish. "That's my gal! Always good for a laugh. Say, you ready for some good news?"

"Fuckin'-A yes I'm ready for some good news," she said, ever the gentlewoman. "All I've had all day is *bad* news."

Fishy chuckled. "Yeah, I heard. You got canned from the deli 'cos Zefowitz caught ya stickin' a leg of lamb in your cookie."

Steam may very well have shot from June's ears. "It was a Chorizo sausage, not a leg of fuckin' lamb! And-and, it's not true! And where did you hear that?"

"Aw, hell, damn near everyone. Whole town's talkin' about it."

Fuck! Fuck-fuck-FUCK! June thought.

"Just don't you worry about that none'a that, Junie," Fishy consoled. "I'se bet every dang gal in this town has stuck all *kinds*'a things in themselves."

Now she was truly close to tears. What could be worse than this? She'd have to move. Everyone would be calling her Sausage Girl. "Come on, Fishy. I thought you said you had *good* news."

"Oh, yeah, that's right. You know ole Captain Kupjack, don't ya?"

June made a face. "Yeah. That perverted old drunk's been trying to get in my pants since I was ten. I'm serious. *Ten.*"

Fishy chuckled. "Yeah, he's a rascal, all right. Anyway, he just pulled into the dock on his 42-footer."

"Shit," June muttered. "I was hoping you were gonna tell me his boat sunk with him in it, that fuckin' old crustcake diaper sniper."

"You're something, Junie, you really are. Anyhow, like I was sayin', he just pulled in, been gone two weeks. Devil Reef, I heard, and he must've brought back one hell of a catch 'cos he was spendin' money like water at the bar. Picked up everyone's tab."

"That scumbag skin-flint never bought anyone anything. Ever," June observed.

"Well, he sure as hail did today, and he's *still* down there buyin' drinks. Oh, and he bought hisself a brand-new Cadillac ta boot."

This didn't sound right. "Unless he brought in 20,000 pounds of rockfish, he couldn't make enough profit to pay off his crew and then buy a Caddie. And rockfish is out of season right now."

"Well, funny ya mention it, about his crew, I mean. When he left he had four fellas with him, but when he come back today, he had none. Said he dropped his crew off on Kent Island 'fore he pulled in. Ain't no one work for him from Kent Island that *I* know of."

June's shoulders drooped. This sounded like a run-around. "Fishy, I don't give a fuck about Kupjack, his crew, Kent Island or *nothin'*. All I care about is good news, and if you don't have any, I gotta go."

"Hold up there, little girl! Don't let your titties get tied in a knot," Fishy said. "Lemme git to the best part. So when I was in the bar drinkin' on Kupjack, he slams like his tenth shot of Wild Turkey and he come to me and say, 'I need my boat painted, inside and out, and there ain't no painters in this town worth of pinch of dog shit, not one, 'cept June."

"Bullshit," June said. "Last time I saw that stewed old perv, he pinched my butt, so I told him if he was the last man on earth and I was hornier than a jackal in heat, I'd hang myself before I'd fuck him, and if he ever touched me again, I'd cut his dick off and use it for fish bait."

"Wow," Fishy laughed, "that's sure sendin' a message! But I'm serious. He knows you and I are friends, so he tells me to tell you he wants to hire you to paint his boat, and if you agree he'll give me $100 for a finder's fee."

June winced. "Are you shitting me?"

"Ain't nothin' but the truth, hon, and I sure could use that c-note."

"Well, you can forget it. I wouldn't work for that creepy two-bit little-girl's-bicycle-seat- sniffing old crock for *any* amount of money," and she took a sip of the cold, two-day-old coffee sitting next to her: the last coffee in the house.

"It's a two month job, Junie, and he'll pay fifty bucks an hour, cash, daily."

June spat the fetid coffee in a wide spray across the room, where it dotted her velvet Elvis portrait. "Tell him I'll take the job!" she gagged. Drunken fat old pervert or not, that much money would solve all of June's problems for the next year!

"Be crazy not to," Fishy said. "Just you meet Captain Kupjack tomorrow mornin' at the dockyard."

"You can bet your ass, Fishy! Thanks!"

When she hung up, she squealed in proverbial glee. *Fifty bucks an hour! Finally, something GOOD happened to me!*

Good, indeed. And perhaps *too* good to be true...

* * *

Bright and early next morning, June walked briskly through the dockyard, whistling, for some reason, the theme for Sponge Bob. She'd been a boat-painter for several years but quit after that time someone had dropped a Micky into her iced tea. She didn't know what had happened to her in the four hours she was unconscious, but her anus hurt for days. *Was probably Kupjack, the dirty prick,* she thought. Even so, for fifty an hour? She'd just have to keep a close eye on anything she drank.

Wow, came the next thought. She was approaching Kupjack's ship when she spied a brand-new gold-colored Cadillac Seville. The gold paint job looked tacky but still, *That's probably sixty grand! Kupjack must've leased it, wants people to think he's a high roller.*

"Thar she is!" cracked a hoarse voice. Did June smell whiskey breath even at *this* distance? The disheveled, pear-shaped man leaned against the railing of his ancient piece-of-shit dock-shed-turned-office. Kupjack was as broken down as the shed, and as old. His distended liver made his stomach stick out like a woman nine-months pregnant, and the big bushy Talibanish beard covered a huge pink face that was benchmarked by a warped nose akin to a rotten strawberry. Lastly, and most ridiculously, he wore a crooked, white captain's hat with a life-preserver on it.

Then he rubbed his crotch through his canvas overalls.

Great, June thought. "Fishy said you had work for me."

"Aw, yeah," the old man crackled. "Just come back from Dunedin Reef with a hold full of Crackjaw eel, done sold the lot to the Japs for top dollar."

"I heard it was *Devil's* Reef. And Crackjaw eel? Isn't that *freshwater* eel?"

When Kupjack hitched in a pause, his man-tits jiggled. "Well, no, we *passed* Devil's Reef, I mean, and you're right, it were hagfish eel. I always confuse 'em see? Ugly buggers all look the same...I mean the *eel*, not the Japs. Then I drop my crew off St. Mary's Island, where I meet up with the Jap fish broker."

"I heard you dropped your crew off at *Kent* Island," June said.

This second challenge gave the fat drunk a jolt of annoyance. "Well, you done heard wrong, little lady, and that ain't neither here or there, and, yeah, I got work for ya. I need my boat painted inside and out, every square inch. Fifty bucks an hour, and it'll likely last all summer."

June couldn't help but ask, "What's the catch?"

"Catch?"

"Come on, Captain. You been trying to get in my pants for as long as I remember, and *nobody* pays fifty an hour to paint a boat. If that pay comes along with me being your nookie, then forget it."

Kupjack threw his old bearded fat face back and cackled like a witch. "Aw, girl, you're a riot, you are! 'Tis true, I was randy in my day, and gals followed my dick down the street like it was the Pied fuckin' Piper, and with *good reason.* But them days is gone. I'm old as Moses and fat as Buddha, and I'm so filled with liquor they won't even need ta embalm me when I die. Shee-it, if ya wanna know the truth, I can beat my dick like a red-headed step-son and I *still* can't get it hard enough to spit."

June sighed. "Actually, Captain, I *didn't* need to know the truth with that amount of detail."

"Believe you me, ain't nothin' I'd like more'n to bury my hardwood in gal's tail and hump 'tll she come so hard her eyeballs switch sockets, but, no, I'se afraid it'd be easier fer me to shoot pool with a piece'a overcooked spaghetti. And the diabetes just makes it worse." The old saltly dog lifted one leg, pulled up a pant cuff, and displayed a discolored ankle close to 6 inches thick. "Damn shit make my ankles get all swole up big around as a Russard Liverwurst, and that keeps the dick down too. Say, speakin' of liverwurst, is it true what I heard? That you got up'n fired from the deli for jack-hammerin' a liverwurst in and out'a your joy-trail?"

"No!" June exploded. "It's NOT!"

Kupjack shrugged lackadaisically. "Nothin' ta be 'shamed of, hon. Woman got every right to stick *anything she want* in her sauce-box, whether it be a liverwurst, a french bread, a bowling pin, one'a them big rolls'a cookie dough, a rotisserie chick–"

"I get the picture!" June yelled, her face turning evermore pink.

"Anyway, sweetie, the paint's on the deck'n boat's unlocked, start right away if ya like. You need anything"–he jerked a thumb backwards– "I'll be in the bar."

That's it? Just like that, I've got a fifty-buck-an-hour job?

It seemed so.

"Uh, thanks, Captain."

"Shore thing, sugar," he said, limping down the ramp. "Oh, I forgot. Do belowdecks first, 'cos I ain't picked up the exterior paint yet, plus I gotta get my hoist repaired," and then he hobbled toward the bar.

June walked down to the slip where the 42-foot *Gwendylyn Rose,* an old rattletrap but still chugging after decades. A pyramid of one-gallon paint cans sat stacked before the gang-ladder. All the supplies she'd need were right there as well, in a stationary storage locker. There was no time like the present so she pried the lid off a can, squatted down, and began to stir. Her first coherent thought to herself was a familiar one: *Shit,*

I'm horny as fuck! June's sudden good fortune put her in a great mood, and when she was in a great mood...the juices got to flowing. *I must be a sex-maniac,* she concluded, and her sex already damp, *even though I never have sex with anything but vibrators, sausages, and vegetables.* The paint, epoxy-based, was hard to stir, yet the exertion didn't consciously occur to her. *I'm an orgasm addict, I guess,* and she supposed there were worse things to be. The position of her squat pressed the crotch of her cut-offs firm against her already throbbing pubis. *What I wouldn't give for a man right now, a great big fuckin' HUNK of a man with a dick the size of a baby's leg and balls like duck eggs.* Yes, something like that sliding into her and banging in and out like a bilge-pump piston would be just what the doctor ordered. So dense was this desire that she felt very tempted to take a break, go belowdecks, and give her "honey pot" a work-over. She could get her fist in there no problem, and only a few twists would be required to set off a powder-keg orgasm. *But, no, with my luck someone would see...* And that would be even worse than her previous humiliation at the deli.

She got back to stirring, and–

Oh, fuck. Not again.

That *Cosmo* article wasn't kidding about women in their forties. Her hormones must be overflowing, for her squat and the continued pressure of the crotch of her shorts pressing against her "secret garden" continued to titillate her. Again she mused of her phantom suitor, the faceless armature of over-muscular flesh, legs wide and hard as railroad ties, and dinner-plate-sized hands manipulating her like a sack of packing peanuts, flinging off her top, hauling off her shorts and laying her out on her belly like a specimen. Her butt-cheeks were parted, then–

Kurrrrrrr-HOCK!

–a golf-ball-sized wad of spit landed right on her anus. *No, not there!* she thought. *No, not there!*

Her mental plea was answered by the prompt insertion of that perfect, throbbing, heavily veined tennis-ball-can-sized cock. June's cheeks billowed; just the first thrust squashed the wind out of her. But once the mindless rhythm got going–

Yes, there! she thought. *Yes, there!*

Indeed, it felt like an *arm* going right up her butt. Was it actually prodding the bottom of her stomach? It occurred to June, in this peculiar moment of abstraction, that sometime what a woman wanted more than anything was simply to be *filled,* to be used as a container of flesh and be *crammed* to the top, to be *stuffed* like a turkey until there was no more room to stuff anything more.

And if that's what women really wanted, that's what June was getting in the midst of this sopping, cringing, nerve-suckling fantasy.

Her heady glee could only be reflected by one word: *Fuck!*

The prodigious erection pistoned in an out, and the fact that it did so with *no regard for her at all* only made it more delicious. Her suitor's need had denuded her of all identity: she was no longer a thinking, living American woman, she was a squirming, flinching, mindless *thing* that was taken to be used solely as a receptacle for the phantom's animal lust.

And that was just fine with June! *My butt's being plungered like a gas station toilet...and I LOVE it!*

The phantom must've weighed 400 pounds, and all of it was muscle, and when it lay down flat it squashed June like a Twinkie under cinder blocks (if she'd been filled with cream, like a Twinkie, it would be all over the place now!) All her breath was vised out of her; her tongue jutted. Every ounce of strength was required to wedge her hand under her belly and inch it toward her steaming sex, and she knew all it would take was a single press of her fingertip against her gorged clitoris and that would be that: Orgasm City.

Still, the brainless suitor humped her butt without relent. June's finger was two inches away, one inch, a half-inch–

Almost, almost...

–and just as the contact she craved would be achieved...

"Hey, girl, I say that's one mighty fine tail you'se stickin' out there!"

The marauding voice shattered the fantasy, and the gates to Orgasm City were slammed shut.

Shit! Who the–

June, transported back to the dull reality of her life in general and the even duller task of stirring a gallon of marine paint on the foredeck of this old rattletrap fishing boat, fired her glare behind her and down.

It was Rummy, the neighborhood dock bum, grinning toothless through a rust-colored beard that encompassed most of his face and scratching the crotch of dungarees that probably hadn't been washed in a year.

"It's rude to stare at people, Rummy!" she yelled.

"Gal with a butt like that make it hard not too, umm-hmm! Look like you had somethin' naughty goin' on in yer head, the ways you was squirmin' and moanin' and–"

"As a matter of fact I did, and you just ruined it!" she barked and kept stirring.

"Well then what say you'n me go belowdecks and pick up where ya left off?"

What say you drink your own piss instead, June thought in a rage. "What do you want, Rummy?"

"'Sides you? Nothin', girl. Only I wanted ta ask if you heard 'bout Kupjack, but I guess ya have, seein' how you're workin' for him now."

"Brilliant observation, and, yeah, I heard he was back in town."

"Naw, naw, that ain't what I meant. I meant about Kelly Point."

June grimaced, stirring away. The paint was like taffy. "What about Kelly Point?"

When Rummy scratched his beard, a snowstorm of dandruff fell. "Well, accordin' to the local talk, that be where Kupjack just come back from, then he drop his crew off on Brewer Island. But when he pulls in here there weren't *nothin'* in his hold. Was *bone-dry's* what the dockmaster say. Then Kupjack up'n pay cash for that new Caddy and start spendin' money like Donald Strump...or whatever his name is. Donald Gates?"

June stopped stirring and whipped around. "Wait a minute. First I heard is was Devil's Reef, then Dunedin Reef, and now you're telling me he just came back from Kelly Point, and that he dropped his crew off a Brewer Island. Well, I heard it was St. Mary's Island after I heard it was Kent Island. What the hell's going on?"

"Gold, that's what."

June looked at him cockeyed. "Say again?"

"That's what I heard my own self...'twas *gold* he come back with, and it must've been a fair amount 'cos he walked out of the gold exchange in Salisbury this morning with a hundred grand, *cash.*"

June frowned. "Even if that's true, Rummy, how would you know?"

The man patted dust off his corroded shirt. "Simple. My sister works there. She told me."

In a town like this, June knew that most every bit of information communicated amongst the local population was ninety-nine-percent grapevine. "Fine, Rummy, but I still don't believe it."

"Then where'd Kupjack get the money?"

It's a good question, but... "I don't care," she resolved, then squatted back down to her stirring.

"And where *is* everybody?" Rummy continued the conjecture. The question was followed by a tinkling sound.

"What do you mean, where is–" but then June winced. Rummy was standing right there on the dockwalk in broad daylight, urinating into the water. "At least turn around when you do that, Rummy!"

"Oh, shee-it, sorry," he said. Were flies actually buzzing around his exposed penis? He put it away but, without surprise, didn't even pull his zipper up. "Look around. Notice anything strange about the marina?"

It took June several moments to blink away the vision of Rummy's unwashed-for-years dick. But then, as her eyes surveyed the long expanse of boat-slips...

Damn near every boat is GONE... "Where'd everyone go?"

"Where you think?" Rummy replied. "They all high-tailed it to Kelly Point, to look for that stash of gold Kupjack found. Probably a lot more there." Rummy stepped down off the dock, into a small dingy, which was where he usually slept. "'S'where I'm a-goin' now, I ain't no dummy. You wanna come with me?" he added with a crack of enthusiasm.

"No," she said. "No, thank you."

"All's right then. See ya later."

Hope not, June thought as her cynical best. Rummy pulled a cord, started a small outboard motor, and puttered out to the bay.

This is some weird shit going on here, she thought. Devil's Reef, Dunedin Reef, Kelly Point, Kent Island, St. Mary's Island, crackjaw, hagfish, etc. *Every time I heard one thing, I hear another thing completely different. And...*

She stared at the thought. *Gold?*

She'd never heard of one speck of gold in these parts, ever. But it *was* odd about Kupjack's sudden spending spree. The only thing tighter than Kupjack's wallet was a bull's ass in fly season. And now that she thought of it, why would he have bought a gold Cadillac, of all colors? It looked like shit.

Salty sea-foam towns like this all had their local legends, but the subject of gold did not fit into any of them. No hidden treasure, no pirates, not sunken Spanish galleons.

The paint was stirred, and the sun was cooking her back. She lugged the paint can down to the companionway steps to the first cabin. Her mind kept swimming in questions as she opened the port-holes to get some cross-breeze. *Wouldn't it be funny as shit if I found a gold coin down here?* Then–

"Oww!"

In a split second, she'd stepped on something and fallen–*thunk!*–right on her butt. She'd need to get some lights on down here; it was too dark, and...

What did I trip over?

She squinted, patting her hand around on the floor. There was nothing– No! Her hand landed on something cool, hard, and irregular. Was it a piece of glazed porcelain? It felt smooth, polished.

June picked it up and took it to the sunlight slanting in from a port-hole.

And stared.

What the fuck IS it?

It was a six- or seven-inch long metallic object with rounded edges and a not-quite-symmetrical contour. The only thing she could think to compare it to would be a Baby Ruth bar, but of course Baby Ruth bars were not made of solid gold.

This thing was.

It's a gold ingot or something! June deduced. *That old fuck Kupjack really DID find gold!*

June's heart pattered. She paced back and forth, wide-eyed. This thing in her hand was obviously only a tiny bit of the entire stash Kupjack had found. *Like when you bite into a sandwich and a crumb of bread falls to the floor,* came a weighty simile. And with the price of gold over a thousand dollar an ounce, here was the nest egg poor June had never gotten even after a life of hard, honest work. And she knew one thing for sure: *This fuckin' Baby Ruth bar is coming home with ME.*

Stealing, schmeeling. It wasn't hers, no, but Finder's Keepers. *Kupjack has ENOUGH gold and he sure as shit knows where there's more. So...fuck him.* She put the gold bar/piece/ingot/whatever it was in her pocket. But, even though she now possessed a small fortune, she'd still have to paint the damn boat or else Kupjack would be suspicious. The piece in her pocket he'd dropped unnoticed, but if she quit on the spot--

He'll know I found something.

Therefore, she resolved to get to work and make it seem that everything was normal, yet as she prepared to retrieve the dropcloths, rollers, etc., the most natural thought occurred to her:

Maybe there's more. Maybe there are a few more pieces lying around that Kupjack dropped and didn't notice!

Some inner-monitor went off in her brain which said, *You've got enough. Don't be greedy,* and to this monitor she promptly replied, *Fuck off.*

On hands and knees, she proceeded, patting the ancient floor in every dark corner, and it must be said that the excitement derived from finding a chunk of pure gold combined with the excitement of possibly finding more....June was not surprised to find the "purse of her loins" beating like a heart and drenching her crotch; and though her mind was quite set on gold, part of her cognizance was overwhelmed by imagery of the most lusty sort: dicks in her mouth, dicks in her butt, dicks in her "honey bucket." All these things and more poured over her mind's eye, and one imaginary cock after another dumped great plumes of sperm in her and on her. June was so horny, as a matter of fact, that she had to force herself *not* to stick her hand down her shorts for some stimulation of a more substantial nature. *Masturbate later, you horn dog! Right now you're looking for gold!*

But, lo, in her extensive, knee-dirtying search, no gold was to be found. However she *did* discover one beer cap, a cigar butt, an M&M (a green one), and--

Yuck!

--a rubber glove with brown index finger. It was clear how the good Captain Kupjack utilized his spare time.

She moved on, next, to a tiny storage closet, which she felt inclined to skip but for some reason didn't.

Perhaps she should have.

She unlatched the narrow door, and--

Holy motherfucking FUCK!

--out spilled a veritable *pile* of skeletons. Easily the bones of four men were in evidence, and she didn't need to be scholar of Euclidean calculus to realize that the bones constituted Kupjack's "crew." June naturally ejected herself from the compartment in a split-second, but a split-second was enough to digest the horror's details.

The skeletons still had their clothes on, the fabric of which seemed half corroded. One would think that the men had rotted down to bare bones while the clothing remained, but how could this be? There was no stench of death at all, if anything just a pleasant sea-scent. The eye-socket of one victim remained filled by a glass eye. This could only be Tommy Ray Swain, a local deadbeat fishing hand who liked to pop the eye out at the bar and put in people's drinks, not an activity which was met with any levity. June had fucked him once in high school but wished she hadn't. For one thing, she'd received no orgasm for her efforts, for another, she got a UTI.

But that was another story.

The bones were clean, too, scrapless. Not a single sinew of flesh, tendon, or cartilage could be found on any of them.

Be that as it may, June ran her 90-pound ass out of there as fast as her coltish legs could carry her. She tore across the main cabin, shot herself up the companionway steps, grabbed the door latch, and–

Fuck fuck fuck fuck fuck fuck FUCK!

The door was locked!

It must've locked by itself when she'd come down. She kicked at it ferociously. It didn't budge. Then...

What the FUCK?!

And errant glance out porthole on the door showed her this:

Good ole Kupjack sitting in the captain's chair in the wheelhouse, swigging a bottle of Wild Turkey.

How could he not have heard me kicking the door, the old fuck? And with that thought, June POUNDED on the door with all her might. "Hey!" she shrieked. "I locked myself in! Open the door!"

Kupjack made no motion, no response.

And only then did June realize that the door *couldn't* be locked accidentally from the outside. It was a deadbolt which required a key...

"YOU FAT DRUNK PERVERT MOTHERFUCKER!" she bellowed. "YOU LOCKED ME IN!"

At this, Kupjack turned around in the chair, faced the outside of the door, and waved, grinning, right at June.

Whatever was going on here, June hadn't time to conjecture but she instantaneously knew three things.

One, there was no breaking through the door without an ax.

Two, there was an ax in the engine room.

Three, to get to the engine room, she'd have to pass the skeleton pile at the closet, and there was a formidable probability that on such a trek, she would encounter whatever it was that had sucked the flesh off the bodies of four men.

Oh, and Four, the only reason Kupjack would've locked her inside was because he must strongly desire June meet the same fate as his crew.

June's teeth chattered as she daintily stepped over the tumble of corpses that had spilled into the narrow hall. To get to the engine room, she'd have to first pass through the bunk cabin, and this she did with some trepidation—so much trepidation, in fact, that she wet herself. *Terrific,* she thought. It was dark here, only one round window deck level on each side, and, wouldn't she know it, the light switch was on the other side of the cabin, next to the engine room door. Stifling heat seemed to pressure-cook her; she was pouring sweat. Not three steps across the floor and she felt the oddest bumps under her flipflops, as if she were walking over pebbles. When she looked down, even in the limited light, she saw that the "pebbles" were marble-sized nuggets of gold.

She noticed something else as well: a creeky low-tide scent. The cabin was only six feet long, but it felt like six hundred. Six bunks, three on each side, lined the walls, and in the occluded light, crumpled sheets and pillows looked like men. June didn't need that illusion. Then again--

What's that smell?

It was earthy, musky without being unwholesome, and, truth be told, it was kind of a turn on.

"This is NOT the best time to be horny!" she whispered to herself.

At last she made it to the door to the engine room, grabbed the latch, turned it, and–

Oh, for dick's sake!

–it was locked.

No recourse now but to return to the main door at the top of the companionway steps. And– *The fire extinguisher!* There was one on the wall. *Maybe I can break the door down with that!*

Just as she would open the door that led out of the bunk cabin–

click

–someone locked it from the other side.

Bugged-eyed, June looked through the little round window and saw Kupjack smiling at her.

She bellowed loud as a trumpet: "You drunk old fat perverted piece of dog shit! Unlock the door! What's going on? What did you do to your crew? I'll KILL YA when I get out of here!"

She could just hear his voice, muffled as it was, through the door, "You WON'T get out of there, sweetie"–then he cackled a laugh. "Look up at the ceiling."

The ceiling? June was stifled, her mind a mix of terror and questions. She looked up at the ceiling and saw nothing of note at first; there wasn't enough light to see anything but the fact that the ceiling was black, or almost black. But as she squinted at an irregularity, her eyes began to acclimate to the low light, and in the corner of her eye, she noticed, right there on a bunk (next to magazine entitled *All Hands On Dick!* and a jar of vaseline), a large flashlight.

Fuck yeah! came the cultured thought, and she grabbed the flashlight, snapped it on and pointed the strong beam of light toward the ceiling....

And peed in her shorts again.

The ceiling...was *moving.*

Think of a 300-pound blob of fresh-made bread dough dropped on the floor, and the way it would slowly spread outward. That's what this reminded June of, only it wasn't on the floor, it was on the fucking ceiling, and this wasn't bread dough, because bread dough wasn't the color of, well, feces.

Then the blob detached itself from the ceiling and fell right on June.

Holy motherfucking SHIT! she thought, struggling at once with the tent of churning slop that had landed on her. It formed something like a bubble over her, whose confines were very slowly drawing in, and June received the strangest impression that the, the, the *thing* was doing this on purpose, to lengthen the time of her terror before it had entirely converged on her. She received several more strong impressions as well, and another was that the mass of surf-smelling poop-brown glop had every intention of eating her.

Whatever the thing was, June didn't care. An alien that had landed in the sea? A secret genetic experiment run amok? Or just some unclassified, previously undiscovered sea-creature?

June didn't give a flying fuck.

She collapsed down on her back, then stuck her legs out straight–a feeble attempt, at least, to put struts between herself and that ever-lowering mass of sea-blubber, excrescence, reef-slop, or whatever it was. The flashlight remained on, and as the top of that "bubble" sunk around her feet, she pointed the light upwards.

I'm WAY out of my league here, she thought quite dismally, and she peed her pants again, too, by the way.

Puckered holes began to emerge from the slop's inner-surface area, like octopus suckers, and all at once, she deduced what had happened to the crew. Once these suckers made contact with her flesh, they would emit slimy digestive enzymes and then they would, well, they would *suck*. They would suck all her flesh off her bones. And once she'd been liquified and digested, any moron knew what happened next. What goes in, must come out, right? June would be processed through the creature's bowels and then excreted through whatever manner of monster-anus this hideous thing had in its butt.

More than that, she would be excreted, not as common poop, but as *gold.*

It began to occur to her, as her feet struggled against the descending wet mass, that she knew far too much than she had any business knowing. These rapid impressions that fired into her mind had no logical explanation, but still the impressions came, and with them the full gist. *This fuckin' ugly pile of shit is TELEPATHIC!* she realized. *It's sending signals to my brain and letting me know all about it!*

Ever-so-slowly, it continued to constrict, those suckers throbbing. Using her legs as struts against the top of the "bubble" did no good at all. Just as she *knew* the mass would collapse on her and begin to chow down, she noticed the strangest thing in the shifting illumination of the flashlight...

A cock and balls.

Or something *like* a cock and balls: a glistening milk-chocolate-brown sack heavy with two fist-sized lumps semblant of testicles, over which lay what could only be a flaccid, veined, uncircumcised *sea-peter.*

June's sentience shifted into a thoughtless, almost automatic mode. She did not consciously *think,* she merely *acted* the only way her instincts knew.

She shot her hand out, and began to fondle the bizarre genitals.

Her fingers played with the testicles for a few moments; she could feel them beating from within, and as she did so, she noticed something of significance:

The entirety of the mass of slop which surrounded her *stopped* descending.

I'll bet the fucker's horny, she deduced. *Probably hasn't a piece of sea-slug ass in a long time. Let's see how he likes a HUMAN piece of ass...*

She kneed her way through dripping ichor, and with no hesitation whatsoever she pulled what could only be the thing's penis into her mouth, all the while maintaining her titillation of its lumpen gonads. The penis did not come erect as a human one would but instead throbbed in her mouth like an animate pile of wet modeling clay. June's tongue roved over it, feeling the fascinating network of beating veins, and once or twice sliding over the meaty, rimmed aperture which she could only guess was the end of its urethra. An inclination directed her to try pushing her entire tongue *into* that aperture, and when it dilated enough for her to do so, she knew she'd made the right choice. The creature actually *shuddered* in pleasure.

And still, the body of the thing did not collapse on her and subsequently consume her. *It wants a blowjob,* she realized. *Gee, why is THAT no surprise?* But this thing's cock was so different from a man's, she wasn't sure how to commence. While weighing considerations, she "fucked" the monster's peehole with her tongue, plunging in and out, and figured the sensation was lengthening her life. The peehole, however, constricted after another minute, and June figured that meant it was time to get down to business. She began to tighten her mouth around the veined wad of flesh but it was too wide for her to rim her lips around as she would a regular dick. But then?

Yowza!

The odd penile mass in her mouth suddenly protracted, narrowing by degrees, and advanced down her throat. This advancement did not abate until it reached her stomach. It was June's good fortune that she possessed no mode of gag-reflex. The situation could be likened to, say, a girthy snake slithering down from her mouth into her belly.

Here goes nothing...

She began to move her head back and forth, the action of which caused her throat to slide to and fro over every inch of that "snake." *Fuck!* she thought. *This isn't deep throat, this is deep stomach!* She could feel the thing tensing, and she sensed in a more psychical way that the creature was going ga-ga over her oral ministration. But evidently, dicks were universal: if you suck one, it blows its load, and so was the case with *this* dick at that very moment.

June's eyeballs nearly started from her head. The thing came in her stomach as though it were a manual feeding tube. *You gotta be shitting me!* Was it a pint? A quart? June's belly filled with hot slop, and when the snake-like penile shaft withdrew from her throat, it was *still* coming. Quart, be damned–this thing was working on a gallon! Upon full withdrawal, her mouth filled with its cum as well.

What was the creature's sperm *like?*

Hot Tapioca pudding? A bucket of shucked raw oysters? A colossal volume of frog eggs? All these similes combined would probably be a just parallel. The amount of it in her stomach was a grim prospect indeed; it seemed to bubble down there, and shift, and percolate. *At least I don't have to worry about buying dinner...* Further considerations bewildered her. For one, after being orally pummeled by a sea-monster's cock, she would expect herself to be repulsed and terrified, not--

Not *what?*

Horny, she realized.

June was horny, all right, hornier than a nun full of Spanish Fly. Her vagina beat like an angry fist banging against a door. She gave up trying to isolate her thoughts when she realized that the *thing's* thoughts were still seeping into her head, but in no language but that of raw emotion: lust, desire, need, and, yes, love!

This great big plop of monster-slime LOVES ME!

And in a moment more, June--with no conscious forethought whatsoever–physically availed herself to *receive* the sea-monster's love. She was out of her shorts, and spread-eagled on her back in less time than it took to say *Fuck the shit out of me!* It was during these few seconds before physical intercourse would ensue that the same *mental/psychic* intercourse became more acute. *Yeah, this thing loves me, all right, and it's about to prove that in spades,* June thought but, by now she was ready for some love herself, some *hard* love. Her feminine channel was drenched, her nipples gorged to size she'd never before experienced, tingling electrically and actually throbbing. Her loins felt like a pot of Sex Stew, bubbling, roiling, cringing to be stirred, and she knew that she was undergoing some serious hormonal or cerebral-chemical change. Was it normal to *want* to be fucked by a sea-monster? Meanwhile, the sea-monster underwent a change of its own. That massive "bubble"-shape of its body began to turn inside-out and backwards, and when this prolapsation had finished, there stood before June some 300 pounds of brown, mottled, low-tide-smelling porridge which bore the most vague semblance of the human form: i.e.: jointless, digitless arms and legs, an undetailed approximation of a trunk, an eyeless, noseless, mouthless earless lump for a head. Think a monstrous gingerbread man, or a shit-colored Gumby doll...

But, of course, Gumby was not possessed of erection, but this thing was, sticking up like a foot-and-a-half-inch length of veined, pulsing radiator hose. Precum ran like a leaky tap from the puckered slit which crowned the glans. Those same malformed, fist-sized testicles to which June had been previously introduced, constricted in their hideous scrotum even as June stared up, drooling, legs spread painfully apart; and somehow, in the most abstract and introspective insinuation, the monster stared back at her with equal desire in spite of the fact no eyes could be found in its lumpen head.

In a sense of need which could only be likened to insanity, June's hands plied her gushing sex, the sensations of which she had never before experienced with such potency. *If this thing doesn't start banging the daylights out of my RIGHT NOW, I'm gonna have to fist myself!*

"Come on, pal!" she bellowed. "Let me have it!" She lewdly thrust her splayed groin forward. "Does it look like you need a fucking invitation?"

We need not accompany June through the preambles which led up to the business at hand; it should suffice to say, instead, that in a hackneyed wink of an eye, that man-shaped heap of ocean-slop landed on her with the urgency of a pit bull on a meat wagon. June wanted to get fucked, and fucked she got. The thing made mewling sounds as it lay atop her, humping away, drawing that malleable cock in and out of June's "love-hole." Just as it had lengthened and narrowed in order to advance into her belly, it now lengthened and narrowed to advance into the deepest depths of her reproductive tract. At the front of her cervix, it seemed to turn semi-solid and then poured farther, farther, deeper, deeper, through the physical limits of the uterus, then impossibly dividing into two squirming tendrils, each of which quivered still deeper up into the fallopian tubes. The spasms of sensation that coursed through June's body were clearly sensations hitherto unfelt before by any human woman. The thing continued to hump her without relent, all the while causing those delectable "dick-tendrils" to quiver and elicit neural pleasures so intense that all June could do was lie there– drooling, tongue out, limp-limbed–and *feel.* The sentient part of her brain shut off so that it might focus solely on the waves of orgasms that pulsed through her being. Eventually her musky lover's orgasm commenced as well, triggered by the release of its pudding-like sperm: gushes of it, which blew against every inner recess of June's reproductive apparatus. When the thing clumsily began to get up, the unearthly penis continued to pour still more sperm into her, and when that was done, it stood upright and looked sightlessly down at June, whose body just went on spasming in orgasm for at least another half hour.

* * *

Captain Kupjack sat above deck under the wheelhouse awning, nearly done with his first bottle of Wild Turkey for the day. A smile of robust satisfaction touched the booze-reddened face, and in further satisfaction he even gave his crotch a squeeze. The idea simply tickled him pink: June being consumed, digested, and pushed out of that hideous thing's butthole. *That smartass cunt finally gets what she deserves,* his thoughts cackled. She'd sassed him for years, and smirked off every advance, even turned down his offers of good money, while fucking and sucking every cock in town, every cock but poor old Captain Kupjack's. *Too good for me, huh, tramp? Think you're too high-*

falutin'for the Captain, huh? Well, how do ya like me now?

Now?

By now that redneck gravyboat is nothing but a pile of solid-gold shit on the floor.

Yes, Kupjack liked that idea very much.

He waited a while longer, idly stroking his beard and giving further errant squeezes to his groin, until the sun pulled off a bit more, and then he got up and creaked his wobbling fat frame down the steps to the lower deck. When he arrived at the engine room door, he smiled into the porthole, looking for the telltale skeleton which would be all that remained of that fickle white-trash sperm depository named June. However–

"Where the hell is she?"

No evidence of June's remains were to be seen, and only then did the Captain notice that the door was no longer locked and that the deadbolt had been broken *outward.*

What kind'a monkeyshines goin' on here? he thought and scratched his bin Laden-style beard, and then he thought that maybe things had not gone as he'd planned and that maybe he should shag his fat drunken ass the fuck out of there without delay, but–

"Looking for someone?" a snide voice that could only be June's issued behind him.

It took a moment for the implication to register through Kupjack's whiskey-fogged perceptions as he turned, squinting, and saw none other than June herself standing behind him, buck naked and sheened in perspiration. "Why, ya conniving jizz-head whore! That thing should'a et ya by now!"

"It was going to," June replied, "until I fucked and sucked it to kingdom come and it fell in love with me." She looked up to the ceiling. "Honey? Be a sweetheart and come down here. You must be real hungry after all that wonderful lovin' you gave me. Well, soup's on!"

Kupjack was already screaming as the sea-slop slithered down the wall and engulfed him. June used a nearby bunk for a ringside seat; the only thing missing was popcorn. The Captain's pathetic fat form could be seen struggling uselessly within the churning, ravenous pile. She had to credit the old perv at least in his resolve to garble every possible sexist expletive at her for as long as his vocal cords functioned. We need not repeat those expletives here...well, on second thought, maybe we will, just a few, in the interests of completeness:

"Ya dirty white-trash cutthroat fuck-toilet!"

"Low-down tramp, done chugged more cock than I've chugged whiskey!"

"Bet you've had more dick going *into* your ass than shit comin' *out!*"

And so on. At any rate, that was the end of Captain Kupjack, and the beginning of a new life for June!

* * *

A week later, June stretched out in a lounge chair on the sundeck of her brand-new 72-foot Stardust houseboat. No more shitty efficiency apartment for her, and no more minimum-wage jobs busting her tail for asshole sexual-predator bosses. Nope, it was the high-life for June from now on. In the trunk of Kupjack's Cadillac (which June had ransacked the night of the Captain's "disappearance") she'd found several million in gold turds, not to mention the additional gold that the man had been turned into by the sea-slug's digestive tract. She'd never have to lift a finger again in her life, and she figured she deserved it.

"Rummy, get me another Long Island Iced Tea, will you?" came her languid request from the lounge chair.

It was great to just lay around all day on the boat, soaking up the sun and getting loaded. She'd hired Rummy and Fishy as her crew–why not? They were shiftless alcoholic idiots, but she figured they deserved a break. They waited on her hand and foot, cleaned the boat, cooked her meals, etc. June liked the idea of being waited on by men.

"Comin' right up!" Rummy replied after having just finished peeing over the side. Then he shuffled off to the galley where there was a fully stocked bar. Fishy was down below in the back, scraping barnacles off the prop, and June simply continued to lie there, in her Bill Blass bikini, her Ray-ban sunglasses, and a $300 Tropicana sun hat, and she would be happy to spend the rest of her days just like this. *Ah, the good life!* she thought.

But one question remained, did it not?

Whatever happened to the sea-slop thing?

Tempted as she was to keep it locked up for use as her personal sex minister, she knew that would be terribly cruel. It was a creature of the wild and an inhabitant of the deep blue sea–whatever the fuck it was–so in the deep blue sea it belonged.

And into the deep blue sea, she released it.

The best piece of male ass I ever had, she lamented, because she would've been perfectly content to let it fuck the stuffing out of her every day for the rest of her life. But how fair would that be to...to...*it?* To the sea-thing, the sea-monster, the...whatever the fuck it was?

This she knew beyond all doubt: no human man would ever be good enough ever again. But there was also something else she knew with equal certainty:

I was the best fuck of that thing's life.

She gazed out into the endless sea and smiled. See, that abstruse psychic connection she and it had shared never really severed with its departure.

And June knew full well that that great big wonderful pile of sea-slop would be stopping by very soon for a booty call.

A Box Full of Kinks
David Owain Hughes

I'd like to dedicate my story to the memory of Christy Thornbrugh; kick-ass mum, wife and friend, horror nut, embroider and maker of all things magic and awesome. I only knew you for a short while, but it was time enough to know you were a great person, Christy, and I continue to wear your patches with pride. Sleep well, my Jason-loving friend.

PS. I've finally got my Puppet Master ink finished!'
D.O.H.

***

"Hope's the rope that keeps you tied in knots."—
W.A.S.P

When she was a child, her parents and teachers had considered her a normal, healthy girl. She liked to play with her tea set, dollies, mock kitchen appliances, and

Hetty Hoover, and dress up with her mother's clothes, shoes, jewellery and make-up.

Throughout her lower and upper school years, Jodie had good friends and bagged solid grades that indicated she would become a professional, career-driven woman with an outgoing personality one day. This notion was later solidified when she gained access to a leading University and joined a law programme.

During her teenage years, Mother Nature blessed her: Jodie transformed from a sweet-looking girl into a striking, dark-haired beauty. Her body became tight, slender and sported an ample bust that had all the boys in her class hounding her for a date. Even the older lads bayed for her attention.

To add to her perfection, Jodie didn't drink, smoke or eat unhealthy foods. She liked to keep her mind sharp and her figure taut, which had filled out a tad by the time she'd started her degree. So, three times a week, she took to her campus gym, where she'd enrolled in kick-boxing and yoga classes. Jodie also liked to use the pool and thought herself a strong swimmer.

"You're like a bloody fish!" her mother would say. "You could be an athlete."

Her peers and a handful of female tutors envied her; even the girls who considered themselves Jodie's 'besties' tried their paramount to bite down on their acidic tongues and hide their green faces in her radiance which cast shadows over them.

Jodie was destined to have it all. She knew it, and, more importantly, the people around her did. She was sure to find herself a rich husband that liked to spoil her; the type of man who drove a Jaguar, had a platinum membership to the local gun club and liked to play golf on the weekends with his poker-playing mates so he could spend time away from her.

However, beneath her glory and Little-Miss-Perfect, butter-wouldn't-melt-in-her-mouth ways, there was something about Jodie – in her make-up – which nobody knew about. It was a secret that could have held her back as a child or, more disastrously, ruined her adult life by resulting in her ending up in jail or dead.

But she'd learned to control and hide it, once it reared itself and she knew it wasn't going away.

It had started as an itch, a fire between her legs, when she was ten years old. Of course, Jodie had been far too young to realise and understand its workings and what it all meant. At such a tender age, she could have told her mummy and tried to explain what she'd felt, but something inside had told her that Mummy and her 'imaginary sky fairy' called God would not like what she had done, or the excitement that had coursed through her. Also, Mummy had no idea Jodie liked to secretively mock her strict religious beliefs. She played along with it and attended Sunday school and church only to appease her.

So, going to her was out of the question.

Not only that, she'd liked the thrill of what had happened to her, even if it had brought her great shame.

Mummy would probably get Daddy to take his belt to me, she'd thought, looking down at her wet, pissed-through bottoms and soaked carpet. Her cheeks had burned. *He'd probably enjoy it!* Jodie hadn't really known what she'd meant, but had giggled nevertheless.

The urge to go to the toilet had come over her as normal, but instead of going to the bathroom as she would, it had come from nowhere and demanded her to leap up and run to the full-length mirror in her parents' bedroom. Once there, it had told her to wet herself. At first, she had shaken her head and bitten her lip, her bladder pinched.

"No," she'd whispered, trying to move but not allowing herself to do so.

And then she'd released and watched the wet patch at her crotch grow into a large, dark patch; her urine had flooded her knickers and run down her legs and splashed against the plush carpet at her feet.

Butterflies had fluttered in her guts, a strange thunderbolt of pleasure running through her as though she'd been struck by lightning. Her eyes had rolled, and her legs had turned to pillars of wibbly-wobbly jelly.

The blame for the pissed-on carpet had been laid at the feet (or paws) of Mr. Ruffles, the family hound.

"Well, he is getting on," Jodie had heard her father say to her mother. "Incontinence is probably kicking in."

She hadn't understood the word her dad had used at the time, but soon came to learn of its meaning when she asked her teacher. This had then given her freedom to keep on wetting herself and getting her kicks from doing so.

Finally, after twelve months of scrubbing piss out of her expensive shags, Jodie's mother had ordered the dog's execution, which had sent a new wave of excitement through Jodie. She'd acted sad for the dog, but inside, she'd loved every treacherous second of it. And, when she'd put on the crocodile tears, her parents had showered her in lavish gifts.

"Maybe we could buy you a bunny?" her dad had suggested.

By the time her periods started, which was a year after her dog's passing, Jodie found multiple new ways to appease her gratifications, now that she was limited to wetting herself outdoors or when standing in the bath. Some of these new methods involved: telling lies and getting people in trouble; bullying children younger than herself and humiliating them by sticking gum in their hair, pulling the trousers and underwear of boys down and raising the skirts of girls; putting vile substances in people's meals and drinks; shaving defenceless animals and sticking her parents' toothbrushes up her bum, which was her favourite.

When the other children threatened to tell on her, she would threaten them with violence or more of the same. She ruled the playground and schoolyard. The ones she couldn't break or keep in line, she had the older boys handle by promising them a glimpse of her 'special place' and a kiss.

After her mid-teens rolled around and Jodie had developed into a swan, masturbation kicked in and she learned more about what it was that dwelled inside her and pushed her buttons through online research.

"I'm a pervert," she'd muttered. It had disappointed her, because she was a normal young woman with a good head on her shoulders when the urge to do racy things didn't kick in. "I'm ninety-percent perfect, and I will go far in life."

Whilst a lot of what she was doing to its power was normal and healthy, most of her practices were unusual and detrimental to her state of mind.

Still, she found it liberating.

When the boys gave her the eye in school, Jodie liked to play the attention off as though she didn't notice. However, the thought of how her sexy body drove their dicks wild with mad frustration delighted her.

What would Mother think? she'd thought at the time.

And, to add to their flustered, prick-teased ways, Jodie hiked her skirt enough for the lads to notice, but not the authority around her. She'd also invested money in make-up and stockings, which she would adorn before school and remove after her last class as to not get caught by her parents.

Throughout her days at her comprehensive school, Jodie developed more kinks, some of which were normal, like the arousal of female feet, men's legs, being spanked and tied up... But when her first serious boyfriend had refused to beat her and then throw her down a flight of stairs, she'd got angry and lashed out at him.

"I get turned on by it!" she'd screamed.

These outbursts normally resulted in her becoming single. And, when she thought they'd tell their friends how kinky, disturbed of fucked up in the head she is, Jodie threatened to make up lies about them to destroy them.

The crack-pot look in her eyes had told them how serious she was.

Not only that, but she took knives and scissors to them and their clothes.

"I'm your worst fucking nightmare, pencil dick!" she'd told one boyfriend after he'd refused to play dead for a second time as she rode his cock to the tune of multiple orgasms.

Playing-dead fantasies turned into voyeuristic ones, as she crept around her campus so she could peep in windows and watch people fuck, pleasure themselves or undress late at night.

When she couldn't get her own way, she hurt small animals or violated someone vulnerable on the streets, such as a homeless child or an old person.

Jodie was as cunning as she was horny.

She kept her tracks covered, and her movements in the shadows.

Anyone who tried or thought they could get in her way, she stepped on. And, when someone was brave enough to call her out, she fluttered her eyelashes or turned on the tears. Either way, she always looked clean.

Her shit didn't stink.

"Don't tell such lies!" others would say in her defence. "She's nothing but lovely."

When one lad had blabbed about how she liked to get fucked with various household objects, she'd spread rumours about him having a tiny dick, and how he couldn't get it up unless he was bedding an underage girl.

The masses believed her.

He became so ridiculed, he left University.

Of course, nobody knew where the rumours had started – Jodie hadn't told anyone. Instead, she'd scribbled it on walls around campus, along with his phone number.

"You'll get your comeuppance one day, *whore*!" had been his parting words to her.

"No idea what you're talking about," she'd said, winking and smiling after making sure there was nobody around.

Voyeurism turned into Nasophilia (a sexual attraction to the nose). This was followed by an exploration into licking and rubbing herself against doorknobs and unsuspecting people. Farting against random folk also thrilled her. It wasn't long before she had men and women pissing on her, and she found pleasure in turning people into human furniture by tying them in placc with bondage equipment.

Most of the fetishes came with names.

However, it wasn't normal to have so many.

"You're like a box full of kinks!" one of her many fuck buddies had quipped after she'd told him she liked exposing herself and walking around a crowded city in a coat with nothing on underneath.

It reached a point where being fucked or having her pussy eaten did nothing for her, as her perversion matured.

One evening whilst bored, Jodie had taken a stroll through the park and surrounding woods. She soon found that she liked being out at the dead of night, especially on cold evenings.

It became a new avenue of filth for Jodie to explore, which excited her. The students had been told never to leave the site after a certain hour, as the crime rates for violence, rape and muggings were at an all-time high.

Of course, this only added to her excitement.

When out and about, she liked to play Fight or Flight whenever she saw someone walk out of the darkness towards her – it gave her unlimited thrills.

Ah, the endless dangers, she thought, sitting on a park bench, ready to play her next game. The seat she had chosen was situated beneath a single light, which drenched her in a weak orange glow. Beyond the circumference of luminosity in both directions, Jodie couldn't see much apart from two other lampposts: the one to her left was out, and the right displayed the same level of feebleness as the bulb she was seated under.

Shapes shifted in the gloom.

Bushes rustled; twigs snapped.

Branches groaned to the might of the wind.

The sound of footsteps carried on the stiff night air, along with distant laughter and conversations, which came from the town nearby. When Jodie looked behind her, she could see the glow of cityscape.

Safety, should she need or want it, was a mere heartbeat away.

I live for danger! she thought. *Nobody's a match for me.*

Tonight, however, she would need to be quick on her feet if she planned to play Flight or Fight, as she wore a tight mini skirt, heels and stockings – the black, racy garments that encased her legs displayed their tops, due to the way she was sat.

I feel like Audrey fucking *Hepburn – all I'm missing is a cigarette.*

But she was getting restless. The park was unusually quiet for a Friday night. She hadn't even come across the resident bums, who'd she'd found splayed out in various positions on benches, in bushes and along the path over the time she'd been visiting the area at night. Some had even stank of piss and shit – the front and backs of their trousers stained.

Jodie fucked with the homeless she found sleeping. The previous Friday night, she'd stolen their clothes and thrown them in a pound, which she'd found highly amusing.

And it wasn't just the winos she messed with. In the daytime, when she passed through the place, she'd like to make little ones cry by shoving them, breaking their toys or popping their balloons – anything that would get a reaction out of them. She was even prone to punching, pinching and kicking them.

The thought made her smile.

Her laugh tore through the night.

"Ugh, how much longer?" she muttered, looking at her watch and then all around her. It was dead. "Maybe If I walk to the bandstand? There's always little fuckheads there smoking crack and drinking cheap cider. I really want to play—"

A healthy sounding snap of a twig cut her dead.

Her ears pricked.

It wasn't unusual to hear such sounds.

More crunching – someone was definitely approaching. Sneaking; using the darkness as cover.

A tingle sparked in her pussy, hardening her nipples. *Time to play...*

"Who—who's there?" she stuttered, trying to sound as scared as she could. Jodie fought hard to keep the smile off her face and the laugh down in the bowels of her guts.

Shrubbery rustled violently to her left, causing her to snap her head in that direction.

Someone was definitely close by – she could hear their harsh, raspy breathing.

Standing on bowed legs, with a hunched back, Jodie squinted. "I have *mace*!" she lied. Again, she battled the urge to laugh.

An orgasm built deep within her core.

A snigger escaped the bushes. "You ain't got shit, slut!" a voice snapped. "We're going to cut you into tiny pieces."

"Yeah, we been watching you, cunt!"

Suddenly, she didn't want to play, as two faces emerged from the bushes before her. They looked familiar. Over their shoulder, three more people appeared.

"Thought it was pretty funny to fuck with us down-and-outs, didn't you?" the first one said.

A glint off something bright flashed in her eyes. *Knife*! her mind screamed.

"Gonna rape your twat," said the second one, who was practically hidden behind his comrade.

"Yeah, that's the fucking bitch!" a faceless person said from somewhere behind.

"Tear her knickers off and stick it to her," another random homeless blurted.

"Ha! You said 'stick it to her'," a fresh voice said. "Rango has a knife," they continued, attempting to explain their poor joke.

Jodie gasped, turned and was about to flee in the opposite direction when she saw more of the homeless crawl from beneath bushes and slip out of the darkness.

"Slice her open, Rango," a female yelled.

"Rip her juicy cunt apart," a man slurred.

A scream lodged in her throat. "No, please!" she begged, collapsing to her knees. And then she gasped when the one with the knife, Rango, stepped out of the gloom and towered over her.

"You're going to get it, tramp!" He spat on her, and then bent over to show her the sharpness of his seven-inch blade. "I'm going to ram this in your twat, once I take what I want."

She tried to get up to run, but Rango held her in place. His breath reeked of whiskey and tobacco. In the poor light, she made out a large scar running from his eyebrow to his jawline. And, when he smiled, she noticed an impressive array of gold teeth.

He was terrifying and brutishly large – his hands were the size of shovels.

Rango gripped the front of her dress and ripped it open, taking her bra with it and exposing her ample tits.

"No!" she pleaded.

The thug then threw her legs apart and reached a rough hand up her measly skirt and tore her knickers off. Before sniffing them, he licked them, and then undid his belt buckle and lowered his jeans and underwear.

"Hold her arms and legs!" he bellowed at his lackeys.

His crew pinned her to the floor. She tried to pull away but stopped when she saw the size of his pulsating cock, which leaked pre-come. It was veiny and lacked foreskin.

A deformed snake, she thought, which also brought to mind the image of a Sphinx cat. "Don't you dare touch me with that…that *thing*!" Jodie screamed. Tears ran down her flushed cheeks.

Whoops and laughter tore through the crowd gathered around her – they were baying for her destruction.

"You want a taste, fuck?" he said, brandishing his knife. She whimpered at the feel of his hard prick pushing at her pussy flaps. "Firstly, I try you… The terror in your eyes turns me on," he said, giggling.

He gasped as her hand smacked against his arse. "What are you waiting for? An invitation?" With that, she pushed on his buttocks, forcing his cock deep inside her.

He groaned at first, but when he pulled back for a further pump, he screamed in pain, causing a hush to fall over the crowd.

"My *prick*!" he squealed.

"Come on, fuck me," she insisted, a laugh escaping her.

"*Aragh*!" Rango screamed, dropping his knife.

Jodie thrust her pelvis back and forth, back and forth, causing her would-be raper to scream more – tears ran from his eyes as he tried fruitlessly to disengage from her vagina.

"Got ya, big boy! Now, fuck me but good, ya black son-of-a-bitch," she whispered down his ear, and then wrapped her arms and legs around him before burying her face in his chest so he couldn't head-butt her.

"Get this crazy—*Argh*!" Rango screamed as he bucked, thrashed and tried pulling away and out of her once again – she could hear his foreskin rip and tear; her pussy was drinking his blood.

"W-what's going on?" a nameless, faceless from the crowd asked.

"She's killing him!" another replied.

"That bitch is crazy. I'm going before she works her hoodoo-voodoo on me."

Soon the sound of rushing feet filled the air around her and Rango. Not that Jodie was paying much attention – she was wrapped up in the throes of orgasm, as she continued to pump her hip.

"Yes! I'm coming, I'm coming!"

His macho mask slipped, his hard, violent talk of threats and yells turning to that of a five-year-old's blubbering ways when they lose their mummy in a supermarket.

"I—I *sorry!*" he squealed. "Get. It. Off!" Tears spilled down his cheeks and splashed her face, along with his stringy snot, which found its way into her mouth.

"Yes! Yes! *Yes!*" she screamed in response like a pig with a ripped-open throat.

And then she felt a gush a fluid between their melded hips and private parts, which she knew was a mixture of his spurting blood and her rushing juices. In the pale moonlight, she could see the colour drain from his face, which, ten minutes ago, had been flushed red with excitement.

His struggling lessened.

"You're going to die in"—she bit her lip as another wave of ecstasy trembled through her—"inside me…" Jodie panted, her orgasm coming, going and building towards another.

Within seconds, he collapsed on top of her.

Dead.

"Oh, shit!" she heard someone say, causing her to snap her head in that direction. One of the homeless had stayed to watch the whole sordid episode. "What you done, miss?" he asked.

"Not me, my Rape-X." She tittered. "It's like a cock-shredding condom that fits all nice and snug in my twat. The inside of the device is covered in small barbs. You see," she continued, rolling onto her side and pushing the dead Rango off her so she could get to her knees and grab the knife, "my kinks have evolved…"

She saw him look at the knife as she slowly turned it in her hand.

"Please… I didn't see—I won't say *anything*! Oh, sweet Jesus."

"Ooh, are you going to run? I might just enjoy playing Hunter and Hunted." Jodie jumped to her feet with eerie rapidity and lunged at the man, who was turning to flee. She landed on his back, taking him to ground. With one vicious swipe, she drew the impressive blade across his throat and rolled around in his spurting blood, getting herself off once more.

By the time she was finished playing in the pools of cold, congealed blood, three hours had passed.

I better get up and go after the rest of them, she thought. With effort, she dragged herself to her feet, stretched and yawned and then looked around her. She heard bushes rustling, voices whispering.

They were watching.

Ooh, how fun!

"I'll give you fucks until the count of ten, and then I'm coming." Her grip tightened around the knife. "One, two, three…"

Her smile widened when she heard the sound of rushing feet.

"Nine, ten… Ready or not, here I come…"

Mrs. DiMarco's Corpse
Ray Garton

Leonard Porter had been a police officer in the small town of Anderson for twenty-two years, and in that time, he had never seen anything as unsettling as the corpse in unit 212 of Riverfront Apartments. It was a low-rent complex, run down and long overdue for a paint job, and most of its residents were on welfare.

One of the residents, a young single mother named Dotty Crendin, had called the police department on that hot July day to complain about a smell that was only getting worse, a smell that seemed to be coming from apartment 212. No one had seen Beverly DiMarco, the old widow who lived in the apartment, for about three weeks. But no one had knocked on her door to see if she was home, to find out if she was all right.

Porter had rung the doorbell and knocked on the door, had even called out to be let in, identifying himself as a police officer. When no one had responded, he'd gone to the manager's apartment and asked to be let into 212.

The manager, a tall, stringy fellow named David Rattiger, had gone upstairs with his passkey and opened the door. The smell that came out of the apartment was overwhelming and Rattiger had backed off down the concrete walkway, waving his hand back and forth in front of his face and coughing.

Porter had gone in with a handkerchief over his face. First, he found Mrs. DiMarco's two cats, an orange tabby and a grey Persian. Then he'd found Mrs. DiMarco.

She was sprawled on the kitchen floor, lying on her back. Porter stood there staring down at her remains, not really wanting to look, but unable to look away.

Beverly DiMarco wore a sleeveless blue-and-white house dress, and over that a green apron. The clothes were taut over her abdomen, which was bloated by gases inside her body. Her scrawny legs were bare and spread wide, and her dress had hiked up around them. Her cats had survived by eating parts of her legs and arms. Her wrinkled skin had a yellowish-grey pallor. The tips of her fingers had been nibbled off by the cats and bone was visible, fingers that were curved on each hand, as if she'd been clawing at the linoleum floor when she died. Her neck appeared impossibly thin. But her face—that was the worst part, her face.

Her deep-set eyes were open wide and milky, lips pulled back over her long, discolored teeth in an unnatural grimace. It was little more than a skull with thin skin stretched taut over its surface, cheeks deeply sunken beneath sharp, blade-like cheekbones. Her silver hair was wiry and spread out around her head in a way that looked, to Porter, as if it were being blown by a strong wind.

The cats meowed loudly and rubbed against his legs again and again.

There was no immediate sign of foul play—at her age, natural causes seemed the most likely—but that would be up to the coroner to determine.

Porter looked around the kitchen. There were dishes in the sink, and it appeared that Mrs. DiMarco had been washing them when she died. There was a needlepoint sampler on the wall beside the refrigerator that read, "God bless this mess." There was a pot of eggs, some with cracked shells, in water on the gas stove, but he found all the knobs turned to the Off position. Apparently, she had just boiled some eggs.

The apartment and its dead resident caused a sudden wave of sadness to pass over Porter. No one had checked on Mrs. DiMarco to see if she was okay, no one had cared enough to knock on her door, or even call her on the phone. She had died alone, and had been left that way by her uncaring neighbors.

Somewhere in the complex, a baby wailed and children laughed. A telephone trilled a couple times before it was answered. A television played in one of the nearby apartments, and Porter could hear a studio audience laughing. And Mrs. DiMarco continued to silently decay on her kitchen floor.

Porter turned to leave, to go out to his squad car and call a detective and the coroner and to make some notes about the discovery for his report. As he stepped away from the corpse, something pulled on his left pant leg. Before looking down, he tugged his leg again, but something held it back.

He stopped, turned back, and looked down.

Mrs. DiMarco clutched his pant leg with her right hand. The bones sticking out of the tips of her fingers were closed tight on the cuff. Her milky eyes looked directly up at him and he saw her bloated tongue move in her mouth.

Porter stopped breathing—for a moment, he couldn't breathe—and his entire body stiffened.

Her lips moved, and the voice that came from her was a low, gurgly rasp.

"You're going to die soon," Mrs. DiMarco said. Her dry, cracked lips, peeled back around her teeth and did not move when she spoke. Then again: "You're going to die soon."

Porter heard a horrible sound then, a high, keening cry, and he realized after a moment that it was coming from him. He was screaming.

The hand holding his pant leg dropped to the floor and Porter tripped over his own feet leaving the kitchen. He fell into the small living room and crawled a few feet on hands and knees across the ratty tan carpet, then scrambled to his feet and ran to the open door. He went out of the apartment and both hands clutched the metal railing that ran along the concrete walkway. His shoulders rose and fell as he gasped for breath, but he could still smell the decaying corpse.

"Oh, God," he said as he exhaled, his voice breathy and broken.

"You okay?" Rattiger said. He stood a couple of yards down the walkway, a good from the open door of Mrs. DiMarco's apartment.

Porter suffered from angina, and he felt a twinge of pain in his chest. He had pills for it, but they were in the glovebox of his squad car. He pressed a hand flat to the center of his chest, took a few deep breaths.

"Is she dead?" Rattiger said.

Porter nodded. He licked his lips and cleared his throat. His voice was dry and hoarse when he said, "Yeah. Yeah, she's...she's dead." He realized he was trembling all over, and his knees were weak. His heart pounded so hard that he could hear it in his ears and feel it in his throat and fingertips.

"You okay?" Rattiger asked again.

Porter didn't answer. He stood up straight, stiffened his back, and went down the walkway, past Rattiger, and down the stairs to the courtyard below. He went to his car, opened it, and got in.

He sat there for what seemed a long time, trying to pull himself together. He closed his eyes, bit his lower lip between his teeth, and took deep, slow breaths through his nose.

"It didn't happen," he whispered to himself. He repeated the words a few times, but they did no good. With his eyes closed, he saw Mrs. DiMarco on the floor clutching his pantleg, her dead, pale eyes staring intensely up at him, her tongue moving in the unnaturally wide mouth.

You're going to die soon.

Pain blossomed in his chest again. He opened the glovebox and took out the orange prescription bottle, took off the cap, and shook a pill into his palm. He put the bottle back, popped the pill into his mouth, then took the can of warm, flat Dr. Pepper from the cup-holder between the seats and drank the pill down.

He reached out for his radio microphone and saw his hand shudder. He clenched it into a fist for a long moment, then relaxed it again, took the microphone from its hook, and called it in.

* * *

Two hours later, Porter drove to the station and parked his squad car. Inside, he went to the desk sergeant, Andy Cole.

"Jeez, Lenny," Cole said. "You look like hell."

"Yeah, I'm not feeling so good," Porter said. "I'm gonna have to go home."

"Okay, sure. You all right?"

"I will be."

Porter drove home in his Honda Accord, to his apartment in Magnolia Estates. He'd lived there for twelve years, ever since his divorce. He'd quit smoking years ago, but he could not remember the last time he'd needed a cigarette as much as he did now. Against his better judgment, he stopped at the 7-Eleven and picked up a pack of Marlboros. He just wanted one smoke, that was all, and doubted he'd ever finish the pack.

He parked in his space, walked past the pool, and up the stairs to his apartment. On his way up, he realized that the layout of Magnolia Estates was not very different from that of Riverfront Apartments, but it was in far better shape, clean and well cared for—

You're going to die soon.

—and there was no foul smell of human decay.

In his apartment, he went to his kitchen, took a bottle of Chardonnay from the cupboard, opened it, and poured some in a water glass. He drank it down in a few swallows and poured some more. He got a pack of matches from a drawer and put it in his pocket. He took the glass, the bottle, and a small bowl with him to the living room and sat down in his recliner, still wearing his uniform. He turned on the television with the remote. He put the bowl and the bottle on a lamp table beside the recliner, leaned back, lit a cigarette, and took a puff.

Porter sucked all those poisons into his lungs for the first time in a dozen years and he didn't cough once. It was a pleasant, familiar warmth. He exhaled in a cloud of toxic smoke as his body experienced a brief reaction to the poisons, that initial, delicious high that smokers futilely chase in every cigarette thereafter.

He closed his eyes as he took a second puff, but he saw her again—arms and legs partly eaten by the cats, milky eyes open wide, mouth pulled back from her old yellowish teeth.

You're going to die soon.

He opened his eyes again and tried to find something on television to watch. He settled on a rerun of *Seinfeld*.

Porter did his best to think around what he'd seen—what he *thought* he'd seen—and keep his mind off of it. But he kept feeling the old woman's hand clutching his pant leg.

By the time *Seinfeld* was over, Porter had drunk most of the wine in the bottle and had smoked four cigarettes.

And still, he could not keep his mind off the corpse.

You're going to die soon.

He got up and went to the bathroom, emptied his bladder, then took off his shirt on the way into his bedroom. The wine had made him sluggish and the cigarettes made him cough. He stripped down to his boxers and got into bed. He rolled over on his side and saw a hand sticking up from the side of the bed closest to the wall. He sat up and saw her lying there, her head at the foot of the bed, reaching up with her right hand, bones sticking out of her eaten fingertips.

Porter screamed as he scrambled to get off the bed on the other side. He became tangled in the covers and fell to the floor—

You're going to die soon.

—but he got to his feet and opened his nightstand drawer, took out his .38 revolver, and held the gun in both hands as he aimed it at the far side of the bed.

The hand was gone.

He slowly walked around the foot of the bed. The gun made a small chittering sound in his shaking hands.

The corpse was gone.

It was never there, Porter thought as he lowered the gun.

You're going to die soon.

He put the gun back in the drawer, put on his robe and slippers, and went back out to the living room. He finished off the bottle of wine and smoked three more cigarettes, then fell asleep in his recliner watching Jerry Springer.

As he slept, he dreamed of Mrs. DiMarco's corpse in the small kitchen of her apartment. In his dream, the corpse rose to its feet and reached out for his throat with bony, eaten fingers.

Porter cried out as he sat up in the recliner. It was dark, and the only light came from the television. An infomercial for a juicer was playing. The clock on the Blu-ray read 1:33.

He did not go back to sleep.

* * *

The next morning, he called the station.

"I'm not feeling too good," he told Carolyn at the front desk.

"Oh, I'm sorry, Lenny," she said. "You gonna stay home today?"

"Well, actually...I've got quite a bit of vacation time coming to me, and I'd like to take some of it now."

"Oh. Okay. How long do you think you'll be out?"

"I don't know yet. I'll give you a call at the end of the week."

After hanging up, he went into the bathroom to take a shower and found Mrs. DiMarco lying in the bathtub, arm outstretched, fingers clutching, tongue wriggling in her mouth.

Porter stumbled backward and fell to the floor, turned around, and crawled out of the bathroom making a groaning sound. He got to his feet and turned, looked into the bathroom.

There was nothing in the tub.

You're going to die soon.

He backed away from the bathroom. In the living room, he smoked another cigarette with a trembling hand.

Porter wondered how he would sound if he told someone what was happening to him. Whom would he tell? One of his fellow officers? One of his neighbors? He didn't even know his neighbors. Porter had kept to himself since his divorce. He was the kind of solitary person who did not clutter his life with other people and put most of his time and energy into his job.

His hands continued to tremble. His heart pounded. He ran a hand down his face and felt unshaven stubble.

He put on some clothes and drove down to Duffy's Liquors, picked up a bottle of scotch, another pack of cigarettes, and went home.

* * *

A week passed.

At the beginning of the week, Porter had called the station again and arranged to take his other two weeks of vacation time, as well. It felt like it would be a little while before he could go back to work.

For most of that time, Porter was drunk. He made a couple of trips to Duffy's liquors, one to 7-Eleven for bread, lunch meat, and milk. But he ate very little of the food he bought. He now wore a beard and mustache. His hair was greasy because he had not bathed. He went to the bathroom only when he needed to, and to his bedroom even less. He did not sleep, although on occasion he dozed in his recliner, only to be awakened by a vision of Mrs. DiMarco's decaying corpse clutching his pant leg.

You're going to die soon, Mrs. DiMarco's rasping voice said in his mind again and again. There was nothing he could do to shut the voice off, to block out the words.

His phone rang a few times, but he did not answer it and he ignored his voicemail.

On Friday afternoon, he went to the kitchen to make himself a sandwich. Mrs. DiMarco lay on the kitchen floor, reaching out for him. Her tongue moved, but she did not make a sound. He heard the words in his mind, though.

You're going to die soon.

Pain exploded in his chest, so intense that he could not make a sound, could not breathe. His legs buckled and he landed on his ass on the floor, eyes clenched shut. He put a hand to his chest and finally sucked in a breath. When he opened his eyes again, the corpse was gone. But the pain did not go away. It continued to explode in his chest, over and over again, radiating into his shoulders and arms, until he fell onto his back, mouth open, making a strangled sound in his throat.

* * *

Leonard Porter had been away from work for three weeks when Officer Kevin Nadry was summoned to Magnolia Estates. He went to apartment 14A to see Mrs. Olivette Spelling, who had called the police. But he smelled the foul odor as soon as he entered the complex.

Mrs. Spelling said it seemed to be coming from apartment 16B, just upstairs.

Officer Nadry was concerned. He knew Porter lived there.

"No one's seen him in a couple of weeks," Mrs. Spelling told him.

Nadry went upstairs and knocked on the door. "Hey, Lenny, you in there?" He rang the bell. No response.

He found the manager, a Miss Fuchs, and she let him into the apartment. The smell was overpowering.

Nadry entered with a sick feeling of dread.

The television was on with the volume low.

He found Porter on the kitchen floor, his body well into the process of decay.

"Oh, God, Lenny," Nadry said, his voice thin and sad.

He turned to leave the kitchen, but something held his pant leg. He looked down and saw Porter clutching the cuff.

"You're going to die soon," Porter rasped.

Nadry screamed as he ran out of the apartment.

The Blackest of Cats
Benjamin Blake

1.

The cat had followed Vinnie home from Earney's, the butcher shop in town.

Which wasn't too surprising, considering the amount of meat he had just purchased, but still, it seemed like something out of one of the old black and white movies his wife, Linda, liked to watch on the TV late at night. And that was rather suiting as the cat was black and white itself – well, mostly black, but it did have a small patch of white on its neck, right dead in the center. It was strangely heart-shaped.

It was a handsome puss, a large male (or so Vinnie thought, he wasn't one-hundred-percent, he had always been more of a dog person), in great condition with glossy coat, and intelligent yellow eyes.

Vinnie's hands had been full on the walk so he couldn't stop to pet the cat (he was already beginning to think of him as "Fat Tony"), but he stopped every now and then, turning around as the cat meowed and walked up to rub himself against his legs.

Linda had turned down his proposal to get a puppy, saying that with a three-month old baby they had enough on their plate. But would she be open to the idea of a cat? Cats were supposed to be pretty self-sufficient, weren't they? Fat Tony didn't wear a collar and did seem pretty damn hungry – though judging by his rotund figure, he was certainly eating well. And, anyway, if the cat chose to follow him home it was by his own free-will – Vinnie hadn't cat-napped the amiable creature.

Vinnie climbed the front stoop and banged on the door with his free hand while clutching his precious cargo to his chest with the other.

'Well, this is the last stop, Fat Tony. I guess this is goodbye.'

The cat bounded up the stairs and proceeded to scratch at the door. Vinnie laughed. 'She's taking her time, isn't she, buddy?'

The cat meowed in response. The door opened and Linda gasped in surprise as Fat Tony sprinted into the house. He moved surprisingly fast for such a chubby specimen.

'Jesus Christ, Vinnie! What the hell was that?!' A look of utter disbelief played across her face.

'That's "Fat Tony." He followed me home from Earney's.' Vinnie handed his wife the packages of sausages, steaks, and dried meats, and stepped inside after the wayward cat.

'Get that thing out of here this instant, Vinnie, and are you certain you got enough meat? You could feed half of New Jersey with all this!'

'The party was your idea, not mine – you wouldn't want to disappoint your guests would you?'

Fat Tony had made himself at home on the leather sofa, and was curled into a ball and purring contentedly away to himself. Vinnie hadn't completely abandoned all hope; he still had the "puppy" argument up his sleeve, and was more than willing to use it. He found himself slightly surprised at how fond of the cat he'd grown already.

'Where's the baby?' Vinnie asked, as he reached tentatively for the cat – you could never be too careful.

'Little Henry's taking a nap in his room, I finally got him to stop crying and pass out.'

'That's good, darling.' Vinnie ran a hand along the cat's fur, causing him to purr even louder. 'That's a good kitty,' he crooned, slipping a hand beneath his sizeable belly and picking him up. Fat Tony meowed, and butted his head affectionately against his cheek. Vinnie followed Linda into the kitchen, waiting for his wife to say something.

'You do realize there's no way we're keeping that cat, don'tcha? Besides, it probably belongs to somebody – strays aren't that fat.'

She opened the refrigerator and bent over to place the meat on a shelf. Vinnie admired her Levi-clad behind. His wife had a great ass, and even after two years of marriage, he still took a great amount of pleasure in admiring it.

Fat Tony meowed irritably as if he had known what Linda had just said - or most likely he just wanted his pick of the meat.

'Aw, look what you've done now! You've upset the poor guy.'

'I'm not joking, Vinnie,' she said as she stood and swept her dyed blonde hair from her pretty face.

'I know, I know! Look, he's a lovely puss and I swear he'd be no trouble. How about we see if he wants to stick around the rest of the day, and then decide, okay?'

Linda scowled, and pursed her lips – a sure sign that she was about to give in to his demands (not that it happened very often).

'How about it?' Vinnie asked, setting Fat Tony down on the linoleum floor and slipping his arms around his wife's waist. Before she could reply, he brushed a stubbly cheek against hers, and lightly started to kiss her neck, knowing that that was her weak-button.

Running her hands through his messy dark brown hair, she said: 'As long as you make sure you shave before tomorrow night, you look like a bum.'

2.

Fat Tony was absolutely no trouble whatsoever for the rest of the day. He spent the majority of it curled up asleep on the leather sofa.

Little Henry woke up again around twelve (bang on lunch Linda noted – he definitely took after his father in that respect), and she fed him a can of apple-cinnamon flavor baby food as well as his bottle.

Even though it was a Friday, Vinnie wasn't rostered on at the restaurant like he usually was. He assumed the boss has taken pity on him due to the long hours he had been putting in lately. He was only a waiter, but the work was still pretty damn exhausting. Especially taking in the fact that he had a baby – a child could tear apart a good night's sleep like a miniature tornado. He had the whole weekend off so had a good chance to fully recuperate if Henry didn't act up, and if he could restrain himself from drinking too much during the party.

Vinnie made chicken cacciatore for dinner, and fed Fat Tony a handful of little scraps he had cut off the thighs. After the meal was on the stove and simmering away, he poured two glasses of red wine and joined Linda on the sofa where she sat watching Rachael Ray on TV next to the baby. The cat trailed him into the living room and jumped on Linda's lap.

'See, he loves you!' Vinnie laughed, trying not to look too amused.

Linda stroked the cat's back.

'Yeah, well, he's still not ours.'

'He could be,' Vinnie smiled, a mischievous look playing in his dark eyes.

As if to accentuate his statement, Fat Tony stretched up and smooched Linda's neck, before settling back down and kneading her jeans with his paws.

'He knows what you like, baby. Kisses on the neck and a good thigh massage.'

Purring away, Fat Tony said; 'Meow!'

That was the clincher.

3.

'I can't believe you got me to agree to keeping Fat Tony,' Linda said, helping herself to more of the cacciatore.

'He's a charmer, alright,' Vinnie replied.

'Where is he, anyway?'

'I actually don't know.'

Right on cue there was a meow from somewhere down the hall that led to the bedrooms.

'That sounded like it came from Little Henry's room,' Linda said, setting her plate down on the coffee table that sat in front of the television set. 'I better go check that he's not disturbing him – the last thing we need is Henry waking back up already, he's been so good today.' She took one more slug of wine, and headed off to check on her son.

A moment later she reappeared, cradling not Henry but Fat Tony in her arms.

'I found this guy inside of Henry's cot, trying to smooch him to death – thank God he hadn't woken up - though, it's a miracle that he didn't.'

Linda sat back down next to her husband, setting Fat Tony between them.

Vinnie couldn't help but think he looked a little pissed.

4.

The evening of the party rolled around in no time at all. Friends and family started to arrive at around six, Linda welcoming them and fixing and fetching drinks, while Vinnie grilled steaks and sausages in the backyard, beer in hand, and enjoying the pleasant spring weather.

He looked up from the grill plate, taking a swig of Bud, and saw his uncle Vito come out the back door, a beer clenched in each chubby hand and a cigarillo stuck in his stubbly face.

'Vinnie!' You son of a bitch! - and I'm allowed to say that cause your mom's my sister, how ya doin'?'

Vinnie couldn't help but smile, Uncle Vito was a loudmouth and a lush, but, boy, was he lovable.

'I'm good, Uncle V, watching my weight and my hairline so I don't end up looking like you.'

'Hey!' Vito said, rubbing his sparse-haired pate with a forearm. 'I'm not *that* bald.'

'The hell you got two beers for? One's not enough, you fat bastard?'

'Hey, one of these's for you, I thought you could use one, being chained to the grill and all.'

Vinnie gave his uncle a hug and a kiss on the cheek. 'Thanks, old timer.'

'Don't mention it, kid. Those steaks look damn good, by the way.'

'They'll be done soon, Uncle V, you're not going to miss out, don't worry.'

'That's what I like to hear.'

Vinnie finished the rest of his beer, and started on the one that Uncle V had given him.

'Jesus! That's a fat cat!' Vito exclaimed.

Vinnie turned to see Fat Tony come padding out of the small patch of shrubbery at the rear of the yard.

'You're not wrong there. That's Fat Tony, come to harass me into giving him a piece of rib-eye, too.'

Uncle V laughed. 'That's a puss after my own heart. When did you get him? I haven't seen him around here before.'

'Followed me home from Earney's yesterday morning, would you believe it? He's a good-natured creature, managed to win Linda over, and seems to have taken a shine to Little Henry, too.'

'Yeah? You better hope the Cat Police don't come knocking at your door, you cheap prick.'

'He came by his own volition, V. I didn't do nothin.''

'You enticed the poor guy with Earney's best cuts of steak! That cat got lured here good and proper.' Vito pointed in mock reproach at Vinnie with the neck of his beer bottle.

Vinnie cut the cat off a small piece of steak and held it out for Fat Tony. He gulped it down with admirable gusto.

'Hey, where's mine?' Uncle V asked, polishing off his beer.

5.

The house party was in full swing by ten p.m.

The turn-out was considerably good. People ate, drank and laughed the night away in the backyard. Bottles clinked, and anecdotes were told for the first or hundredth time – depending on who was recounting them.

Vinnie was feeling quite merry – though, not as high-spirited as Uncle Vito, who was doing some kind of crazy dance in front of some of Linda's girlfriends – who were finding it extremely entertaining indeed.

Vinnie had just finished his current beer (he had kind of lost count), when Linda came over, her glass of wine sloshing over the rim in the process. 'Vinnie, can you check on Little Henry? I'd do it, but I'm a little drunk and I don't wanna spill my drink on the carpet.'

'Why don'tcha just put your wine down somewhere?'

'Vinnie!' Linda said, looking melodramatically horrified.

'I was joking, I was joking,' Vinnie laughed. 'Of course I'll go and check on him.'

Uncle Vito continued to dance like a loon as Vinnie headed in to check on the baby.

6.

The bulb in the hall blew when Vinnie flipped the switch.

Warm yellow light spilled out of the baby's room. 'Goddamn thing,' he muttered as he made his way toward the soft glow of the nightlight. Once through the doorway, he found himself frozen on the spot. The cat sat upon his son's small chest. His face bent in close to the baby's.

Right away he knew that there was something wrong. The cat wasn't just smooching Little Henry, it was as if he was sucking the breath right from his tiny lungs. Vinnie noticed in horror that Henry's face was turning a shade of blue.

The covers had been pulled back and Fat Tony's claws were digging through Little Henry's pajamas and into his skin. The baby made a terrible choking sound, and his father broke free of whatever spell was holding him. He lunged toward the cat, a guttural cry of rage ripping from his throat.

Grasping the cat with both hands, he tore it from his poor child. A small piece of flannel fabric from Henry's pajamas was stuck on the cat's claws. Fat Tony yowled, and twisted in Vinnie's grasp, raking a razor-studded claw against his right cheek. It left a jagged wound that instantly started to pour blood.

Vinnie cried out in pain and reflexively dropped the cat, which bolted out of the room and disappeared down the hall.

No time for him, Vinnie thought, as he stumbled to Henry's cot. He grabbed hold of his son, praying out loud that he was alive. He held his baby's angelic little face against his ear. He could neither hear, nor feel any breath.

Vinnie tore Henry's pajamas open and felt for a heartbeat. There was none. His son was dead.

He sunk to his knees, sobbing relentlessly. Droplets of blood spilt from his wounded cheek and fell on his son's forehead.

Footsteps grew louder in the hall, his wife's frantic screams, and his uncle's drunken shouts.

He blacked out.

Epilogo

Katie thanked the elderly gentleman who held the door for her, as she wheeled the pram out of the butcher shop. The small package of pastrami that she had purchased sat in her daughter's lap.

She swept a strand of brown hair from her face, and started wheeling baby Lily toward the small apartment they had moved into the week before.

She didn't notice the rather large black cat which trailed along the sidewalk behind them.

La Fine

Comfortable in the Harness
Lance Tuck

Static blared from the speakers as lightning arced across the night sky, a powerful blue-white burst of energy that infused every electrical system within ten miles, a belch of charged particles forcing its voice overwhelmingly into every one of the senses of the men who drove through the stormy night. An orchestra of light, sound and motion seemed to try its best to distract them from their tasks.

"Jesus, that one was close!" the driver muttered as he reached for the volume knob on the radio. He had nearly swerved off the road, blinded by the elemental fury unleashed upon them as they raced along (too fast, if one was keeping track) toward their destination. "It figures that they have to do this during the stormiest goddamned night of the past decade!" Thunder boomed mightily, as if in response to the pale bald man's complaint, a dreadful shearing explosion that sounded as if some monstrous horror were trying to rend apart the heavens themselves. "Jesus, that one was right on top of us!" he added nervously, his blue eyes wide with fear.

"Don't take it too personally, Doc. You didn't design the damned thing. Is there anything coming in on that radio?" The man in the passenger seat shook his head as he inhaled lightly on the aromatic, cone-shaped bidi cigarette. His window was lowered just a bit, in a vain effort to draw the smoke out the window, away from his companion. He presumed that Dr. Laudick did not smoke.

As a general rule, Dominic Laudick *did not* smoke, but tonight was exceptional on many vectors. "Give me that!" Dr. Laudick snapped, snatching the cigarette away from the slouching engineer in the seat beside him. It was more brittle than an American cigarette, more like a little dry cigar, and the strange sweet smoke brought back memories for Dominic. Memories of the time he had spent in Iraq, where he had picked up the habit for a brief period. He stared intently at his companion, his icy blue eyes giving no indication of approval or disdain, only a hawk-like focus. Dominic Laudick took a deep pull from the Indian cigarette, then handed it back to Lloyd Morfran. "Nothing on the radio...not this far out. Not in weather like this. Just dead air," he said as he turned the radio off, coughing slightly as he exhaled.

Lloyd shook his head as he accepted the bidi, a slight, bemused smile playing briefly across his otherwise bleak features. He looked like a condemned man, ironically enough, as they sped along toward the New Panopticon site, far away from any major population center. Lloyd thanked God for that little kindness...at least if any of the subjects had somehow escaped, they would need to travel for some distance before they would find anyone to victimize.

"Maybe I didn't design it, but I sure as hell oversaw their medical care. If they really did escape, there will be questions. This isn't the desert, or Guantanamo Bay! There will be consequences, and I intend to make sure that I am not found at fault." Lightning forked across the sky again, lighting up Dominic's eyes with a brilliant blue.

"The jackass that woke me up didn't tell me much. He said we had a security situation; that doesn't mean it was necessarily an escape." Lloyd knew damn well what it meant if even one of their test subjects had escaped. He knew what they were capable of; he had to. He was the one that translated Dr. Gaston's profiles and diagnoses into actionable program architecture to keep the subjects contained. And it had worked perfectly for three years...up to now.

"What could it be? Why would they call for us at this hour...in this weather?!" Another flash of photonic rage cracked the sky as thunder shook the ground. Rain swept across the road, pouring from the darkened skies. "It's got to be Rothwell. He was the one with the weird EEG's. I bet he stroked out." Dr. Laudick continued to pursue fruitless speculation about the reason they were called out. But Lloyd Morfran had a pretty good idea of who the problem was. The whole network had been running screwy since they brought him in. They had just chalked the irregularities up to overtaxing the grid, running too many cons through it at once.

Something told Lloyd that it wasn't just stress on the network, not just too many demands on the memory grid. He knew that there was enough memory and power to simulate a damned mini-multiverse. His designs were not at fault. The trouble hadn't started with Rothwell. His sensory system was anomalous, it was true, but he was responsive to the simulation and showed no signs of wakefulness during the diagnostic evaluations.

"I told you it felt like he could see us. I knew something was wrong with him. He probably woke up and panicked. He probably had a stroke." Dr. Laudick shifted his hands uneasily on the leather-wrapped wheel. He had forgotten his driving gloves, and the storm had made him tense. He was an expert driver, but the conditions in the storm were absolutely relentless. The tobacco was now pushing through his system, calming him by stimulating his processors. That was why he was suddenly so chatty.

"It isn't Rothwell. It's Milton." Lloyd took a too-deep pull from the bidi, finishing it off. He squeezed the glowing coals of the roach between his fingers, the last tiny bits of fire extinguishing against bare skin that sizzled slightly in protest. "The trouble all began when they brought in Raymond Milton."

The wind howled around the towncar as it raced through the coursing rain. Dominic Laudick could see the lights of the facility up ahead. It was bigger than the ones he had worked at overseas, in Iraq and Dubai, but smaller than the camp in Cuba. It looked smaller still in the downpour, its lights muted by the driving rain, but he wasn't looking at the approaching prison.

He was staring incredulously at Lloyd Morfron.

"You'd better watch the road. It could have washed out or something." Lloyd knew what Laudick was thinking, but it wouldn't do them any good to wreck way out here in the boonies. Dr. Laudick seemed to recover his senses and snapped his attention back to the road.

"Why are you so sure that it's Milton?" the doctor demanded. There was an underlying concern in his voice, an annoyed expectancy. It was clear that he had a pretty damned good idea of what had persuaded Lloyd. "Please tell me that you haven't been listening to that hack headshrinker Baylor-"

"He is a certified clinical psychologist. But he hasn't influenced my reasons."

"More like certifiable," Dominic muttered humorlessly as he fiddled with the radio knob again. Anything would be better than hearing more of Jim Baylor's insane theories about why Ray Milton went on his killing sprees.

"Yes, I have read his evaluations, but that has nothing to do with why I suspect Milton. Those evaluations are...bizarre, at best, barely worth reading by the end. He isn't the first doctor to come to fear his patient, though his explanations are somewhat...colorful." No, it wasn't that. It was the way that the simulation reacted when it interfaced with Milton. Lloyd could tell that the AI was having trouble synchronizing with his sensory inputs. He could sense that his creation was having difficulties with the killer's perceptual style. It wasn't normal, when everything else seemed to be. But how do you explain such an instinctive appraisal to a man like Doc Laudick, whose whole career is based upon diagnostic aberration? *Too normal* was bound to sound crazy.

"I would have preferred to have read Dr. Gaston's evaluations," Dominic sniped. The storm had him quite agitated.

Lloyd Morfron answered almost without emotion, "Yes, so would I, but Dr. Gaston is dead, so he can't help us with that." Lloyd noted that Dr. Laudick usually did not bitch this much. But Dr. Gaston's death was unexpected. Had Gaston still been alive, it was likely that Dr. Laudick would not even have been contacted about tonight's event. Lloyd wondered how the man had maintained his security clearance for so long, as much as he talked. That security clearance was the main reason Dr. Laudick was brought into the project. "I need to see the readouts...see what happened. Once we learn who woke up, we can figure out how they bypassed the wake-up protocols."

"*If* they did," Laudick added. The sky lit up again with another river of blue fire. They were nearly at the Supermax. Something was really wrong, they both knew it. "Where the hell is the escort? Did they miss us in the rain?" Dominic peered into the darkness, straining to see if he could recognize the features of the landscape. He felt lost.

"No way. It has to be the storm...messing with the gear. The security cameras had to have seen us." Lloyd had seen the tech used to monitor the wilderness around the prison, both active and passive systems. If they hadn't sent out interceptors, it meant that they had their hands full. If it weren't for the rules about cell phones, he could just call the warden. But they had left their cell phones behind because of the rules at New Panopticon.

The project had been put together by the bigwigs from Luminary Investment Group as part of their bid for a piece of the private prison market. Arclight Financial Services had tried before, but it wasn't profitable enough because of the extreme cases. For lower tier incarceration, there was money to be made, but the maximum security cases blew the profitability curve. New Panopticon was supposed to correct the capital imbalance.

The notion was to create a low labor, high security containment unit that would allow for the safe monitoring of incarcerated, high-risk, super violent offenders. The corporation was willing to financially back an experimental facility that allowed maximum monitoring with minimal manpower. Each model that was proposed resulted in a failed test run. In every case, the convicts themselves were able to manipulate their jailers, resulting in favoritism, and that led to disaster in each case. The problem was the human element. Without the right kind of jailer, it was impossible to provide fair and proper supervision for the inmates without utilizing a rotating roster of overseers or inhuman conditions of isolation.

The solution was simple. Eliminate the human element that allowed for the detrimental behaviors; eliminate the interaction itself.

Obviously, physical isolation had terrible ramifications for the psychology of the inmate, but what if the inmate didn't realize that they were isolated? What if the inmate could be convinced that they were in fact interacting intensely with a staff of rehabilitation specialists all working toward the goal of the inmate's eventual release?

Most options of this sort were simply not financially feasible; android jailers...holograms…artificial intelligences on view screens. Too scifi...too 1984. Too expensive to even test. But Lloyd Morfron had been developing brainscan technology for visualizing and recording dreams, and he had learned the means to stimulate the sensory pathways of sleeping patients in a fashion that allowed him to control what the dreamers perceived as they slept. That was why Luminary Investment Group contacted him.

The bigwigs wanted to know if people in medically induced comas could be made to think that they were in fact out living their lives in the real world. Lloyd presumed that the research he was doing would be used to better the lives of the injured and incapacitated. He envisioned a technology that would free the catatonic, the comatose. He imagined his creation helping innocent victims of disease and misadventure to participate more fully in society than they could have ever done before!

He couldn't have been more wrong.

By the time old Lloyd had figured out what Luminary Investment Group of Highland, Texas had intended to do with his technology, he was in too deep to extract himself. As a psychologist, he would have been ashamed of how his efforts were being used. But he wasn't a psychologist. He was an engineer. And at this point, the best he could do was see to it that his creation wasn't used for even more nefarious purposes.

That was why Dr. Laudick had such little confidence in Lloyd's integrity. Dominic believed that technologists were intrinsically less moral than biologists, though he would never admit to this irrational prejudice. He felt that a certain level of inhumanity was necessary to work with hard, unyielding components, that the ability to intuit the properties of elements and forms somehow precluded one from having the delicateness to navigate the rivers of human decency. After everything that Dr. Dominic Laudick had done in the name of God and country, he needed to believe that he saw human beings as more than simple automatons of meat and chemicals.

He needed to believe that he was still one of them.

And Lloyd knew that that was how they kept Dr. Laudick quiet and loyal to the program. If the team pulled this off, then it would be the conclusion of Dominic's journey, the vindication of his methods, no matter how questionable they might have seemed. If, in the final analysis, he had protected the innocent by his actions, no matter how morally reprehensible those actions might have been, then his career would be legitimate. His "special service" as a civilian contractor for the military would never be questioned.

Dominic Laudick would never have to remember what they had unknowingly done to hundreds of innocent men who had refused to admit to being terrorists. His team had found ways to make them admit it. Even if "the terrorists" were innocent. Some died from the distress. It haunted him, as a professional and as a human being. He needed to make amends, even if in only the smallest way. If Panopticon was effective, he knew that he could lay those ghosts to rest.

"Alright, we're driving past the prison now. We should be at the facility in fifteen minutes." *Where the hell are the escorts?* Dr. Laudick wondered, not daring to voice the words. Riot wasn't a possibility in the Supermax. Power failure was an inconvenience of moments. On site generators would kick in after three minutes, and the cell locks and surveillance systems had six hours of primary battery power, not including backup cells. Something cataclysmic would have had to have happened to compromise security enough to suspend intercept and escort protocols.

As if on cue, a nearly simultaneous eruption of charged particles and sonic shock waves rattled the fabric of reality just above their towncar, making both men jump in their seats. The blinding blue-white cracks in the sky burned temporary shards of frosty white into the retinas of the two men as the gods sounded their mighty judgment through the power of the storm.

"Maybe a direct lightning strike took out their surveillance. A power surge from that might take ten, maybe fifteen minutes to complete a reboot," Dominic rambled on, speculating endlessly. It wasn't helping anyone feel better.

"Maybe they have better things to do than risk men on escorting a couple of dumbasses who don't know better than to drive out in the middle of a fucking monsoon," Lloyd mused absentmindedly, not even entirely aware he had said it aloud.

"I just hope everyone's alright." Dr. Laudick pretended he hadn't heard the last comment. Perhaps he hadn't; the thunder had been deafening.

"They're psychopaths and monsters. Believe me, we'd all be better off if they had died before anyone even knew their names. They'd probably thank us for letting them die now." Lloyd didn't really believe the last part. He had seen their psych profiles. The test subjects were pure predatory rage. They lived to feed on the softest parts of society in the most brutal fashion possible. They had all been sentenced to death for their crimes, and each had received clemency in exchange for volunteering for the project. There was just one detail that was left out.

None of the candidates had any idea that they would be put into medically induced comas. They were told that they would be provided with an intensive inpatient rehabilitative experience that would last up to five years. Upon completion of the study, each candidate would be remanded to life in the Supermax facility.

But the experiment was conducted at the site beyond the prison, close enough to the prison medical facilities, but far enough to be certain there was no contact between the experimental group and the Supermax inmates. Some of these bastards were very bright...genius level. If there was some way for them to contact one another, coordinate some sort of escape attempt, these people would find and exploit it. That was a reality that they had to accept as overseers of the experiment, but it had somehow never seemed real until now.

Lightning seared the skies again, briefly illuminating the bleak wilderness. In the driving rain it was nearly impassible. Only the most savage could survive here. Nothing human could last for long, especially in a storm like this. Still, Lloyd had a very strong sense that something was out there, watching them.

Supermax protocols were in effect at the experimental facility. No cell phones, no broadcast radios, no satellite phones. No way to upload location data, like coordinates. No hired guns would be sent in to free their comrades or bosses; some of the experimental subjects were career military, others were high-level cartel operatives. Visitation was suspended for the duration of the study, but most participants had long since stopped receiving visitors. Even their therapists visited only out of medical necessity.

Before tonight, Lloyd could have believed that God might not see you out here. Now, as the thunder rolled across the valley, he couldn't have felt more exposed, as if something had taken an unholy interest in what they were doing out beyond the edges of civilization. Something...not God.

"Surely you don't truly believe that?" Dr. Laudick asked. "You honestly don't believe that these people have any chance for redemption?" He paused, waiting, but Lloyd didn't answer. "Then why did you even join up with this project? If you didn't believe they should be rehabilitated, why did you even agree to try?"

"It was never about rehabilitation, Dominic," Lloyd Morfron said without any emotion. How could a murderer like Sal Grimaldi, who fed his victims to innocent families, ever hope to be normal again? How could you fix a woman like Annie Stotts who put poisoned pills deep into the bottles of vital medicines of elderly people in her care, making sure that they wouldn't use them until long after she was out of the circle of suspicion, raising the concept of premeditation to new heights? Sadistic perverts that entertained their sickness at the expense of innocent children...can you wipe away the awful stains that such acts leave on the minds of everyone involved?

No. No, it wasn't possible to forgive and forget. But by diligent study of the known examples, one could develop an early diagnostic system, to recognize the thought patterns of dangerous minds before they unleashed themselves on the public at large. Such patterns could only be identified in the environment that generated the hostility, that prompted the rage that resulted in the criminal acts. That was where Lloyd's machines came in.

They were designed to generate the complete sensory experience of a low-security medical rehabilitative facility. Comatose subjects were plugged in to the virtual reality architecture without their knowledge. For all intents and purposes, they were forced to take part in a simulation that afforded them complete freedom to act and respond as they chose, without fear of reprisal by their captors. Each subject was exposed to a reality carefully crafted to test their ability to resist their homicidal impulses. Dr. Gaston's profiles were used to create stressors and irresistible temptations meant to evoke the worst in the test subjects.

It worked like a charm. The subjects embraced the artificial reality wholeheartedly, participating unknowingly in the investigation into the roots of their own criminality. It was illuminating. And every bit of it was recorded for posterity. As new subjects were brought in, the program was expanded to accommodate their unique histories and psycho-pathologies. They all seemed to be oblivious to the nature of their incarceration. Most of them experienced relapse, lashing out at virtual family members or fellow patients, some even murdering members of their surrogate society.

This simulation was regarded as a safe, experimentally controlled virtual exercise, only allowing victimless crimes it was argued. The final rationalization for building a murder simulator was that it allowed the study of extreme criminality without risking the lives of innocent people. Those who touted this justification failed to consider the greater harm of reinforcing the murderous behaviors of the human subjects involved. Just like Lloyd, they considered the subjects to be "monsters," subhuman beasts not worthy of even the most rudimentary expressions of decency or mercy.

After all, hadn't each of them been sentenced to die for their crimes? Had any of them shown mercy?

Raymond Milton was the last subject selected for the program. He had been convicted of a series of bizarre ritual homicides that were coordinated with Christian holidays in honor of the Saints. He was arrested with "religious accessories" manufactured from the skins of three of his victims, all priests of different denominations. Milton had a solid shot at a "not guilty by reason of insanity" plea, but he wouldn't hear of it. He was lucid, positively charming in court. Raymond plainly admitted his guilt, almost boasting as he recounted the specifics of his crimes to the jury, a wry smile on his narrow face all the while. He demanded to be found guilty, and was not disappointed. He was found guilty on thirteen counts of premeditated murder and sentenced to die.

Milton waived his rights of appeal. He was represented by a high-dollar attorney from a Boston firm who provided the services *pro bono*. It was this attorney who steered Milton into the program. He was an ideal candidate. No diagnosable psychiatric disorders, no organic mental defects or abnormalities. No family or other "entanglements." He was accepted without hesitation.

Raymond Milton was medically fit, in excellent health for a thirty year old man. He gave no indication that he was even remotely repentant, on more than one occasion stating sarcastically, "Send in the clowns, baby...let the healing begin!" He truly enjoyed describing his victims' suffering in lurid detail, mocking their pleas and suffering. Milton held particular scorn for religion.

For that reason, it was determined that Raymond Milton's therapeutic simulation would be charged with religious elements and miraculous displays of the power of faith. Dr. Gaston was not in support of this choice, a decision made at the highest levels of Luminary Investment Group without any apparent medical consideration. He said that he had not had adequate time to interview and evaluate Milton to determine the best way to confront his pathology without entrenching him in the aberrant behavior, or worse, causing him to become unhinged.

That was always a risk with Hyber-Reality, as the team had come to jokingly call the mental state. Some just called it braindance. If the subject realized that the environment was not real, that it was constructed and manipulated, it could trigger a dangerous neuro-chemical cascade that might render the subject irrevocably insane. Such complete dis-integration from reality was a real risk when dealing with borderline personalities, and if such a psychotic break did occur, the subject could awaken, have seizures, stroke out or even die. In the induced coma, the only way to tell was to monitor the vital signs and the graphic display readout that Lloyd had created to observe the perceptions of the test subjects.

Dr. Gaston was afraid that Raymond Milton might be more likely to suffer such an event because of the deeply personal nature of his motivations. Religion was at the root of his murderous sprees, and until they had a full understanding of exactly how Milton thought he was fulfilling a religious imperative by killing those innocent people, it was foolhardy at best to expose the subject to simulations of supernatural religious activity. The doctor finally threatened to publicly out the program to the media, to see what the people thought about the company's plan. He was instructed to not return to work for the rest of the week, to consider his level of commitment to the program.

It was during that week that Dr. Marcus Gaston was murdered in his own home during an apparent burglary break in. Had he been at work, he would not have been home to face the intruder that killed him. His notes and interviews with Raymond Milton, though incomplete, were forwarded to Lloyd to construct the sensory architecture for the murderer's own private hell.

He loaded it with religious imagery and religious personnel. He created scenarios that would force Raymond to engage with virtual people who would challenge his twisted views of religion. Lloyd went to the limits with this one, maybe a little bit too far. He had forgotten how smart these bastards really were, no matter how addle-brained they might seem.

"Look! Look there!" Dominic yelled out, gesturing widely out into the blackness of the storm. Lloyd strained to see what he was pointing at as a flash of lightning lit up the terrain.

Lloyd saw three prison escort vehicles mangled beyond reason, black scorch marks betraying what had befallen them. Lightning.

Dominic slowed down as they drove past the wreckage, not certain what to do. He saw no signs of life, but in spite of the rain, the wasted hulks were still smoldering. It looked like they got hit while traveling in a column, creating a chain reaction crash. As the towncar slowed, it began to bog down on the rain soaked dirt road. The thickening mud began to drag the vehicle sideways.

"Don't stop, Doc! Jesus, don't stop!" Lloyd spoke with an imperious tone, a bad habit he expressed when he was stressed out. It did not win him many friends. "Ease into it, or you'll bury it for sure!"

Dominic Laudick knew how to drive, his uncle David was a professional driver and had taught him well. He turned his wheels, accelerating gently, gathering enough speed to straighten out and resume the course along the muddy dirt road. He was scared now. "What the hell happened to them? How does a whole group of escort vehicles wipe out like that?"

"Lightning. It's just the storm," Lloyd said nervously, no longer believing the words. It was the religious themes that got him thinking. There was a commonality among the test subjects that he had failed to consider until now. All of them believed that they were evil incarnate, that is, that they had literally become vessels for the devil. He originally saw it as simple dissociation, or even bravado. But now, another horrible possibility began to fulminate in his mind.

"Just a little farther...right up here!" Dominic was overjoyed at the prospect of not driving as he pulled up onto the paved road that led to the barbed wire enclosure that surrounded Panopticon. He was struck by how close the escort vehicles had been. "Almost there," he said quietly. As he slowed down safely on the mud-covered pavement, he saw a vehicle that did not belong here. "What the hell?" Dominic asked, unable to believe his eyes.

Standing beside his old Ford pickup in the driving rain was Dr. Jim Baylor, Raymond Milton's original defense attorney. He looked haggard as he waved one arm at the towncar, covering his head in a futile protective gesture with the other. His long trenchcoat was barely keeping the pouring rain off of him as he waited for the two men who were authorized to be there to get out of their car.

"Dr. Baylor...what the fuck are you doing here?" Lloyd was very to-the-point. His tone showed that he was not amused. "More importantly, how did you find this place?" If there was some sort of security leak, Lloyd wasn't gonna swing for it. He'd read Baylor's briefs about Milton, but hadn't actually spoken to the man.

"Please, gentlemen...we must go inside!" Dr. Baylor spoke with an urgency not often heard in sane men. His eyes seemed wild. Perhaps it was just the storm.

"Not a chance. What do you think you're doing here? This is trespassing." Dr. Laudick clearly disliked Jim Baylor. "Do you have any idea where you are?" Dominic was angry, because he knew exactly what Baylor was thinking: *they will have to let me inside with weather like this!*

"Please...you must listen to me. He shouldn't be here. I tried to tell you all, but no one would listen. This place...it will only make him more dangerous," Dr. Baylor spoke as if they were all old friends. "I warned you...he does not belong here!"

"Yeah, well your buddy confessed to thirteen killings, so everybody else seems to think he does belong here," Lloyd scowled as he looked at the shivering wretch pathetically trying to shield himself from the cold rain. "You realize that you will go to jail for this? This is restricted access! How the hell did you find it?"

"Google maps," he answered. "It wasn't that hard to do. I was guided. After all the time I spent with it...with him...I can sense the evil." Dr. Baylor's eyes were bright as he spoke, sparkling like those of a true believer.

"Great," Dr. Laudick scoffed. "So, does your amazing psychic power tell you how long you'll be in prison for this stunt?"

Dr. Baylor glared at Dominic Laudick, a flash of lightning illuminating his grim features as he replied, "For the rest of my life, doctor. The rest of my life. But, if we can stop what is happening here, it will be worth it. You have to let me in."

"You are not getting inside this facility," Dr. Laudick reaffirmed. "You will be escorted back to the prison and held until it is determined which agency has jurisdiction. What did you do, follow one of us?" He was convinced that Baylor was deranged, and these behaviors confirmed it. The crazy sonofabitch was probably trying to kill Raymond Milton himself.

Lloyd pushed the button to alert the on-site guards; they carried nonlethal compliance weaponry, no firearms. He didn't imagine they would need more to keep Dr. Baylor under control until they could get him to somewhere he could be dealt with by the proper authorities. Tense moments passed but the electronically locked door did not open.

"What the hell?" Dominic rolled his bright blue eyes in annoyance. "What is taking them so long?" The exterior lights were on, there was no indication of a power failure.

"We need to get inside, now!" Dr. Baylor demanded, his voice more pitched now.

Lloyd Morfran pushed the button again, then jabbed at it three or four times in rapid succession. Lightning flared as the cold rain pelted the three men. Lloyd had had enough. "Fuck this," he muttered as he entered his personal access code. He hadn't used it since twenty-four hour security had been established, and wasn't certain it would work. As he keyed in the final numbers, there was a loud buzz before the solid clank of the electronic bolt opening. The door thunked open as Lloyd caught it.

Dominic paused as he realized what had to happen now. Without the help of the guards, they would have to bring Jim Baylor inside. He stared at the gaunt man in the rain-drenched trenchcoat, and he swore that the smug bastard was silently laughing at him. "Alright...let's go. Inside." Laudick glared at Jim Baylor as he motioned for the trespasser to follow Lloyd into the Panopticon facility.

Something was definitely wrong. Emergency power was engaged, but there was no sign of any of the three guards, Beau Riggs, Mick Norbert and Perry Drake. Security cameras were active, and everything seemed to be quiet.

"Dr. Laudick...you stay here with our guest." Lloyd hissed the word, speaking with obvious derision. "I'm going to go see what the hell is happening in the lab. Don't let him get away from you," he added with an angry glare. The engineer walked down the corridor past the security station and through the heavy metal doors to the inner lab.

"You heard the man, Dr. Baylor. Let's find somewhere to sit down while we wait for the boys to come back." Dominic Laudick's mind was moving too fast. Too much was happening at once, he was having trouble making sense of it. He seemed to think that the security guards might pop right back in at any moment. Dominic pointed to the door to the security station, a small room crammed with security camera monitors and archaic file cabinets. Dr. Baylor stepped to the door and opened it as Dominic Laudick followed him inside.

"We are wasting time," Jim Baylor warned. He looked like he was about to go into another tirade about the evil that was Raymond Milton.

"Not another word, Jim. Remember, I am a doctor, and my medical opinion will count in court when I testify against you. Your crackpot ideas about Mr. Milton are a matter of public record. Coming out here tonight was not a good idea." Dr. Laudick was lecturing as he examined the bank of security monitors. He could easily access tonight's tapes and find out what in the hell had happened here.

Jim Baylor nodded as he removed his wet trenchcoat, draping it over one of the chairs. "Of course. I understand." He looked around the room and saw a mini-fridge with an electric coffee maker sitting on top. There was a pot ready to go. Jim glanced back over toward Dominic and said, "Look, at least let me get you some coffee." He nodded toward the steaming pot.

Dominic was accessing the video logs, barely paying attention to Baylor. "Sure, sure," he said dismissively as the gaunt man walked over to the coffee maker.

Lloyd had a bad feeling about all this. The two people who were supposed to be overseeing the lab were good people, it wasn't like them to be so slipshod. As he pushed the doors open to the observation room, it took him a moment for his eyes to adjust. The room called the Bedchamber was visible through the observation window, giving the overseers clear views of each test subject and their containment tubes, which were brightly lit and filled with a bluish nutrient fluid. This was almost blinding compared to the dim lighting of the observation room where banks of computers monitored everything that happened in the minds and bodies of the comatose subjects.

The first thing he noticed was that someone had moved the containment tubes around. This was no easy task, each one weighing around 1200 pounds. Nevertheless, they had been moved. And worse, some of them had gone dark.

Lloyd panicked. Dark meant one of two things: death or containment failure. He quickly scanned the room, trying to figure out which tube was which. They were arranged in a larger circle of eight lit-up tubes, about thirty feet across from each other. Inside that radius, the phantom mover had crafted another smaller circle of five tubes, all silent and dark. Lloyd could not see if they had been breached. He immediately turned his attention to the monitors, studying the readouts. Five had gone flat, but it was impossible to tell if it was because the subject was deceased or unplugged.

He read the names of the murderers in the dark cocoons. Kenneth Tennent, aka Mr. Clean, a brutal murderer who invaded his victims' homes and tortured them with "purification rituals" consisting of bleach baths and drain cleaner enemas over the course of weeks, in some cases. Monty Lee Gerardo, aka Alastor, an enforcer for the Brimstone Brotherhood MC. He was convicted of criminal mayhem and depraved indifference for his tender ministrations to enemies of the MC, as well as 6 admitted murders. Walter Pennycuff, aka Roadrage, a sexual predator that made Ted Bundy look like a boy scout. He murdered 25 people across 6 states. Keynan Arbuckle, the infamous Mr. Mulch, a greenskeeper who forced his still-living victims into a woodchipper to finish their time with him. He was an enthusiastic torturer and rapist as well. And finally, Lyndon Lee Pearl, a pale-skinned monster, slight of build and of quiet demeanor. He was called Morning Sunshine, and was the one who terrified Lloyd the most of all because of his absolute, studied evil. Lyndon would target religious families where one parent woke and left the home a few hours before the rest of the family woke. He would break into the home and horribly disfigure the children, who usually bled out before they were found. His calling card was using a severed body part to write "Morning Sunshine!" on the walls of the family room in the blood of the youngest child.

The group of names struck him. His heart froze as he realized why he saw a connection between them. Each one of these killers claimed to have been killing in service to the Devil. He looked around the dark monitor room, his eyes finally adjusting to the dim light. He recoiled in horror as he saw, written in blood that was still fresh and red, "Morning Sunshine!" scrawled in crude letters over the doorway.

"Lloyd..." a quiet, almost feminine voice purred from the darkness of the hallway as Lyndon Lee Pearl walked into the room, his pale naked skin glistening with streaks of scarlet gore. "So good of you to come..."

Dominic had accessed the security files and was watching as Jim Baylor poured two big mugs of hot coffee. Dr. Laudick was watching as Beau Riggs and Mick Norbert seemed to be drawing something on the floor around one of the containment tubes. He couldn't believe what he was seeing.

"What are they doing?"

Jim Baylor squinted as he strained to make out details. "Looks like they're making a magic circle. Probably to contain something."

"Yes, Jim, I read all about how you believed that Raymond Milton was actually possessed by demons. That doesn't mean that anyone else believes it." As Dominic watched, the two guards finished their artistic endeavor, but the camera angle wasn't right. Mick pulled a small prayer book out and began to read aloud. Dr. Laudick was stunned. "What the hell? They weren't authorized to do that! Who the hell told them to do that?!" Dominic demanded rhetorically.

Jim Baylor answered back, "Why I did, of course." Before Dominic could even turn around, Jim knocked him out cold with the hot coffee pot.

Dominic woke from a bleary dream, his scalp and neck burned, a dull throb piercing through his skull. He looked around, saw that he and Lloyd had both been taken. They were now restrained, seated in the Bedchamber, positioned in the center of the circle formed by the containment tubes. Someone had been carving on Lloyd; his face, caked with blood showed evidence of a good beating.

Jim Baylor was there. And Lyndon Lee Pearl. So was Mr. Mulch, and Mr. Clean, and even Monty Lee Gerardo, Alastor, himself. Their eyes were not right. Now, in control, they allowed themselves to be seen through the windows of their hosts' souls. Jim Baylor leaned in close, his bright, unnaturally green eyes more akin in character to a goat than a human being as he chuckled. "I knew we could get you boys out here. We just had to make you think your machines had failed."

"So it was all a sham?" Laudick asked, trembling. He had never put much stock in stories about devils and demons, but now, confronting them...his mind was beginning to unhinge. "Why? What did we ever do?"

"Well, pretty much everything you did in Iraq and Cuba, for starters. Oh, don't look so surprised. I can smell your sins. Your guilt." Jim Baylor smiled as he wrinkled his nose in jest. "But that wasn't what demanded action. No, Dominic, it was your friend's machine that forced our hand."

Lyndon Lee Pearl stepped forward, slashing at Lloyd's face with a piece of broken glass. "Wake up, Sunshine! No more sleepy time!" Lloyd moaned and jerked his head away from the agonizing assault.

"How? How did you get the guards to turn?" Dominic had seen the tape, seen Riggs and Norbert performing some sort of ritual around Raymond Milton's container.

"I didn't. You told them about my "unorthodox" beliefs about old Raymond here. A couple of god-fearin' patriots like them, they jumped at the chance to do battle with the Devil." The thing in Jim Baylor rolled its luminous green eyes as it laughed. "Too bad they didn't know the difference between an exorcism and a summoning!"

All of the assembled demons laughed at that one.

"Yeah, Lloyd, your machine worked a little too damned well!" Raymond said, his voice cold and lifeless, his eyes deep black with a distant point of liquid blue occasionally catching the dim light. "The first couple that you snatched from us, we let it slide. After you took The Gristleman...well, we had to get involved."

"No!" Dominic protested. "No, the program was supposed to help them...to rehabilitate them!"

"No it wasn't. It was to study them." Jim laughed openly at Dominic's naivety. "Do you think an asshole like Lloyd Morfran would actually be a philanthropist?" He kicked Lloyd, making the bound engineer gurgle in protest. "He's as bad as you are...worse. He actually got off on reading what our servants did. Said he needed to know it to design 'rehabilitation programs'. What a load of shit. What your friend actually did was created a means for your kind to indulge your darkest passions without the slightest stain on your souls!"

"What? No! It was to condition them against their violence...it was to make them confront what they had done!" Lloyd tried to speak in his own defense, but it was distorted. He wasn't going to last much longer.

"You can lie to yourself, homes," Alastor said in a soulless echo of a voice, "but you can't lie to us! We see your thoughts...smell your sins."

"But your machine allowed our minions to indulge in their murderous little habits without incurring any punishment from us," the thing wearing Jim Baylor chided. "Inside your `virtual architecture' there were no victims! Without victims, there is no need for punishment! No need for us!"

"And that simply can't be allowed," Alastor added ominously.

"But why us? Why did you have to drag us into it?" Dominic's blue eyes were welling with tears of rage. "Why us?"

"Because you helped them try to cut us out," Raymond Milton said angrily. "We are part of this game, until the end, whether your kind likes it or not. Your machine fooled me. I thought I was in a paradise of death and mayhem, but I was starving. No souls to feed me when I destroyed simulations...beings of light with no souls! I would have wasted away to nothing if Nebiros here hadn't arranged this little jailbreak."

"It was my pleasure, brother," Jim Baylor crooned. He stared mercilessly at Dominic while addressing him. "In response to your earlier query, I found my way out here after ripping the location from the late Dr. Gaston's mind as I drained the blood from his still-living flesh. Yes, it was me that did him." He smiled pleasantly before continuing. "Your friends, the guards? We used them to summon Adramalech out of your simulation...I told them how to make an 'exorcism circle', and the fools believed me without so much as an internet search. Of course, they were scorched out of existence when Adramalech emerged...such fragile little bags of grease and piss."

"Once I was here, I woke the others. We dealt with your friends, the whitecoats who watched us sleep. They were delicious. Once we had control, I called in Nebiros...Jim...whatever you want to call him."

Jim Baylor smiled broadly, bowing slightly as he spoke. "And of course, I led the escorts into the trap...one of the guards' vehicles, parked right in the middle of the road. So hard to see on these dark roads at night, especially at such high speeds." Jim/Nebiros was gloating as he remembered. "Then I came back here and waited for the cavalry...you two assholes...to arrive. So eager to cover your own asses. You never spoke to me professionally in person, you didn't recognize my voice as the one that called you. Woke you. Summoned you here. And now...you will be coming with us."

"We have simulations as well...and we think you will find them as distracting as we found yours," Adramalech smiled malevolently. Fire began to erupt from any inflammable surface, including Dominic and Lloyd's clothing. Their skin began to sizzle as the gathered demons began to chant an ominous dirge. "We shall watch how you react...we shall make certain you are alert...aware. Just as you did for us...for our slaves. You tried to spare them death...that was never your right." The flames engulfed everything, burning the fleshy facades away, revealing the Infernal spirits inhabiting the gathered evils. In their faces, Dominic Laudick saw the faces of all the men he had forced to stay alive...all the men he had driven mad. He was beginning to grasp the basics of Hell.

The fire consumed everything, destroying the lab and the equipment, as well as the data stored onsite. No fire crews responded, and the blaze burned itself out. Perry Drake, the third security guard, was found dead of smoke inhalation tied up and gagged in the charred remains of the break room, where his companions had left him while they performed the ill-fated "exorcism." Only one of the containers survived the fire, and it contained the remains of Nathan Rothwell. He was the subject who Lloyd had noted had unusual sensory readings. Offsite recordings of what he experienced that night, before being boiled alive in his own hyberchamber, were dismissed as a malfunction. Apparently, there was some crossed signals on his sensory monitors resulting in the machine recording a vivid hallucination about an attack by demons who were bent on destroying the entire project.

Executives from Luminary Investment Group of Highland Texas quietly shelved their New Panopticon project as unfeasible. All records of the study are classified.

Other HellBound Books Titles
Available at:
www.hellboundbookspublishing.com

Shopping List 2: Another Horror Anthology

Once again, HellBound Books Publishing brings you an outstanding collection of horror, dark, slippery things, and supernatural terror - all from the very best up and coming minds in the genre.

We have given each and every one of our authors the opportunity to have their shopping lists read by you, the most wonderful reading public, and have the darkest corners of their creative psyche laid bare for all to see...

In all, 21 stories to chill the soul, tingle the spine and keep you awake in the cold, murky hours of the night from: Erin Lee, The Truth Artist, John Barackman, Serena Daniels, M.R. Wallace, Isobel Blackthorn, Pamela Morris, Alex Laybourne, Jason J. Nugent, Josh Darling, Jovan Jones, Nick Swain, Douglas Ford, Craig Bullock, Craig Bullock, Jeff C. Stevenson, PC3, David F Gray, Sergio Palumbo, Donna Maria McCarthy, David Clark & Megan E. Morales

Shopping List

A simply superlative collection of spine-tingling horror from the very best minds in the business!

We decided upon the shopping list theme for this particular volume as an antithesis to those wildly successful writers (they know who they are) of whom it is often said *'we would read their damned shopping list if they published it!'*

Well, we have given twenty-one of the hottest authors in the independent horror scene the unique opportunity to have their own shopping lists read by you - along with their most terrifying tales of course!

Stories of gut-wrenching terror from:
Kathy Dinisi, Robert Over, Christopher O'Halloran, Eric W. Burgin, Russ Gartz, Mark Slada, Jeff Baker, Tim Miller, Nick Swain,JC Raye, Jovan Jones, Ben Stevens, David F. Gray, Brandon Cracraft, M.S. Swift, Kevin Holton, David Owain Hughes, Bertram Allan Mullin, Jeff C. Stevenson, Sebastian Crow and S.E. Rise

Demons, Devils and Denizens of Hell Vol, 2

The second volume in HellBound Books' outstanding horror anthology fair teems with tales of Hades' finest citizens – both resident and vacationing in our earthly realm… -

Compiled by the inimitable P. Mattern and featuring: Savannah Morgan, Andrew MacKay, Jaap Boekestein, James H Longmore, Stephanie Kelley, Ryan Woods, James Nichols, P. Mattern, Marcus Mattern, Gerri R Gray, and legion more…

The Big Book of Bootleg Horror 2

The second volume in HellBound Books' flagship horror anthology - this one bursting at the seams with even more fantastically dark horror from the cream of the rising stars in today's horror scene!

Featuring: Tracey A. Cross, Elizabeth Zemlicka, Shelby Thomas, Matthew Gillies, Spinster Eskie, Stephen Clements, Ken Goldman, Nathan Robinson, K.M. Campbell, Cody Grady, Sebastian Bendix, Leo X. Robertson, David Owain Hughes, Timothy McGivney, Kane Gordon, Todd Sullivan, Mike Mayak, Edward Ahern, Rose Garnett, Jaap Boekestein, Brandy Delight, Stanley B. Webb, D. Norfolk, and Thomas Gunther.

Blood and Kisses

The definitive short story collecting from James H Longmore - an eclectic mix of dark horror, bizarro and Twilight-Zone style tales of the downright disturbing.

Welcome to the long awaited collection from the writer of horror novels *'Pede* and *Tenebrion*; a foreword by Richard Chizmar (co-author of *Gwendy's Button Box* and author of *A Long December*), 18 short stories, 5 flash fiction and even a poem - all skin-crawling, soul-shredding tales of terror, of the darkest things that skulk amongst the night's inky shadows, and of the everyday gone horribly awry.

Discover the alternative implication of technology becoming self-aware, enjoy the acquaintance of a charismatic new pastor who promises his flock a brand new place in which to worship his God, and spend a little time in the company of a nice young man who is inexorably caught up in his home town's terrible secret. Then there is Cupid's revelation that personally he has never experienced love, yet we discover that very emotion alive and not so well amongst the ruins of a post zombie apocalypse world, and we bear witness to a childhood innocence forever destroyed in a war-torn city. There is more, Dear Reader, much, much more; for within these pages we have devils, demons and ghosts, lycanthropes and demi-gods, all rubbing nefarious shoulders with vilest of Hell's offspring who have slithered from the netherworld to doff their caps and wish us all the sweetest of dreams…

A HellBound Books LLC Publication

http://www.hellboundbookspublishing.com

Printed in the United States of America